**Maureen Child** writes fo[...]
and can't imagine a better[...]
prestigious Romance Writers of America RITA® Award,
Maureen is an author of more than one hundred romance
novels. Her books regularly appear on bestseller lists and
have won several awards, including a Prism Award, a
National Readers' Choice Award, a Colorado Romance
Writers Award of Excellence and a Golden Quill Award.
She is a native Californian but has recently moved to the
mountains of Utah.

*USA TODAY* bestselling author **Janice Maynard** loved
books and writing even as a child. But it took multiple
rejections before she sold her first manuscript. Since 2002,
she has written over forty-five books and novellas. Janice
lives in east Tennessee with her husband, Charles. They
love hiking, traveling and spending time with family.

You can connect with Janice at
www.janicemaynard.com
Twitter.com/janicemaynard
Facebook.com/janicemaynardreaderpage
and Instagram.com/janicemaynard.

# BILLIONAIRE'S BARGAIN

## MAUREEN CHILD

# HIS HEIR, HER SECRET

## JANICE MAYNARD

**MILLS & BOON**

First Published in Great Britain 2018
by Mills & Boon, an imprint of HarperCollinsPublishers,
1 London Bridge Street, London, SE1 9GF

*Billionaire's Bargain* © 2018 Maureen Child
*His Heir, Her Secret* © 2018 Janice Maynard

ISBN: 978-0-263-93605-6

51-0618

MIX
Paper from
responsible sources
FSC® C007454
www.fsc.org

This book is produced from independently certified FSC™ paper to ensure responsible forest management.

For more information visit: www.harpercollins.co.uk/green

Printed and bound in Spain
by CPI, Barcelona

# BILLIONAIRE'S BARGAIN

## MAUREEN CHILD

To the Canterbury girls—Teresa, Patti, Mary, Colleen and Peggy. For the memories, for the laughs and because I love you guys.

# One

"Fifty thousand dollars and the baby's all yours."

Adam Quinn swallowed back a quick jolt of anger and studied his adversary. Kim Tressler was about thirty, with white-blond hair cut into a sharp wedge that clung to her cheeks. She wore a black, body-hugging dress that left little to the imagination. Her heavily lined blue eyes were narrowed on him and her mouth was a grim, red slash. She stood hipshot, with her infant son propped on her left hip.

Deliberately, he kept himself from looking too closely at the baby. His dead brother's son. Adam had to keep his head on straight to deal with this woman and that wouldn't happen if he looked at Devon's child.

Adam was used to handling all sorts of adversaries. Owning one of the world's largest construction and property development companies ensured that Adam regularly went head-to-head with many different types of personalities. And he always found a way to win. This time, though, it wasn't business. It was personal. And it cut damn deep.

Glancing down at the DNA test lying open on his desk, Adam saw proof that the baby's father was Devon Quinn, Adam's younger brother. He kept his gaze fixed on the paperwork even as he admitted silently that the test hadn't been necessary. The baby boy looked just like Devon. So that meant there was no way Adam could leave the baby with his mother. Hell, he wouldn't want to leave a dog with her. Kim came across as cold and mercenary. Exactly the kind of woman Devon would go for. Adam's brother had always had miserable taste in women.

With one major exception. Devon's ex-wife, Sienna West.

Adam felt a flicker of something he didn't want to acknowledge, then deliberately pushed all thoughts of Sienna from his mind. He was dealing with a very different kind of woman at the moment, and he needed to focus.

"Fifty thousand," he repeated, slowly lifting his gaze to hers.

"It's fair." She lifted one shoulder in a careless shrug and when the baby started fussing, she jiggled him furiously to try to silence him. Rather than looking at her child, she slid a fast, careful glance around Adam's office and he knew what she was seeing.

His inner office was huge, with a massive, mahogany desk that now stood between him and the woman. Wide windows offered a spectacular view of the Pacific, where surfers and boaters plied the water's surface.

Framed photos of some of his company's more famous projects lined the battleship-gray walls, and wood floors were softened by deep, ruby-colored rugs. He'd worked hard to put his company where it was at the moment and damned if he cared for having her look around like everything in the place had dollar signs on it.

When the infant subsided into whimpers, she shifted her attention back to Adam and said, "Look. This is Devon's child. He promised to take care of me and the baby. He's the one who wanted a kid. Now that he's dead, all of that's over. My career's taking off and I don't have the time to take care of it. I don't want the baby. But since he's Devon's, I'm guessing you do."

*No more motherly instinct than a feral cat. In fact, less*, he told himself, immediately feeling sorry for the baby. At the same time, Adam couldn't help wondering what the hell his brother had seen in this woman. Even considering that Devon had always been as deep as a puddle, why would he choose to make a child with a woman who was so clearly mercenary? She didn't give a flying damn about her own child—or Adam's brother.

He swallowed hard at how easily she dismissed Devon and his memory. Adam's younger brother had had his issues, but damn it, he deserved better than he was getting from his former lover. But that was Devon. He'd never thought beyond the next adventure. The next woman. Sadly, he'd never had a chance to move on from this one. And though he'd known about his child, he hadn't left a will because he'd expected to live forever.

Instead, he'd died in a horrific boating accident in the south of France just a little over six months ago. That wound was still fresh enough to bring a wave of pain that washed over Adam. When Devon died, it had been a year since Adam had spoken to him. Now he never would.

"Does he have a *name*?" Since she'd only referred to the child as "the baby," Adam wouldn't have been surprised to find she hadn't bothered to name him, either.

"Of course he has a name. It's Jack."

After their father. Adam didn't know whether to be moved or angry. Devon had cut himself off from the family, and then named the child he'd never know after a grandfather dead long before his birth.

*Time for introspection later*, he warned himself.

"What took you so long to bring the baby to me?" Adam leaned back in his chair and studied her, still keeping his gaze from straying to the child.

"I've been busy." She shook her hair back from her face and winced when the child slapped one hand against her cheek. "Since all of the publicity revolving around Devon's death, I've had several modeling gigs in France."

Money made on the broken bones of his dead brother. Kim was trading on being Devon's last lover and clearly her child was slowing her down. Fury, ripe and rich, boiled and bubbled in the pit of his stomach and he knew he couldn't afford to let her see it. Damned if Adam wanted to give the bitch a dime, but he also couldn't see himself leaving a defenseless kid with such a cold woman.

She sighed and tapped the toe of her high-heeled sandal against the hardwood floor. "Are you going to pay me or do I—"

"What?" He stood abruptly, planted both hands on his desk and stared into her eyes. He was willing to call her bluff. Remind her that *he* was the one in charge here. She'd come to him, not the other way around. He had the power in this little scuffle and they both knew it. "What exactly will you do, Ms. Tressler? Drop him off at an orphanage? Try to sell him to someone else?"

Sparks fired in her eyes, but wisely, she kept silent.

"We both know you're not going to do either of those things. Mainly, because I'd put my lawyers on you and they'd tangle your career up so tightly you'd be lucky to get a job posing beside a bag of dog food."

Her eyes narrowed and she breathed in fast, shallow gasps.

"You want money, you'll get it." He'd avoided looking at the baby, but he couldn't stand the thought of her even touching Devon's kid a moment longer. He came around the edge of his desk, scooped the baby boy out of her grip and held him uneasily. The child stared at him through wide, unblinking eyes, almost as if he were trying to decide what he thought about the whole thing.

Adam couldn't blame him. The boy had been dragged halfway across the globe, and then handed off to a stranger. It was a wonder he wasn't howling. Hell, it was a wonder *Adam* wasn't howling. He hadn't been around kids much and babies, almost never. By design.

That was, apparently, going to change. Fast.

"Fine. Then let's finish our business and I'll be on my way."

He dismissed her with a cool look, then hit the intercom button on his desk phone. When it took a few seconds for his assistant to answer, he knew Kevin had probably been listening at the door. No doubt, the man was ready to toss Kim Tressler out on her welltoned ass.

"Kevin," he said curtly. "Get legal in here. I need them to draw up an agreement. Now."

"On it."

"Legal?" Kim's eyebrows lifted into high arches.

"You think I'm handing you fifty thousand dollars without making sure it's the *last* time you come to me for money?"

Adam knew her type. Hell, before Devon died, Adam and the company had paid off dozens of women he'd grown tired of. Again, with the exception being Sienna West. When she and Devon had divorced, Sienna had refused a settlement—in spite of the fact that Adam had done everything he could to change her mind.

"What if I don't sign?" Kim asked.

"Oh, you'll sign," Adam told her. "You want the money too much to refuse. And, I'll warn you now, if you try anything—like renegotiating—I'll file for custody. I'll win. I can afford to fight you for years. Hell, by the time everything's settled, you'll be bleaching gray roots. Understood?"

Her mouth worked as if words were gathering there, trying to spill free, but she was holding them back. Finally, she managed to say, "Understood."

There was no way she'd fight him on this. Mainly because she just didn't care enough.

Adam looked at the baby boy in his arms and wondered what the hell he was supposed to do now. Adam knew nothing about babies. There was no family for him to call on for help. His dad was gone and his mother was living in Florida with her latest boyfriend—and she wasn't exactly a "typical" grandma, anyway.

He was going to have to hire someone. A nanny. But until then… Reaching for the intercom button again, he pressed it and said, "Kevin, come in here, will you?"

A second or two later, the office door opened to reveal Kevin Jameson. Tall, with dark blond hair and sharp eyes the same shade of blue as his silk tie, Kevin paused long enough to give the woman in the room a hard look, then walked to Adam. "What do you need?"

Instantly, Adam handed the baby over and just managed to swallow a sigh of relief before it could escape. If the situation had been different, he might have laughed at the expression of pure panic on Kevin's face, but Adam had a feeling his own features hadn't looked much different a minute or two ago. "Take care of him while Kim and I get this situation resolved."

"Me?" Kevin held the baby as he would have a stick of dynamite with a burning fuse.

"Yeah. His stuff is in that bag," Adam added, then waved to the two men in staid black suits entering the room. "Thanks, Kev."

As the lawyers huddled around the desk, Adam didn't watch Kevin and the baby leave. But he knew he'd hear about it later. Kevin and he had been roommates in college, so they went far enough back that he'd feel free to let Adam know just what he thought about being made an instant babysitter.

With the doors closed, Adam looked at Kim and said, "This is it. A onetime payment and you'll sign away all parental rights. Are we clear?"

She didn't look happy—probably because she'd imagined coming back for more money whenever she felt like it. Adam wasn't stupid enough to allow room for that.

"Fine."

Nodding, Adam said, "Gentlemen, write it up. I want a document that turns over care of Devon's infant son to me. And I want one that will stand up in *any* court."

Kim's eyes narrowed. "Seriously? You don't trust me to keep my word?"

"You're selling your son," Adam reminded her tightly. "Why in the hell would I trust you?"

An hour later, Kim Tressler was gone and Kevin was back in Adam's office, his feet propped on the edge of the desk. "I'll get you for handing that baby off to me."

"I figured you would," Adam said, lifting his own feet to the desk. He leaned back in his chair, took a sip of coffee and wished to hell it was scotch. "You heard all of it, right? I mean before you came in to get the kid."

"Damn right I did." Kevin drank his own coffee. "As soon as I saw her come in with that baby, I knew there was going to be trouble." He shook his head. "Kid looks just like his father. Adam, we both know Devon picked some crappy women in his time, but that one I think takes the prize."

"If they gave prizes for selling your own kid, yeah, she would."

"Man, it's days like these that make me glad I'm gay."

Adam snorted, then stopped. Looked around. "Where's the baby?"

Kevin laid his head back and closed his eyes. "I put Kara in charge of him. She's got three kids of her own, so I figured, hey. Experience counts."

"Plus, then you didn't have to watch him."

"Major bonus, yes." Kevin opened one eye to look at Adam. "I noticed you weren't real anxious to cuddle up, either."

"Well what the hell do I know about babies?"

"And you think I magically know something?" Kevin shuddered. "Kara's taking care of him and I sent Teddy from accounting out to buy diapers and food and whatever the hell else it needs."

"He. Not it."

"Excuse me."

"Okay, so the baby's fine for now. But that won't last." Adam frowned. He needed help and he needed it now. "I have to find a nanny."

"Well don't look at me."

"I wouldn't do that to the kid."

"Funny." Kevin took another sip of coffee and sighed. "So do you want me to set up interviews or something?"

He could trust Kevin not only to advertise, but to interview and find the best possible person for any given job. Still, this was something he should probably do himself. "I'll take care of it. But I need someone *today*."

"Yeah, that's not gonna happen."

"What about your mom?" Adam asked, delighted when that brilliant idea popped into his mind. Kevin's mother had practically adopted Adam into the family years ago. She was warm, kind, funny and already a grandmother thanks to Kevin's sister Nora. "You think she'd help me out for a while?"

"She'd love it," Kevin said, nodding. "Nothing Anna Jameson likes better than a baby."

"Good—"

"Unfortunately for you," Kevin added, "she's on that Alaskan cruise you gave her for her birthday…"

"Damn it." Scowling, Adam took another drink of his coffee.

"Got a video email from her last night," Kevin said.

"She and Aunt Noreen are having a great time. Mom bought Nick and I fur coats for winter."

"We live in Southern California."

Kevin shrugged. "Didn't seem to matter to Mom. Oh, and she said to say thank you again."

"She's welcome again. Your sister lives in San Diego, so I can't ask her."

"Nora's got three of her own. If you don't mind the drive she probably wouldn't even notice a fourth."

"Funny. I just wish—never mind." Adam looked at his friend. "Who else do we know?"

"Any number of people." Kevin shrugged. "None of whom I'd trust with a baby. Except for maybe Nick— and before you suggest it, no."

Kevin's husband, Nick, loved kids. He was already an uncle many times over through not only Nora, but his own two sisters and a brother, as well. "It wouldn't be for long."

"Overnight is too long." Kevin shook his head firmly. "Nick's still talking about us adopting and I don't want to give him more ammunition."

"Fine." But it wasn't fine at all. He'd done the right thing—saved his nephew from a mother who didn't deserve him, and now Adam had to come up with some answers. He couldn't think of anyone who might ride to the temporary rescue. Not as if he could ask his own ex-wife. Even the thought of that made him laugh quietly. Tricia was a TV reporter and had less knowledge of kids than he did. Besides that, he and Tricia hadn't spoken since their marriage ended more than five years ago. They'd had nothing in common then and even less now. And to top it all off, Tricia was working at a Seattle station now, so geographically undesirable anyway.

Frowning, Adam realized how insular his world was. He set his coffee cup down and tapped his fingers against the desktop. Most of the people he knew were business acquaintances. He didn't have time for friendships, so anyone he knew was just as busy as he was.

"You're tapping."

He stopped, looked at Kevin. "What?"

"Your fingers. Tapping. Either start playing a tune or cut it out."

"Right." Adam pushed to his feet and shoved both hands through his hair. "It shouldn't be this hard to figure out."

"What about Delores?"

Adam shook his head. "She's a housekeeper, not a nanny."

"But temporarily…"

"She leaves tomorrow to visit her sister in Ohio."

"Perfect."

"It's the beginning of summer. People take vacations." Of course, the reason his people were currently gone was because *he'd* bought them tickets. Was this some kind of weird Karma? Make him suffer for doing something nice for Anna Jameson and Delores Banner? It seemed like the universe itself was conspiring against him. And damned if Adam would surrender. There had to be someone—

As one particular thought sailed into his mind and settled in, Adam examined it from every angle. Okay. It could work. If it didn't blow up in his face, first.

"Who are you thinking about?"

He looked at Kevin. "Sienna."

Kevin's mouth dropped open. "You want Devon's ex-wife to take care of Devon's kid with someone else."

Frowning, Adam murmured, "It didn't sound that bad in my head."

"Well it should have. Adam, she left Devon because he didn't *want* kids."

He waved that aside. "That's only one of the reasons."

"Exactly." Kevin stood up and faced his friend. "Devon was an ass to her and now you want to continue the Quinn family tradition?"

"This will be a straight-up business arrangement."

"Oh well, that's different then."

Ignoring the sarcasm, Adam stalked across the room to the wide window that overlooked the sea. Kevin was right, but that didn't matter because Adam couldn't think of anyone else *but* Sienna.

One part of his mind took in the scene before him, the impossibly small boat, red sails billowing in the wind. A pod of dolphins leaping from the water like ballet dancers. Surfers riding waves toward shore. But while he could enjoy the view, most of his brain was talking himself into his best chance. "She's the only one I know who could do this."

"Maybe, but why should she?" The argument was a good one and they both knew it. Kevin walked over to stand beside him. "When she divorced Devon, she didn't want his money. What makes you think she'll take yours?"

Adam looked at his oldest friend. "Because I won't give her a choice."

Sienna West gently tucked the newborn's arms beneath its chest, turned that perfect little face toward her, then stepped back and took the shot. The lighting was perfect. The pale, lemon yellow blanket beneath the baby highlighted the tiny girl's copper skin tone and the yellow-and-white daisies scattered around and across the impossibly small, naked body gave an almost fairy-like impression.

Sienna took a few more shots in rapid succession, then her assistant, Terri, stepped in to gently lay a daisy against the baby girl's ear. More clicks of the digital camera and finally Sienna sat back and smiled. She checked the screen on her camera and felt that familiar flush of accomplishment. They'd already been at it for half an hour while the baby quietly slept through prop changes, hair brushing and lighting changes. This couldn't last forever. Quickly, she scrolled through the shots, seeing ones she liked, ones she would edit and others she would delete.

Glancing up at the proud parents hovering close by, she said, "I think that's got it."

"They're going to be beautiful," the young mom said, hurrying in to scoop up her daughter and hold her close.

"Hard to be anything else," Sienna assured her. "She's a gorgeous baby."

"She is, isn't she?" the baby's father mused, reaching out to run one finger along his daughter's cheek.

Quickly, Sienna lifted her camera and took several shots of the family, connected, touching, sharing a moment they weren't even aware that they'd created. The tenderness of the young mother. The protective stance and gentle touch of the father and the sleeping baby nestled close. Checking her camera screen, Sienna smiled to herself. Since they hadn't asked for a family print, this would be a gift from her. And, with their permission, she'd showcase it on her website, as well.

Standing up, she said, "In about a week, I'll have some proofs to show you. Terri will give you the sign-in code for the website. Then all you have to do is decide which ones you want."

Kissing her baby tenderly, the mother laughed a little. "That's going to be the hard part, isn't it?"

"Usually, yes." Terri spoke up and began to herd the family from the room. "If you'll come with me, you can get Kenzie dressed and I'll get that code for you."

Sienna watched them go, then turned to her equipment. Terri was good with the clients. As the mother of four and grandmother of six, she knew her way around babies. Plus, she had a calming touch with nervous parents and jittery kids. Hiring her had been the best move Sienna had ever made.

She took the memory card from the camera, inserted it into the computer and opened a new folder for the Johnson family. Once the images were done loading, she flipped through them with a critical eye, deleting those that didn't meet her expectations and marking those that would be the winners.

Already, she loved the last-minute shots she'd taken of the family as a whole. It said something to her. The love in the mother's eyes. The trusting curl of the baby's body against her mother's chest. The protective gleam in the father's eyes and the visual element of his much bigger hand against his tiny daughter's cheek.

Sienna's heart gave a hard squeeze. Once upon a time, she'd dreamed of having kids herself. Of building a family with a man she loved, who would look at her and see everything in the world he wanted. She'd made a grab at the brass ring a few years ago—only to discover that she hadn't really caught it at all. Instead, she'd been grabbing at fog. Wisps of dreams that in the light of day lost all cohesion.

Devon Quinn had been both the dream and the nightmare. So handsome. So charming, with a wicked smile and a twinkle in his eyes that promised adventure and love. But she'd only seen what she'd wanted to see and it hadn't taken her long to figure out that marrying Devon had been the biggest mistake of her life. Now Sienna was divorced, with a struggling business taking pictures of children that weren't hers.

"Wow." Shaking her head, she ordered, "Snap out of it, Sienna."

She usually didn't wallow. Sienna was a firm believer in letting the past go and concentrating on the now. She didn't spend much time remembering Devon or the marriage that had been such a disappointment.

"Sienna?"

She looked up at Terri. "The Johnsons have a question?"

"No," the older woman said. "They paid and left. But someone else is here to see you."

Terri didn't look happy about it, either. Which only made Sienna wonder who could have put the uneasy look on her friend's face. "Who is it?"

"Me."

Terri jumped when the deep voice sounded out from right behind her. Sienna's gaze was locked on the man standing behind her assistant as she stood up slowly. Even if she hadn't seen him, she would have known that voice. Though she hadn't heard it in two years, she'd have recognized it anywhere. That voice was not just deep, it carried the ring of power, letting everyone know that the man speaking was used to being heard and obeyed.

Which just didn't fly with Sienna.

Still, her gaze locked with his and a rush of heat filled her stomach, swirled around for a heartbeat or two, then rose up in her chest.

Adam Quinn.

Her ex-brother-in-law. Funny, looking at Adam now, she could see the family resemblance between him and Devon. But she could see so much more than she once had. For example, Adam's chocolate eyes met hers squarely. They didn't shift around the room as Devon's had, as if he were looking for someone more interesting to talk to.

Adam's mouth was firm, and some would say grim, but Devon's smile, she'd discovered, was used to disarm, deceive. Adam's hair lacked the wave of Devon's, but somehow the expert, somewhat shaggy cut suited him. Devon had boasted a dark tan, which had come from so much time spent playing on lakes or ski slopes while Adam's skin was paler, letting her know that he was still more focused on his business than in entertaining himself.

He was taller than she remembered, Sienna thought. At least six foot two, and even wearing the elegantly tailored navy blue, three-piece suit, he looked more of a pirate than a businessman. Maybe, she told herself, it was because he carried an air of, not danger, exactly, but as if he were issuing a silent warning to stay out of his way or be mowed down.

And just watching him had her heartbeat speeding up. It happened every time she was around Adam. Sienna hated acknowledging that, even to herself. Devon's brother was off-limits. Or should be. While Devon had been completely self-indulgent, Adam was too strait-laced. Too much the corporate raider for her. What she needed to do was find a man right in the middle of those two extremes. The problem was, Sienna didn't think she'd ever meet a man who could turn her insides into a blazing inferno with a single look like Adam could.

Two years since she'd spoken to him. Seen him. And the internal fire was sizzling away. Ridiculous or not, she really wished she were wearing something more flattering than a long-sleeved white shirt and an old pair of jeans.

When she realized the humming silence between them had been stretching out interminably, she cleared her throat. "Adam. What are you doing here?"

He stepped out from behind Terri and the woman sort of skittered sideways to keep out of his path. Sienna couldn't really blame her. Adam was intense.

"I need to talk to you," he said, slanting the other woman a look. "Privately."

# Two

*Giving orders again.* Sienna shook her head. The man hadn't changed a bit. The last time she'd seen him, he'd begun their meeting by telling her exactly how to handle *her* divorce from his brother. He'd worked out a financial settlement that would have had most women flinging themselves at his manly chest, thanking him profusely. Instead, Sienna had told him what she'd told his brother. She didn't want the Quinn money. She just wanted the marriage to be over.

Now here he stood, two years later, still trying to take charge. Well, she'd hear him out, then go back to her life. The sooner she could put out the fire slowly boiling her blood, the better.

"Terri," she said, "would you mind?"

"Sure," the woman said, but added, "If you need me, I'll be right up front."

Sienna stopped her smile before it could get too big.

Good to have friends. Even though the thought of the older woman trying to rescue her from Adam was ludicrous. "Thanks. I appreciate it."

Terri left, closing the door behind her. When she was gone, Adam asked, "What does she think I'm going to do?"

"Impossible to say," Sienna admitted. "But you do look scary and she has an excellent imagination."

"Scary?"

Well, she mused, he didn't look happy about that. "To someone who doesn't know you, yeah."

"So I don't scare you." He tucked his hands into his pockets and watched her, waiting for an answer.

"No, Adam. You don't." *But*, she added silently, *you worry me.*

"Good to know." Frowning, he glanced around what she called her "shoot room." While he looked, so did Sienna, seeing it as he did.

This was by no means her dream studio, but it would do for now. The images that came to life here shone when the building itself didn't. It was a plain room, really, the walls were a cool cream and unadorned. There were props stacked neatly on a series of shelves—everything from silly hats to baby blankets to old-fashioned slates that children scrawled their names on with chalk to be held in their photos. Right now, a sturdy table with the lemon yellow throw draped over a series of small pillows took up the middle of the set, with the lights focused down on where the baby had been lying. There was good light from the wide windows and when she had a night shoot, there were literally armies of lighting scaffolds scattered around the room.

Sienna studied him while he was unaware. To her,

he looked way too good, and instinctively, she lifted her camera. Light and shadow played on his features, making him an irresistible target for her lens. In the late afternoon, she was losing the light, but there was enough to make him look almost dangerously alluring as he stood, half in shadow. She took two quick shots of him before he slowly swiveled his head to stare at her.

"I didn't come here to pose for you."

"I figured that. So why are you here, Adam?" She glanced down at the screen on her camera. Even the photo of him was hypnotic. Oh she was in bad shape.

"I need your help."

Surprised, she looked up at him. That, she hadn't expected. "Really? That's so unlike you."

His eyes narrowed. "Why?"

"You're just not the kind of man to ever ask for help."

"Know me that well, do you?"

"I think so," she said. As well as anyone could know him, she hedged silently. Sienna was willing to bet that not even his ex-wife could claim to know him completely. Adam Quinn kept his thoughts and his feelings to himself. He had the best poker face in the universe and trying to see past the shields in his eyes could give you a migraine.

After she and Devon were married, she'd met Adam for the first time and thought then that two brothers couldn't have been more different. The fact that she'd also felt a quickening inside her for the quiet, stern-faced Adam was something that had embarrassed her at the time and was strangely even more mortifying now.

Tipping her head to one side, Sienna looked at him from across the room and wished she could flip the lighting on so his eyes wouldn't be in the shadows. "I was sorry to hear about Devon," she said abruptly, as a niggle of guilt pinged in the center of her chest. "I thought about calling you—after. But I didn't know what to say."

"Yeah." He pulled his hands from his pockets and reached down to pick up a tiny stuffed rabbit she'd used in the photo shoot with little Kenzie Johnson. He turned the soft, brown animal in his hands. "I get it. Devon didn't exactly treat you well."

Regret jabbed at her in twin stabs with the guilt. As much as she'd like to completely blame her failed marriage on her ex-husband, she just couldn't. Her mom always told her that it took two to make or break a marriage. So she had to accept her own share of the blame.

"It wasn't entirely Devon's fault," she said. "I wasn't what he wanted, either."

One eyebrow winged up. "Awfully generous."

"Not really," she said. "Just honest. What's going on, Adam? It's been two years since I've seen you, so why now?"

He tossed the little rabbit onto the table, then turned to face her dead-on. "I had a visit today from Devon's latest woman."

That news didn't even sting, which told Sienna as nothing else could have that she was truly over Devon Quinn. Heck, he'd had other women *while* they were married.

"And?"

*"And,"* he said, reaching up to rub the back of his neck in a gesture of complete irritation. "She *sold* me Devon's son."

"She sold her child?" Sienna said it again because

she could not believe what she was hearing. "And you *bought* him? You actually paid this woman for a *child*? Your own nephew?"

Adam stiffened and his features went even more grim. Eyes narrowed on her and she noticed a muscle in his jaw twitch as if he were grinding his teeth.

"I can't believe this. My God, Adam." She thought about little Kenzie Johnson and the love that had surrounded her. How her parents had practically beamed with pride and adoration. She actually winced, thinking about Devon's son being sold off like a used car. "You actually *bought* your nephew."

"What the hell choice did I have?" Adam sounded furious and seemed to be asking himself the question as well as her. He started pacing, in quick steps fueled by rage. "Was I going to leave the boy with her? Jesus, she hardly looked at him the whole time she was negotiating." He snorted and repeated the word. "No, she had a price, demanded it and waited for me to pay it. It wasn't a negotiation. It was extortion."

Watching him quieted her own anger in sympathy for his. He'd lost his brother and then six months later, his brother's only son had been held hostage by a mercenary woman with her own agenda. Sienna was almost too stunned to speak. Almost. The reality was hard to get past. "She sold her child. Her own child."

A tiny ripple of pain washed through her. When she'd married, she'd assumed that she and Devon would have a family eventually. But that was one of the things that had driven them apart. He'd flatly refused, saying he didn't want kids slowing down the "fun." He hadn't cared how Sienna felt about it. His dismissal of her told her more than anything that their marriage was doomed.

Now he'd made a child with a woman who clearly didn't deserve or *want* the baby.

"Fifty thousand dollars." Adam snorted again, but there was no humor there. Through gritted teeth, he added, "Apparently *motherhood* was getting in the way of her career."

"You shouldn't have paid her a dime." What kind of woman would sell her own child? And what kind of man would pay her price?

His head snapped up and his gaze pinned hers. For a split second, Sienna felt a jolt of white-hot fury sizzle in the air between them. His expression was thunderous and maybe she should have been intimidated. But she wasn't. Maybe that expression worked on his employees, but not her. A second or two later, he seemed to understand that.

"What the hell else was I supposed to do?"

She threw her hands up. "Oh, I don't know. Have her arrested for trying to sell a baby? Take her to court? You've got legions of lawyers at your beck and call, and instead you wrote her a check."

He scrubbed both hands over his face and she could feel his frustration. "All I was thinking about was getting Devon's son away from her. This was the fastest solution."

Okay, she could see that, but her insides were still fisted and her heart pounding. "And what keeps her from coming back for more? For haunting that poor baby's life, constantly letting him know that he's nothing more to her than a bargaining chip?"

"I'm not an idiot," he snapped, firing a look at her that was designed to silence her arguments. "My lawyers wrote up a contract. She signed away her parental rights to me. I'm Jack's legal guardian now. God help us both."

Sienna blew out a breath. "Jack?"

"Yeah." He pushed one hand through his hair again and it occurred to Sienna she'd never seen Adam this *unsettled* before.

"Apparently," he continued, "Devon named his son for our father. And now the boy will never know either of them."

A twinge of sympathy for Devon, for Adam and mostly for the baby tugged at Sienna's heart. She'd thought when she left Devon that she was finished with the Quinn family. She'd made it a point to stay out of Adam's way over the last two years and that wasn't always easy. She and Adam didn't move in the same circles, of course. He was rich, powerful and she wasn't.

But she did take photos of the wealthy and famous. She did do photo spreads of some of the buildings he'd designed and built. But somehow, for two years, Sienna had managed to avoid him. Yet now, here he was, standing right in front of her.

She took a steadying breath that didn't really do the trick. "Fine. So the Mother of the Year took the money and ran, I'm guessing?"

"She was nothing but a blur when she hit the office door and she probably didn't stop until she got to the airport."

Disgusted, she muttered, "That's something, anyway."

Slanting her a look, he agreed. "Exactly how I feel about it."

She watched him as he wandered the room, looking at the props on the shelf, reaching out to pick up the wooden framed slate.

"So now what?" she asked.

He took a piece of chalk and scribbled something on the chalkboard while he talked. "That's why I'm here."

"Uh-huh. That doesn't tell me anything, Adam," she pointed out.

He flipped the slate around to her and Sienna read what he'd written.

*I NEED A TEMPORARY NANNY.*

She read it again, then lifted her gaze to his. "And you're telling me, why?"

"Because I need *you*."

"Me?" Her brain was racing and her thoughts flew scattershot through her mind. Her? A nanny? For Devon's baby? What the hell? Shaking her head, she said, "I'm not a nanny, Adam. I'm a photographer with a growing business."

"I'm not asking you to give up your business."

"Sounds like you are."

"Look." He tossed the slate back onto the shelf, and then faced her. "I know this is weird, but damn it, Sienna, you're the only woman I know I can ask to do this."

"Oh come on." She laughed shortly and perched on the edge of a table. "You're hardly a monk, Adam. You know plenty of women."

"I know plenty of women who are great in my bed. Not so much with a small, defenseless human."

"I'm not quite sure how to take that," she admitted, even as her mind tried to settle down enough to figure it out. Naturally though, her brain went instead to images of Adam in bed. Naked. Not that she'd ever seen him naked, but Sienna had an excellent imagination.

"Take it as a compliment," he said tightly. He pushed

one hand through his hair again and Sienna noted that the excellent cut meant his hair fell neatly back into place. She wondered if that idle gesture was done deliberately.

"Sienna," he said, releasing a long breath, "I know Devon treated you like crap and you have no reason to do any Quinn a favor—"

"Devon wasn't that bad, Adam," she interrupted him. "And I have nothing against you…"

To put it mildly. She had already been married to Devon when she met his older brother for the first time and Sienna hadn't been able to deny she felt a flash of something tantalizing the minute Adam had shaken her hand. And as her marriage crumbled, she'd often wondered what might have happened if she'd only met Adam first. But that was *not* the point at the moment.

"Good to know," he said, nodding. "I need you. That baby needs you."

She sucked in a gulp of air. "That was low."

"Yeah," he smiled briefly. "I know. But I learned a long time ago that you use whatever weapons you have to win the day."

He'd picked a good one to use on her was all Sienna could think. There was a reason most of her work centered around images of babies and children. "Great. That poor baby's a bargaining chip to his mother and a weapon to you."

"You know what I meant," he argued.

"Yes, I do." And she could see that he was really trying to do his best by his brother's child. Most men, she thought, would probably be trying to slip out of caring for the baby entirely. But that fact didn't make this any easier.

"Temporary, you said."

He nodded. "Just until we find someone permanent. You could help me with that. Pick out the right person."

"I don't know…" She looked around the room, at her equipment, the business she'd built from the ground up. If she did this, she'd be taking time away from the very thing that was most important to her. But how could she *not* help care for a baby who'd really been given a lemon from the garden of mothers?

"I'll pay you whatever you want."

Sienna stiffened and lifted her chin as her gaze met his. "Just because you bought off the baby's mother doesn't mean that *every* woman is for sale. I don't want your money, Adam. I told you that when Devon and I divorced. I wouldn't take it from him. Didn't take it from you when you offered. Nothing's changed. I make my own way."

"Fine." He walked toward her, his eyes flashing as he stared at her. "I respect that. Admire it even. But I can't be in your debt like this, either, Sienna. So instead of paying you, why don't I help you with your career?"

She laughed shortly. "How do you plan to do that? Pose for me, after all?"

"No." He came closer. Close enough that Sienna was forced to tip her head back to meet his dark brown eyes. His scent came to her and she noted it was just like him. Subtle, rich and tempting. She held her breath.

"Your studio's a little on the small side," he mused, giving a quick, assessing glance around the space.

Insulted, she argued, "It works just fine."

His gaze snapped back to hers. "You should never settle for 'fine,' Sienna."

"I don't plan to. I'll get something bigger one day."

"Why wait?" He gave a shrug that was deliberately careless, but she didn't believe it for a minute.

"What?" He couldn't be saying what she thought he was saying.

"Here's the deal. You help me out with the baby—"

"Stop calling him 'the baby,'" she interrupted. "You said his name is Jack."

"All right. Help me with *Jack* and you'll get your dream studio out of it."

"Adam—"

"You find the building you want," he continued, steamrolling over whatever argument she might have made. "And my company will take care of the rest. We'll rehab, remodel, set it all up to your specifications."

Her heart was pounding. His words hung in the air like helium party balloons, bright, pretty. Her studio now was small, but she'd been saving her money, building her reputation. The long-term plan was to have a higher-end studio that would draw bigger clients. Eventually, she dreamed of being the top photographer in Huntington Beach, California, maybe even on the whole West Coast.

And if she did this for Adam, that could happen a lot faster. God, she was so tempted. But if she did this…

"What?" he demanded. "You're thinking and they're not good thoughts."

Irritated, she muttered, "Stop trying to read my mind."

"Don't really have to try when whatever you're thinking or feeling is stamped all over your face."

"Well that's insulting." And unsettling.

"Didn't mean it that way."

She waved one hand at him. "I was just thinking…

if I do this, would I be any better than Jack's mother? She used him for profit. Wouldn't I be doing the same thing?"

"No." One word. Flat. Final.

She looked into his eyes and saw that he meant it. Too bad it didn't convince *her*.

"You're nothing like her, Sienna." He paused. "Hell. No one is. If you do this, it's not about Jack at all. It's a favor to *me*."

God help her, she was wavering. Shaking her head, she continued her argument against doing this by saying softly, "I have a job, Adam. And I can't take a baby along with me on photo shoots."

"I understand and we'll work it out. I don't know how yet, but I'll find a way."

He would, too. Nothing stopped Adam Quinn from doing whatever it was he wanted to. According to Devon, his older brother was a human bulldozer, plowing down everything in his path. Once, she'd thought Devon was like that, too. She'd met him and seen ambition where there was only charisma. She'd thought him charming but hadn't realized the charm was practiced and not at all genuine.

Adam, on the other hand, clearly didn't care a damn about charm. He was practically a force of nature. He'd come here for the express purpose of getting Sienna's help no matter what it took and he was very close to succeeding. Adam didn't need Devon's easy smile or quick wit. He had the power of his personality going for him. He was absolutely up-front about what he wanted and how he was going to get it and that could be hard to take even if it was safer in the long run.

"I'm not asking you to give up your work," he said.

"Hell, I'm offering to give you a dream studio so you can build your business faster than you would have been able to. I just need some temporary help."

His mouth screwed up as if even the word *help* left a bad taste in his mouth. This was not a man accustomed to needing anyone.

"In exchange," he added a moment later, "I'll give you the best photography studio in California."

He'd laid her dreams out for her on a silver platter. They were right there, within reach and Sienna felt a little light-headed at the prospect. She wanted it. Fine, she could admit it, to herself at least, that she really wanted a beautiful, state-of-the-art studio. She could build the career she'd dreamed of with the right tools. And if she didn't take Adam's deal it could take her years to earn that reality on her own.

This was a bad idea, though. There was history between them, not to mention the ghost of his dead brother. She didn't want to be attracted to him but she most definitely *was*. And as that thought skittered through her mind, she deliberately kept her features blank. She really didn't need him reading her expression at the moment.

He was watching her and Sienna fought to keep what she was feeling off her face. Now that she knew he was reading her expressions, it put her at a real disadvantage. But how could her mind *not* wander to his broad chest, his deep brown eyes, his strong hands? *Oh God.* One corner of his mouth lifted briefly as if he knew what she was trying to do.

So she took a breath and got it over with. "Okay, I'll do it. But—"

"Great." He pushed his sleeve back, glanced at the

heavy platinum watch on his wrist, then looked at her. "What time are you finished here today?"

"Just hold on a second. We need to talk about a few things and—"

"We will," he said quickly. "Later. So, when can you leave?"

"Uh—" If he kept cutting her off in an attempt to hurry this arrangement along, she'd never be able to say what she needed to. She had a few ground rules of her own to lay down and she knew he wouldn't be happy to hear them. But the man was like the tide, pushing inexorably toward shore. No point in arguing with him here. "Fine. I can leave in about an hour."

"Good. That'll work. I'll meet you at your house, help you move your stuff to my place."

She blinked at him. "You'll what? I'm sorry. *What?*" She shook her head as if to clear her hearing.

"If you're going to take care of the baby, you'll have to be where he is, right?" He looked at her steadily and his gaze was strong enough that she felt the power of the man slide into her.

That hadn't occurred to her at all and now she had to wonder *why.* Of course she'd have to be with the baby to take care of him. But she just hadn't put that together with living in Adam's house. And now that she was, Sienna was pretty sure this was a bad idea.

"I didn't think I'd be living with you."

"Not with me. At the same address."

"Oh." She nodded and shrugged. "Sure. That's a whole different thing."

He blew out a breath at her sarcasm and that told her he was a lot closer to the edge of exasperation than she'd thought. "It's a big house, Sienna. You'll have your own suite."

Her eyebrows arched. A suite? *Not the point, Sienna.* "I don't know…"

"Remember our deal. You find any building you want, Sienna. You can design the remodel yourself."

The snake in the garden had probably sounded a lot like Adam Quinn.

"Put in shelves and workrooms and prop rooms and any kind of lighting you need."

She ignored the inner tug she felt toward that tasty carrot he was holding out in front of her. He knew all too well that he was getting to her. And she imagined her expression told him everything he wanted to know. "You're still selling me on an idea I already agreed to. Feeling a little desperate, Adam?"

For a second she thought he'd deny it, then he clearly thought better of it.

"Not quite," he admitted. "But it's close. Look, Sienna, we can help each other here. That's it. So are you in or not?"

She met his gaze for a long second or two. She could say no, but why should she? There was a baby who needed to be cared for and a man completely out of his depth asking for her help.

And okay, the photography studio.

But there was another reason to do it. One she didn't really want to think about. It was Adam, himself. It was his eyes. The deep timbre of his voice. And the way he looked at her. Foolish? Probably. Irresistible? Absolutely.

"Okay," she said before she could talk herself out of it. "I'm in."

Relief flashed across his features briefly. "Good. That's good. So I'll meet you at your place in two hours. Help you move what you need to my house."

"Okay." Decision made, her stomach was still spinning. She'd have to get her neighbors to watch the house and bring in the mail and— "I'll write down my address."

"I know where you live."

She looked up at him. "You do?"

His gaze locked on hers. "I've always known, Sienna."

# Three

Two hours later, as promised, Adam pulled up in front of a small bungalow in Seal Beach and parked beneath the shade of an ancient tree. A hell of a day. He had a headache that pounded hard enough to shatter his skull and it didn't look as if it would be going away anytime soon.

Staring at the house, Adam frowned a little. Bright splashes of color lined the front of the house, flowers spilling out of the beds onto a lawn that hadn't been mowed in a while. The paint was faded and the roof looked as old as the tree.

"Why the hell would she refuse a settlement when she divorced Devon?" he wondered aloud. There was a place for pride—no one understood that better than he did. But damn it, pride shouldn't get in the way of common sense. Clearly, she could have used the money.

The street the house sat on was old and settled. Most

of the houses were small, but well kept. A crowd of kids across the street were playing basketball against a garage and the throaty roar of a lawn mower sounded in the distance. He tapped his fingers against the steering wheel and glanced at Sienna's faded green sedan parked in her driveway. The rusted bumper irritated him more than he could say.

"Hardheaded woman," he muttered. "She should have taken Devon for millions."

Climbing out of his car, he walked up to the house, noting the cracks in the sidewalk, the chipping stucco alongside the garage door. Grinding his teeth together, he made a dozen mental notes on the short walk to the porch. They had a deal, but he was adding to it whether she liked it or not. His company would give her the best damn photography studio in the state, but they would also redo this house. And if she argued with him about it—which she would—he'd steamroll right over any objections she came up with.

Sienna had married his brother and Devon had proven quickly just what a bad decision that had been. Adam couldn't ignore his family's mistakes. He'd fix them if he could, and this he could definitely take care of. By the time he was finished with this tiny house, Sienna would think she was living in a damn palace.

She answered the door before he'd had a chance to knock, which told Adam she'd been watching for his arrival. Her eyes were wide and her expression wary. Had she changed her mind? Was she going to try to back out of their deal? If so, she would fail.

"You don't look happy to see me," he mused.

"Stop reading my mind."

He laughed shortly. "Well, that was honest anyway."

"That's not what I meant. I mean, of course, I'm happy to see you. Well, not happy, but I was expecting you and—" She stopped, scowled and took a deep breath. Once she'd released it again, she started over.

"Hi, Adam."

"Hi." He liked knowing that he made her nervous. Liked that she got a gleam in her eyes when she looked at him. He knew that same gleam was in his own eyes every time he saw her. How could it not be? Tall and curvy, with those big blue eyes, Sienna was enough to bring most men to their knees.

She pushed the screen door wider for him, then turned back into the house as he stepped inside.

His gaze swept the interior quickly, with a professional eye that missed almost nothing. Inside at least, the house appeared to be in better shape than the exterior. The walls were jewel toned, a deep scarlet in the living room, fading to a soft rose in the hall. He could only imagine what the rest of the house looked like, but realized he was curious about her home. About her.

The old, scuffed wooden floors had been polished and she had what looked like fifties-style braided rugs in a variety of colors spread throughout the hall and the front room. Her furniture wasn't new or contemporary but it suited her. There were framed prints of photos on the walls. Her work, he imagined. Seascapes, meadows, people and, for some reason, babies dressed up like flowers and fruit.

She followed his gaze and grinned. "They're so cute when they're tiny—it's fun to dress them up."

"Sure." He shook his head, studying one baby in particular. "What is that? A peach?"

"Yes."

"Hmm." He shrugged and looked at her. "I like the beach scenes."

"Thanks."

"We've actually got a new building going up down in Dana Point," he said thoughtfully. "Sits above the beach and it's a different kind of design."

"Really?"

It was easy enough to see how intrigued she was, so Adam kept talking. The idea had only just occurred to him, but now that it had, he went with it. "The architect really outdid herself. The building is a curve of glass that faces the ocean, but there are open areas all over the face of it, too."

"What do you mean?"

"Sort of mini balconies, I guess you'd call them," he said, staring again at one of her framed seascapes. "There will be some kind of ivy trailing on the railings so that the whole thing will give the impression of the building itself growing out of the land." He could see it now, in his head, as he could every project he'd ever done. Adam liked doing projects that challenged him. That worked his imagination as much as his skills. "With the sky and the ocean reflecting off the glass panels, it will make the trails of ivy even more alive, I think."

"Wow."

One word, spoken in a kind of hush. Adam looked at her. "What?"

Smiling, she shook her head and said, "I've just never heard you talk like that. I mean, you're obviously good at what you do, but—"

"But most buildings these days are fairly boring?"

he asked, one corner of his mouth tipping up. "Sort of generic."

"Well, yes." She led the way into the living room and he looked around as he followed her.

More framed prints here. His gaze swept them, empty beaches, lonely people, cheerful babies. Each one was perfectly lit, with shadows sliding in giving them all a depth they might not have had otherwise. But he had to wonder if she was aware of just how much of *herself* was displayed on her walls.

"I don't mean they're not beautiful, but this project you're talking about sounds amazing."

He nodded. "It will be, once it's finished. But now I realize I'd like some pictures taken during the process of building."

"So you want a before, during and after series?"

"I guess so. Interested?"

Her eyes lit up and he was glad he'd asked her, just to see that brightness fill her eyes. "Absolutely. Yes."

"Okay, in a day or two, we'll take a ride down Pacific Coast Highway so I can show you around."

"Good." She nodded. "That's good."

She was close, Adam realized. Standing so close to him, he inhaled her scent with every breath. Her eyes caught his and held and Adam felt a throbbing tension erupt between them. He read her expression easily and knew she was feeling the same thing. For a long second, he stared down at her and fought the urge to pull her in close and—

*Yeah. Don't go there.* "You ready?"

"Yes. At least, I think I've got everything," she said, grabbing up a lightweight jacket off a nearby chair.

His eyebrows lifted as he looked at the duffel bag

and a small, wheeled suitcase sitting beside the front door. "That's it?"

She looked too, then turned to meet his gaze. "Yes, why?"

Chuckling, he said, "Most of the women I know take more luggage than *that* for an overnight trip. I don't even want to think about what they'd be hauling for two weeks."

She grinned and a ball of fire flashed instantly to life in his gut. It was all too familiar to him. From the moment they'd first met, Adam had felt that jolt of something hot and dangerous. Naturally, he'd kept it on a tight leash, since she was his brother's wife. Then when Devon and Sienna divorced, Adam had kept his distance because he'd figured she'd had enough of the Quinn family to last a lifetime.

Now here he was, taking her to his home. If he couldn't find a way past the hard tug of desire, it was going to be a *long* couple of weeks. He would handle it, though. That's what Adam did. When faced with a situation, he found a way through it, or around it. And if there was one thing Adam was good at, it was focusing. That's all he had to do. *Focus.* Not on what he wanted, but on what he needed. And damn it, he needed Sienna's help.

"Adam?" she asked, dropping one hand onto his forearm. "Are you okay?"

"Yeah. I'm fine." A light, friendly touch, and yet, it felt like lightning striking between them. She felt it too because she let her hand fall away. Brusquely, he stepped back from her. Distance would be key, he told himself. Best to stop now. "You're sure this is it."

"If I need something else, I can always come back

here to get it. Not like I'm going to the other side of the country." She smiled again. "Besides, I'm not like most women. I travel light."

And a part of him was impressed by that. The women who came and went from his life were interchangeable in their attitudes toward clothes, jewelry and being in the right place at the right time. After a while, they all seemed to be practically clones of each other. None of them were interested in anything beyond the next society function or charity fund-raiser. They didn't even care what the charity was for. It was mainly a chance to see and be seen and it bored Adam beyond the telling of it.

He couldn't imagine Sienna bothering to put on makeup before she so much as left her bedroom in the morning. Hell, all she was wearing now as far as he could tell, was a little mascara and some lip gloss. And damned if she wasn't the most beautiful thing he'd seen in a long time.

"You really didn't have to come pick me up," she was saying, and Adam paid attention. "I've got my own car and I remember where your house is."

"I don't know," he mused. "*Car* is a pretty generous description of what's parked out in your driveway. I doubt you'd have made it all the way to Newport."

His home in Newport Beach was fourteen miles from Seal Beach, but as far as neighborhoods went, it might as well be light-years from here. Adam frowned at that random thought and wondered when the hell he'd become a snob.

"Hey." Insulted, she insisted, "Gypsy is a great car."

"Gypsy?" he snorted. "You named your car?"

"Don't you?" She shook her head as she swung

a giant brown leather purse onto her shoulder, then wheeled the suitcase closer.

"No."

Now she shrugged. "Cars are people, too. We yell at them, bargain with them—'please don't run out of gas here'—why shouldn't they have names?"

"That is possibly," Adam said thoughtfully, "the weirdest argument I've ever heard."

"Think about it the next time your car doesn't start and you're cursing it."

"My cars *always* start."

"Of course they do." She laughed. "No adventure in that, is there?"

"Adventure?" This was the strangest conversation he'd ever had with a woman. And Adam realized that he was enjoying himself more than he had in a long time.

"Well sure," she said. "If everything goes right all the time, where's the fun in that?"

"I don't consider a car breaking down to be fun."

"It can be." She dug in the oversize bag and came out with a set of keys. "The last time my fan belt snapped, I found the greatest bakery/coffee shop. I waited for AAA there and had an amazing slice of German chocolate cake."

"Fascinating." And she was. Not only did her looks appeal to him, but the way her mind worked intrigued him.

"You just never know. One time I got a flat tire and took the most amazing sunset pictures." She sighed a little as if remembering. "I was on my way to an appointment and never would have seen it if I hadn't been forced to stop."

So, in Sienna's world, a flat tire or a snapped fan belt was a *good* thing. "You're an interesting woman."

Her smile brightened. "Isn't that a nice thing to say?"

A laugh shot from his throat, surprising them both. "Only you would find a compliment in there."

"I'd much rather be interesting than boring," she quipped. "So maybe you're hanging out with the wrong women."

"Maybe I am," he admitted. Hell, he hadn't laughed with a woman in far longer than he liked to think about.

She tipped her head to one side and her blond hair swept out in a golden fall. A smile teasing her mouth, she looked up at him. "There may be hope for you, Adam."

His gaze locked with hers. "Hope for what?"

"Well," she countered, "that's the question, isn't it?"

His body stirred and his mind filled with all kinds of things he might hope for. Then he got control again and reminded himself that no matter how much he wanted her, Sienna West was off-limits. "Is every conversation with you going to be this confusing?"

"If we're lucky." Still smiling, she lifted her suitcase.

"I'll get that."

"Nope. You can carry the bag with my clothes. Nobody carries my cameras but me."

"Cameras? Plural?" he asked, looking at the rolling suitcase. "How many do you need?"

"Well I don't know, do I?" she said patiently. "That's why I bring a selection."

The tone in her voice was patient, as if she were talking to a three-year-old. Irritating. Amazing how quickly she could turn what he was feeling from attraction to annoyance. And it would be best all the way around if he just *stayed* annoyed. "Right."

"And remember, I'll be going to work when I have to, Adam." She looked up at him. "You already agreed to that. I've got four appointments this week."

He nodded. Safe ground. Hell, he was willing to compromise. After all, the baby wasn't really *her* responsibility. No, little Jack Quinn was now Adam's charge. Just for a second or two, Adam's legendary self-confidence wavered. He knew next to nothing about raising children. Hadn't exactly had prime role models in his own parents. He'd be feeling his way through this blind, but he was determined to succeed.

Devon's son deserved a happy life and Adam was going to see to it that the kid got exactly that. "Not a problem. We'll work around your appointments."

"Okay, good." Nodding, she turned to lock the front door, then started down the front steps.

"I appreciate this, Sienna." He frowned briefly. Adam wasn't accustomed to being so damn humble and he realized it left a bad taste in his mouth. Asking for assistance was just out of his normal world. He did what needed doing. He was the one in charge. Finding answers, solving problems. Now everything was different. "In case you were unaware, I'm not used to having to ask for help."

"Yeah, I got that," she said. "But everyone needs help sometimes."

"Not me," he muttered, then said louder, "Look, I realize this might be…awkward. You. Devon's child."

Sienna held up one hand and shook her head. "Don't. Don't read things into this that aren't there. It's not like that for me. So we should probably get this out of the way right from the jump. Devon and I were divorced two years ago. And it was over for me for at least a year before that."

Her voice was soft, but her eyes flashed, letting him know that this was important to her. That she wanted him to not just listen but to *hear* her.

"I'm sorry Devon died. I really am. But not for my own sake, Adam. For you. For your mom." She reached out and laid one hand on his forearm. "I'm happy to help with the baby, but I'm not hurt that he had a child with someone else. Devon and I were much better friends than we were a couple. I'm not a victim, Adam. I'm doing fine on my own."

He studied her for a long minute before nodding. "Okay, yeah. I can see that you are. I'm glad for that. It will make things easier on all of us."

"Good." She gave him a quick smile. "We'd better get going. I'll just follow you."

Frowning again, Adam countered, "I was going to give you a ride to the house."

"And without a car, I'll get to work how?" Shaking her head, she said, "Nope. I need Gypsy, so I'll follow you. And don't worry about losing me. Like I said, I remember where you live."

He didn't like the idea of her driving what looked like a hunk of metal held together with prayer. The damn car was an accident waiting to happen. But one look into her eyes told him if he said anything, he'd have a battle on his hands.

Ordinarily, Adam wasn't against a good battle; nothing he liked better than getting into the middle of a debate and proving just how right he was. But today, he didn't have time for it. Once she was at his house, he'd take care of the car situation. He had half a dozen cars at his place; she could take her pick of them. Hell, he'd make it part of their deal if he had to. She'd go for it.

"Fine," he said, willing to let it go for now.

"So is Delores watching the baby at the house?"

"Just for tonight. She's going on vacation tomorrow." He carried her out to the drive. "Kevin drove the baby to the house."

She laughed and the sound lifted into the air and hung there like a rainbow shining through gray clouds. Turning to grin up at him, she repeated, "Kevin? How'd you talk him into that?"

"He works for me."

"Uh-huh." She waited, watching him knowingly.

Finally, Adam sighed. "I'm buying lunch for the rest of the month."

"Oh. Good bribe."

"I don't bribe people—" He stopped and nodded. "I incentivize." When she didn't say anything, he admitted, "Fine. It was a bribe."

"So, how is Kevin? He and Nick still together?"

"Yeah. They got married a year ago."

"That's great," she said. "Did Nick ever open the restaurant he was always talking about?"

Adam carried her bag to the back of her car. "He went into catering instead. Decided it was less frustrating to deal with one picky client than an entire restaurant of customers. His place is called Tonight's the Night."

"Oh, I like it."

"Yeah, he's doing really well."

She walked straight to her car, stabbed the key into the trunk lock and—nothing. "Come on, baby, just open up..."

"Let me try," Adam said, taking the keys from her.

Sienna tried to snatch them back, but Adam evaded her.

"I can do it," she argued. "It just sticks sometimes, that's all."

"Right." Adam tried the key himself with the same results. Scowling, he tried a few more times before crying defeat. "Yes, this is the car you want to depend on."

"There's nothing wrong with my car." She grabbed the keys, walked to the driver's side and opened the passenger door. Carefully, she set the suitcase on the backseat, then motioned for him to hand over her duffel bag. When he did, she tossed it inside as well and closed the door. "See? Everything's fine."

"Except you can't open the trunk."

"Turns out, I didn't need to."

"Are you this stubborn with everyone? Or just me?"

"Everyone."

"Great."

"Now, if we're finished dissing Gypsy…" She gave the car a pat, then opened the driver's door. "I'll meet you at your place."

"Just follow me." It was an order, not a request.

"Sure."

She'd already dismissed him, climbing into her car and firing up the so-called engine that coughed and hacked like a tuberculosis patient. Leaning down, he peered into the window. "Straight down PCH, past Fashion Island to—"

"Adam, I *know*." Shaking her head, she asked, "Honestly, are you this bossy with everyone? Or is it just me?"

Frowning as she tossed his words back at him with a twist, he grumbled, *"Everyone."*

"I actually knew that." She grinned and shoved the gear stick into Reverse.

He bit back his frustration and turned for his own car. Once inside, he fired up the engine, then made a U-turn and waited to make sure she followed him. Hell, to make sure her vehicle could keep up. He didn't trust that rusted-out piece of junk she was driving.

Sienna was irritating, attractive and hardheaded enough that he could only think that the next two weeks were going to be a nightmare. Especially because he wanted her now more than he ever had. What Adam couldn't understand was why arguing with Sienna left him more intrigued than a polite conversation with anyone else. Aggravated with himself, he deliberately pushed all thoughts of Sienna out of his mind for the rest of the drive.

Fifteen minutes later, Adam turned off Pacific Coast Highway and waited for Sienna to catch up. Cars had moved in and out of the space between them like blips in a video game, but she shouldn't be more than a minute or two behind him.

He waited. Five minutes. Ten. Then grumbling, turned his car around and backtracked, looking for her. "That fossil she's driving probably broke down and she's waiting for a rescue," he told himself. "Well if she'd listened to me in the first place—"

It wasn't long before he spotted her car parked on PCH not far from the Huntington Pier. She wasn't in the car. And she wasn't standing beside it, looking for her rescuer.

"Of course." Adam blew out a breath as he drove past her. Turning around as soon as he could, he parked behind her so-called car, got out and walked to find her.

The wind whipped past him, rushing inland, carrying the scent of the sea along with it. The palm trees danced in the wind like chorus girls in a Vegas review and a froth of foam dotted the waves headed toward shore. And there was Sienna—crouched at the edge of the greenbelt, holding her camera to her eye, focusing on the ocean and the surfers gliding on their boards.

He studied her for a second or two, admiring her complete concentration, her focus. She was unaware of him or anything else that wasn't outlined in the center of her camera lens. Her blond hair waved like a flag in the wind and the faded jeans she wore cupped her behind lovingly. He took a breath and deliberately looked away from that particular view.

"What're you doing?"

Sienna didn't even glance at him and that fried his ass just a bit. "I'm taking some pictures."

"And you had to stop to do this now?"

"Had to capture the light on the waves," she said, not answering the question at all.

He glanced out to where her camera was pointed. "Yeah. Sunlight. Happens every day."

Now she did swivel her head to look up at him. There was a mixture of pity and exasperation in her eyes. "You have no vision."

It wasn't her words so much as the expression in her gaze that slapped at him. "My vision's good enough."

"Is it?" She turned away to take a few more pictures, the quiet, repetitive click of the shutter the only sound between them. Finally, though, she stood up and looked him in the eye. "You see what you have to see, Adam. What you expect to see. Anything that isn't on your agenda gets overlooked."

"Because I don't daydream while driving or get distracted from the task at hand, that makes me what? A barbarian?"

She laughed and shook her head. "No, it just makes you...*you*."

"Glad to hear it," he snapped, though he had a feeling he'd just been insulted. But he wasn't dealing with it now.

"What I *expected* to see was your pitiful car right behind me."

Her mouth twitched once, then she sobered again. "Well, I'm finished now, so we can go."

Adam was torn. He admired a strong will and a woman with the strength to go toe-to-toe with him. But he also wanted to set the tone for this arrangement. He would be the one calling the shots, whether she liked it or not, so she'd better get used to the idea.

"Before we go—"

"Yes?" Her hair twisted in the wind and she shook it back from her face.

"When you're watching the baby I expect your 'vision' to be focused on him."

"What's that supposed to mean?"

"It seems pretty clear to me." He shrugged. "You were supposed to be following me and instead you detoured to do something else entirely." He shoved his hands into his pockets and flicked a quick glance at the sea. "I don't want that happening around Jack."

"You really think I would?" Insult colored her words and a dangerous glint flashed in her eyes.

"I didn't say that."

"You did everything but."

"Then you agree I didn't say it."

She took a deep breath, closed her eyes and a second later said, "Nine, ten." She opened her eyes and fixed her gaze on his. "Look, Adam. I agreed to help you out and that's just what I'm going to do, but you're not going to micromanage me while I do it."

"I'm not?" Amused now, he gave her a half smile that disappeared again an instant later.

"No, because if you can't agree to back off, I won't do it at all."

"You already agreed."

"And I keep my word," she said, then added, "unless provoked."

He could argue the point with her. Because when it came to provocation, he had more to complain about than she did. They could stand there beside the palm tree that continued to sway with the wind and talk circles around each other until late into the night. But the bottom line was, he *needed* her. So for now, he'd give her this point. But he'd manage anything in his own damn house that he wanted to manage and there wouldn't be a thing she could do about it. Because he *knew* Sienna West. She would never walk away from a baby who needed her. No matter the provocation.

"You'll be provoked," he said, not even sure himself if it was a warning or a promise. "Clearly," he added, "so will I."

"Are you irritated? Again?"

"The feeling's becoming alarmingly familiar," he admitted. "And we both know you won't back out on a deal."

Her blue eyes were squinted against the afternoon sunlight as she turned to look out at the sea. The first hints of sunset were staining the cloud-spattered sky, lavender, pink, deep gold. While she took her sweet time answering him, Adam studied her. Her profile was sharp and strong. Her blond hair whipped around her face and lifted into the same wind that plastered her white, button-down shirt against her body, defining her high, full breasts to such a degree that Adam had to curl his hands into fists to keep from reaching for her.

His body tightened, his heartbeat jumped into a gallop and he told himself that if he was as smart as he thought he was, he'd call this whole thing off. Having this woman in his home for at least the next couple of weeks and not being able to have her was going to be torture.

One stray thought slid through his brain. *His brother had been an idiot.*

Adam wouldn't make the same mistakes. Devon had married Sienna, and then let her leave. Adam wasn't going to be involved with her at all, because if he allowed that, he'd never let her go. And he'd already proven that he sucked at relationships.

So Sienna was off-limits.

Damn it.

"I said I'd stay and I will," she told him flatly. "But, Adam, you make the decisions for the baby. You don't make *mine.*"

"Agreed." With reservations, he added silently. If he saw something that needed doing then he'd damn well arrange for it to happen.

Whether Sienna West liked it or not.

# Four

Adam's house was as spectacular as Sienna remembered.

She followed his car through the scrolled ironwork gate along the drive edged with flowers and trees, and then parked beside him. She got out of the car and took a moment to let her gaze slide across the house and grounds.

The house itself was Tuscan style, with lots of aged brick, cream-colored stucco and heavy wood shutters at every window. Along the second story was a balcony with a black iron railing and terra-cotta pots boasting rivers of flowers in bright colors that spilled onto the deck. It sat high on a hill above Newport Beach, boasting an amazing view of the ocean and the bay, where hundreds of luxury boats dipped and swayed in their berths.

The entry, she remembered, was a long, tiled walkway lined with arches adorned by bougainvillea vines in rich shades of red, purple and coral. The yard was a wide sweep of meticulously tended green dotted by trees along a high wall separating the estate from the street.

It was perfect—and to her photographer's eye, a dream house, begging to be documented.

"You ready for this?" Adam was right beside her and she hadn't heard him move.

He was so close she swore she could feel heat pouring from his body to wrap itself around her. And in spite of that warmth, or maybe because of it, she shivered a little.

"I'm ready," she said, swallowing hard before turning her head to meet his gaze. "It's just two weeks, Adam. What could happen?"

One corner of his mouth lifted and Sienna took a quick breath. The man was so damn confident already, she didn't need to let him know that his slightest smile was enough to make her knees quiver.

"That's what we're going to find out, Sienna." He turned to open her car door. "I'll get your stuff."

She was grateful he wasn't looking at her face at the moment. If he read her expression now, Adam would know exactly how much he affected her. And that was one secret she didn't want to share.

"I'll get the cameras," she reminded him. Idle daydreaming over gorgeous homes was over. Now it was time to begin the bargain that would open the way to her creating her own dreams. She took the bag with her cameras and Adam grabbed the duffel, then led her toward the house.

"I called Delores to let her know we were coming."

"How is she?" Sienna remembered the older woman as warm and friendly. Of course, that was when Sienna and Devon were married. There was no telling how the woman would react to her now.

"Same as always," he said, not bothering to look back at her. "Like I told you before, tomorrow she's leaving to visit her sister in Ohio for two weeks, which is why I need the help."

Reminder: It would be just her, Adam and the baby in the beautiful house for the next two weeks. Her stomach did a quick dip and spin at the thought and a treacherous tingle set up shop just a little lower. Oh, this could be really bad.

Keeping a tight grip on her suitcase, Sienna followed Adam down that beautiful entry and through the double, hand-carved doors. To avoid watching him, she shifted her gaze to take in the interior of the house. It was even more impressive than the outside and that was saying something.

Wide, rust-colored tiles swept through the entire first floor, with huge, floral rugs in faded shades of blues and greens offering warmth. The ceilings were open beamed and every wall boasted floor-to-ceiling windows to take advantage of the ocean views. The furniture was heavy and oversize, but comfortable and seemed to set a welcoming tone in a place that would otherwise have felt intimidating by its sheer size and opulence.

A red-tiled staircase swept off the entryway in a wide curve accompanied by hand-carved wooden banisters. She knew the bedrooms were upstairs because she and Devon had stayed here a couple of times. And she knew the views from the second story would take her breath away.

"There you are!" A woman's voice carried to them, followed by the smart clip of heels against the floor.

Sienna turned to watch Delores Banner walk into the room, a beautiful baby perched on her hip. Delores was about fifty, with graying blond hair that swung around her face in a long bob. Her eyes were blue and her mouth was curved in a smile.

"Sienna. It's good to see you again."

A small wave of relief swept through Sienna at the other woman's greeting. She'd been half-afraid that she might somehow blame Sienna for what had happened to Devon. Which made Sienna wonder if there wasn't a small part of herself that felt blame, too. Silly of course. She'd had nothing to do with Devon's death. They'd divorced two years before he died, but maybe guilt was harder to let go of than she would have thought.

"Thank you, Delores. Good to see you, too." But it was the baby on the woman's hip who had Sienna's attention. She set her suitcase of equipment down carefully and walked across the room. "This must be Jack."

The baby looked up at her with big golden-brown eyes and a smile tugging at his mouth. His dark brown hair stood up in tufts and a dimple winked in one cheek. Sienna's heart melted.

"The image of his daddy, isn't he?" Delores bounced a little, making the baby chortle and wave both hands. Shaking her head, she looked at Sienna. "Such a shame. Devon will never—" She stopped talking abruptly, lifted her chin and said, "Never mind that. It's good of you to take care of him while I'm gone, Sienna. I swear if my sister hadn't made so many plans, I'd cancel."

"You're not going to cancel anything," Adam said in a tone that brooked no argument. "We'll be fine without you for two weeks. Sienna will be here and she's going to help me find a nanny, too."

"There he goes again," Delores said to Sienna, then turned a heated gaze on her employer. "I told you we don't need a nanny. I'm perfectly capable of taking care of this baby."

"And when you want to visit your sister again?" Adam asked.

"Well—"

"Why don't you let me hold him?" Sienna reached out and scooped little Jack into her arms. Instantly the tiny boy patted her face and smiled.

He was small but sturdy and had that special smell that all babies seemed to have. Something soft and innocent that made Sienna want to cradle him close and protect him from the world. While Jack played with her twist of silver earrings, she listened in on the argument between Delores and Adam. Fascinated, she admired the housekeeper even more than she had before. Not many people could stand up to Adam Quinn without blinking.

Delores countered, "We can work something out or my sister can visit me here until Jack's older…"

"Delores." Adam frowned at her. "It's not your job to deal with the baby."

"So you don't trust me to do it?"

"I didn't say that."

"Then I can do it."

"I didn't say that, either."

"I don't know what you're saying, or not, but I'll tell you right now, Adam Quinn," Delores warned with a shaking finger in his direction. "If I don't like the look of this 'nanny' you hire, I'll show her the door."

Sienna buried a smile at the frustration splashed across Adam's features. He couldn't afford to offend his housekeeper, but he couldn't stand there and take orders, either. This baby had already thrown Adam's world out of balance and it was enthralling her to watch him find his feet and stand his ground.

"We'll deal with that if we have to," he said, and mollified Delores even without agreeing to her demands.

He was good. And, Sienna told herself, she should keep that in mind. Adam was fast, smart and unwavering when he wanted something. Why did she like that about him?

"Did Kevin send the things for the baby?"

Delores's lips twisted as if she were considering continuing the argument, but then she thought better of it and blew out a breath. "He did. There've been delivery trucks in and out of here all afternoon."

"Good. Where'd you set up the nursery?"

"Right where you told me to," she said. "The guest suite across from yours."

Sienna knew that room. It had once been Devon's whenever he was in town. Appropriate, she thought, that his son would sleep there now.

"Everything's in place?"

"It is." Delores walked to Sienna, threaded her arm through hers and led her to the staircase. "And Sienna, I've put you in the suite beside Adam's."

Oh boy. That might not be such a good idea. Being in the same house with Adam was going to be hard enough. Being in the bedroom right next door could be one temptation too many. Maybe she should just sleep on a couch in the baby's room. The minute that thought raced through her mind though, she was ashamed of herself for even considering using a baby to protect her from her own desires.

"Of course," Delores said, watching her, "if you'd rather a different room…"

"No." Damn her easy-to-read expressions. "No, it's fine. Thank you for taking care of it on such short notice."

"Oh, it's my pleasure. With just Adam in the house, I've little enough to do. It's nice having to scurry about occasionally." Together, they climbed the stairs with Delores talking a blue streak, the baby jumping up and down on her hip and Adam's silent footsteps right behind them.

Sienna could feel his presence and told herself that was not a good sign. She was going to have to be careful. To remember that she was only doing this for the sake of building her business. There was nothing personal between her and Adam and there wasn't going to be. Wanting him was one thing, having him would be something else altogether. That would be a complication she didn't need in her life. So she'd take care of the baby and keep to herself as much as possible. The best thing to do would be to find a good nanny. Fast.

Climbing the stairs to the second floor, Sienna focused on the house, the hall, the paintings on the walls, anything but the sensation of having Adam so close behind her. Cuddling the baby to her, she gently held his hand when he gave one of her earrings a hard tug and made a mental note to avoid dangling jewelry while she was here.

When Delores turned into a room on the left, Sienna

followed her, and then stopped dead. For once in her life, she was stunned speechless. All she could do was walk to the center of the room and make a slow circle, taking it all in.

"All of this was done in one day?" The baby on her hip cooed as if in appreciation. And she couldn't blame him. It was the ideal nursery. Okay, yes, if given the opportunity, she would change the wall color from a boring soft gray to something a little more cheerful, but other than that, she was wildly impressed.

A cherrywood crib stood along one wall, all made up and ready for the baby, complete with a teddy bear in one corner. There were two dressers, an overstuffed rocking chair near one of the windows, low shelves holding a few books and toys, and a colorful rug covering the hardwood floor.

"I told him I wanted it ready by this afternoon," Adam said, giving the room a careful, thorough look.

"So naturally, it is." Sienna shook her head. She wasn't sure whether to be bemused or appalled. The man could order up something like this and not be surprised in the slightest when it was all just as he'd commanded.

"Problem?" he asked.

"No, of course not." Annoyance bubbled inside her and even Sienna couldn't have said exactly why. "You make demands and the world jumps."

One eyebrow lifted. "Not the world. Just the people who work for me."

*Which now included her.* At least temporarily. So she gave him a not so gentle reminder. "I don't jump."

One eyebrow lifted and his eyes narrowed on her. If that was the look he gave to recalcitrant employees,

Sienna could see why they would hurry to do his bidding. But she wasn't so easily intimidated. She didn't need Adam Quinn's job for her livelihood. And it would save them both a lot of time if he got used to her defying him right from the beginning.

"I didn't ask you to jump," he pointed out.

"You might. I'm just letting you know beforehand that it's not going to happen."

"I'll make a note," he ground out.

"All right," Delores said, looking from one of them to the other. "I'll just take the baby downstairs and feed him while you two settle…whatever it is that needs settling." She plucked the baby from Sienna's hip. She didn't give either one of them another look before slipping out the door.

"I don't want to fight about this," she started saying.

"But you're going to anyway."

Sienna blew out a breath and shook her head. "Adam, you're entirely too used to people leaping into action whenever you speak."

"Is that right?" He folded his arms across his chest and stared down at her as if she were a fascinating bug under a microscope. Great.

"When was the last time someone told you no?"

"You mean besides you?" One eyebrow lifted.

"Yes, besides me." She wandered the baby's room, snatched the teddy bear from the crib and held it in both hands as she studied its ridiculously happy face.

"People argue with me all the time," he said.

She glanced at him. "Do they ever win?"

He didn't say anything to that and she knew she had him.

"So, no."

"And you know that, how?"

Her gaze snapped up to his. "Because it's who you are, Adam."

"Got me all figured out, do you?"

"Oh please," she said, dropping the bear back into the crib. "Don't look so offended. You know I'm right. But here's something you don't know." She lifted her chin defiantly. "Try to order me around and I'll leave."

A tight half smile curved his mouth briefly. "No you won't, Sienna." He reached up and loosened the knot of his tie, undid the top button of his shirt.

Just that simple action made him less formidable and even more attractive. Why was that open collar so sexy? Her stomach swirled with nerves that she tried desperately to tamp down.

"I saw the look on your face when you held the baby," he said, amusement coloring his words.

Annoyed, she said, "Stop reading my mind."

"And even if you didn't already love Jack, you wouldn't leave because you don't quit," he added, staring into her eyes.

True. It wasn't just the baby who would keep her here. She'd made an agreement and, for Sienna, that was now nonnegotiable. In fact, the one and only time in her life that she'd given up was when she'd ended her marriage. And she still felt a pang of guilt for it. As if he'd heard that thought, he spoke up.

"Don't." Adam held her gaze. "You stayed with Devon far longer than any other woman would have."

"He was my husband."

"Yeah." He nodded, scrubbed one hand across his face and muttered, "And my brother, so I know what I'm talking about."

"This isn't about Devon," she said, interrupting whatever else he might have said. "This is about me. Being here. With you. Earlier, when I agreed to do this, you didn't give me a chance to lay down a few rules of my own."

He stuffed his hands into his pockets, tipped his head to one side and waited.

Looking at him was hard, because it tested her own will. He was just too gorgeous. Too crabby. Too everything. "I'll take care of the baby, but I won't do it alone."

He frowned. "What're you talking about?"

"You." When he still frowned, she went on. "Jack is your nephew. You're his guardian so you'd better get to know him."

"He's six months old."

"He won't be forever, and even with a nanny, he's going to need *you*."

Adam inhaled sharply and for the first time since she'd known him, he looked worried. Was there really something Adam Quinn wasn't supremely confident about?

"Believe it or not," he muttered, "I'd already worked that out on my own."

"Glad to hear it. He's a baby, Adam. He just wants to be held. Loved. You don't have to have all the answers right now."

"Maybe not, but I prefer having all the answers."

"Who wouldn't? But sometimes it just doesn't work out like that."

"Getting philosophical on me?" he asked.

"Hardly. Just settling a few things." As if to prove to him—and herself—that he wasn't getting to her, she walked across the room and stopped right in front of him. "I'll do my job, Adam. But I don't take orders. Not from you. Not from anyone."

Gazes locked, they stared at each other for several humming seconds as tension built between them. Every instinct Sienna had wanted her to speak up, to smooth things over. To somehow take the sting out of the challenge she'd just tossed at his feet, because she knew powerful men could never resist flaunting that power. But she held her tongue. Because she and Adam had to understand each other before this little experiment started.

She gritted her teeth to lock her jaw shut and didn't even speak when he moved in close enough that his scent flavored every breath she drew. Tipping her head back, she continued to hold his gaze, and after another second or two of taut silence, he started talking. "Everyone who works for me takes orders—one way or another. You're no different, Sienna."

"Yes," she assured him with a smile. "I really am. You came to me, Adam. You needed my help."

A muscle in his jaw twitched and his dark eyes suddenly went even darker. She almost felt sympathy for him because clearly he didn't like being reminded that he'd had a problem he couldn't solve himself.

"I'm here now and I'll do what we agreed on," she continued. "But don't think you can pull the King of the Universe thing with me."

In an instant, the darkness in his eyes lifted and his mouth curved slightly. She really hated what that simple facial expression did to the pit of her stomach. "King of the Universe," he mused. "I like it."

Laughing, she said, "Of course you do." As her

laughter faded, her smile remained because the tension had been broken and because, damn it, she liked him. Bossy attitude or not.

"You've got a great smile."

"What?"

"You heard me," he said, and reached out to lift a long, wavy lock of her hair. "I like your hair, too."

Her breath caught. "Thank you?"

His gaze locked with hers, he asked, "You know the only thing I ever envied of Devon's?"

Her heart was hammering in her chest. "What?"

"You."

"Adam…" Sienna took a long, shaky breath and though she tried to look away from his eyes, she couldn't quite manage it. So she saw the spark of heat flash there. Saw his eyes narrow as he bent his head to hers. Someone must have hit a supernatural pause button. Because the world stopped. Everything went quiet.

Outside, beyond the wall of glass, the June sky roiled with gray clouds, and in the distance, fog lay thickly on the surface of the ocean. A sea wind sent the flowers on the balcony into a twisting dance and the vibrant colors looked like a kaleidoscope. Inside, though, the world was still.

She should say something. *Do* something.

Her mind shouted warnings that she paid no attention to. Sienna's insides jumped up and down in excitement. Then she did exactly what she shouldn't have. She leaned into him. When his mouth met hers, Sienna felt the reaction shaking in her bones.

Electric. That's what he was to her. Dazzling. Sensory overload. One touch and her skin sizzled. Her blood burned. Her mouth went dry; her heart hammered in her ears. Her chest felt tight as his mouth moved over hers in a kind of hunger she'd never known. It was as if he was fighting his own desire even while feeding it. She knew how that felt because she was caught in the same sensations.

Her mouth opened beneath his and their tongues tangled desperately. He let one hand slide down her body until he was cupping her core. Even through the denim of her jeans, she felt the heat of him, the insistence of him as he pressed and rubbed. Riding the thrill of the moment, the rush of sensations, Sienna rocked her hips, riding his hand, building on what he was doing to her.

Adam groaned and Sienna echoed the sound. Her hands snaked up to hold on to his shoulders, luxuriating in the strength of him. His hand pressed harder against her center and all she could think was that she wished her jeans were gone so she could feel his touch on her bare skin. She trembled, tore her mouth from his and struggled for air.

"You're killing me," he muttered as his clever, clever fingers undid the button and zipper of her jeans.

"I don't want to kill you," she whispered. "I just want you."

He actually growled, a low, harsh scrape of sound that sent shivers coursing through her body. In one part of her mind, Sienna couldn't believe this was happening, and yet, another part of her sighed in satisfaction.

Then he slipped his hand beneath the slim band of her panties and touched her. She was hot, slick and ready and the moment he touched her, Sienna felt a *pop* of release. Her body bucked, she trembled and sucked in air like a drowning woman coming up for the third time.

She looked into his eyes as she whimpered his name

and rode out the last of the tremors claiming her. When it was over, he withdrew his hand, released her and took a long step back.

Sienna swayed unsteadily, and clumsily did up her jeans while she fought for air. Her mind was a blur of thoughts, emotions, and her body was struggling just to remain upright. It had been so long since she'd felt anything like that ripple of pleasure, it was hard to slow down her racing heart.

Adam stared at her and she watched as desire drained from his gaze. His eyes were shuttered. Blank slates. She couldn't read what he was thinking, feeling, and she hated that in the span of moments, he could distance himself from what had just happened. Was he simply trying to pretend nothing had happened here?

Well, she wasn't going to let him. She was shaken, but she didn't believe in lying to herself—or anyone else for that matter. Sienna preferred to face things head-on.

Her mouth still vibrating from the pressure of his, her body still humming, she asked, "Why?"

"Good question." He took a step back, shaking his head. "When I have an answer, I'll let you know."

Shaking her head, she swallowed hard. "Adam—"

"Don't start talking about it, Sienna, or we won't be stopping with some kissing and groping."

"What if I don't want to stop?" There it was. Out in the open. So much for maintaining control. But the simple truth was, now that she'd had his hands on her, she wanted his touch again.

"It doesn't change anything. I don't want to stop, either," he admitted through gritted teeth. "And that's a damn good reason why we should."

"That makes zero sense," she said, getting her breath back, steadying herself as she faced him.

"Damn it, Sienna." He pushed one hand through his hair and blew out a breath. "For once, try not to argue with me on something."

"So we're just going to ignore what happened?"

"We're gonna try," he muttered, and grabbed up her duffel. "Meanwhile, I'll take your stuff to your room."

"Okay…" She waited until he started out the door to speak again and when she did, he stopped and turned his head to look at her. "But what if we can't ignore it, Adam?"

His gaze burned into hers for what felt like forever and the taut silence between them practically screamed. "Then I guess we'll have to find out what happens next."

He left and she stared at the empty space where he'd been as if she could find answers to what she was feeling. Thinking. She hadn't counted on the desire she'd felt for him to be so easily stoked into an inferno. But now that it had been, she didn't want to deny it, either.

Since Devon's death, Sienna had been alone. By design. She'd concentrated on her business, on rebuilding her life. There'd been no time for men, even if she'd been interested, which she really hadn't been.

But now there was Adam.

And her emotions were so all over the place she couldn't pin a single one down long enough to examine it. She wasn't here to play house, though. To give in to the need for him that had always been there, just beneath the surface. And she'd do well to remember that.

When she was steady enough, she followed Adam to the suite that would be hers and told herself that she was going to have to be very careful for the next cou-

ple of weeks. Moving in with Adam was going to be a
test. Yes, she wanted the new photography studio. Yes,
she loved babies and looked forward to taking care of
Devon's son.

All of that said, though, there was Adam to be considered. He was both drawing her in and pushing her
away in equal measure.

But his kiss, his touch, was going to haunt her.

# Five

"It's taken care of, Mother." Adam carried his cell phone across the office and stopped in front of one of the wide windows. While his mother ranted through the speaker, he stared out at the sea. Usually, he could find calm there. Not, it seemed, today.

*More surfers than usual*, he thought idly, but then there was a storm out there somewhere, making the waves higher than normal. And, he told himself, there was clearly a different kind of storm brewing with his mother in Florida.

"How?" Donna Quinn demanded. "How is anything being taken care of? You can't expect me to believe *you're* caring for that baby."

Was that really so implausible? God knew he couldn't do much worse than his own parents had. He was already regretting calling Donna Quinn to let her know about her grandson's existence. But, she'd had a right to know that her favored son had become a father just before he died.

"I'm going to hire a nanny," he said, working hard to hold on to a temper that seemed to flare into life at just the sound of his mother's voice.

"Your housekeeper is unqualified," she told him flatly. "You need a proper nanny."

Both eyebrows rose as did the temper beginning to bubble in the pit of his stomach. "As I said, I'm going to hire a nanny."

The door behind him opened and he turned to wave Kevin into the room.

"And until then?" Her voice went higher, more demanding and he was regretting putting her on Speaker.

"I've got someone temporarily."

"Who?"

Kevin grimaced and Adam knew just what his friend meant. His mother wouldn't be happy if she knew it was Sienna caring for the baby. Donna Quinn still blamed Sienna for the divorce and even for Devon's death, insisting that if Sienna had stayed in the marriage, Devon wouldn't have been in that damn speedboat. His mother was irrational, but unmovable.

"Don't worry about it," he hedged. "It's handled."

"If I weren't so far away," she vowed, "I'd do it myself."

Kevin snorted and Adam frowned at him. Though, hell, that remark had been laughable. Donna wasn't exactly maternal. Oh, she hadn't run out on them, but she'd turned Adam and Devon over to a procession of au pairs as soon as she could.

"Kevin just came in—" Devon told her and watched with evil satisfaction as Kevin paled and waved both hands as he shook his head in blind panic. God, it was tempting to get rid of his mother by handing her off to Kevin. But if he did, the other man might quit just to get even.

"Well." Donna sniffed, and her voice went even cooler than usual. "You tell him for me that I've still not forgiven him for not inviting me to his wedding and—"

"I'll tell him," Adam interrupted. "I've got work, Mother."

"Fine. I want regular reports on Devon's child."

"His name is Jack."

She huffed. "After his father. Why would he do that?"

"I don't know," Adam said.

"Probably to irritate me," she said, because in Donna's world all things were about her.

Adam didn't have the time or the inclination to listen to his mother rail about how she'd suffered during her marriage and how Adam's father had crushed her girlish spirit. Since he'd lived through it, he knew damn well there'd been plenty of crushing on *both* sides.

"I'll keep you posted, Mother." He hung up then, before she could say another word.

Adam took a deep breath and deliberately loosened his grip on the cell phone before he could shatter it.

"I thought you were going to throw me to the wolf," Kevin said.

"Thought about it," Adam admitted with a shrug. "Hell, anything to get the wolf off me."

He scrubbed the back of his neck, trying to ease the tension, but it didn't work. Nothing did when he had to deal with his mother. They'd never been close—Donna had devoted whatever motherly interest she possessed to Devon. Just as well, since her constant plotting, planning and conniving had driven Devon crazy enough that when he married Sienna, the two of them had moved to Italy—partly to escape Donna.

"We probably should have just invited her to the wedding," Kevin mused.

"Oh hell no." Adam shook his head, walked back to his desk and dropped into the chair. "She'd have turned the whole thing into a circus."

Kevin shuddered. "Yeah, I guess. But I'll be hearing about it forever."

"The price we pay for sanity." Adam leaned back and closed his eyes. "At least she's in Florida."

"True. From what I heard, it sounds like she's already focusing on the baby. Substitute for Devon?"

"That's probably her plan." Adam opened his eyes and gave Kevin a hard look. "But that's not going to happen."

"Good luck stopping her."

Adam picked up a stray pen and tapped it furiously against the desk. "Oh, I'll stop her. I'm not a kid anymore. She doesn't make the rules. I do."

"Okay, good." Kevin nodded and leaned back in his chair. "So how'd your first night as a daddy go?"

Adam winced. "I'm his uncle not his father."

"Uh-huh. Technically. In practice, you're a brandnew father. Got cigars?"

"You're not as funny as you think you are." Adam frowned, sighed and admitted, "It was a nightmare. He cried for two hours straight. Sienna and I traded off walking him. Think I did twenty miles."

Of course, the hardest part of that had been being with Sienna and not touching her again. He'd had just a small taste of her, and that had fed his hunger until it was now gnawing on his bones. His soul.

He'd told Sienna they were going to ignore what had happened. So far, that wasn't working. At least, not for him.

Kevin groaned in sympathy. "Be sure to tell Nick that story, will you?"

"Happy to." Pushing Sienna from his mind, he said, "The kid's got a good set of lungs on him anyway."

"Uh-huh. How'd it go with Sienna?"

Adam speared him with a look. "What's that mean?"

Kevin shrugged. "It means she's gorgeous and you've always had a thing for her."

Adam sat up straight, tossed the pen down and then picked it up again. "You know, some people go their whole lives without a know-it-all best friend."

"Poor souls." Kevin grinned. "Talk."

"It went fine."

Kevin snorted. "You're a master storyteller."

"I don't *share,* Kevin, and you damn well know it."

"I live in hope, though. Seriously, Adam, you're wound so tight, keeping everything so locked down that one of these days you're just going to snap."

"Thanks for the warning. I'll keep it in mind."

"Or you could just tell me what the hell's going on," Kevin said, eyes narrowed on him.

"What do you want from me?" Adam shook his head and avoided eye contact. "She's there to take care of Jack. That's it."

"Well," Kevin said slowly, "that's about the saddest thing I've ever heard."

Adam wasn't going to get into this with Kevin. Hell, he was trying very hard to not even *think* about Sienna—

so far with no success. But talking about her wouldn't help the situation. Especially since Adam knew damn well that Kevin would encourage him to seduce Sienna. To go after what he wanted and worry about the fall-out later.

Well hell. He didn't *need* encouragement.

"I'm not looking for a woman, Kevin." And before the man could make a smart-ass remark, he added, "*Or* a man."

"Don't knock it till you've tried it."

Adam snorted. "Yeah, I tried marriage once. Remember?"

"That didn't count."

"Really?" Leave it to Kevin to rewrite his own rules when it suited him. "Why not?"

"Tricia wasn't exactly the settle-down type."

"Maybe she wasn't the problem."

Kevin narrowed his gaze on him. "Feeling all introspective? Lack of sleep getting to you?"

"No." But if his short-lived marriage had done anything, it had proven to Adam that he sucked at sharing. Tricia wasn't good at it either, so between the two of them, they'd created the marriage from purgatory. Hardly hell, since they were never together enough to make each other miserable. It had just been a slow slide into indifference and then oblivion.

He liked his life just fine now. Living on his own meant no one was counting on him. No one else's needs depended on Adam. He could go home, have a drink and get some work done in the peace and quiet.

Of course, he reminded himself, all of that had just changed dramatically. Quiet was going to be hard to find now that he had Jack to think of. He would do his best by his nephew—but that didn't change one very important thing. He wasn't a commitment kind of guy. He liked women fine as long as they came and went from his life without causing a ripple.

Then memories of that kiss, the feel of Sienna's body trembling in his arms as she reached a quiet climax, flooded his mind. The look in her eyes, her mouth parted, breath coming fast, quick. The slick heat of her body and the driving need he'd been forced to strangle before he could toss her onto the nearest bed and find what he wanted most.

A ripple. The thought was laughable.

Those stolen minutes with Sienna had proven to him that her presence in his life would be more like a tidal wave. A tsunami that would wipe out the world he'd created for himself. And even knowing that, he couldn't deny that his body was still hard, tight, painful.

Desire continued to pound inside him. He'd spent what was left of the night before lying awake, with his body aching for what he refused to give it. He wasn't going to start up something with his brother's ex because it couldn't go anywhere. And damned if he'd use Sienna as badly as his brother had.

All he had to do was make it through the next couple of weeks without touching her again. And that meant he had to keep his mind from wandering to thoughts of her, too.

"Haven't we got some actual *work* to do?" he asked abruptly, desperate for something else to think about.

Kevin gave him a long, considering look. "That's actually why I came in here in the first place. The Davidson Group called about the project in San Diego. They want an in-house meeting."

"Good. Set it up." This was what he needed. To keep his mind so full of work it had no room to torment him with images of Sienna.

Adam's company was behind a luxury hotel going up in the place of a derelict building that had been left to rot. "Get the latest sketches from the architect. Tell them we want the finals ready to roll. Get the Davidson people in here tomorrow afternoon. I want to move on this."

"Right." Kevin stood up. "One of our crews are on-site now, clearing it. Mike Jonas says it should be ready for the new foundation by the end of the week."

"Good. Keep me posted. If they run into any trouble, I want to know about it." Adam grabbed a thick stack of files and opened the one on top.

"You will, but they won't." Kevin tapped his iPad, calling up one of the lists he lived for. "Oh. Tracy said to tell you she's got the bid from the landscape gardeners on the Long Beach project. Said it's too high, but she'll get them down lower."

"Okay, and call the Realtor in Santa Barbara about that property we put a bid on. I want to know what's taking so long."

"Got it." Kevin headed for the door.

"Wait a minute," Adam said, and Kevin stopped, turning to look back at him. "Did you arrange for a crew to take care of the repairs at Sienna's place?"

He'd told Kevin what he wanted done as soon as he got to the office that morning. Whatever happened between him and Sienna, damned if Adam was going to let her live in a place that looked so run-down. Naturally, Kevin had argued with him about it, insisting that Adam talk to Sienna before they did any work, but

Adam wasn't interested in an argument. The woman had too much pride for her own good. So he'd just take the decision out of her hands. She'd be grateful. Eventually.

"I did," Kevin said reluctantly. He pulled up the schedule on his iPad. "Toby Garcia's going to take a few of the guys off the school building in Mission Viejo."

"Are we on schedule there?" Adam signed one of the letters Kevin had brought him and looked up at his friend.

"All on track. They're wrapping things up this week, so Toby felt safe pulling a few of the guys off that job." Kevin looked at him. "But I still think—"

"Yeah, I know what you think." Adam waved one hand at him dismissively. "I told you what I want. New roof, paint, any repairs, fix the damn cracks in her sidewalk, too," Adam muttered. "She's always staring into a camera lens so she'll kill herself on that walk sooner or later."

Kevin laughed. "Got it."

"And the garage door." Adam tossed his pen aside. "It looks like it's original to the house and that puts it around the forties. I want an automatic door installed so she can park that crappy car of hers inside without having to get out and try to wrestle the door into submission."

Still laughing and shaking his head, Kevin made more notes. "And since we're not talking to the owner of the house, what color would you like for the new paint?"

"Had to get a shot in?" Adam asked wryly.

"Just a reminder that you're asking for trouble doing this without talking to her first."

"Thanks. Look. I could have asked her, but she'd

have said no, so why bother?" Adam grabbed his pen and signed another letter after scanning it quickly. "Go with blue. Soft, not bright. White trim. Paint the damn porch, too. Looks terrible."

"Adam, I say again, she's going to be pissed."

"She can be as mad as she wants to be. The house will still be fixed."

Kevin's eyebrows went sky-high and he shook his head. "Better you have to face her with this than me."

Adam snorted. "Stop worrying. She'll love it so much she'll get over the mad fast enough." And if she didn't, Adam knew that he'd at least enjoy the argument. That woman had a head like a rock, but eventually, she'd be grateful he swooped in and fixed her house. Now all he had to do was replace that car.

"Right." Kevin nodded. "Please let me be there when you tell her what we did. I'd love to see how fast she gets over the mad."

Adam scowled at him. "Think you know her better than I do?"

"I think you just ride in and take over."

Hard to argue with that.

"And," Kevin continued, "I know I'd be furious if you just *decided* on your own to redo my house without asking."

"Then I won't do your house."

Kevin shrugged. "It's your neck. Anyway, once Toby's done at Sienna's, he'll head the crew doing the church job in Lake Forest."

"That'll work," Adam said, pleased at the change in subject. "We've got a meeting in Santa Barbara next week, right?"

"Yeah, with the group looking to fund a new golf course."

Adam smiled and leaned back. "How's the design coming?"

"The team's working on it, but they hit a snag." Kevin waved his hand. "Something about a par three overlooking the ocean but needing more room for the bunkers they want to add."

"Send me the specs. I'll take a look at home tonight."

"Already sent them to your email."

"Great. Thanks."

Kevin turned to leave, but Adam stopped him. "I'll be bringing Jack in tomorrow. I'm going to need help with him."

"Yeah," Kevin said, laughing as he closed the office door. "You really will."

Sienna took dozens of pictures.

Little Jack Quinn was the perfect subject. Of course, even if the adorable baby hadn't been there, Sienna would have had plenty of targets for her lens. The house. The grounds. The views. On the second-floor balcony, surrounded by terra-cotta pots filled with flowers that spilled over onto glass-topped tables, she shot so many images, she'd be sorting through them for hours.

And Jack was there, at her feet, laughing, bouncing in a walker that contained far too many bells and other assorted noisemakers. Once Delores left for her vacation, it had been just Sienna and Jack in the big house. And after a couple of hours alone with a baby, Sienna had a whole new respect for mothers.

"Who knew you could be so demanding?" she asked,

smiling and talking in a singsong tone that made the tiny boy laugh in response.

Instantly, she felt a flutter around her heart and told herself that Adam wasn't the only danger in the Quinn household. She could easily fall in love with this baby. Which wasn't a good idea, since the moment Adam hired a nanny, Jack would no longer be a part of her life.

"But I'm going to love you anyway, aren't I?"

He giggled, slapped both arms against the walker and kicked his chubby little legs. She took another quick shot and admired it on the view screen. "You just don't take a bad picture, do you? Sort of like your father. And your uncle."

She sat back into the deep cushions of the couch and watched Jack push off on his tiny feet and roll along the floor of the great room. Watery sunlight slipped through the gray clouds to lay what seemed like a mystical glow on the scene. The house was quiet but for the baby's gurgles, laughs and slaps. She lifted her ever-present camera and took a few shots of the tiny boy with the magnificence of the house surrounding him. As she looked at her view screen, Sienna thought about what it would be like for him, growing up here with Adam.

Would the baby find the father he needed? Would Adam turn Jack's care completely over to a nanny? She frowned at the thought, then reminded herself that Adam had been right there with her the night before when they couldn't get Jack to sleep. They'd taken turns walking through the house, murmuring and consoling the baby who had to have been confused at his new surroundings. Adam had been patient and kind, and being that close to him in the stillness of the night had made her feel too much.

Of course, he'd been even closer yesterday afternoon. With his hands on her. His mouth on hers. Sienna trembled, remembering those few stolen moments when she'd shattered in his arms. A swift jolt of heat swamped her and sent flames licking along her bloodstream. She wanted to feel it all again. Feel *more*. For years, Sienna had tried to ignore what Adam made her want. Need. Now it was as if her body and mind had been unleashed and she wanted to revel in it.

This was so not good.

Before she could get any further on that train of thought, her cell phone rang and Sienna grabbed at it like a lifeline. "Cheryl, hi."

Best friend, mother of three and the voice of sanity when Sienna needed it.

"Hi back. Weren't we supposed to have lunch over here today?"

"Oh God." Face palm. She sat back and let her head drop against the dark brown leather couch. Jack paused in his play to give her a quizzical look. She smiled at him as she said, "I completely forgot. I'm so sorry."

Cheryl laughed. "Hey, no problem. Just glad to know it's not *my* mind dissolving."

"No, it's totally me." Sienna watched the baby roll over across the floor, slapping both hands onto the bells attached to the walker tray. "Something came up yesterday and—"

"And apparently is still going on today?" Cheryl interrupted. "Intriguing."

*Intriguing.* Well, that was one word for it. Another was *crazy.* Or *masochistic.* Or, given enough time, she could no doubt come up with plenty of words to describe what was going on right now. Sienna sighed.

"You're not going to believe this, but I'm at Adam's house."

There was a long pause. "Adam? As in Adam your ex-brother-in-law? Adam Sex-on-a-Stick Quinn?"

In spite of everything, Sienna laughed. "He's not on a stick."

"Maybe not," Cheryl mused, "but I'm betting he's got a '*big* stick.'"

Instantly, her mind conjured up images of Adam, naked, and everything in Sienna curled up and whimpered. "Really? You're not helping."

"Disagree," her friend countered. "You've been telling me about Adam for two years. Do you really think I haven't done a little imagining from time to time? For example, my Charlie has a terrific stick."

Sienna laughed. "I do *not* need to know that."

"How can I make my friends jealous if I don't brag?"

Shaking her head, Sienna rolled her eyes and asked, "Does Charlie know how often you brag?"

"Why do you think he loves me so much?" Cheryl paused and asked, "But enough about my love life—what're you doing at Adam's house?"

"It's a long story." And it felt as if she'd been involved in this story for a lot longer than just a couple of days. But then, she'd first met Adam, first felt that quick zip of attraction for him, almost four years ago. So was it any wonder that as soon as they were really alone together, it was almost as if they always *had* been?

"I've got a hot cup of tea and the kids are outside playing. I have the time, so if it's a long story, then you'd better get started."

So Sienna launched into an explanation, and the more she talked, the more improbable it all sounded, even to her. Adam had appeared in her life, turned it upside down and here she was, still trying to make sense of it all.

Then she looked at baby Jack and smiled as he slapped at the tray of toys with two chubby fists. "Bottom line, I'm staying with Adam until he hires the right nanny."

"Wow." Cheryl took a breath and sighed it out again. "It's a soap opera. You're even living in that mansion you drove me past one time."

"I am, and it's still more impressive inside than out," Sienna said, glancing round the great room, admiring the soft warmth of the place with the view of the cold ocean beyond the glass. A sea wind tossed the flowers on the balcony into a riot of colors and the thick gray clouds scuttled back and forth across the sky like prizefighters waiting for their chance to enter the ring.

"It's amazing. You, a baby and the Lord of the Manor. I was wrong. It's not a soap opera. It's a gothic novel." Cheryl warned, "Whatever you do, stay out of the attic. That's where the hero stores his crazy wife."

Laughing, Sienna said, "Sorry to disappoint, but there is no attic. There is however, a terrific view of the ocean from almost every room."

"Well, that's just mean," Cheryl said, a whine evident in her tone. "While you're there, I have to come over and see it."

"Absolutely. I'd love the company. When I'm not working, it's just Jack and I here in the house." Sienna grinned at the baby, bouncing up and down on his toes. "He's adorable, but not much for conversation."

"You think that's a bad thing," Cheryl said on a chuckle. "Then they start talking. So when do you work next?"

"Tomorrow I've got two shoots, back-to-back at Huntington Central Park." She still had to get her equipment together and ready, but there was time.

"What'll you do with the baby?"

Smiling, Sienna said, "Tomorrow, he's all Adam's."

Cheryl laughed. "I'd actually pay to see that."

"Me, too." Sienna took a breath and smiled at the thought. "But can you come over the following day?"

"You bet. I'll take the kids to their grandmother's."

"You don't have to," Sienna assured her. Cheryl's kids were great and she was sure Jack would enjoy them.

"Trust me—it's a win-win. I'll have a couple of hours to myself and my mother-in-law will be happy with me for a change."

"Okay, I'll have wine and snacks."

"You don't have to sell me," Cheryl said on a laugh, "but good to know."

When she hung up, Sienna looked down at the little boy who had managed to scoot across the room and right up to her. He grinned and a long line of drool slid from his open mouth. His eyes were shining and when he squealed in delight, Sienna smiled. He was already burrowing his way into her heart, and she knew that when she left she would miss little Jack desperately.

But she had a feeling that leaving Adam was going to be the hardest thing she'd ever done.

# Six

A few hours later, Adam walked in the door to find Sienna in the great room and no sign of the baby. He took the moment before she noticed him to look her over, top to toe. Hunger stirred inside him in a wave that was so high, so powerful, it was all he could do to control the urge to grab her and indulge himself with the heady taste of her again.

She was curled up in a big chair, long blond hair hanging over her left shoulder and across the top of her breasts. Her legs were tucked up beneath her and she had her head propped on one fist as she flipped through an open magazine on her lap. For a second or two, he wondered why it was *she* who drove him crazy.

She wasn't trying to be seductive. She was dressed simply and was totally unaware of his presence—and yet, Sienna West tied him into knots that were only tightening by the hour. Taking a breath, he steadied himself and spoke up. "Baby wear you out in one day?"

She jolted a little in surprise, then her blue eyes shifted to him and locked on. "Turns out babies are *not* easy." Then she smiled teasingly. "But you'll find that out for yourself tomorrow."

"Yeah," he said, as an unfamiliar feeling he thought might be *cowardice* whipped through him. "About that."

Sienna gave him a stern look that did nothing to dissipate the desire he felt for her. "No way you're backing out, Adam. We have a deal."

He met her determined gaze for a long moment before nodding. "You're right. We do." He shrugged out of his suit jacket and loosened his tie and collar button. Tossing the jacket onto the nearest chair, he plopped down in another one. "I'll take him with me to work tomorrow."

Sienna grinned and he really hated that his body fisted in reaction, but there didn't seem to be anything he could do about it. "I'd love to see you dealing with the baby during some high-powered meeting."

"You think I can't?" Even though he'd thought the same himself only seconds ago, he brushed aside her disbelief. "I absolutely could, but I don't have to. When I'm in a meeting, Kevin will take care of him." In fact, he was looking forward to the expression on his friend's face when Adam handed Jack over to him.

She tipped her head to one side and watched Adam with a slight smile curving her mouth. "He might quit."

"Not a chance," he said, shaking his head. "He'll complain, but he'll do it."

Adam thought about getting a beer from the wet bar

across the room, but it seemed like too much trouble. Then she spoke, and he had to wonder if Sienna was reading *his* mind for a change.

"Want a beer?"

He frowned. "You don't have to wait on me, Sienna."

"Oh, if I *had* to," she assured him, "I wouldn't."

He grinned briefly. "In that case, yeah. I would like a beer."

She unfolded from the chair and he watched her walk barefoot across the room, admiring the view. Her jeans were worn and faded and hugged her legs like long-lost lovers coming together. The tail of her pale blue dress shirt hung past her butt and he was disappointed that particular view was hidden. She bent to the bar refrigerator and came out with two cold bottles. She delivered one to him and kept the other, twisting off the top and taking a drink.

"Long day?" he asked, sipping at his own beer.

"You could say so." She studied the label on the green bottle, then looked at him again. "Jack's a sweetheart, but he needs constant attention. It's exhausting. I don't know how parents do it."

"Some don't," he muttered, and was surprised when she picked up on it.

"Yes," she said softly. "Devon told me a little about your folks."

Adam chuckled and lifted his beer in salute. "Oh, I'm sure he had plenty to say."

Shaking her head, she said, "Not really. Just that they were divorced and that your mom was a little...clingy."

"Nice word for it." Adam rested the bottle against his abdomen and studied her silently as he decided whether or not to say any more about it.

Then he realized there was no one to protect—Devon was gone, so was their father and as for Adam's mother, no woman had needed protection less. Besides, Sienna had obviously been told some of it already, so why bother pretending the Quinn family was anything but dysfunctional?

"Devon was the golden child," he said on a sigh. "Our mother really wasn't a hands-on parent when we were little. She was too busy with clubs and charity and society. But once Devon hit twelve or so, she started hanging on his every word." He frowned, remembering. "Maybe it was because Dad started cheating on her about that time. Maybe she wanted Devon to love only her. I don't know. She probably doesn't, either.

"Anyway, if that was her plan, it didn't work. She lavished attention on him until all Devon could think about was getting away."

Sienna picked at the label on her beer bottle with her fingernail. "He did say that your dad was easier to deal with…"

Adam laughed shortly when he glanced at her again. "He was. Because Dad didn't really give a damn what we did as long as our jobs got done."

Gritting his teeth, he clammed up, rethinking the decision to talk about the past. What the hell? He never told anyone about his parents. Even Kevin only knew bits and pieces of it and only because he'd actually seen some of it for himself when he'd gone home with Adam during college vacations.

What was the point of rehashing the past? It was useless and served nothing. When Sienna spoke, she broke his train of thought and he was ridiculously grateful.

"So does your mom know about Jack?"

"She does now." Remembering that phone call earlier, he took another sip of beer. Giving a snort of derisive laughter, he added, "She's so worried she's going to stay right where she is."

Sienna laughed a little, too. "Sorry. But in her defense, it's a lot to take in and she did just lose her son."

He looked at her and noticed that she was silhouetted now against the wall of windows behind her. Streaks of pink and gold and deep red shot through the clouds as the sun began to set and her eyes shone in the shadows. Her features were again easy to read and he saw sympathy for his mother written there. He couldn't really say why that annoyed him.

"You don't have to defend her," Adam said. "Or feel sorry for her. She's not coming, and it's better for all of us that she's not."

Sienna bit down on her bottom lip. "Does your mother know I'm the one watching Jack for you?"

The question came soft and low. So low he almost missed it. "No," he said, taking another sip of his beer. "I didn't see the point in stirring her up."

Sienna sighed and set her beer on the table in front of her. "She still blames me."

Adam shrugged that off, sat forward and braced his forearms on his thighs. Meeting her gaze squarely, he said, "If she does, that's her deal, Sienna. Nothing you should even think about. She has to blame someone— God knows she'd never blame herself for Devon's problems—so you're handy."

Sienna smiled sadly and shook her hair back from her face. "Or, maybe she's a little right."

"No. She's not." He wouldn't let Sienna accept his mother's implied accusations as if they were deserved.

Donna Quinn had always been unreasonable when it came to Devon. She'd seen only what she had wanted to see and disregarded the reality that didn't quite measure up.

Sienna tipped her head to one side and her hair fell like a golden waterfall. He'd spent most of the day with her face, her voice, her scent, haunting him. He never should have kissed her, and he knew it because now all he could think of was tasting her again.

"You sound sure," she said.

"I am. Hell, Sienna, you stayed with Devon two years. That's a damn record." He pushed to his feet, because he couldn't remain so close to her without reaching out to touch her. And if he touched her, he wouldn't stop. Riding the energy pulsing inside him, Adam walked to the bar, set the beer down and turned back to look at her from across the room. It was safer, keeping a distance between them.

Too bad this wasn't far enough.

He took a deep breath, grateful that her scent wasn't filling his lungs. Didn't know if he could take that just now. "Don't get me wrong. I loved my brother but that didn't make me blind to who he was."

She frowned slightly. "He wasn't a bad guy."

Adam rubbed one hand across his eyes as if he could wipe away the memories suddenly flooding his mind. "Oh, I know that. But he wasn't a *good* guy, either."

She didn't comment on that and Adam almost congratulated her on her restraint. Yeah, she'd been married to the man, but Adam had grown up with Devon. Had known him better than anyone else possibly could. And he still felt a tug of shame for how Devon had lived his life.

Adam believed that a man was only as good as his word. In that respect alone, Devon had been a disappointment. The man constantly made promises that weren't kept because something more interesting came up. It wasn't that Devon went out of his way to be a dick. It came naturally to him. But his smile, his charm had always been there to dig him out of whatever hole he found himself in.

"I don't know what you want me to say, Adam."

"Not a damn thing. You don't have to explain my brother to me or why you finally left him." He sighed and shook his head. Devon was gone and there was nothing to be gained by wishing things had been different. "But you don't have to pretend you were happy with Devon, either."

She laughed a little, but there was a tinge of sadness in the sound, too. "No point in that, really. If I'd been happy I wouldn't have divorced him."

"Well yeah, that's true enough." He looked at her as she stood up and walked toward him. Adam stiffened and hoped to hell she didn't come too close. Those eyes of hers held his gaze and he couldn't have looked away if it had meant his life. As she came near, he said, "Devon cared about Devon. He was my brother and I loved him. But I watched him blow up every relationship he ever had. Before you and after you, he couldn't be happy with anyone else because *he* wasn't happy."

"He thought he was," Sienna said.

"No he didn't. Not really." Adam took a drink of the beer he didn't want anymore. "He just kept himself so busy—yachts, jets, parties—that he didn't have time to sit down and realize that his life was so damn empty, every breath he took echoed."

"He did what he liked doing, Adam."

"Mostly," he acknowledged. "But he lost something when he left the business. Hell, I think he lost himself. He thought it'd be easier, being away from the family. From expectations. Not his fault entirely. Our dad was hard on both of us," he mused. "But he rode Devon all the time. Maybe because our mom went hard the other way."

Over the years, Adam had seen Devon change in response to his position in the family. To their father, Devon was the errant boy. The screwup. The guy who never got anything right. To their mother, he was the golden child who should be coddled and adored.

Devon became the bone that two dogs were fighting over. And Adam was on the outside, looking in. He couldn't change his parents, couldn't reach his brother, so he'd channeled everything he had into building his business. And when his father died, he'd merged the two companies. He'd bought Devon out when it became all too clear that his little brother was only interested in indulging himself and that his lifestyle was starting to affect the business.

"I let him go," Adam admitted, though the confession stung, even so long after.

"What do you mean?"

He looked into her eyes and for the first time, he couldn't read what she was thinking. Was that because he didn't want to know? Didn't want to see her blame him for what had become of Devon?

He set his beer onto the wet bar, then stuffed his hands into his pockets. "Devon wanted out. Wanted to get away from our mother, out from under the company and I let him go. Instead of kicking his ass, making him see that he should stay, work through whatever the hell was bugging him—I bought him out because he was driving me batshit. And I watched him leave. Never tried to stop him."

Sienna moved to the bar and leaned both arms on the cool, sleek polished top. "It was his decision."

"Was it?" Adam shook his head, then pushed one hand through his hair, irritated with himself. With Devon. With the whole damn situation. "I don't know. By the time he left, he was rarely at the office anyway, but if I'd said something, maybe he'd have straightened up. No way to know."

"He couldn't stay, Adam. You couldn't have changed his mind." She walked behind the bar and opened the fridge.

Adam spoke up quickly. "No thanks. I don't want another beer. Hell, I don't want this one."

"Me, either," she said, and stood up, handed him a bottle of water instead.

Ruefully, he smiled. He should have known she wouldn't do what he expected. "Thanks."

Opening her own bottle, she said, "Y'know, Devon told me about how much fun the two of you had when you started your business."

Surprised, but pleased, Adam said, "He did?"

"He missed those days, I think." She took a sip of water. "He missed *you.* But your mom drove him crazy, though he never said much about your father."

"Not shocking," Adam told her, and took a drink to ease his suddenly dry throat. "Dad and Devon never got along."

"He wouldn't have stayed, Adam," she said again, her tone practically demanding that he believe her. "He wanted to get away and you couldn't have changed his mind."

"Yeah, probably not." At least, he hoped not. Adam hated to think that when his brother had needed him most, Adam had taken the easy route and given Devon exactly what he wanted—instead of what he needed.

Frowning, he took another drink of water and watched the woman standing too close to him. He'd never talked about any of this before. Not even to Kevin. Adam had hung on to the tattered threads of his own guilt about Devon for years.

Because his father hadn't resented him and his mother had mostly ignored him, Adam hadn't had the same problems his younger brother had had. It wasn't his fault, Adam knew, but that knowledge didn't stop the guilt that crept up and slapped at him when he least expected it. Still, Devon was gone now and the best Adam could do for his little brother was to make sure Devon's son was happier than his father had been.

Thinking of Jack, Adam changed the subject abruptly. "I didn't even ask you about the baby. Where is he?"

She smiled and Adam tried to ignore the burn he felt in response.

"He's sleeping. I've got the baby monitor over there on the coffee table so I can hear him."

"Right. Of course." He capped off the water bottle. "Well, him sleeping's a good sign. Maybe he won't be up all night again."

"I think he'll be okay," she said. "He was probably just scared of a new place and new people."

"Hope you're right," he muttered. "How'd the first day with him go? Any problems?"

"No," she said with another smile.

"So, any tips for tomorrow?"

"You bet. Don't take your eyes off of him for a second." She shook her head and gave a little laugh. "He can't even walk yet, but put him on the floor and he's scooting and crawling a million miles per hour. And in his walker? Forget it. He figured out really fast how to make that little sucker move like a race car."

"Great…"

"And he's really picky about his food," she mused. "We went through a couple different kinds of baby food with him spitting most of it out. Thankfully, my friend Cheryl suggested banana slices. Those, he chowed down."

This was all so far out of his experience, Adam had a momentary pang. He was responsible for a tiny human. It would be up to him to make sure Jack was always secure. Safe. How would he be able to find a nanny in the next two weeks who he could trust enough with Jack's safety? How did parents do this?

"Oh, and he tried to pull himself up and bonked his forehead on the coffee table."

"He hit his head?" Adam blurted out as a quick jolt of what felt like *fear* scrambled through his veins. Before this baby entered his life, Adam had never been afraid of a damn thing.

"He's fine, Adam," Sienna said. "He didn't even cry, really. Just rubbed his forehead and looked surprised. As if the coffee table had betrayed him or something."

"Okay." He relaxed a little and scrubbed one hand across the back of his neck. "Who the hell can I trust with him?" he asked as his new reality came crashing down on him. "Basically, I have to find a nanny who's a world-class sprinter, a paramedic and a chef."

Sienna laughed and shook her head. "Don't make it all sound so impossible. People have been raising children for thousands of years."

"I haven't," he reminded her. Taking a long swig of water to ease the knot in his throat, he muttered, "I never wanted kids, you know."

"Like Devon, then."

He looked at her. "Yeah. Can't really blame either of us. We were raised by wolves. What the hell did we know about how to treat a kid?"

"Easy," Sienna replied, and reached out to lay her hand on top of his. "Just do everything your own parents *didn't* do. You know what you wanted from them when you were young. Give Jack what you needed and didn't get."

Sounded reasonable. And yet, there was still a slender thread of fear spooling inside him. It was a huge obligation and he didn't want to screw it up. *So, don't.* Even as those words echoed in his mind, he reminded himself that he'd never failed once when he went after something. If Jack was his goal, then he'd do it right. Adam didn't accept failure.

He looked at Sienna's much smaller hand on his and concentrated on the heat passing back and forth between them. Lifting his gaze to hers, he saw a flash of understanding in those blue eyes just before she pulled her hand back.

"You're a smart guy, Adam," she said blithely. "You'll figure it out. Now how about dinner?"

He accepted the change of subject, the coolness in

her eyes because damned if it didn't make things easier. Right now, easy sounded pretty good. "You *cooked*?"

"No, I dialed." She shook her hair back from her face. "I found a nearby Chinese restaurant and called. Turns out you have an account there."

Adam smiled. "When Delores isn't here, it's better I don't try to cook."

"No breakfast in bed for me then, huh?" She grinned. "I'll keep that in mind."

His eyes narrowed on her and he picked up her hand, rubbing his thumb across her knuckles. "When I get you into bed, trust me when I say you won't be thinking about food."

Adam had the satisfaction of seeing heat burst in her eyes like fireworks. Then she pulled her hand free again. "Well right now, I'm hungry."

"Me, too," he assured her.

"For food," she said.

"That, too," he murmured. Until just that moment, they'd both been ignoring the damn elephant in the room. Time to notice it. "You avoided me this morning."

She pressed her lips together. "I evaded. That's different."

"No, it's not."

"Okay, you're right." She crossed her arms over her chest in an unmistakable, self-defensive posture. "I wasn't ready to talk to you about what happened. So I hid out with the baby. How pitiful is that?"

"I did the same thing," Adam admitted with a shrug. "Hell, I left the house without coffee. Trust me when I say, that's pitiful. Avoiding you didn't work. though. I still thought about you today."

"Did you?"

How could he not? he wondered silently. Hell, just look at her. Blond, blue eyes, long legs, full breasts and a smile that curved her delicious mouth into tempting lines. "I don't want to think about you, Sienna."

She took a deep breath and he couldn't help but notice the rise and fall of the breasts he wanted his hands on.

"I don't want to think about you, either," she admitted.

"Well then, seems we have a problem."

"Probably," she agreed. "But we can worry about that *after* we eat, right?"

*Before, during, after...* But all he said was, "Yeah, we can do that."

"Come on, Gypsy. Don't make us look bad in front of all those snooty cars."

The next morning, Sienna glanced at Adam's fleet of vehicles with a touch of envy mixed with exasperation. How did one man need six cars? The garage and carport area behind the house was enormous. He'd moved his Land Rover out of the garage to make room for her car and she had to admit that alongside the sleek, waxed and gleaming autos, Gypsy looked a little worn.

"But looks don't matter," Sienna soothed as she patted the dashboard. "You're just as good as those other cars. Now, come on. Show them all. Be a good girl." She tried turning the key again and got exactly nothing. Not even an engine cough. As if her car wasn't even *trying* to start.

Defeated, Sienna slumped in the seat, and then jolted when Adam leaned down and asked, "Problem?"

She gave him a sneer. He was probably enjoying this.

Nothing the man liked better than being right. "Gypsy won't start."

"Imagine that." He straightened up and jostled baby Jack into a more comfortable position on his shoulder.

Things had been tense between them since last night. They'd retired to their separate bedrooms and Sienna had spent most of the night lying awake, wondering if he was regretting the decision to *not* have sex as much as she was.

But there were a lot of good reasons.

First, Devon, naturally. And, did they really know each other well enough to take that step? Sienna wasn't a one-night-stand kind of girl. Never had been. Yet, if she slept with Adam, she had to admit to herself that it would just be a fleeting thing. The man hadn't made a secret of the fact that he hated the very idea of commitment. So there was a lot to consider that was absolutely no consolation at all, when what she wanted was to jump into his bed and enjoy herself.

Looking down at her, he asked, "So. Is this the kind of 'adventure' you like, or would you rather drive one of my cars to your appointment?"

Oh, she wished she could refuse the offer, but if she didn't leave in the next few minutes, she'd be late. Swallowing her pride with a good dose of irritation, she said, "Thanks. I'd appreciate it."

He waved his free arm toward the cars waiting in the spotless white and stainless steel garage. "Take your pick. The keys are in a cabinet on the far wall."

Said the king to the peasant. Rolling her eyes, she climbed out, retrieved her camera bag and then muttered, "Thanks."

"I'm sorry, what?"

She shot him a look, then reluctantly smiled at the glint of amusement in his eyes. "Fine. Thank you. You were right, oh, King of the Universe. My car needs work."

He snorted. "Your car needs a burial."

Jack laughed and slapped Adam's cheek. He caught the baby's hand in his and held on. Why did he look so damn sexy holding the tiny boy?

"I'd be insulted by that, but—" She looked at Gypsy and had to admit he had a point. Her car had definitely seen better days. Gypsy was really old and she'd lived a hard life. It was time to find a new used car. "I'll take your Explorer if that's okay."

"Fine. I've got his car seat set up in the Rover." Adam looked at the baby as he would an alien being.

He was way out of his depth and yet, Adam wasn't trying to evade the new responsibility dumped on him. She admired him for that. Heck, there was a lot she admired about him. This wouldn't be easy, incorporating a child into his life, but Adam was already making concessions. As she watched, Jack gave Adam a wide, toothless smile and just for an instant, Adam smiled back. Then he glanced down at his suit jacket. "Drool. Perfect."

She laughed. "Okay, really I have to go. You want me to stop at the office to pick him up when I'm finished?"

Adam's whole face lit up. "You do that and I'll buy you a *car*."

Laughing again, Sienna started toward the Explorer. "Not necessary. Dinner would be good, though."

# Seven

Jack became the office mascot.

Adam ran his meeting, settled a few things with the Davidson Group, wound things up with Kevin, who'd also been in the meeting while Tracy in accounting watched Jack, and then Adam had to hunt down his nephew. Apparently, tiny Jack Quinn was now the star of Quinn Development Enterprises.

First, he went to Tracy, who was supposed to look after Jack during the meeting. But when one of their top clients dropped by, she'd handed Jack off to Kara. Then Kara was needed to research one of the new projects, so Tom in IT took over. Like Kara, Tom had kids of his own, so one small baby was no problem. But then a computer crashed and Tom handed Jack off to Nancy at reception and by the time Adam finally caught up to the traveling baby, Jack was eating banana slices in the employee break room with Sienna.

"Not surprising," Adam murmured. "The kid's been all over the place…"

Standing in the doorway, Adam watched the baby squash bananas in his fists, and then laugh up at Sienna. She smiled at the little boy and everything inside Adam fisted. Her blond hair hung loose around her shoulders. Her blue eyes were shining. She wore a lemon yellow T-shirt that hugged her body, with a neckline that scooped low enough to give him a peek at the top of her breasts. Her jeans were faded and her sneakers were purple. He laughed to himself. Of course she would wear purple shoes.

A wild, barely controllable surge of pure lust rose up inside him, making breathing difficult and walking near impossible. Last night had been the longest of his life. Logically, he knew they'd done the right thing, pulling back from each other after dinner rather than giving in to what they both wanted. But logic didn't have a hell of a lot to do with what he was feeling right now.

"You're staring," she said, and slowly swiveled her head around to look at him.

"I like the view."

Her eyes flashed and he went so hot it was a wonder he didn't simply spontaneously combust. There she sat holding a laughing baby and all Adam could think about was tearing her clothes off and stretching her out on the break table. Damn it, he never should have touched her in the first place. Those few stolen moments, her quick breathing and soft sighs as her body trembled at his caresses had reawakened every damn instinct and urge he possessed.

Jack squealed in delight when he saw his uncle,

then threw a slice of banana at him and Adam almost thanked the boy for shattering the tension in the room. Staring at Jack's round little face, with his wide-open mouth blasting a huge smile and his big eyes twinkling, Adam felt a surge of warmth he really hadn't expected. He'd never wanted children, yet here he was now, a surrogate father. And if he were being honest, he could admit at least to himself, that he hadn't been at all sure he was up to the task of giving the boy the kind of love he deserved. Yet now, love simmered warmly inside him and he could acknowledge that in an incredibly short period of time, Jack had completely claimed Adam's heart.

Oh, the kid was a lot of work. Didn't like to sleep. Went through enough diapers for a small army. But when he laughed, when he laid his head on Adam's shoulder, or patted his cheek with a gooey hand, it felt right.

"So," Sienna asked, "did you go out and conquer more of the planet today?"

One corner of his mouth lifted. He liked her attitude. Liked her smile. Her eyes. Her scent. Her taste. Hell.

"I did my share. What about you?" He moved into the room and sat down next to her. "Get all your pictures taken?"

"It was great," she said with a wide grin that lit up her eyes and made him want to take her mouth with his. "The park was perfect. And in the shots I got by the lake, I caught a flock of ducks swooping in. Caught them on the wing, with the trees bending in the wind and the blue sky and fat white clouds in the background."

She sighed in satisfaction. "That was perfect, but one

of the kids got stuck in a tree and their father stepped in a mud hole, but all in all…"

Adam stared at her for a few seconds, then laughed. "Well, it's not the usual description a workday."

"It's pretty usual for me." Jack leaned toward Adam, so Sienna handed the baby off to him.

Instantly, Jack slapped his banana-coated hands on the sleeves of Adam's pin-striped jacket. "Perfect."

"Oops." Sienna laughed, dug in the diaper bag for wipes and cleaned the baby's hands.

"A little late, but appreciated," Adam said wryly.

"Yeah, sorry." She wiped off his jacket sleeves and as she bent over, he could see down her shirt. He stared unabashedly and wished to hell he could touch her as easily as he could admire the view.

Gritting his teeth, he deliberately shifted his gaze and started talking to take his mind off what it really wanted to concentrate on. "The Explorer work for you?"

"I can't believe you gave me a brand-new car to drive around."

"I got it six months ago," he argued.

"He's still got that new car smell," she said, with a shake of her head.

"He?"

"Absolutely. No way is Thor a girl."

She sat up and Adam met her gaze. *"Thor?"*

"Well, he's burly and beautiful and there when I needed him." She grinned. "Besides, he just feels like a Thor to me."

"Right." Why Adam found her naming his car charming instead of just loony was beyond him. Shaking his head, he said, "Well you can use him—*it*—whenever you want."

"Thanks, I will until my car's fixed."

Yeah, they'd see about that. Her car was a nightmare. And all he'd had to do was disconnect the battery in "Gypsy" to make sure Sienna was driving something safe and reliable. He'd find a way to make the change permanent, too.

The baby jumped up and down on Adam's leg as if he were riding a horse, bringing Adam back to the situation at hand. "Kevin contacted a nanny employment agency."

"Oh." Sienna frowned a little. "Well, that's good, right?"

"Yeah," he said, nodding. "Hell, I didn't even know there *were* employment agencies strictly for nannies. Anyway, they have our requirements and they'll be sending people out for interviews. The first one is tomorrow."

"Tomorrow," she repeated, as if trying out the word. "Will you be interviewing them here?"

"Actually," he said, resettling Jack when the baby started trying to lurch forward, "I thought it'd be better if you talked to them first. Let whoever it is meet Jack at the house. See if it looks good. If you think it does, I'll do the final interviews." He met her gaze and wondered why all of a sudden he *couldn't* read what she was thinking. "Does that work for you?"

"Sure." She swallowed, took a breath and said, "That makes sense, really. I mean, if the baby doesn't like the nanny, we don't want her—or him—do we?"

"Right. That's what I was thinking. So, you'll be there tomorrow?"

"Yes. My next appointment isn't for a couple of days."

"Okay, great then." They sounded so stiff. Polite. A damn weird situation. Sienna was staying with him until he could find a nanny, and now that they had an appointment to interview one, neither of them was thrilled by the idea. Weird.

Jack squirmed on Adam's lap and reached out for Sienna. She scooped him up and stood.

Adam rose too and realized how much he liked that she was tall. Kissing her was easy, just a dip of his head and he could taste her again. He looked into her eyes and saw the same heat he felt swamping him. Like the night before, he shook his head and said, "This is crazy."

"I know," she said. "We weren't going to do anything about this." But her breath was coming faster and when she licked dry lips, Adam had to force himself not to take that mouth with his.

"We agreed it would be a mistake," he said, forcing each word from his throat.

She hitched the baby onto her hip, licked her lips again and whispered, "We already made one mistake. You know...when you..."

"Yeah." His memory of caressing her damp heat was seared into his brain. The feel of her when her body shuddered. The sound of her sighs and gasps. Bad move or not, it was something he hungered for. "Yeah, we did. And I want to do it all over again. And more."

"Oh me, too." She pulled in a long, slow breath. "But you said we were going to ignore it."

"I said we would *try* to ignore it."

She huffed out that breath. "How's that going for you?"

"Not good," he admitted.

"Me, either," she confessed.

He reached out and stroked one finger across the top of one of her breasts, then dipped into her cleavage and watched her eyes haze.

"Adam…" She shivered again and his body jolted in response.

He stopped touching her, pushed his hands through his hair. "We'll probably regret this."

"Maybe," she said, her gaze locked with his. "But I think I'd regret it more if we didn't make another 'mistake.'"

Now her eyes met his and he read her desire shining there. She wanted him. She wasn't being coy. Wasn't after his money or prestige or a first-class trip to Paris. Sienna was nothing like any woman he'd ever known. And right at that moment, he was grateful.

She wasn't playing games and he wouldn't, either.

Adam reached over and grabbed the diaper bag off the table. "Let's get out of here."

She blew out a breath, shook her hair back from her face and nodded, hitching the baby higher on her hip. "I'll take Jack in Thor and meet you at the house."

"Screw that." He wasn't taking the chance of her getting distracted on the drive home by another beach scene. He needed her and needed her *now*. "I'll get Kevin to bring my car to the house later. We'll both take Thor. Where did you park?"

"Just behind the building." He led her through the offices, waving off anyone who tried to get in his way. From the corner of his eye, he saw Kevin, and paused. "Kevin, I'm going home with Sienna. Have my car brought around, will you?"

"Sure." The man's smirk came and went so fast, only

someone who knew Kevin as well as Adam did would have noticed it. Clearly, his best friend knew that Adam and Sienna were off to do exactly what Adam had insisted they wouldn't. "Have a good night. Nice to see you, Sienna."

"You too, Kevin. Hi to Nick." She said that last as the elevator doors closed between them. Looking up at Adam, she said, "Kevin knows why we're leaving together."

He glanced at her. "Does that bother you?"

She thought about it for a moment. "Maybe it should, but it doesn't."

"Good." He didn't want to waste any more time talking about or thinking about anything but what was bubbling between him and Sienna. The tension in the elevator was so thick it was hard to draw an easy breath. When the doors swished open, Adam herded Sienna and Jack along as quickly as he could.

In a few minutes, they had Jack secure and were driving down PCH. Traffic was thick. Even this early in the summer, beach lovers were crowding the coast. Teens with surfboards, moms with herds of kids, bikini-clad girls, they were all there and they were all contributing to slowing down the trip home.

The ride took forever but finally they pulled into the drive, only to see a white van with the slogan Tonight's The Night painted in black script on the side, parked in front of the house.

"Nick's here," Adam said on a groan. "You've got to be kidding me."

Glancing at Sienna, he expected to see the frustration he felt clearly marked on her features. Instead, her lips twitched, and then she laughed. An explosion of sound that rolled on and on as if she couldn't quite stop. In a second or two, Adam let go of the grinding aggravation lodged in his throat and smiled with her. Shaking his head, he said, "Maybe Somebody's trying to tell us something."

"Oh, I don't think Somebody bothers with the details of our lives."

"Well then, this is either a setup by Kevin or a weird coincidence."

Sienna laughed again and laid one hand on his forearm. He felt the heat shoot right down to his bones.

"Why would Kevin go out of his way to make sure we're interrupted?"

Thinking about his best friend and the man's sense of humor, Adam muttered, "He thinks he's funny."

"Well," Sienna said, "he is, usually. This? Not so much. Still, it'll be nice to see Nick."

From the back seat, Jack laughed, as if in on the joke, and Adam conceded that he'd lost this round. But he swore he'd get rid of Nick as fast as possible.

"How'd he get into the house?" Sienna asked as they unloaded the baby and all of his stuff.

"He and Kevin have an emergency key," he grumbled. "Which I'm seriously reconsidering."

Sienna laughed again as she headed for the house with the baby, and Adam followed, settling for watching the sway of her hips, telling himself that eventually, he was going to get his hands on her.

If the wanting didn't kill him first.

As soon as they opened the door, a blend of incredible scents greeted them.

Even Adam whispered, "Okay, it might be all right that Nick's here."

Grinning at him, Sienna started down the wide, tiled hall toward the kitchen, where they found Nick stirring a gleaming, stainless steel pot on the stove. When they stepped into the room, the big man spun around, took one look and shouted, "Sienna! It's so great to see you!"

Being hugged by Nick Marino was like being enveloped in warmth. He was tall and broad shouldered with the body of a weightlifter. He had once told her that working out was the only way he could combat all the calories he consumed having to taste everything he made before serving it. Nick's hair was black as night and held back in a short ponytail at the back of his head. His eyes were the deep brown of dark chocolate and his skin was burnished gold, revealing his love of the sun.

Sunlight poured through the windows, illuminating the white cabinets, the acres of forest green quartz and the honey-toned hardwood floors. There was a copper range hood over the stove and a copper faucet at the wide farmhouse sink. The windows offered an amazing view of the ocean and Sienna had already discovered that the sunsets from the balcony were incredible.

When Nick let her go, she smiled up at him. "I'm so happy to see you. Congratulations on the wedding."

"Thanks, sweetie. Married life is great." He stepped back and gave her a quick once-over. "You look spectacular."

Before she could answer, Adam asked, "What're you doing here, Nick?" and set the diaper bag on the kitchen counter.

"Well, Kevin told me about Sienna staying here for a couple of weeks—with no Delores to actually *cook*, so

I took pity. I stuffed your freezer with enough fantastic dinners to last ten days. The rest of the time you can take Sienna *out* to dinner. Meanwhile, all you'll have to do is heat and eat, and then sigh in contentment." Nick winked. "Blessing my name, of course, for having saved you from canned soup and cheese sandwiches."

"You're the best," Sienna said, and jiggled Jack on her hip as he started to fuss.

Nick looked at the baby and his eyes went soft. "Devon's son." He lifted his gaze to Adam. "God, he looks just like him, doesn't he?"

"Yeah, he does."

Sienna didn't like the brief hint of sorrow she read in Adam's eyes, so she spoke up quickly and a little too brightly. "Do you want to hold him, Nick?"

Nick grinned. "You bet I do. I'm trying to talk Kevin into adopting, you know."

"I heard," Adam said knowingly.

Nick winced. "Yes, and I know you heard nothing wonderful. What I don't know is *why*. Kevin's great with kids. When his sisters bring their kids over, we all have a great time. I don't know why he's so hesitant." He lifted the baby and grinned when the tiny boy smiled at him.

"It's a big step," Sienna said with a shrug. "Takes some getting used to the idea, maybe."

"I wish he'd hurry up then." Nick did a fast turn to make the baby laugh in delight. A grin still plastered on his face, Nick glanced at Adam. "I called Kevin a few minutes ago to tell him I was here. He said to tell you that he was on his way with your car. That way he and I can just go home together."

"Kevin's on his way?" Adam asked, and sent her a glance that said, *See? I told you Kevin was behind this.*

"He is." Nick lifted the baby high in the air and giggles rained down on the room. "I've already got a lasagna in the oven, so we can all have dinner and visit for a while."

"Nick Marino's lasagna?" Sienna sighed. "No wonder it smells like heaven in here."

"Nick Marino Jameson, now," he told her with a quick grin.

She hugged him again. "I'll remember. So. Is there anything I can do to help?"

Nick winked at her. "Want to make a salad while I play with the little guy?"

"Sure."

"And Adam can pour us both some wine." Nick carried the baby into the adjoining den and did a few more spins just to hear little Jack laugh again.

Adam followed her to the fridge and leaned on the edge of the door when she opened it up.

"So much for great plans," he whispered, stroking the back of her hand with the tips of his fingers.

Funny—they'd gone from insane with desire and exploding passion into having dinner with friends, and still, he could make her sigh with a simple touch. She looked up into stormy brown eyes and said softly, "They won't be here all night."

"Damn right they won't. Even if I have to physically toss Kevin out the door. We've still got 'mistakes' to make."

"Oh yes." She reached into the fridge and pulled out a bottle of wine. Handing it to him, she said, "I'm looking forward to it."

Nodding, he leaned in, took the wine and then brushed his mouth over hers. It was quick, hard and the taste of him lingered even after he pulled back. "I plan on making a *lot* of mistakes tonight."

Everything inside her quivered at the inherent promise in his tone, his eyes. "You're not making it easy to wait."

"Who wants easy?"

Nothing about this was the slightest bit easy, so she gave him a slow smile. "Clearly, neither of us." Taking a deep breath, she said, "Nick was right. I could use a glass of that wine."

"Or two," he said, and kissed her again.

"Hello? Wine steward?" Nick called from the other room.

Rolling his eyes, Adam muttered, "Can't catch a break here." Then to Nick, he spoke up. "It's coming, Your Majesty."

"Hey," Nick called back, "I like that."

"Of course you do." Shaking his head, Adam went for glasses.

Sienna laughed again and dug into the fridge for lettuce and vegetables. Passion could simmer through an evening with friends, she told herself, and maybe even make those feelings hotter, more desperate, for the wanting. Just thinking about what would come later made her blood sparkle like champagne.

Three hours later, Sienna realized she hadn't had so much fun in way too long. She'd been so busy the last couple of years, working on her business, staying focused, that she'd forgotten how good it was to simply *be.* Kevin entertained them all with stories about clients or the crews that worked for them. Nick's stories about the different catering jobs he'd done were just as entertaining. He and Sienna then commiserated with each other over how hard it was to establish a new business. And Adam made sure Kevin got plenty of one-on-one time with baby Jack—which Nick loved.

Sitting around the table in the big, beautiful kitchen, Sienna watched Adam with his friends and realized just how different he and Devon really had been. Devon had always had to be the star of the show. The entertainer. As if he thought no one would want to be with him if he wasn't constantly "on."

Adam didn't need to claim the center stage. The understated power of his presence, his personality, was enough. And now he seemed content to laugh at Nick's stories or argue with Kevin or to simply meet Sienna's gaze across the table and share a long, silent look.

As she'd suspected it would, rather than easing the desire that had been plaguing her for two days, this dinner with friends had only made it stronger. Watching Adam relaxed, laughing, had allowed Sienna to see him more clearly than she ever had before. The shields he usually kept up to protect himself were down and she felt as if she was getting to know the *real* Adam. So when Kevin and Nick finally left, Sienna was more than ready to make those mistakes they'd planned.

"I told you Kevin did that on purpose," Adam said. "Did you catch him smiling to himself when he first got here?"

"Yes. And I saw that you handed Jack off to him at every chance."

He shrugged and gave her a half smile. "Payback's a bitch. Besides, he's not as antikid as he wants Nick to think. I watched him with the baby tonight."

She looked up at him briefly as the white van's engine fired up. "So did I. He was having a good time."

"You can bet Nick saw it, too," Adam mused. The van headed down the driveway and they both waved until the taillights disappeared into the growing darkness.

Sienna had forgotten just how much she enjoyed Kevin. But after her divorce, she'd thought it best to stay away from all things Quinn. Which, unfortunately, had included Kevin and Nick. It seemed silly to her now, but at the time, she'd thought that keeping a distance was the right thing to do.

She smiled and gave him an elbow-nudge in the side. "They're so great. You're lucky to have them."

"Usually I feel that way. Tonight," he said, turning to wrap his arms around her, "I wished them halfway across the planet."

He pulled her in tightly to him and she felt the racing beat of his heart. Her own jumped into a gallop and she took a deep breath as she lifted her gaze to his. "They're gone now…"

He grinned down at her. "So they are."

"And the baby's asleep," she said softly, lifting her arms to hook them behind his neck. Nick had insisted on putting the baby down for the night and had even cajoled Kevin into helping him.

"News keeps getting better." He bent his head, took her mouth and stole her breath in the wash of heat that swamped her.

Sienna sighed as Adam's hands swept beneath the hem of her shirt, and up, along her spine. His fingers traced wild patterns on her skin as his tongue stroked her into a frenzy of need that clamored in her mind like fire alarms.

"Inside," he groaned when he tore his mouth from hers. "Inside, now, or I swear, we're going to do this on the porch."

She shivered and wondered if maybe she was a little bit of an exhibitionist, since that threat didn't sound so bad. She looked up into his eyes and saw his hunger, read the need etched into his features. "Yes," she said, and turned for the door. "Inside."

He was right behind her and when she would have headed for the stairs, he grabbed her hand and dragged her into the great room.

"Bedrooms are too far away," he muttered, and took her shirt, dragging it up and over her head. The cool air kissed her skin and her nipples went hard and erect when he undid her bra and pushed the straps down her arms to fall onto the floor.

"Beautiful," he whispered. "So damn beautiful." His hands cupped her breasts, his thumbs caressing her rigid nipples until she swayed on her feet, undone by what he was making her feel.

"You're driving me wild," she murmured, then gasped when he dipped his head to take first one nipple then the other into his mouth. Lips, tongue and teeth teased her sensitive skin until she whimpered in the back of her throat and half collapsed in his arms. Sienna knew that at any second, her knees were going to give out completely and she'd be in a puddle on the floor.

She didn't get the chance. Adam straightened up, tore off his shirt, then tipped her backward onto one of the couches. Sienna *whooped* in surprise, then grinned up at Adam as he tore off the rest of his clothes. She took a moment to relish the look of him, from his broad chest, long legs, narrow hips and *more*. Her eyes went wide in appreciation, and her stomach did a series of flips and spins in anticipation. She lifted her gaze to his and took a breath. "Well, hello…"

His eyes flashed and the faint smile curving his mouth faded in a blink. Eager now to feel all of him, she worked at the button and zipper of her jeans then pushed them and her panties down her legs to kick them off entirely. The couch was soft and cushioned and roomy enough for both of them to lie side by side. All she was interested in at the moment, though, was the man looming over her.

He covered her body with his and Sienna sighed at the simply delicious sensation of his bare, tanned skin brushing against hers. His chest was sharply sculpted muscle, telling her that he worked out regularly. She skimmed the flats of her hands across that expanse, loving the feel of him.

He smiled as he lowered his head to kiss her, tasting, teasing her lips with his tongue and teeth. She tried to catch his mouth with hers, but he managed to keep tantalizing her even as his hands swept up and down her body, exploring every line and curve. He slid one hand across her abdomen and down to the juncture of her thighs and Sienna braced herself for that first, magical touch.

She'd wanted to feel it again ever since that first night. Now, with his first caress, Sienna shivered in response. Sliding her hands up and down his back, over his shoulders and down his powerful arms, she indulged herself by touching him as he touched her. She ran one foot up his calf and sighed when he buried his head in the curve of her neck, tasting, nibbling. She tipped her head to one side to offer him access.

"God, you smell good," he murmured against her neck.

"Mmm, jasmine," she whispered.

"Tastes good, too," he said softly.

"Hope you're hungry…" She laughed when he nibbled at her neck, then sighed as his hands continued to caress every inch of her body. He lifted his head, looked down at her for what seemed forever, and then kissed her as if he were a dying man getting one last wish. Sienna held on to him, palms flat against his back. She opened her mouth for him and sighed at the sensual invasion of his tongue. Hers tangled with his and breathlessly, they chased each other up the rungs of sexual tension. Every second that ticked past, she felt her heartbeat quicken, her breath catch in her throat.

At the very heart of her, heat engulfed her. She wouldn't have been surprised to see actual flames dancing along her skin. A tingle of expectation dropped into the center of the fire and spun quickly out of control.

Arching up into him, Sienna met his kiss with a hunger that raged inside her. She'd waited for this. Maybe she'd been waiting since the very first time she'd met Adam. Her husband's brother. Out of bounds. Until now.

When he dropped one hand to the juncture of her thighs and cupped her heat again, she groaned. He pushed one finger, then two, into her depths and stroked her core until her hips rocked of their own accord. She surrendered control, arching into him, struggling, nearly screaming as tension built to an unbelievable height. Finally, she tore her mouth free of his and cried, "Adam, please. Inside me. Now."

"Now," he agreed. "I've got to have you." Adam shifted, then stopped. "Damn it."

"What? What? Why'd you stop?" She blinked wildly, trying to see through the passion-induced haze. Aching, needing, she demanded, "What's wrong?"

"Protection," he muttered grimly. "I'll be back. There are condoms upstairs."

"No!" She shook her head and grabbed his arm to keep him with her. "Don't go. I'm covered. I'm on the pill. And I'm clean."

He gave her a slow, satisfied smile. "I'm healthy, too."

"*Really* glad to hear it." Sienna pulled him closer. "Now, back to business."

"I admire a woman with a one-track mind…"

"You have no idea," she assured him.

Then all talk fled. Her mind, her soul, her body, were all too overwhelmed with sensation. Thinking, talking, were unnecessary and completely out of the question. She held her breath, lifted her hips and moaned when he entered her. Sienna gasped and held her breath as her body accommodated his. He felt right.

Then Adam went perfectly still and stared down into her eyes. Sienna read the passion shining down at her, and knew he was seeing the same thing in her eyes. Then he slowly began to move inside her, rocking his hips in a rhythm that quickly sent Sienna into a frenzy. She chased that tingle, raced after the flames. Her breath heaved in and out of her lungs. She moved with him in perfect tandem, as if they'd been born to come together in this ancient dance.

He pushed her higher, faster, and Sienna raced to keep up. She looked up into his eyes, saw the heat, saw the passion and lost herself in it. As her body peaked, she tumbled eagerly into the abyss opening up beneath her. Surrendering to the inevitable fall, Sienna trusted him to hold on to her. And when he shouted her name and fell with her, she closed her eyes and savored the crash.

# Eight

By the time her heartbeat was back to normal, Sienna's brain was working again. The feel of Adam's body on hers, the brush of his ragged breath against her neck, combined to create a satisfied sigh that slipped from her throat.

Adam lifted his head, looked down into her eyes and smiled. "I don't make mistakes often," he admitted, "but this one was well worth it."

Sienna lifted one hand and stroked his hair back from his face. In the darkness, his eyes shone down at her. He was still buried deep inside her body and she felt as if even their souls were touching. She couldn't remember another time when she felt such a connection to someone. Yet, as he'd just said, it had been a mistake. And though it had been wonderful, Sienna knew that she also had to consider this time with him a major slip in judgment.

But her mouth curved as she spoke on a sigh. "It was right up there for me, too. Top two at least."

He shifted, pulling away from her, sitting up and grabbing his clothes. It seemed, she thought with a sinking heart, the moment was over. Since she was at a distinct disadvantage naked, Sienna picked up her clothes, as well. She swung her hair out of her face, tugged her jeans on and shrugged into her shirt.

God, her body felt loose and relaxed, while inside she was a churning mess of mixed emotions and feelings that she would worry about sorting out later and— She caught him looking at her through narrowed eyes. "What?"

"You seem happy."

*Funny*, she thought. The first time he was wrong in reading her expression. But she went with it, because why admit to being so confused?

"Why wouldn't I be?" She lifted both arms over her head and stretched.

His frown deepened and she had to wonder when exactly Mr. Sexy had become Mr. Crabby. Was he feeling as torn as she was? "What's going on, Adam?"

"I just don't want you to get the wrong idea, that's all." His dark eyes were completely shut down. He could have been a robot for all the emotion she read there. How did he do that so quickly? So completely?

Tipping her head to one side, she stared up at him. "What wrong idea?" she asked. "Be specific."

He glanced around the room as if checking to make sure they were alone—after what they'd just done, they'd better be, Sienna thought. Then he turned his gaze back to her. "I was married before," he blurted.

"Hey, me, too." Frowning a little, she asked, "This

is not a news flash. So where are you going with this, Adam?"

He pushed one hand through his hair. "I just want you to know up-front, that I'm not looking to get married again."

Stunned, she could only blink at him as her mind raced to figure out where *that* had come from. Nope, she acknowledged a moment later, couldn't do it. "Did I propose or something in the throes of passion?" Sarcasm colored her tone. "Because that would just be tacky."

He blew out a breath, scrubbed one hand across his face and said, "It's not a joke, Sienna."

"I'm not laughing, Adam." In fact, she'd never felt less amused. Did he really think she'd had sex with him just to trick him somehow into marrying her? Did he think she'd done that to *Devon*?

"No point in getting mad. I just want us to know the lay of the land right from the start," Adam said. "Devon swept you off your feet and into a marriage. That's not going to happen with me."

"Well, good. I didn't ask to be swept," she reminded him, letting the first bubble of anger rising in her chest grow and swell. Damn it. "If you think I somehow seduced Devon into marrying me, you're wrong. And you're even *more* wrong if you believe I've got some nefarious plan to snag *you*."

"Sienna…"

"Believe me when I say that you can relax, Adam. You're completely safe from the gold-digging femme fatale."

"I didn't say that," he blurted out.

Her gaze fired into his. "Do you realize how often you say those words? 'I didn't say that.' It's like your mantra or something. Maybe you should get some calling cards printed with that phrase so you can hand them out to everyone you manage to insult without even trying."

"Sienna—"

"Or you know what?" She walked closer to him and poked him in the chest with her index finger. "Instead of overusing that one particular phrase and confusing everyone around you, maybe instead you should rethink the things you *do* say *before* you say them."

"You don't sound confused." He glanced down at her finger, still jabbing at his chest, then up into her eyes again. "You sound mad."

"You'll be happy to know that your powers of perception are still A+. Congratulations, Adam."

"I'm not trying to make you angry—"

Her head snapped back and her eyes went wide. "Wow, and look how well you're doing without any effort at all." Sienna folded her arms across her chest and tapped the toe of one bare foot against the rug. Amazing that he could stir her up as easily as he did. Passion. Fury. Befuddlement.

He was always so damn sure of himself. And apparently convinced that he was such a magnificent catch that any woman who wormed her way into his bed was there for the express purpose of making it permanent. She took several deep breaths in an attempt to keep her head from exploding.

His gaze was still detached. Cool, while she was burning hot. Adam was always so positive that his way was the right way he would never be dissuaded by temper. Hers or anyone else's. Now logic, on the other hand, might just get through.

"I just want us both to be clear on what this is," Adam said tightly.

Deliberately, she pushed her anger aside and focused instead on convincing the man that he was being an idiot. An insulting idiot.

"Oh, I'm perfectly clear on that. It seems to me that *you're* the one having an issue. This is *sex*, Adam. It's not a declaration of forever. It's passion, desire." Shaking her head, she let the last of her fury fade because in his own completely stupid way, he was trying to be fair to her. "We're both adults. Why can't we just be together until it's over, and then walk away friends?"

Now it was his turn to simply stare at her as if she were speaking Martian. Sienna almost laughed in spite of the situation. Irritation smoothed out. Honestly, she found she really liked being able to confuse him. Obviously, the women he was accustomed to weren't quite as forthright as she was.

"Friends."

"Why not?" she asked. A part of her mind was shrieking *You'll never be his friend*, but she ignored that and moved in closer to him. Sliding her palms up his bare chest, pushing back the open edges of his shirt, she felt his heart pounding. However cool he wanted to act, she knew he was feeling more than he pretended, and somehow, that cheered her up a little. Staring up into his eyes, she said, "Just stop thinking, Adam. And for heaven's sake, stop talking."

A moment or two passed before a smirk lifted one corner of his mouth. "I've never had a woman tell me to shut up before."

She grinned back at him. How could she not? He was everything Devon hadn't been. Everything she'd ever really wanted and he wasn't hers. Wasn't going to *be* hers. Except for now. For whatever stolen time they had together before it ended and the world returned to normal.

"Well then," she said, "I'm proud to be the first."

"Of course you are." He shook his head, gave her a wry smile, then cupped her face in his palms and bent his head to kiss her. Just before he did, he paused and said, "So lovers now, *friends* later."

Sienna's blood began to boil again. "We can be friends now, too, if you want."

"No, thanks." His smile faded. "What I want to do to you, I don't do to my friends."

She quivered, told herself to enjoy every moment of her time with him and leaned in close. "Show me."

He did.

Adam wasn't used to waking up with company.

He didn't spend the night with any woman and he sure as hell didn't let them stay over at his house. That way led to too many assumptions. In his experience, once a woman stayed over, she tended to think more proprietarily. Soon, there'd be little things left behind, as if she were marking her territory. So it was easier—and more honest—to end the night early and sleep alone.

*So what the hell had happened to that rule last night?*

Yes, Sienna was staying at the house anyway, but staying in his bed was different. She was still sleeping, her blond hair a tangle across her face. Her eyelashes lay like silk fans on her cheeks and the pale gray sheet covering her body dipped over one breast, as if tempting him to taste her.

Dawn was just streaking the sky with ribbons of rose and gold, turning the dusky light to soft lavender. Adam went up on one elbow to look down at her. With the tips of his fingers, he lifted a strand of her hair, then bent to kiss her bare shoulder. Soft. Naked. Sienna.

She sighed and instinctively moved closer to him. All night, they'd had each other. Fast, slow and everything in between. He couldn't seem to get enough of her. Every touch only fed the need for more. Every climax made him burn hotter.

*Friends*, she'd said last night. Adam almost laughed. He didn't want to be her friend. And temporary lover wasn't enough. But what was left? Anything beyond temporary wasn't in his game plan.

And Adam always kept to the damn plan. Knowing where he was going, what he was doing, kept him focused on his goals. But with Sienna, he felt as if he were always a step behind. He didn't like it.

That said, he liked everything else about her. Her wit. The stinging sarcasm and the way she stood up for herself. Her scent. Her taste.

He bent his head, took that tantalizing nipple into his mouth and as he suckled her, he felt her wake. She threaded her fingers through his hair, held his head to her and gasped, "Good morning."

He smiled against her breast, then lifted his head to look down at her. Even first thing in the morning, not a drop of makeup, her hair wild from sleep and sex, she was the most beautiful thing he'd ever seen.

"It is now," he said, and rolled her over onto her back. Moving to cover her body with his, he parted her thighs and slipped inside her before she could take another breath. Warmth spilled through his veins as he watched her take him. Her eyes closed briefly on another sigh, then she opened them and fixed her gaze on his. Adam thought wildly that he could drown in the blue of her eyes and it wouldn't be a bad way to go.

And then the rhythm caught them, held them. In the soft hush of dawn, he watched her eyes glaze with the kind of heat that torched everything inside him. She lifted her legs and locked them around his hips, pulling him tighter, deeper. Their gazes locked, they watched each other as the end rushed toward them.

The morning light brightened and her eyes glittered fiercely. "Go over," he whispered, controlling his own need in favor of watching her shatter first. "Go and I'll follow."

She arched her head back, closed her eyes, and he felt her body clench around his. Digging her short, neat nails into his shoulders, she cried out his name and let the internal explosions take her.

Adam felt her pleasure as his own and knew that she was touching something inside him no one else ever had. What it meant for him, for *them*, he didn't know. And when his own release claimed him an instant later, he didn't care. All that mattered was the woman in his arms and the silent clock in his mind, slowly counting off their days together.

A few hours later, Sienna was exhausted. She was working on about two hours' sleep and though her body felt wonderfully well used, she really needed a nap. That was not in the cards though, as she went back and forth between caring for Jack and working on her laptop. Doing the drudge work of owning your own business was time-consuming and less than fun. She went through the bills, paying some, delaying others. She looked up her calendar and made notes about what she wanted to do on the photo shoots.

And finally, she welcomed her creative side and pulled up her digital files. Going through the images she took in Central Park the other day, she made some corrections, some deletions, then turned to editing and got lost in refining her favorite shots. And she did it all on way too little sleep.

Which was probably why the nanny interview didn't go well.

"Thanks for coming by, Ms. Stryker," she said, Jack cuddled close to her chest.

Evangeline Stryker was tall, thin with a sharp blade of a nose and ice-blue eyes. Middle-aged with a ramrod-straight posture, she was, in fact, the cliché of a mean governess. All she needed was a wart on her chin and a hideous cackle. Sienna felt a little guilty for the thought, but then the woman spoke again and her English was so precise, Sienna felt like a peasant before a grumpy duchess.

"I appreciate your time. If I am hired, I can assure you that the child will receive care and discipline." The older woman reached out toward Jack and the baby cringed like a vampire from a cross.

*The child.* Sienna smothered a sigh. Ms. Stryker was perfectly qualified, but seemed cold and Jack hadn't taken to her at all. So that was a no go on the nanny front.

The woman's eyebrows arched high on her forehead and her disapproval was evident. Oh well. "Again, thanks for coming."

"Certainly." As the nanny walked across the drive to

her sedate black sedan, Cheryl arrived in her VW bug. The bright yellow car was like a splotch of sunshine in the grimness, and right then, Sienna really needed it.

Cheryl climbed out of her car wearing jeans, flip-flops and a pink, button-down shirt. Her short, dark hair was a perfect bob at her jawline and the purse she carried slung over one shoulder was almost as big as she was.

Giving the nanny a quick look as she passed, Cheryl gave a dramatic shudder, then grinned. When she walked close enough, she said, "Hi, who's that?"

"A would-be nanny," Sienna told her as the woman drove away.

"Oh, don't do that to this sweet cutie." Cheryl plucked Jack into her arms and the baby laughed and slapped her cheeks. Okay, Cheryl had the stamp of approval, which just proved that Jack was a baby of discernment.

"So." Cheryl gave Sienna a hard stare. "You had sex."

"What?" Was it stamped on her forehead?

"Please, am I blind?" Cheryl hooked her arm through Sienna's and pulled her into the house. "Tell me *everything*. But first, a tour." She craned her neck to look around the hall and into the great room. "I have to see this place."

An hour later, the tour was over and Cheryl was feeding Jack in the kitchen while Sienna sipped coffee.

"And now," she said, "I've got to find a nanny."

"Why you?" Cheryl asked. "Jack is Adam's nephew. He should be doing the interviewing."

"That's what I thought at first, too," Sienna admitted, practically inhaling the caffeine. "But he had a point. Whoever gets hired will be living here. Taking care of Jack. So why shouldn't they come here first?

See how the baby reacts to them—and Jack did not like Ms. Stryker."

"Good for him," Cheryl said, leaning forward to plant a quick kiss on Jack's forehead. "She even scared *me*."

"Me, too, a little." Sienna yawned and Cheryl gave her a knowing smile.

"Busy night?"

"Jealous?"

"Desperately."

"You should be."

"Oh," Cheryl said, "that's just mean. So if you're this tired, why don't you look happier?"

"Because it's…complicated," Sienna admitted, getting up to refill her cup.

"All the best things are," Cheryl said.

She looked at her friend, sitting in the sunshine-filled kitchen. Then her gaze fixed on the laughing baby slapping both hands against the tray of his high chair. Sunlight gilded his hair and sparkled in his eyes and Sienna's heart squeezed.

"You're falling in love," Cheryl said softly.

"What?" Sienna jolted, shook her head and said, "No, I'm not. Adam and I are just…*not*, that's all."

"Interesting," Cheryl said, smirking at her. "I meant you were falling in love with this baby. But it's fascinating how you went straight to Adam…"

Sienna closed her eyes and sighed. "Don't start."

"I didn't start it—I just remarked on it. Isn't that right, Jack?"

The baby giggled and Sienna sighed again. "Fine. Maybe I feel a little more for Adam than I want to admit to."

"Blatantly obvious, and…?"

"And, nothing," Sienna said firmly. "This is temporary, Cheryl. Once I find a nanny and a place for Adam to renovate for my business, then this is over."

Cheryl wiped the baby's face, and then gave Sienna a long look. "Do you *want* it to be over so soon?"

"Doesn't matter what I want, does it?"

"Of course it matters," Cheryl snapped. "What are we, in the Middle Ages or something? If you want him, go get him."

"You make it sound easy."

"It's not," Cheryl said. "But it's also not impossible. Let him know you're interested in more."

Sienna shook her head firmly and folded both hands around her coffee cup. "No. He already gave me the 'don't get any ideas' speech."

"He did not."

Sienna just looked at her. "Yes, he did. But he didn't have to. I knew going in that he wasn't interested in more than *now*. And I assured him that I'm fine with that. That I'm not looking to be swept away into a romance."

Cheryl gave her a smile. "But you are?"

"I don't know," she said, then added, "I mean I do know, but no, I'm not, even though I am, because there's nothing waiting for me there but the Valley of Pain."

"That was completely convoluted and I still got it." Cheryl reached over and gave Sienna's hand a pat. "All I'm saying is, if you found something you want, go for it."

"Even if there's no hope of getting it?"

"The only way you absolutely cannot have something is if you never try."

While her friend lifted Jack out of the high chair, Sienna wondered. She thought about spending time with Adam the last few days. The laughter, the conversations, the kisses and then, oh, my, *last night.* She felt as if he'd been branded into her skin and she really wanted to do it all again. As soon as possible.

Waking up with him that morning, him sliding deep inside her, Sienna had felt a sense of completion she'd never known before. They shared so much and at the same time, they were so far apart. And that's how it should stay, for her own good.

Deliberately, Sienna reminded herself that once she found a nanny and a building for her photography business, their relationship would be over.

And with that thought in mind, she opened her eyes, looked at Cheryl and said, "Want to go for a ride? I need to find the perfect photo studio."

She didn't expect to find something so quickly, but an hour later, Sienna knew she'd stumbled on the perfect property. On the outskirts of Long Beach, the Craftsman had probably been built in the forties. It boasted a wide front porch with stone columns, windows that overlooked Ocean Avenue and beyond that, the sea. It was surrounded by other old homes that had been turned into law offices, art galleries and even a ceramics shop.

"It'll take a lot of work," Cheryl mused.

"True, but when it's finished…" Problems with Adam momentarily forgotten Sienna grabbed her camera to take a quick picture of the For Sale sign, to get the agent's phone number.

Once that was taken care of, Sienna said, "You know, as long as we're here in Long Beach, we could stop by my place, pick up my long lens. I want to get some shots of the view off Adam's balcony."

"That's not all you want off Adam's balcony…"

"Seriously?" Sienna laughed and shook her head. Sadly, the action didn't shake the image of her and Adam on a chaise on that balcony out of her mind.

"I'm with you." Cheryl settled back in her seat. "Mike's got the kids and I have the afternoon off."

"Great. We'll go to my house, then maybe stop for a coffee and brownie?"

"Now you're talking."

Sienna shot a quick look at Jack, sleeping peacefully in his car seat, then she put Thor in gear and headed for her home. Ten minutes later, she was parked in the driveway staring at a house she didn't recognize.

"Wow," Cheryl said from beside her, "when did you do all of this? And why didn't you tell me?"

Sienna climbed out of Thor and spared her friend a glance. "I didn't do it. Adam did. And he didn't tell *me*."

"Uh-oh."

"Damn right." Her gaze swung back to her house and she struggled to take it all in. The house was now sky blue with bright white trim. The porch was painted a navy blue and she had to admit, through her fury, that it really added something to the curb appeal.

Her ancient front door now boasted a high-gloss finish of sunshine-yellow paint and there were even fresh flowers potted on the porch. She took a longer look at the place. Her front walk had been replaced. The cracks were gone. Even the one that looked like the Big Dipper.

Plus, she could tell at a glance that Adam had replaced her roof and there was a brand-new garage door complete with stained glass inserts along the top. The whole place looked like an old woman who'd been given a makeover by the best in the business. You could still tell her age, but she looked shiny.

Cheryl got out of the car, walked around and stood beside her. "How did he get all of this done so fast?"

Good question. He must have put a crew on her house the day she agreed to help him out. Well, she hadn't asked him to do it, had she?

"What was he thinking?" Sienna demanded, not really expecting an answer. "He didn't ask me if it was okay to do this. No, not Adam Quinn. He just decides something needs fixing and he does it."

"Well hell, he should be shot," Cheryl said sharply.

Sienna shot her an exasperated look. "This is *my* house, Cheryl. Not his."

"And now it looks like it won't blow over in the next wind." Cheryl looked at her. "Didn't you lose like thirty shingles in last winter's big storm, and then spend the next few nights emptying pots of rainwater?"

Remembering the nights filled with the plops and drops made her bite back a groan. Naturally, when her roof was leaking, they got near Biblical rains. "Yes," she agreed. "But that's not the point—"

"Didn't you tell me you were going to have the roof repaired this summer?"

"Yes…"

"So now it's done."

And it looked beautiful. Blue shingles. Of course Adam would think about details like that. Irritating man. "But I didn't do it. *He* did."

"Bonus, if you ask me, which you didn't."

"You don't get it," Sienna said, whipping her head back to glare at the high-gloss yellow paint on her front door. She really loved that and it went perfectly with the navy porch and the white trim and— Irritating man. "He did it because he clearly doesn't think I'm capable of taking care of my own life."

Cheryl snorted. "Oh, come on. Maybe he's just a nice guy."

"Nice guys bring you flowers. They don't put a new roof on your house."

"They do if they're *rich* nice guys," Cheryl said.

"No." Sienna shook her head. "No, I have to make him stop or he'll run right through the rest of my life. He's already got me living at his house, driving his car, taking care of his nephew and picking out buildings that he can renovate for me."

"Again. Call the executioner."

Scowling at her friend, Sienna muttered, "You're on his side."

"In this, so far, yeah," Cheryl said, and leaned in to check on the still-sleeping baby. "From what I can see, he's fixed your house, agreed to give you a fabulous new office and he's provided sex great enough to put a glow on your face. How is any of that a bad thing?"

When she put it like that, it was hard to argue. But Sienna's pride kept throttling her. How could she let Adam do all of this without so much as discussing it with her?

"I have to talk to him," Sienna muttered.

Cheryl sighed. "Of course you do. Okay then, go in and get your lens, then you can take me to get my car before you face Adam."

"Fine." A few minutes later, Sienna climbed into Thor and turned the key. She was so furious she didn't even enjoy the purr of the engine. "He's got to stop, Cheryl."

"Good luck with that, sweetie," her friend said as she

got in and buckled her seat belt. "In my experience, it's easier to move a mountain than it is to get a man to do what you want him to do."

She had a point, Sienna told herself as she backed out of her newly asphalted driveway. How had she missed *that* when she pulled in?

"Maybe you're right," Sienna said thoughtfully. "But Adam is going to learn that it's not easy to bulldoze Sienna West."

# Nine

By the time Sienna dropped Cheryl off, and then made the trek back to Adam's office, her initial anger had burned off. But the irritation bar was still pretty high.

Walking through the office with Jack on her hip, Sienna smiled and nodded to everyone, then stopped at Kevin's desk.

"Well hi," he said, giving her a quick glance up and down. "You look gorgeous."

Surprised at the compliment, Sienna took a quick look down at herself. She'd completely forgotten that she was wearing a simple summer dress and high-heeled red sandals. She'd wanted to look nice for the nanny interview, and then simply hadn't bothered to change later.

"Oh, thanks. Um, is Adam free?"

"He just finished up a meeting, so yes." Kevin stood

up as if to walk her to Adam's office. "You caught him at a good time."

"Great. Here. Will you watch Jack for a few?" She handed the baby off without giving the man a chance to object. "He should be fine, but there are diapers and bottles in the bag."

Kevin looked wildly panicked for a second, but Sienna was on a mission and couldn't take the time to soothe the man. She did, however, manage to say in exasperation, "He doesn't bite."

"We'll see…" Warily, Kevin held the tiny boy, who laughed at him in delight.

Sienna had already turned, heading for the set of double doors leading into the lion's den. She opened one, stepped inside the inner sanctum and closed the door behind her. For just a moment, she leaned back against the doors and stared at the big man across the room, sitting behind a wide desk.

Adam wore a charcoal-gray suit with a black shirt and a bloodred tie. He looked every inch exactly what he was. A power broker. A rich, successful man who ran the world around him exactly as he wanted to.

Sunlight poured in from behind him, gilding him in a way that made it look as if the office had been designed to showcase Adam as the absolute ruler. Her stomach did a quick spin and dip in automatic reaction to him, before she reminded herself that she was here because Adam thought he could run *her* world, too.

He caught her eye and gave her a slow smile that made her toes curl. "Well, hello. You look beautiful."

She really should wear a dress more often.

"Thank you." He was disarming her with a compliment and a smile that hinted of wicked thoughts and even more wicked deeds. Damn it. "Adam, I went by my house this afternoon—"

He leaned back in his chair, comfortable. In charge. "Yeah? What'd you think? I haven't seen it in person, but Toby Garcia took some pictures when it was finished. Looked good to me."

She blinked at him. Sienna had expected defensiveness. The King of the Universe tone saying something along the likes of *Too bad if you're not happy, I wanted it done and it's done*. Instead… "It's beautiful, but—"

"Glad you liked it." He slapped both hands on the arms of his chair. "I thought the garage door was nice."

"Yes," she said, remembering how elegant the arched windows along the tops of the door looked. "The stained glass is gorgeous, but—"

He stood up, came around the desk and walked toward her in long, lazy strides. "It's a thirty-year roof, too. So you won't have to worry about leaks anymore."

This was *not* going how she'd thought it would go. "That's great, Adam—"

"Kevin chose the yellow paint for the door. I wanted a bright red, but he said the yellow would contrast better."

Kevin had a good eye, because that bright yellow made the whole house just *sing*. "Yes, it's gorgeous."

He was so close now she could see her own reflection in his eyes. She looked confused. Hardly surprising since not only had he taken the wind out of her anger sails, he actually had her complimenting him on the work they'd done.

"It was Toby's idea to lay down new asphalt on the driveway, but I think it was a good call."

"Sure. Toby who?"

"Garcia. He's the crew chief."

She'd have to find him. Tell him what a good job they'd all done. *For heaven's sake, Sienna, you were mad, remember?*

"Right, well the driveway's nice, but—"

"And with the new walkway to the porch," he continued, "you won't trip and break your neck."

She'd tripped on those cracks more than once, but she didn't have to admit to that. Besides, "The Big Dipper's gone."

"What?"

Sienna sighed as she realized that she'd not only lost the upper hand, she didn't have a clue where it had gone. "One of the cracks looked like the Big Dipper."

He snorted. "Only you would see the stars by looking *down*."

Sienna took a deep breath. "Adam, I came here to tell you that you can't do this kind of thing."

"Too late," he said, one corner of his mouth quirking. "It's already done."

And there it was. Exactly what she'd expected to hear. "See, you're not even sorry."

"Why would I be sorry?" He looked bemused at the very idea.

"Because you didn't bother to consult me when you decided to do a makeover on *my* house?"

He shook his head and waved that away with one hand. "You would have said no."

How were you supposed to win a battle with a man who used that kind of logic? "Exactly."

"So we avoided that argument and the work's done."

Dumbfounded, she stared up into his eyes and saw a flash of amusement that really should have made her angry. But what would have been the point? He was right. The work was already done, no reason to argue about it now. And she really hated that she loved what he'd done to her house, too. Hard to maintain righteous indignation when a part of her was thinking *Ooooohhh*... But he knew that. Had counted on it. And Sienna didn't like being played, either.

"Don't do something like that again, Adam."

"Do you own another home?"

"No."

"Then no problem," he said amiably. "Although..." He walked back to his desk, picked up a folder, then came back to her. "You should probably just take this now."

She frowned and stared at the folder as if it were a snake. Sienna was wary now, so she asked, "What is it?"

He shrugged. "The pink slip to the Explorer. Car's been signed over to you."

*"What?"* She gaped at him. Sienna knew she must have looked like a landed trout, with her eyes bugged out and her mouth hanging open in shock, but she couldn't help it. "No, you didn't—"

He shook the folder in an imperious manner until she instinctively reached out to take it. Then helplessly she opened it to see all the paperwork. A pink slip. The insurance paperwork and cards. Registration. Shaking her head, she lifted her gaze to his. "You're crazy. I don't need Thor. I already have a car."

"No you don't. You have a metal doorstop shaped like a car."

Insulted on Gypsy's behalf, Sienna stiffened. "You can't just do this."

"Why not?" Again, he sounded completely sincere.

As if it were a usual thing for a person to give another person an amazing SUV free and clear.

"Because—" She reached for words. For outrage. For *something*. And came up empty. Finally, she settled for, "I don't want you to."

"Oh, well, if that's all…" He gave her a lopsided grin that tugged at everything she was.

God, she really loved that smile. She shook her head firmly. "Adam, seriously, you have to stop this."

"Sienna," he said on a long exhalation of breath, "this is all your fault, anyway."

*"What?"* There was that word again. She laughed and heard just a tinge of hysteria. "How is this my fault?"

"You're the one who named the car Thor. I can't even get into the thing now. It'd be like sitting in the lap of a huge guy with long blond hair and a hammer."

She laughed again. "That's ridiculous."

"You painted the mental picture," he said slowly, "I just see it."

Sienna took a deep breath and let it out again. "So you expect me to just accept a new car—*and* everything you did to my house."

"Yes."

"Why is it so hard to argue with you?"

He shrugged. "Because you know I'm right?"

She shook her head. "No, I don't think that's the reason." Staring up into his eyes, she said, "Before I saw the house, before you gave me a *car*, I was going to tell you that I found a place for the photography studio."

"Yeah?" His face brightened and curiosity shone in his eyes. "That's great."

"Yes, well, now I don't think I'm comfortable with

our deal. You've already done too much for me—doesn't even matter that I didn't ask you to."

"You can't back out of our deal, Sienna." He reached out and rubbed his hands up and down her bare arms. And it felt like a match touched to kindling.

"Adam…"

"You know, I really like this dress."

"Oh." He threw her off deliberately. She was beginning to think he enjoyed it. "Thanks. I wanted to look good to interview the nanny who didn't work out anyway, so—"

"Let's not waste that dress."

She was almost afraid to ask, "What do you mean?"

"Do you have your camera with you?"

"Of course. It's in Thor."

"Naturally." He took her arm and steered her out of his office. "Okay, let's go."

"Go where?"

"First to the place you found—"

"Adam we have to talk about that."

"—then to Dana Point. You can take those pictures of our new project."

They walked into the big outer office and stopped dead. Kevin was playing peekaboo with Jack. The baby laughed, Kevin grinned, then looked sheepishly over at Adam when the man cleared his throat.

"Fine," Kevin said. "You caught me. I don't actually hate babies. Don't tell Nick."

"He knows," Sienna said, and smiled to herself. She had a feeling Kevin was going to stop fighting the idea of adoption. That should make Nick happy.

"Glad you're having a good time." Adam kept a firm grip on Sienna as he said, "Keep it up. Take Jack back to my place, will you? You can drive the Explorer—the car seat's in it. I'm taking Sienna down to Dana Point to get some shots of the wave project."

Kevin shrugged. "Sure. I can do that."

She was being steamrolled—again—but for some reason it wasn't bothering her. Sienna was starting to worry about that.

"If you get hungry," she said, "Nick left some meals in the freezer."

Grinning, Kevin said, "If I get hungry, I'll call Nick and get him to come over and feed me."

"That works, too. We'll get dinner out, so you and Nick enjoy yourselves," Adam said, already walking away. Sienna looked over her shoulder at Kevin, who gave her a thumbs-up as she hurried to keep pace with Adam.

She had no idea how she'd lost control of this confrontation. She had gone there to lay down the law and instead, she was being swept off on an adventure. She threw him a quick, sideways glance as they stepped into an elevator. He was so damn bossy. Why did she find that so attractive?

"I didn't say I'd go to dinner with you," she said.

He looked down at her and smiled. "I didn't ask."

"I can't believe you did that."

Adam watched her from across the table and relished the mixture of excitement and bafflement in her eyes. "You keep saying that," he said. "But you were there. You heard the conversation."

"I know." She picked up her glass of wine, took a sip, then shook her head.

That action sent her long hair sliding back and forth

across her shoulders in a sinuous movement that was hypnotizing. Adam's breath caught in his chest until it felt like he might explode from the pressure.

"It's just," Sienna said for at least the third time, "I've never heard of someone calling a real estate agent and making a cash offer on a house they haven't even inspected."

"You have to let that go."

"I don't think I can." She laughed a little helplessly. "I don't think the agent's going to recover anytime soon, either."

"Yeah," he said, remembering how the woman had sputtered and gasped over the phone. He shrugged and took a long drink of his wine. "Look, bottom line? You found what you wanted. Good spot for it. Lots of walk-in traffic and drive-bys will see you easily. Plenty of room, and the house itself has good bones. Once we get the deed, we'll take a walk through and you can tell me exactly what you want."

"You mean I get to have input this time?"

One corner of his mouth lifted. "That was the deal."

The restaurant was crowded, even so early. They had a table by the glass, with a view of the cliffs below and the surf pounding against the rocks as steady as a heartbeat. There were candles on the tables, weeping violins pumping through the stereo system and the most beautiful woman he'd ever known sitting across from him.

She wore a summer dress that was a soft, white fabric with dark red flowers scattered all over it. Wide straps curved over her shoulders and a square bodice drew attention to her breasts without displaying them. The skirt was full and hit just above her knees and the high-heeled red sandals she wore showcased shiny red toenails. Her long blond hair was loose and caressing her skin with every tiny movement. Her smile, when she looked at him, lit up her face and shone in her eyes.

And damn it, Adam felt something. He didn't want to admit it—hell, even think about it. But it was there.

She was encroaching too deeply into his life. His world. Thoughts of her were constantly swimming through his mind, and when he was anywhere near her, all he could think about was getting her naked and losing himself in her arms, her heat, her eyes.

Warning bells went off in his mind, but Adam was too far gone to listen. Sienna crossed her long, tanned legs and claimed his full attention. She was too beautiful. Too talented. Too funny. Too damn smart. She was too much of everything, which meant he'd been with her too long.

He needed some space. And not just from Sienna. He needed room to seriously think about Jack. Yes, he loved the baby, but that didn't mean he'd be any damn good at raising him. He needed help, and so far the nanny situation wasn't working out. Sienna had told him on the drive about how their first applicant had had mean eyes and made Jack cry. What the hell was he supposed to do with *that*?

Good thing he had a trip to Santa Barbara coming up. He could get away. Think. Try to make sense of what was happening in his life.

"Adam?" The tone of her voice told him it wasn't the first time she'd spoken to him.

"Sorry. What?"

"Are you okay?"

No, he wasn't okay at all. But damned if he was

going to confess that to the woman who was the *reason* his usually centered, logical mind was suddenly going off on tangents.

"I'm just thinking." Frowning, he said, "You didn't like that nanny. I talked to the owner of the agency today and she sounded so cold I damn near got frostbite over the phone."

She frowned, too. "That doesn't sound good."

"No," he admitted. "It doesn't. I'm thinking now that maybe Delores was onto something when she offered to care for Jack."

"Really?" Candlelight reflected in her eyes.

"For now, anyway," he said. Actually it had only just occurred to him a few minutes ago. But the more he thought about Sienna, the more he wanted her—and the more he knew he had to get her out of his life. He was getting drawn in too deep and he couldn't allow that.

So if Delores took care of the baby, then as soon as she came back from vacation, this time with Sienna would end. They wouldn't be together even longer, searching for some mythical nanny they might *never* find. If they did that, this thing between them could drag on forever and he'd get pulled deeper and deeper into something he knew damn well would never work out.

Better to end it now. For her sake, he reminded himself.

"Well, good." She lifted her glass again. "So no more interviews?"

"Not necessary. Delores will be back in a little over a week. If you can stay until then, I'd appreciate it." He told himself to be polite. Businesslike. No point in making this ugly as he worked to end it. He wouldn't be her friend. He couldn't continue to be her lover. Didn't mean he had to be her enemy, though.

Confusion etched itself into her features. "I thought we'd already decided that I would stay."

"Okay. That's good. Thanks."

*Don't look at the rise and fall of her breasts. Ignore it when she licks her bottom lip.*

He'd have to tell her that what was between them was over. But damned if he'd do that to her over dinner.

He already knew he was terrible at relationships. And his brother had already caused Sienna enough grief for one lifetime. So really, he would be doing this—*ending* this—for her, more than for him. Sienna deserved better than another Quinn screwing with her life.

"You're welcome. Adam…what's wrong?" Concern glistened in her eyes and he hated that he wanted to ease it. So he didn't.

"Nothing's wrong. Just a long day."

She reached across the table for his hand and he pulled back, instead lifting his wineglass. He saw the flash of hurt in her eyes and told himself not to acknowledge it. Pain was transitory. She'd get over this.

They both would.

Dinner had been long and quiet, Sienna thought a couple hours later. She'd sensed Adam pulling away from her even as he sat within touching distance. It was as if the man she'd known for so long had vanished into an icy shell.

And it had only gotten worse once they got home. *Home.* When had she started thinking of Adam's house as *home*? When had she begun to think that there was more between her and Adam than either of them had counted on?

When did she start to love him?

Sienna stopped on the stairs and clutched the banister. Kevin and Nick were long gone, and Adam had disappeared into his office the moment they returned. She was alone when this new, staggering realization hit her and Sienna was grateful for it.

Four years ago, when Devon Quinn rushed her through a romance, seduction and marriage, she'd convinced herself that she was in love. Now, what she felt for Adam just *eclipsed* what those feelings for Devon had been. It was like comparing a doughnut to a seven-course meal. Or a tent to a mansion.

Not only was there *more* love. There were more layers. More definition. More colors in a rainbow that she'd once thought was complete.

She sat down abruptly and looked through the black iron railing to the floor below and the hall that led to Adam's office. She remembered the sudden coolness that had sprung up between them over dinner. He'd looked at her and she could see that he was simply being polite. The heat she was accustomed to from him was banked behind a wall of distance.

Was this why? Had he guessed how she felt? Had he somehow sensed it? Was that the reason he'd changed toward her so suddenly? Oh God, she hadn't meant to love Adam. Now though, as with her house and the car, it was too late to change anything.

And she wasn't entirely sure she would change it even if she could. Love, when it finally arrived, was too big, too overwhelming, to put aside. Adam might not want it, but Sienna was going to relish these new feelings, even if it meant living with pain later.

"But for right now," she murmured as she pushed to her feet again, "he's going to talk to me. I'm not going to spend the next week or so with this cold silence surrounding me."

Wow, she sounded brave. If only she *felt* that way, too.

She wore a dark green T-shirt, denim shorts and she was barefoot, so when she took the stairs, she didn't make a sound. Sienna walked along the hall just as quietly, then tapped gently on his office door. Opening it, she peered inside. "Adam?"

The office was dark but for the brass desk lamp that sent out a small puddle of golden light. It wasn't enough to eradicate the shadows entirely, but it did manage to paint a soft spotlight on the man sitting at the edge of that glow.

Adam was lounging in one of the two burgundy leather club chairs opposite his desk, with his long legs kicked out in front of him. He had a drink in his hand, and though he looked relaxed, Sienna could nearly *feel* the tension emanating from him coming toward her in waves.

Turning his head, he looked at her and she saw that his eyes were still shuttered. "What is it?"

Hardly a warm welcome, but she'd take it. She walked to him and stopped right in front of him. "Exactly my question. I want to know what's going on. What's happened?"

*And please don't know I love you.*

He took a sip from the heavy crystal tumbler he held. Then he pushed to his feet, set the glass down with a hard *click* on the desktop and swiveled back around to face her. "Nothing's happened, Sienna. It's just that playtime's over."

She swayed a little. Playtime. "What do you mean?"

He sighed, and leaned against the desk. Feet crossed at the ankles, arms folded across his chest, he couldn't have been more silently defensive.

"I mean, I'm leaving for Santa Barbara tomorrow."

Sienna frowned. "I thought your meeting was next week."

"I'm going early," he said, each word clipped.

"Why?" She had to hear him say it, though she was pretty sure she already knew the answer.

"Because this thing between us has to end, Sienna." His gaze fixed on hers, but there was no warmth in that steady brown gaze. "We both knew going in that it wouldn't last. Well, now that Delores will be taking care of the baby, we're done."

Her heart ached as if someone were squeezing it. Her stomach roiled and ice seemed to flood her veins. "Because you say so."

"That's right."

In spite of the chill she felt, Sienna faced him squarely. "You know what, Adam? That's fine. It's over. Because *I* say so."

"Whatever helps," he muttered.

Her best intentions went right out the window. She didn't want him to know she loved him? At the moment, she couldn't have explained to herself why she *did* love him.

"Don't do that," she snapped, and stepped closer. "You don't get to brush off my feelings or act as though nothing between us has mattered—"

"Sienna..."

"—because it *has* and you know it." Her breath came fast and furious from her lungs. She was a little light-headed and starting to think she might be hyperventilating. Just what she needed, to keel over in a dead faint.

"Why does it have to mean anything beyond what it was?" he asked, his voice lazy, as if nothing mattered to him. That, more than anything else, infuriated her.

"My God, the arrogance," she said on a harsh breath.

He pushed off the desk and stood, legs braced, as if ready for a fight. Well he'd come to the right place.

"Stop it, Sienna."

"No. Not because you tell me to. Not because I promised myself I wouldn't say *I love you*."

He winced and shook his head and the ice in his eyes went deeper, colder, going from simply winter to an arctic frost. Pain opened up inside her and tears stung the backs of her eyes, but she blinked frantically, determined not to let him see them.

"Oh, you didn't want to hear that, did you?"

"No, because what would be the point?"

"Feelings are their own point, Adam." She took a breath and blew it out in exasperation. "I knew that would be your response, so I wasn't going to say it. Wasn't going to let you know how I felt because I didn't want to put you on the spot or set myself up for your dismissal." She whirled around, stalked off three paces, then spun right back again. "But you know what? The *hell* with that. Why should I keep *my* feelings to myself for *your* sake? It's clear you don't give a flying damn what I'm feeling or thinking. You've already decided that this is over.

"Well news flash, Adam. You don't decide how people feel. Or what they say or do."

Sienna couldn't remember ever being this furious. This sad. This tortured.

"I never said—"

She laughed and it sounded strained even to her. "There it is again, telling me what you didn't say instead of actually saying what you really mean. Or feel." Sienna looked him up and down and avoided meeting that cold, hard gaze again. "Your problem is that you *do* care for me. You just don't want to."

His mouth tightened until a muscle in his jaw twitched with the force of him grinding his teeth. "Damn it, Sienna, do we have to do this? Aren't you the one who said we could be friends when this was over?"

Having her own words tossed back at her was an extra slap. My God, had she really said that? Believed it?

"I was wrong. I'm not your friend. Apparently, I'm no longer your lover, either." She took a deep breath, swallowed hard and said, "But I am the woman who loves you—in spite of you being the most arrogant jackass on the face of the planet, I love you.

"I'm going to try to stop though, so spare me your pity." She turned and headed for the door. When she got there, she paused and looked back at him. "If you really think running to Santa Barbara is going to make this easier, I wish you luck with that, but you're going to be massively disappointed."

"I'm not running," he ground out.

"Keep telling yourself that." Grabbing the doorknob, she pulled it closed behind her. "Have a nice trip."

*  *  *

For the next two days, it was just Sienna and Jack. She didn't call Cheryl, didn't even check in at the shop beyond telling her assistant, Terri, to postpone the two appointments she had for another week or so. She was in no mood to try to be creative. To try to find the sunshine in life and capture it digitally.

How could she, when it felt as though the earth had opened up beneath her feet? Yes, she'd known going in that there would be no future with Adam. But she'd at least had the *present*. Now she had nothing.

"Just you, sweet baby," she murmured, smoothing her hand over Jack's baby-fine hair. "You, I won't give up. I can't."

She'd already lost Adam, how could she lose Jack, too? She would just have to be careful. Come to the house when she was sure Adam was at work or something. Sienna was pretty sure Delores wouldn't rat her out to Adam.

"Adam. God, I miss him," she whispered, and heard her own voice echo in the great room. Just being here now, walking through this lovely house, she saw Adam everywhere. And his absence was like a gaping hole in her heart.

She'd spent the last two nights on the sofa in the baby's room, lying awake because if she tried to sleep, Adam came to her in dreams. Cowardly maybe, to use a sleeping baby as an emotional teddy bear. But she didn't want to be alone. And couldn't bear the thought of being in Adam's room without him.

"Was it really only a little more than a week ago that this all started?" she wondered aloud as baby Jack patted her cheeks with both hands. How could everything have changed so dramatically in such a short time? How had she not noticed that she was falling in love?

"Maybe because a part of me has always loved him. And how pitiful is that? But don't worry. I'll be okay, sweetie," she said, holding Jack close, nuzzling his neck, inhaling that clean, fresh scent that spelled baby, love. "And I'll always love you, even if I'm not here. You're going to have to be patient with your uncle Adam because he loves you, too. He's crabby sometimes, but don't hold that against him."

The baby reared back and gave her a wide, toothless grin.

"Boy, I'm really going to miss you."

Before she could get all teary again though, the doorbell rang and she walked to answer it. When she opened the door, Sienna's heart dropped.

"I knew it would be *you*." Donna Quinn sailed past Sienna into the house, then spun around to face her. "One of my sons wasn't enough for you? Now you're making a play for the other one, as well?"

# Ten

"I won't have it."

Donna Quinn was practically trembling with fury. Her brown eyes snapped with the force of her rage. "I won't have you here. In this house. In my son's life." She stabbed one finger at Sienna. "An old friend of mine saw you out to dinner with Adam. She called and delighted in telling me that Devon's ex was moving up the food chain in the Quinn family."

Just when Sienna had thought she'd hit rock bottom, it seemed there was further to fall.

Oh God. Adam's mother had never liked her. Never thought Sienna was the "right" woman for Devon. According to Donna, the divorce was Sienna's doing, and when Devon died, the woman had blamed Sienna for that, too. It hadn't mattered to her at the time, because Sienna never had to deal with Donna.

Looked like those days were over.

Sienna closed the front door and held on to Jack just a little tighter. She watched Donna stride up and down the entryway, her heels clacking noisily against the tiles. Her blond hair was styled into a layered bob and she wore cream-colored linen slacks and a sapphire-blue silk shirt. She would have looked the picture of elegance, but for the fury pumping off her.

"Whatever you're thinking," Donna accused, "worming your way into Adam's house, caring for Devon's son—" She stopped abruptly. Her gaze left Sienna's and landed on the baby as if she was just noticing him.

"Give him to me," Donna demanded.

Sienna actually took a step away. She didn't have the right, of course. Her former mother-in-law was Jack's grandmother, after all. But the baby's fingers took a tight grip on her hair and Sienna understood. This stranger with the loud voice was scaring him, so Sienna stood fast.

"He doesn't know you, Donna. You're scaring him."

The woman's head snapped back as if she'd been struck. "How dare you. He's *my* grandson."

"And he doesn't know you," Sienna said again, keeping her voice quiet and low. "If you could calm down a little—"

"Calm down?" Donna choked out a laugh that sounded to Sienna like nails on a blackboard. "I find it ironic that the woman who is the cause of my anger is actually telling me to calm down."

Sienna took a breath and reminded herself to be polite. The cool quiet of the house had been shattered. Donna stood in a slash of sunlight that reflected in her eyes and almost looked like flames. In a flash, she remembered everything Adam had told her about his mother. About the way she'd hovered over Devon and pretty much ignored Adam. Sienna remembered Devon ducking his mother's phone calls. Moving to Italy to get out from under her thumb.

And yet, none of that mattered because Donna was here now, and like it or not, she was Jack's grandmother. Adam's mother. So Sienna kept a tight leash on the anger beginning to build in the pit of her stomach and reached for patience.

Then she watched as Donna swept her gaze up and down Sienna, taking in the jeans shorts, the bare feet and the gray T-shirt with a sneer. "How can I calm down when I find *you* back in our lives? My God, you're like a specter haunting the Quinn family. Wasn't it enough that Devon died because of you?"

Sienna gasped. She'd known all along that Devon's mother blamed her for his death, and she'd let it go. Because Donna wasn't a part of her life anymore and everyone needed someone to blame when tragedy struck.

But damned if she'd stand still for it now. "We were divorced for a year and a half when he died, Donna. How was it my fault?"

"Because if you had *stayed* with him," she cried, the glimmer of angry tears shining in her eyes, "he wouldn't have been on that damn boat. Or in that *stupid* race."

"God, Donna, you knew him better than that," Sienna said, trying to reach past the woman's grief. "Of course Devon would have been in the race. He always did exactly what he wanted, when he wanted. He took every chance he could because he thought he was immortal."

"You don't have the right to speak to me about *my* son."

"I have every right," Sienna said quietly, smoothing her hand up and down the baby's back in an effort to comfort him. "I was his wife."

"You never should have been. If he'd listened to me…"

Sienna sighed and Donna reacted.

"Your plan is to be Adam's wife now, isn't it?"

"No," she said, and the single word cost her because the truth was, if he had asked her to marry him she would have said yes in a blink. But he hadn't. Never would. So how she felt didn't matter.

"You'd better not even consider it," Donna said, and swiped one hand across her cheeks to angrily wipe away a stray tear or two. Then she narrowed her gaze on Sienna. "Because Adam will never tie himself to you."

No, he wouldn't. Not because of anything his mother might do, but because Adam had decided to cut her out of his life. And it tore at Sienna to admit that to herself. She looked at Donna and tried to look past the woman's anger. Whatever she was, she had loved her son and Sienna couldn't even imagine the pain of losing him. Whether she qualified for mother of the year or not really didn't come into it.

"There's nothing between Adam and me," Sienna finally said, though it cost her. Donna didn't look convinced.

"And there won't be. I'll see to it."

Sienna could have laughed at that. No one made Adam Quinn do anything he didn't want to do. And he didn't take orders from anyone, either. Especially his mother. No reason to point that out though, since no matter what she wanted to believe, Donna knew all of this as well as Sienna did.

"Now," Donna said, her voice low and throbbing with banked emotion, "I want to hold my grandson and I would like you to leave this house."

Pure reflex had Sienna tightening her hold on the baby. "Adam's expecting me to be here, taking care of Jack."

"I'm here now. Your assistance is unnecessary." Donna reached out and scooped Jack up.

Instantly, the baby wailed and leaned toward Sienna, holding out both arms to her. Sienna's heart physically ached as she looked from the baby to the hard eyes of his grandmother. She really didn't have a choice. This wasn't her home. That wasn't her child. And Adam wasn't hers, either. The hardest truth to face.

"All right, Donna, I'll leave." Deliberately, she avoided looking at the baby, still crying for her. "Jack's food and bottles are in the kitchen pantry."

"I'll find them," Donna assured her.

"Okay, then. I'll pack and go." The other woman watched in silence as Sienna turned and walked up the stairs. Jack's heartbroken wails followed her, and Sienna's gaze blurred with tears. She held tight to the railing as she took the stairs with the slow deliberation of someone climbing the steps to the gallows.

She felt as if she'd been hollowed out and could only think that *this* was how it felt to lose everything that mattered.

Three days in Santa Barbara and it was all over but for the celebrating.

The golf course was a done deal and work on the project would start in the next couple of months. It was one of the best deals Adam had ever undertaken, and he realized he didn't give a good damn. He'd had to fight every minute to be able to concentrate because his mind had kept drifting back home to Sienna and the baby. Somehow, he thought in amazement, the three of them had become a *family*.

He scrubbed his hands over his face and tried to wipe away the thought that he'd thrown away something most people never found. But what other choice had he had? None. His track record with relationships sucked. Adam didn't want to give Sienna more pain. If she was hurt now, then that was better than more pain later on. He'd done the right thing.

So why did he feel so crappy?

Adam paced the length of the luxurious living room in the Presidential Suite. He and Kevin were in the best hotel in the city in a room that would have had Sienna sighing in pleasure—and no doubt taking pictures from every angle—and he couldn't have cared less. The place could have been a flooded-out cave for all he noticed. Or cared.

"Man," Kevin said, dropping into a chair, "we cleared this up in record time. Once we get the papers signed tonight, we can head home."

"Yeah. Thanks for taking care of that last meeting."

"I've never seen you in such a rush to get things settled and signed."

"No point in waiting around, is there?" Adam opened the French doors onto the stone balcony and leaned both hands on the wrought iron railing. It wasn't that he was in a hurry. More like he couldn't focus for the first time in his life. He leaned into the wind and hoped to hell it would blow his mind clear. But chances of that were slim.

It had been three days and he'd been reliving that last scene with Sienna ever since he left the house. He could see her face clearly, how she'd struggled to bank down tears of fury and frustration. He heard her say *I love you*. He saw her walk out of his office and close the door quietly behind her.

Didn't matter that she was hundreds of miles away. She was with him, no matter where the hell he was. He couldn't get her out of his mind. And wasn't sure he ever would. Hell, Adam figured he'd probably spend the next forty years with her image front and center in his thoughts. Torturing him. Showing him what he could have had. "Maybe that's just what I deserve."

"What's that?" Kevin called.

"Nothing," Adam told him. "Wasn't talking to you."

"Well, talking to yourself is a bad sign, son."

Adam frowned as his best friend walked out onto the balcony to join him. He was carrying two beers and handed one to Adam. "So, want to tell me why you raced through this deal like the hounds of hell were after you?"

"I didn't. Hell, you did most of the work."

"And don't think I won't remind you of that come bonus time," Kevin said cheerfully. "But I think there's more to it than that. I think you're in a hurry to get home. Hmm. Wonder why."

Adam snorted. "You couldn't be more wrong." Though a part of him wanted nothing more than to hop on his private jet and get the hell back to *her*, he knew it wouldn't do any good. When he went home, Sienna would leave. Even if Delores wasn't back from vacation yet, Sienna wouldn't stay in that house with him. Not after everything they'd said to each other.

Not after they'd ended so brutally what had started out so well.

"Okay, that's a lie," Kevin said amiably.

Adam gave him a hard look.

"The patented Quinn glare never worked on me, so save it," Kevin said. "We both know you're in a hurry to get back to Sienna, but you're lying about it to me and yourself. Why?"

Adam sighed. Having a best friend who knew you so well could be a real pain in the ass sometimes. Yes, Adam wanted to get back home, and also, no, he didn't. Because once he was back home... "Let it go, Kevin."

"Not a chance." Kevin took a sip of his beer, stared out at the sea for a minute or two, then looked at Adam. "So. What did you do?"

Adam stared at him. "What makes you think I did anything?"

"Because I know you, Adam." Kevin shook his head in disgust, took another sip of his beer and leaned back against the railing. The ocean wind whipped past them both. The sun dipped behind a bank of gray clouds and below them on the sea, surfers shouted joyfully to each other as they rode waves to shore.

"Nobody likes a know-it-all, Kevin."

"Sure they do." Looking straight at him, Kevin narrowed his eyes and said, "Let's see how close I get. You told Sienna to get lost because you're sacrificing yourself to save her."

He was close but damned if Adam would admit it. He snorted. "I don't do sacrifice."

"Bull. You spent most of your whole damn life jumping onto a sacrificial altar."

"I'm not that altruistic."

"Bull again." Kevin scowled at him. "Family is what counts to you, Adam. And Devon was family."

"What's that supposed to mean?"

The sun was just beginning to set and Kevin was backlit against it. Adam had to squint to see his friend's expression and when he finally made it out, he wasn't surprised to see aggravation there.

"You took the heat with your mother to try to keep her off Devon's ass."

"Didn't work. Thanks for the reminder." Adam lifted his beer in salute and took a drink.

"You pulled all the weight with your dad to cover up the fact that Devon was a screwup."

"Nobody could please our dad," Adam countered, thinking back to just how many times he himself had taken the blame for some mishap on a construction site because their father went easier on him than he did Devon.

"Right. Okay, still defending him." Kevin pushed off the railing and stood there, with the wind whipping through his hair. "You forget. I saw a lot of this crap, Adam, so you can't fool me."

Good point. "Fine. Whatever. I tried to help my brother. Shoot me."

"You're doing a good enough job on your own," Kevin snapped. "I've seen you and Sienna together. The two of you *work*. And you know it. Hell, there's so many sappy butterflies flying around you both I expect cartoon hearts to appear in the air over your heads."

"I could say the same about you and Nick," Adam pointed out, taking another sip of his beer, though it didn't even taste good anymore.

"Yeah, you could. The difference is, I found who I

wanted and I went out and got him. You're going to let Sienna dance out of your life. Why? Because of Devon again? Just how much do you have to give up because of your no-good brother?"

"Just hold on a minute…"

"No. Screw this, Adam." Kevin set his beer down on a nearby table and crossed his arms over his chest. "Devon was selfish and lazy and didn't deserve half of the loyalty you always gave him."

Adam stiffened in automatic defense mode. Hell, he'd been standing up for Devon their whole lives. Apparently, even death couldn't stop the knee-jerk reaction to save Devon's reputation. "He was still my brother."

"Too bad he never seemed to remember that," Kevin said grimly.

"Damn it, Kevin, he's dead. Isn't that enough?"

"Apparently not, since you're still jumping in front of bullets for him." Shaking his head, Kevin stared him down and Adam listened. "Devon never had the brains to know a good thing when he had it."

Adam raked one hand through his hair and wished he could argue with him.

Kevin's chin jutted out as if asking Adam to plant his fist on it. But they both knew that wouldn't happen. "Devon threw away his partnership in the firm you two started together."

"Yeah—"

"He turned his back on his parents, practically cutting them out of his life completely because it was easier than dealing with the family crap we *all* deal with."

"True, but he—"

"And finally," Kevin said hotly, "he let Sienna go so he could chase other women. And *these* are just some of the reasons why you've always been a better man than Devon."

"Damn it, Kevin." As much as he hated to admit it, everything his friend said was true. Hell, Kevin was more a brother to Adam than Devon ever had been and though it hurt to admit it, it was a relief to acknowledge it at last, too. Kevin had always been the one Adam could count on. Even if it was to say all the things Adam really didn't want to hear.

Grabbing up his beer, Kevin clinked his bottle to Adam's and took a drink. "So you're a better man than your idiot brother."

"Thanks. But according to you, that's a low bar."

"Now we have to find out if you're smarter than he was, too."

Adam knew exactly what he meant and said, "Hasn't she had enough of the Quinn family messing with her life?"

"Adam," Kevin asked on a sigh, "does Sienna seem like the type of woman who's going to let *any* guy run her life for her?"

He thought about that for a minute, then smiled. "No, she's really not. You were right about us redoing her house. She was so furious…"

"Yet she didn't leave you," he pointed out. "You left her."

"For her sake," Adam muttered. "I failed at marriage once before."

"Takes two, man," Kevin told him. "Believe me, I *know*. Tricia didn't hold up her end, either. Neither one of you cared enough to fight for it."

Nodding, Adam silently agreed, remembering that he and his ex-wife hadn't even really had a fight. They weren't invested enough to care, so they'd eventually just drifted apart. Now, Sienna, on the other hand—he actually enjoyed going head-to-head with her. Arguing was fun, but making up was amazing.

"You're smiling."

"Stop looking at me," Adam said, and took another sip of his beer.

"I'd rather be looking at Nick," Kevin allowed. "So? What's the plan? We get back home and you straighten this mess out while you still can?"

"If I don't, are you going to bug me about it forever?"

"I think we both know the answer to that," Kevin said, smiling.

"Yeah, we do." Adam nodded at his friend. His brother. "Let's get the paperwork wrapped up and go home."

"I'll drink to that." Kevin lifted his beer and Adam tapped his own bottle against it.

One more day and he'd fix this. Fix it all. He'd marry Sienna, they could both adopt Jack and they'd have a damn family that would make everyone who knew them jealous.

And if she argued with him about his decision?

Bonus.

Adam walked into chaos.

Jack was screaming, Donna was crying and the great room looked like a bomb had gone off in the center of it. Where the hell was Sienna?

"Mother?"

Her head snapped up and her wild gaze fixed on him. "Oh, thank God. He won't stop crying." She waved both hands at the baby. "Do something for him. It's driving me insane. There's no one to help. I'm at my wit's end…"

Adam dropped his bag, walked to the baby and lifted him out of the walker. His skin was hot and flushed; tears tracked down his cheeks and into the rings of fat around his little neck. His hair was plastered to his head and the minute Adam picked him up, Jack laid his head down on Adam's shoulder and snuffled loudly.

"What the hell is going on here?" he asked, turning his head to look around the room. "Where's Sienna?"

Donna gasped. "I sent her away. As you should have."

"You did what?" His voice went too loud and Jack cringed against him. "Sorry, sorry," he murmured, patting the boy's back while he fired a hard look at his mother.

"She didn't belong here. In your *house*. Caring for Devon's *son*. *My* grandson."

"She was invited to be here, Mother," Adam pointed out. "You weren't."

She gasped again and color rushed into her cheeks. Adam sighed. It wouldn't do any good to fight with his mother. Better to just placate her and get rid of her.

"If you think you can take up with that woman, you're wrong."

Adam went still. "Excuse me?"

Jack's toys were strewn across the floor. There were four empty coffee cups on different tables and a few bottles of water. Cookie crumbs littered the floor under the walker and a box of diapers was sitting on the wet bar. His place was a wreck, the baby was hysterical and his mother was ready for war. Perfect.

"If you allow that woman back into our family, I'll never speak to you again."

Drama. His whole damn life had been drama.

Donna Quinn knew how to create a scene better than any Hollywood director. She was known for being able to bloodlessly flail someone alive until they were nothing more than a hank of hair and a bag of bones. But Adam hadn't played her game since he was a kid, so he wasn't quite sure why she thought this would work on him now.

"Mother," he said evenly, "you don't run my life. Never have. I make my own choices and I'll see any woman I want to. I don't need your permission."

"She's *evil*," Donna insisted. "She as good as killed your brother because she didn't care enough to stay with him. Take care of him."

"Oh for God's sake." He hitched Jack higher on his shoulder when he realized the baby had fallen asleep. "Devon cheated on her regularly and didn't bother to hide it. Sienna would have been crazy to stay with him."

"You don't understand. You never did," Donna said as tears welled up and spilled down her cheeks. "You were always more your father's than mine."

"I don't know, Mother," he said, tiredly. He'd come home to face Sienna. To find a way to make a future. To convince her to take a chance on yet another Quinn. Instead, he was thrown into a B movie starring a woman who seemed determined to cling to the drama he wanted to avoid. "Maybe that's true. What I *do* know, is that I'm going to see Sienna. And I'm going to bring her home. Here. If you can't handle that, I suggest you go back to Florida."

"You're throwing your own mother out?"

"No," he corrected, looking into her teary eyes. A part of him felt sorry for her. She'd been a ghost in his life, never really putting in the time, but he didn't doubt that she had loved him and Devon. In her own way. But Adam's priority was Sienna now. Sienna and Jack. If his mother couldn't accept that…

"I'm asking you to stop blaming everyone but Devon for what happened," he said quietly.

"If I can't?"

"Then I'll be sorry about it. But, you can take my jet back home. I'll call the airport and tell them to get it ready for you."

She stared at him, horrified for a moment or two. "You've chosen her over me."

"I've chosen the future over the past," he corrected and the moment the words left him, they felt right.

"Then I'm leaving."

"That's your choice," he said, wishing things were different—as he had most of his life. "I'll call the airport."

Donna stared at him for a long moment as if she couldn't quite believe how this scene had gone. In her mind, he was sure, she'd imagined Adam apologizing to her and promising to turn Sienna out of his life forever. Well, she'd have to learn to live with disappointment.

Donna sniffed heroically, then hurried from the room, one hand to her mouth as if holding back more tears. She would go back to Florida and whether she came back to visit or not would be up to her. But it was time she realized as he had, that Adam was done with what Kevin had called *jumping onto the sacrificial altar*.

"Okay, kiddo," he whispered, kissing the baby, who lay sound asleep against his chest. "Time to go find our woman."

\* \* \*

Sienna hunched over her computer, studying the photos she'd taken the day before at the beach. Since leaving Adam's house, she'd tried to focus. To reclaim her own life and lose herself in her job.

So far, it wasn't working, but she had high hopes. She hadn't cried all day today, so that was a plus. She still wasn't sleeping though and spent the nights curled up on her couch watching dreadful old movies, just for the company.

But every day it was bound to get a little better, right? Because the way she was feeling, there was just nowhere to go but up.

When the doorbell rang, she went to answer it and caught a glimpse of a shiny black Jaguar parked at her curb. Her heart leaped in her chest and she had to swallow hard past a knot of longing that lodged in her throat. She knew it was Adam. It had to be—because she simply didn't know anyone else who owned a car like that one.

Why was he here? What could he want? Hope lifted in the center of her chest and she batted it back down. She couldn't stand to pump up her balloon again only to have it popped.

Steeling herself, she opened the door and simply stared. His hair was shaggy and windblown. He wore a dark red T-shirt, blue jeans and a worn pair of brown cowboy boots. She was so used to seeing him either naked or in elegantly tailored suits, she had to take a second to appreciate the casual Adam.

He held Jack in his arms and as she looked at him, the baby squealed and threw himself at her. Sienna grabbed him and snuggled him close, reveling in the warm, solid weight of him. Then she looked up into Adam's eyes and her heartbeat stuttered. There were no shutters in those brown depths. He wasn't trying to keep her out anymore and she didn't know what to make of that.

Jack squirmed excitedly and she laughed as she wrapped both arms around him. "Oh, I've missed you so much," she whispered, and planted a kiss on his forehead.

"Did you miss me, too?" Adam asked, walking into the house, forcing her to back up so he could come in and close the door behind him.

She'd missed him as she would have her arm. Her leg. Her heart. "Adam…"

"Just answer the question, Sienna."

"Of course I missed you," she snapped, irritated that the moment they were together, he started issuing orders again.

He grinned. "You don't sound happy about that."

"Why would I be? I tell you I love you and you basically say 'go away'?" She blew out a breath. "Not exactly hearts and flowers, Adam."

"Yeah," he said, frowning, "about that. That's why I'm here." He took a deep breath and said, "I was wrong."

Sienna blinked at him.

"Surprise." He scrubbed the back of his neck and for the first time, Sienna realized Mr. King of the Universe looked nervous.

"Yes," he continued, "I can admit when I'm wrong. It doesn't happen often because I'm usually right."

"Of course you are." Sienna laughed helplessly. "So what were you wrong about exactly?"

He walked past her into the tiny living room and

began to pace it like a tiger in a too-small cage. "Nice room. Tiny, though."

"Thank you," she said wryly.

He glared at her. "You know, I already failed at marriage once."

"Yes, we've been over that," she reminded him. "I have, too."

"Yeah, but that's different. Devon was an ass. Wasn't your fault. Me? I'm no good at sharing." He shot her a look and Sienna saw the flash of worry in his eyes. This was the first time she could ever remember seeing Adam less than supremely confident.

"Adam—"

"Oh, and I'm sorry for any hideous thing my mother said to you."

She flushed and leaned her forehead against the baby's. "Not necessary. I understand."

"Well I don't." Adam scowled again, came to a stop and crossed his arms over his chest. "I want you to know, I don't care what my mother—or anyone else for that matter—thinks. I don't care that I sucked at marriage before, either, because being married to *you* would be different."

"Married?" Her heartbeat jumped into a gallop. Was he proposing? If so, it was a terrible one and she wished he'd be quiet long enough for her to say yes.

"You love me, Sienna. Even if you hadn't told me, I'd have known. It's written all over your face." He walked right up to her, tipped her chin up and stared down into her eyes. "I see it whenever I look at you. And I don't think I can go another day without seeing it again."

She took a breath and said, "Oh, Adam, I—"

"No point in you saying no, because this is just the

way it has to be." He gave her a hard look. "You love me. I love you. We get married. Delores can help us out with Jack when we need it—you know, if we both have to work and neither of us can take him with us…"

"I'm sure she could, but—"

Adam stared at the ceiling for a second, thinking, then said, "Of course, when we have more kids, Delores will need help—"

"More kids?"

He shrugged. "Big house. You don't want Jack growing up alone, do you?"

"No, but we should—"

"Maybe we could get Delores's sister to move here. We could build a casita in the backyard, big enough for both of them and—"

"Casita?"

"You know, small house—mother-in-law quarters—" He broke off. "Don't worry though, not for your mother-in-law."

Her head was spinning, her heart was racing and breathing was really becoming an issue. "Adam, what exactly are you trying to say?"

"I'm trying to tell you you're going to marry me," he said.

Jack squealed, reached for Adam. He took the tiny boy into his arms so easily it was as if he'd been born handling a baby. Funny how quickly things could change, Sienna thought. Yesterday her heart had been broken. Today, Adam was here, offering her love. A family.

"I'm going to marry you?"

"Damn straight you are." With his free arm, Adam pulled her up close. "I love you, Sienna. I tried not to. I thought about staying away from you. To protect you.

But I can't. If that makes me a selfish bastard, I'll have to live with it.

"I can't let you go. Don't want to live without you and I'm not sure I could. I want us—the three of us—to live in that big empty house. I want us to have more kids, too. Jack needs some brothers and sisters and we're getting pretty good at the kid thing, so why not?"

"Why not?" she repeated, nodding, crying, blinking her eyes because she didn't want to miss a moment of this.

"I think we should adopt Jack right away," he went on, and ran the palm of his hand over the back of the baby's head. "Be officially his parents, you know?"

She laid one hand on Adam's chest and felt his heart racing as quickly as hers. "I think that's a wonderful idea."

"Good. That's good." He kissed her, lingering over her mouth as if he were savoring the most delectable taste in the world. When he finally lifted his head again, he said, "We'll have to find a way to deal with my mother. But I promise you, she won't ever interfere with what's between us."

"I know that, Adam," Sienna said, reaching up to cup his cheek in the palm of her hand. Donna Quinn was an unhappy woman, but maybe someday, Sienna thought, there would be peace between them all.

He bent for another kiss and the baby slapped them both, laughing gleefully. "Okay," Adam said with a grin, "I think he approves. So. You still haven't said. Are you going to marry me or not?"

Sienna laughed. God, she felt wonderful. "Wow. A question. Sure you don't want to just order me to marry you?"

"It would be easier," he admitted. "But yeah. A question. That needs an answer."

"Then here it is. Absolutely yes, Adam." Sienna smiled up at the man who had held her heart almost from the moment she'd first met him. It had taken time for them to find each other. But the waiting had only made this beginning that much sweeter.

She wrapped her arms around Adam and laid her head on his chest alongside the boy who was already the son of her heart. The three of them completed a circle that Sienna hadn't even known she'd been searching for. And now that she'd found it, she knew she was home.

"So," Adam whispered. "To go ring shopping, we'll have to leave Hermione here and take Thor."

She tipped her head back to look at him, a smile curving her mouth. "Hermione?"

Adam shrugged. "You're not the only one who can name a car."

"But Hermione?" Sienna was grinning now, so happy she felt like she just might explode with it.

"It's British and I liked those Harry Potter books."

Laughing, Sienna said, "I really love you."

Adam kissed her hard. "Don't ever stop."

# Epilogue

*One year later...*

"Lift Jack a little higher," Sienna ordered. "And move Maya more to the left. No my left. Your right."

"Sienna," Adam grumbled, "this shot is for us, not the Sistine Chapel. Can you just take the picture?"

"Just a minute," Nick said, and darted in front of the camera to straighten Maya's tiny, pale green dress. "There you go, my little goddaughter. You look beautiful." He turned to Jack to tickle the little boy's ribs, gaining a giggle for his trouble. "And that handsome boy." He slipped out of the way again. "Okay, Sienna, get it fast!"

She did, the click of her camera sounding like a whole herd of crickets set loose in the photography studio. When she was satisfied, she straightened up, walked to her family and scooped the two-month-old girl into her arms. "There we go, sweet baby girl."

Adam swung Jack up to his shoulders as he stood up and looked over at Nick. "Where's Kevin?"

"He took the boys into the backyard." Nick grinned. "All three of them get a little antsy when they're forced to sit still for pictures."

Sienna listened to everyone and smiled. The last year had been the most perfect one of her life. Married to Adam, mother to Jack and then, like a blessing, a mother again to baby Maya.

The world was pretty much a beautiful place and she thanked Whoever was listening every night for the wonder of her life.

"Hey," Adam said, coming in close to claim a kiss from her and to drop one on his daughter's forehead. "You okay?"

She looked up into brown eyes that were never closed to her these days. Sienna read warmth and happiness in his steady gaze and her heart simply filled up and spilled over into her soul.

"I'm excellent," she assured him.

"Good, I settle for nothing less than the best." Adam dropped one arm around her shoulders and hooked his other arm across Jack's feet, holding him in place.

"I'll get Kevin and the boys, then we can head to our place for dinner." Nick grinned and headed down the hallway toward the backyard. No doubt, the boys were on the swing set or drawing at one of the tables. Sienna kept several items in the yard to use as props for kids' pictures, and to occupy children who hated being cooped up inside.

Sienna watched him go and leaned into Adam with

a satisfied smile. "Who knew that Kevin would be so into being a daddy?"

"I think Nick always knew," Adam said, dropping a kiss on the top of her head. "Those kids already have Kevin wrapped around their fingers."

Two brothers—Max, three and Tony, five—had joined Kevin and Nick's family as foster children six months before. And already they were talking adoption. Nick had never been happier and Kevin carried so many photos of the boys around to show off, people at the office were actively avoiding him now.

Adam's mother hadn't exactly turned into Mary Poppins, but she had made an effort in the last few months. The woman was crazy about her grandchildren—in small doses—so Sienna had hope that one day, old wounds would heal over.

Meanwhile, Sienna had her perfect photography studio and she'd sold her little house in Long Beach to a lovely young couple who promised to take good care of it. Her business was growing by leaps and bounds, and every day, she got to go home to the people she loved most in the world.

"What're you thinking?" Adam whispered.

"About how much I love you. And the kids. And our life."

"Our life together is everything to me. I don't know how I lived before you, Sienna," he said softly, and his eyes showed her the love that colored those words.

"I love you, Adam," she said, stroking her fingertips along his cheek.

"And when we get these kids to bed later," he said with a wink, "I'll show you how much I love you."

"More mistakes?" she teased, reminding him of how they started.

Staring deeply into her eyes, Adam said, "Best mistake I ever made. It brought me to you."

\* \* \* \* \*

# HIS HEIR, HER SECRET

**JANICE MAYNARD**

For all of my friends who have ever fantasized about owning a quaint bookstore in a charming small town…this one's for you… ☺

# One

The Scotsman was back. Heart pounding, hands sweating, Cate Everett leaned over her old-fashioned, nicked-up porcelain sink and eased the curtain aside with one finger. From the vantage point of her upstairs apartment, she had a perfect view of the comings and goings across the street.

Brody Stewart. The man she hadn't seen in four months and believed she would never see again. Brody Stewart. Six feet and more of broad shoulders, sinewy muscles and a rough-velvet brogue of a voice that could shuck the panties off a girl before she knew what was happening. The Scotsman was back.

She wasn't ready. Dear Lord, she wasn't ready.

Her freshly brewed cup of tea sat cooling on the table behind her. The late February day had been icy and drear, a perfect match for the mood that had plagued her since climbing out of bed at dawn. She'd thought the comforting drink would cheer her up.

Instead, a clatter of slamming doors and deep male voices had distracted her…driven her to the window. And now she knew. The Scotsman was back.

In all fairness, Cate had never seen disaster coming four months ago. When a man's grandmother introduces you to her grandson, a woman usually thinks the guy can't get his own dates.

Only in this case, it wasn't true. Brody Stewart could have any woman he wanted with one twinkle of his long-lashed, indigo-blue eyes. She still remembered the tiny lines that crinkled at the corners of those gorgeous eyes when he smiled. Brody smiled a lot.

*Oh, jeez.* Her legs wobbled in sync with the drunken butterflies in her stomach. She needed to sit down. She needed to drink her tea. But she couldn't tear herself away from the window.

On the street below, a tiny, gray-haired lady gave orders to two remarkably similar men. Brody was one. The other must be Duncan, his younger brother. Suitcases came out of the trunk of a rental car. Hugs were exchanged. Snow-flakes danced on the breeze.

None of the three people she spied on seemed to notice the cold. Perhaps because they hailed from the Scottish Highlands…a place where winter winds scoured the moors, and bloodlines went as far back as the hearty stock of warring clans and beyond.

Cate wiped damp palms on her faded jeans. She needed to focus. Voyeurism and dithering weren't going to accomplish a thing. Besides, she had a shop to run.

Forcing herself to step back and abandon her intense fascination with the tableau on the street, she cradled her teacup in two trembling hands, drank most of the cold liquid and set the delicate china aside before making her way downstairs. Lunch break, such as it was, was over.

For five years she had found solace and pride in her charmingly eccentric bookshop, Dog-Eared Pages. The little store with the uneven hardwood floors and the rows of antique bookshelves held a place of honor on the main street of Candlewick, North Carolina. From the spring solstice until almost Thanksgiving, tourists came and went, bringing dollars and life to the region.

Tucked away in the Blue Ridge Mountains an hour from Asheville, Candlewick hearkened back to a simpler time. Neighbors knew each other's business, crime was rare and the quality of life made up for the lack of first-run movie theaters and big-name restaurants.

Cate straightened the local History section and dusted one volume at a time, congratulating herself on avoiding the front of the store. She didn't need to know what was happening across the street. It had nothing to do with her.

Without warning, the tinkling of a bell above the door announced the arrival of a customer. Cate's heart stopped for a full three seconds, and then lurched ahead with a sickening whoosh when she recognized her visitor.

She cleared her dry throat. "Miss Izzy. What can I do for you?"

Isobel Stewart stood barely five feet tall but carried herself with the personality of an Amazon. Decades ago she had left her parents' home in Inverness for a secretarial job in the big city of Edinburgh. While there, she met a charismatic American who had come to Scotland for a study-abroad semester.

After a whirlwind courtship, Isobel married the lad and followed him back to the United States—Candlewick, North Carolina, to be precise. She embraced her new life with only one request, that she keep her maiden name. Her new husband not only agreed, but also legally changed his last name to hers so that the Stewart line would continue. Together, the young couple launched a business building cabins in the mountains.

The intervening years produced vast wealth and a single son. Unfortunately for his parents, the young man felt the pull of his Scottish roots and after college settled in the

Highlands. *His* two sons were the two men Cate had been spying on across the street. Izzy's grandsons.

Isobel Stewart scanned the titles on the New Release shelf. "I want ye to come to dinner tonight, Cate. Brody is back. And he's brought Duncan with him this time."

"You must be thrilled," Cate said, avoiding the question. Actually, it was more of a command. Isobel rarely accepted no for an answer.

The little woman suddenly looked every one of her ninety-two years. "I need you," she muttered as if mortified by her weakness.

The smell of lemon polish permeated the air. Cate leaned a hip against the oak counter that supported the cash register. "What's wrong, Miss Izzy?"

When the old Scottish lady blinked back tears, Cate couldn't tell if they were genuine or manipulative.

Isobel's bottom lip quivered. "I don't have room in the apartment for *two* huge men, so I've told the lads they have to stay up at the big house."

The *big house* was Isobel's lavish and incredibly beautiful property on the mountaintop above Candlewick. Izzy hadn't been able to spend the night there since her husband died six months before. Like many of the businesses in Candlewick, Stewart Properties was housed in a historic building on Main Street. Izzy had taken to sleeping on the second floor above her office.

"Makes sense," Cate said carefully, sensing a trap. "But what does that have to do with me?"

"The boys wanted to surprise me for my birthday. They've hired a caterer to prepare dinner for us tonight. I hadn't the heart to tell them I didn't want to come."

"Oh, I didn't remember it was today. Happy birthday. But Brody was here before. Surely the two of you spent time up on the mountain."

"He did a few chores for me. Checked on things. I pretended like I was busy. And since it was just Brody, he slept on the sofa, ye know…in the apartment…with me."

"Miss Izzy…" Cate trailed off, searching for words. "Your grandsons must have an inkling of how you feel. Maybe this is their way of breaking the ice. It's been six months. The longer you stay away, the more difficult it will be. I'm guessing they planned the birthday dinner to lure you up there."

"It doesn't feel like months," the old woman said, her words wistful. "It seems like yesterday. My dear Geoffrey's spirit is a ghost in every room of that house. Go with me," Izzy pleaded. Gnarled, arthritic hands twisted at her waist. For a split second, Cate witnessed the depth of Isobel Stewart's anguish at losing the love of her life.

"It's a family celebration," Cate said. "It will seem odd if I come."

"Not at all," Izzy said. "It was actually Brody's idea."

Five hours later Cate found herself on the doorstep of Stewart Properties, bouncing from one foot to the other in a futile attempt to keep warm. At the curb, she had left the engine running in her modest four-door sedan.

At last, when Cate's fingers were numb, Izzy appeared. She looked remarkably chipper for someone who was about to face an unpleasant experience. "Right on time," Izzy said. "You're a lovely young lass. Men don't like a woman who can't be punctual."

Cate helped the old woman into the car. Izzy was wrapped from head to toe in a brown wool coat and a heavy woven scarf in brown and beige. "That's a stereotype, Miss Izzy. I'm sure there are as many men as women who have trouble being on time."

Isobel snorted and changed the subject. "I thought ye'd wear a dress," she complained.

Cate extracted the car from the tight parking space and adjusted the defroster. "It's going to be close to twenty degrees tonight. These are my best dress pants." She'd worn them back when she was on her way to becoming a doctor...in the days before her world fell apart.

"Pants, schmantz. Brody and Duncan are hot-blooded men. I'm sure they would have enjoyed seeing a glimpse of leg. Yours are spectacular, bonnie young Cate. When you're my age, you'll wish ye'd appreciated what ye had when you had it."

There was no arguing with the antiquated, sexually regressive logic of a woman in her nineties.

Cate sighed. Unfortunately, the road up the mountain was easily traversed and not long at all. When they pulled up in front of the Stewart mansion—Cate would be hard-pressed to describe it as anything else—they had time to spare. Izzy's home was spectacular. Weathered mountain stone, rough-hewn lumber, copper guttering, giant multi-paned windows that brought the outdoors inside... This magnificent architectural gem had once graced the cover of *Southern Living*.

Cate touched the petite woman's arm. "Are you going to be okay?"

Izzy sniffed. "Outliving your friends and contemporaries is bollocks, Cate."

"Miss Izzy!" Her friend's lack of respect for social convention still caught her off guard at times.

"Don't be prissy. What's the point of getting old if ye can't say what ye please?"

"So back to my original question. Are you going to be okay?"

Izzy gazed through the windshield, her cheeks damp.

"He built that house as a thank-you to me. Did you know that?"

"No, ma'am, I didn't. A thank-you for what?"

"Giving up Scotland. My family. My home. Coming here to America with him. Silly fool." She stopped. Her throat worked. "I'd have given all that and more for one more day with the auld codger."

Cate felt her own throat tighten, and not only because of Izzy's emotional return to the house where she had spent a decades-long marriage. Izzy had pledged herself and her heart to a man who was her soul mate. Cate had never even come close. And now she had made the most wretched mistake of her life.

She turned off the engine and gripped the steering wheel. Brody was inside that house. What was she going to say to him?

Izzy moved restively. "Might as well get it over with," she muttered. "I'll not cry, mind you. Too many tears shed already. Besides, I don't want the lads to think they've done wrong by me. Let's go, Cate, my girl."

The two women scuttled up the flagstone walkway, buffeted by an icy wind. Moments later the double, burnished-oak front doors swung open wide. The massive chandelier in the foyer spilled light into the darkness. The diminutive Scotswoman was caught up in the enthusiastic hugs of her two über-masculine grandsons.

Brody's thick, wavy chestnut hair shone with strands of reddish-gold mixed in. Duncan's was a darker brown and straighter. He had the rich brown eyes to match. Though the brothers were alike in many ways, Izzy had once upon a time explained to Cate that Brody favored his Irish-born mother while Duncan was a younger version of his Grandda.

Now that Cate had finally met Duncan, she agreed. It

was astonishing to see how much Brody's younger brother resembled Geoffrey Stewart. She wondered if it was painful for Izzy to look at Duncan and see the memory of her young husband in the flesh.

Cate hung back, still not sure why she had come. Izzy seemed to be handling things with grace and bravery. It was Cate whose stomach quivered with nerves.

Izzy drew Cate forward. "Cate, my dear, meet Duncan."

Duncan Stewart lifted her hand and kissed the back of it. "Charmed, Miss Everett."

Brody snorted. "Knock it off, Duncan."

Duncan held up his hands, visibly protesting his innocence. "What? What did I do?"

"Go check on the caterer, would you?"

Moments later Duncan bore his grandmother deeper into the house, leaving Cate alone with Brody.

The man who had avoided eyeing her until now, gave her a crooked grin. "Surprise, lass. I'm back."

Brody wasn't an idiot. He knew when a woman was glad to see him and when she wasn't. Cate Everett looked like someone who had swallowed bad milk. His pride took a hit, but he maintained his smile with effort. "It was nice of you to come with Granny. I know she's been dreading this moment."

Cate took off her coat slowly and handed it to him. "Then why force the issue?"

He shrugged, turning to hang up Cate's wrap. "There are decisions to be made. My ninety-two-year-old grandmother has been sleeping in a closet-sized room with the barest of essentials. Grandda is gone. This house is still here. We can't pretend anymore."

Cate's jaw tightened. "Are you always so sure you know what's best for everyone?"

He cocked his head, studying her from a distance, even though he thought about grabbing her up and kissing her soundly. The last time the two of them had seen each other, they had been naked and breathless in Cate's bed.

"Have I upset ye in some way, Cate? I had to leave. You knew that."

A month after his grandfather's funeral, Brody had returned to Candlewick to spend time with his grandmother and to assess the state of the family business. Stewart Properties was a thriving company with a stellar reputation in the United States.

Unfortunately, Geoffrey Stewart was gone now. Brody's own father had no desire to return to the States permanently. So something had to be done about Granny Isobel.

Brody had spent four weeks in North Carolina, two of them wildly in lust with the beautiful and brilliant Cate Everett. By day he had been a dutiful grandson. At night he had found himself drawn time and again to the woman who had a reputation around the small town for being kind but standoffish. With Brody, she had been anything but…

To be honest, the depth of his physical infatuation had made him the tiniest bit uncomfortable. He understood the mechanics of sexual attraction. He'd even had his share of serious relationships. But when his grandmother introduced him to her friend and neighbor, Cate Everett, Brody had felt like a tongue-tied adolescent.

Cate was a mix of femme fatale and spinster schoolteacher. Her pale blond hair was like sunshine on a winter afternoon, though she kept it tucked up in a tight knot on the back of her head most days, the kind of knot that looked headache-producing from the get-go.

But when she let it down…hot damn. Even now Brody's fingers itched to touch the fall of silk that had spilled across his chest and still featured in his fantasies.

She was tall, five-ten at least. Brody knew the curves and valleys of her alluring shape, but Cate kept her body mostly hidden beneath loose cardigans and below-the-knee jumpers. He had no clue why a woman as intensely feminine as she was would make a concerted effort to hide in plain sight.

After a long, awkward silence, she cast him a sideways glance, her small smile rueful. "I'm sorry. It's been a long day. It's nice to see you again, Brody."

He wrinkled his nose. "Nice?"

"I didn't want to give you any ideas."

"About what?"

"You *know* what," Cate said crossly. "I'm not interested in picking up where we left off."

"Maybe I wasn't going to ask." He taunted her deliberately. Her prickly attitude was both frustrating and a challenge. He'd never met a woman with as many complicated layers as Cate Everett.

Cate sighed. "It's cold here in the foyer. Do you mind if we go find the others? I'm starving."

"Of course. I do remember how ye like to eat."

When Cate flushed to her hairline, he smiled inwardly. On one memorable occasion last fall, the two of them had climbed out of Cate's bed at midnight and fixed scrambled eggs and bacon, because they had skipped dinner in favor of urgent, mind-blowing sex.

Cate knew her way around Isobel's house, so he let her lead. She and Granny had been friends for several years. Although Brody had pumped his grandmother for information about the aloof American, she had fed him few details.

They found Duncan and Isobel in the dining room. The caterer who was preparing dinner had set an elegant table with Stewart china and silver and crystal. Brody's grandmother stood behind the chair that had been her husband's and rested her hands on the tall back. "One of you boys should sit here," she said with the tiniest quaver in her voice.

Brody and Duncan looked at each other. Cate winced. Finally, Brody shook his head. "I can't, Granny. Neither can Duncan."

"Then why did ye make me come up here?" she snapped, her eyes welling with tears. "If my own grandsons won't move on, how am I supposed to?"

# Two

To Brody's relief, Cate stepped forward. "What if I take Mr. Geoffrey's chair tonight, Miss Izzy? It would be my honor. You can sit here beside me."

Brody mouthed a *thank-you* to her over his grandmother's head. Izzy had some definite ideas about how the future was going to play out, and she wasn't above emotional manipulation to get her way. He and Duncan had spent hours discussing possibilities, but no single solution had presented itself as of yet.

Without extra leaves in the antique table, the four adults sat in an intimate enclave, Cate and Duncan at the head and foot, Brody and Izzy to Cate's left and right. Fortunately, the caterer was on his game, and the elaborate meal kicked off immediately, helping ease the moments of tension. The brothers had ordered all of Izzy's favorites: fresh brook trout, seasoned carrots and potatoes, flaky biscuits and tender asparagus, all washed down with an expensive zinfandel. Though the elderly woman's capacity for food was modest, she ate with delight, her worn, wrinkled face aglow.

Cate did her part, not only by sitting in for the ghost at the table, but also by contributing with her quick wit and stimulating conversation. The four adults covered books and politics and international affairs.

Duncan, much to Brody's dismay, seemed especially taken with Cate. That was a really bad idea. Maybe Brody should have given his little brother a heads-up that the lady was spoken for.

He choked on a bit of carrot and had to wash it down with half a glass of water, red-faced and stunned. If Duncan ended up being the one to move here with Granny and keep the business afloat, it made perfect sense that he and Cate might hit it off.

Apparently, Brody did a poor job of disguising his emotions. Granny Isobel waved a fork at him. "Ye okay there, my lad? Did you find a bone in your fish?"

Brody grimaced. "I'm fine."

Cate gazed at him curiously with catlike green eyes that always made him uncomfortable. He didn't particularly want a woman peering into his soul. Surely it was his imagination that suggested she could read his every thought.

Desperate to deflect the attention from himself, he nudged his brother's foot under the table. "Duncan here has some good ideas about the company, Granny."

Isobel perked up. "I'm listening."

Duncan glared at his brother with a fierceness that promised retribution. He cleared his throat. "The thing is, Granny, I think it makes a lot of sense to put Stewart Properties on the market. The American economy has rebounded. It's an optimal time to sell. Ye shouldn't be living alone at your age anyway, and just think how happy Dad would be if you moved back to Scotland."

Everything in the room went silent. The four adults sat frozen in an uncomfortable tableau. The caterer was nowhere to be seen, undoubtedly in the kitchen whipping up a fabulous dessert.

Cate cleared her throat and stood. "This is family business," she said quietly. "If you'll excuse me, I'll go to the library and amuse myself."

Before Brody could protest, Isobel lifted her chin and stared them down with the arrogance of a queen. "Ye're not leaving, Cate. I asked you to come with me tonight, and I consider ye one of my dearest friends. It appears I may need someone on my side."

Brody frowned. "That's not fair, Granny, and you know it. Duncan and I love you dearly and want the best for everyone involved. There are no *sides* in this conversation."

His grandmother huffed, a sound he recognized from his childhood and all the years in between. "When I'm dead, ye can do whatever you like with your inheritance. For now, though, this company Geoffrey and I built with our sweat and tears is all I have left of him. To be honest, I'm glad you forced the issue of me coming back to the house. I didn't realize how much I had missed it."

"We could keep the house," Brody said. He had thrown his brother under the bus. Now it was time for Brody to take some of the heat.

Isobel glared at him. "What part of *not selling* didn't you understand? I'm old. Don't you get it? I won't be here much longer. Besides, I have two excellent managers who are working out very well in Geoffrey's absence."

Cate brought in reinforcements, giving Brody a look of sympathy. "But remember, Miss Izzy, Herman is getting ready to move to California...to be near his ailing parents, and it's too huge an operation for Kevin to manage all on his own. You said so yourself."

Instead of being cowed, Isobel seemed energized by the conflict. "Then one of these two will pick up the slack. Surely that's not too much for an old woman to ask of her grandsons."

Again, silence descended, heavy with the weight of familial expectations. Cate tried to help, God bless her generous soul. "Brody has his boat business in Skye, Miss Izzy. Surely you wouldn't ask him to give that up. And Duncan is a partner in that, right?" She lifted an eyebrow.

Duncan nodded. "I am. Brody still owns the controlling share, but I handle all the financial operations."

Izzy wasn't impressed. "So sell *your* business. You can both move here. Stewart Properties is going to belong to you both one day anyway. Your father doesn't need anything of mine."

Isobel's son, Brody and Duncan's father, was a world-famous artist with galleries all over the British Isles. He was wildly successful and obscenely wealthy. Even so, he had insisted his boys get good educations and find their own paths in life. Brody appreciated his father's contribution to the launch of the boating business, but that financial obligation had been repaid long ago.

Brody ran a hand through his hair. Never in his wildest dreams had he imagined his grandmother was going to be such a handful. Whatever happened to sweet, docile old women who knitted and crocheted and went to church on Sundays and let the menfolk take care of them?

"Maybe we should all sleep on this, Granny. Duncan and I are jet-lagged anyway. I vote we enjoy the rest of dinner."

The caterer entered the dining room bearing a tray of warm apple tarts drizzled with fresh cream. The interruption was timely as far as Brody was concerned. The only reason he and Duncan had been dispatched to North Carolina was to settle their grandmother's business affairs and bring her home to Scotland.

The chances of that happening were becoming more remote by the minute.

Unpleasant subjects were abandoned over coffee and

dessert. Brody allowed himself, for the first time that evening, to truly study Cate. He had hoped his four-month-old recollections of her were exaggerated. Surely her skin wasn't as soft as he remembered…or her voice as husky.

When she laughed at something Duncan said, Brody actually felt a pain in his chest. She was everything he had dreamed about and infinitely better in person. Which only made his dilemma all the more complicated. He sure as hell couldn't play fast and loose with a woman his grandmother held in high regard.

Not that it mattered. For some reason Cate had changed. Four months ago she had smiled at him as if she meant it. Now her gaze slid away from his time and again. Even if he wanted her in his bed again—or hers—it seemed unlikely that Cate was on the same page.

By nine o'clock, Isobel was visibly drooping.

Cate noticed, too. She touched the elderly woman on the hand. "I think it's my bedtime, Miss Izzy. Are you ready to head down the mountain?"

"Soon," Isobel said. "But since these boys forced my hand, and I'm here, I'd like to walk through the house before I go. Duncan, you come with me. Brody, entertain Cate until I get back."

When the other two walked out of the room, Brody chuckled. "I swear she doesn't weigh a hundred pounds soaking wet, but she's got all of us at the end of a tight leash."

Cate nodded. "I don't envy you and Duncan. Changing her mind won't be easy."

"And it might be impossible. Which means removing her by force or finding a way to maintain the status quo until it's her time to go."

Cate picked up a silver chalice on the mahogany sideboard and studied it intently. "Have you given any thought to relocating for a few years? For her?"

Brody sensed a trap in the question, but he couldn't pin it down. "My life is in Scotland," he said flatly. "I've spent seven years building my boat business. I need the water. It speaks to me. Nothing here compares."

"I see."

He walked around the table that separated them and touched her hair. "I'll ask again, Cate. Have I done something to upset you?" He wasn't adept at playing games, and he would have sworn that Cate was not the kind of woman to give a man fits.

"Of course not," she said, though her tone belied the words.

He took her wrist in a gentle grasp and turned her to face him. "I've missed ye, Cate." Yearning slammed into him with the punch of a sledgehammer. His hands trembled with the need to drag her close and kiss her.

His head lowered. She looked up at him, big-eyed, her gaze a conundrum he couldn't understand. "I missed you, too," she whispered.

And then it happened. Maybe he moved. Maybe she did. Suddenly, his mouth was on hers and she was kissing him back. Their lips clung together and separated and mated again. She tasted like apples and pure heaven. His heart pounded. His sex hardened. For a single blinding moment of clarity, he knew this was one of the reasons he had come back to North Carolina. "Cate," he muttered.

The caterer returned to clear the table, and Cate jerked away, her expression caught somewhere between horror and what appeared to be revulsion…which made no sense at all. They had been good together. Sensational.

Cate swept the back of her hand across her mouth and whispered urgently, "You have lip gloss on your chin."

He picked up a napkin, wiped his face and looked at the pink stain on the white linen. Before he could say anything, Duncan and Isobel walked into the room.

Brody's grandmother had been crying…her eyes were red-rimmed. But she seemed calm and at peace. Brody shot his brother a quick glance. Duncan grimaced but nodded. Apparently, all was well.

"We'll go now," Cate said.

Isobel followed her through the house and into the front foyer. While Duncan helped the women with their coats, Brody brooded. "I'll drive you down the mountain," he said. "It's dark, and it's late."

Cate frowned. "Don't be ridiculous. I'm perfectly capable of negotiating this mountain. Unlike you, I like it here."

Brody winced inwardly. He hadn't been wrong. *Something* was going on with Cate. He lowered his voice. "Will ye walk Granny upstairs and make sure she's settled?"

"Of course." Cate pulled away from him and put on her gloves. "I've been looking after Miss Izzy for a long time. You people came over for the funeral and left again. She's important to me. I won't let her down."

"The implication being that I'm a disappointment."

Cate shrugged and lifted her hair from beneath her collar. "If the shoe fits."

Duncan intervened. "If the two of you can quit squabbling, I think Granny's ready for bed."

Isobel spoke up. "I can wait. At my age, I don't need as much sleep. Besides, watching Brody try to woo Cate is a hoot and a half."

"There's no wooing," Cate protested, her cheeks turning red. "We were merely having a difference of opinion. Cultural differences and all that."

Now Brody felt his own face flush. "I'm Scottish, not an alien species."

She sniffed audibly. "It doesn't really matter, does it? Miss Izzy is a North Carolinian, and so am I. You and Duncan are merely passing through."

With that pointed remark, Cate ushered Isobel out into the cold and slammed the door behind them.

Duncan whistled long and loud. "What in the hell did you do to piss her off? We haven't even been in Candlewick twenty-four hours."

"I don't know what you're talking about," Brody lied.

"I may be a wee bit younger than you are, but I've tangled with my share of fiery lasses. The sexual tension between you and the lovely Cate is nuclear."

"Don't call her *lovely*," Brody snapped. "Don't call her anything."

Duncan rocked back on his heels and wrapped his arms across his chest. "Damn. You're a fast worker, bro, but even *you* aren't that good. Something happened four months ago, didn't it?"

"None of your business."

"You messed around with that gorgeous woman and then went home. Cold, Brody. Really cold. No wonder she looks as if she wants to strangle you."

"It wasn't like that. Granny introduced us. Cate and I became…close."

"For the entire four weeks?"

"The last two. It wasn't anything either of us planned. Can we talk about something else please?"

"Okay. What are we going to do about Granny?"

*Hell.* This topic was not much better. "We have to convince her to sell. She's too damned old to be here on her own."

"She has Cate."

"Cate's not family."

"I don't think Granny cares. That old woman crossed

an ocean with a brand-new husband and started a brand-new life. She's tough. Losing Grandda was a huge blow, but she's still upright and fighting. What if we make her go home to Scotland, and it's the final blow? She hasn't lived there since she was a very young woman. Candlewick and the business and this house are all she knows."

"Aren't you forgetting our father, her *son*?"

"Dad is an eccentric. He and Granny love each other, but it works really well long distance. That's not a reason to kidnap her. She's an independent soul. I don't want to break her spirit."

"And you think I do?" Brody's frustration spilled over in a shout. "Sorry," he muttered.

Duncan locked the front door and turned off the lights. "We're both beat. Let's call it a night. Maybe we'll have a flash of inspiration tomorrow."

"I doubt it."

Brody fell asleep instantly, but surfaced four hours later, completely disoriented and wide-awake. After a few seconds the fog cleared. It was midmorning back home. On a good day he'd be out on the loch with the wind in his hair and the sun on his back. He slung an arm across his face and told himself not to panic. No one could *make* him move to America. That was ludicrous.

Without warning, an image of Cate Everett filled his brain. He would never admit it, but even with an ocean between them, Cate had been on his mind most days over the past four months. There was something about her gentle smile and husky laughter and the way her hair spilled like warm silk across his chest when they were in bed together.

She wasn't exactly uninhibited between the sheets. In fact, the first three times they had been intimate, she'd insisted on having the lights off. He'd thought her shyness was charming and sweet. He'd considered it a personal triumph when she'd actually let him strip her naked in broad daylight and make her scream his name.

The memory dampened his forehead and caused his jaw to clench. The house was plenty cool, but suddenly the bed felt like a prison.

*Bloody hell.* He pulled on a clean pair of boxers and wandered barefoot through the silent hallways to the kitchen. The generous space had been renovated a decade ago. Despite Isobel's advanced age, she had never fit the stereotype of a little old lady. She embraced change and even loved technology. Stewart Properties was a sophisticated, cutting-edge company with an incredibly healthy bottom line.

He poured himself a glass of orange juice and downed it in three swallows. Brody owed his grandmother a great deal. She had helped him through a very painful period of his life when his parents divorced. He'd been fifteen and totally oblivious to the undercurrents in the house.

When the end came, life had become unbearable. Isobel insisted that her two boys come to North Carolina for a long visit, long enough for the worst of the trauma to ease. These mountains had provided healing.

Under the circumstances, Brody had a very serious debt to pay.

Even knowing that, his gut churned. Staying in Candlewick would mean dealing with Cate and his muddled feelings.

It was far easier to live on another continent.

After half an hour of pacing, his feet were icy, and sleep was out of the question. Without second-guessing himself, he returned to his bedroom and dressed rapidly. Duncan wouldn't need transportation at this hour.

Brody guided the boring rental car down the winding mountain road, careful to stay on the correct side of the road. It helped that no one else was out at this hour. Soon he reached the outskirts of town. Candlewick still slept. Main Street was deserted.

He parked the car and filched a small handful of pea gravel from the nicely landscaped flower beds at the bank. Then he eyed Cate's bookstore with a frown. The striped burgundy and green awning that covered the front of the shop was going to make this difficult.

Though he had sucked at geometry in school, even he could see that he needed a longer arc. Looking left and right and hoping local law enforcement was asleep, as well, he backed up until he stood in the middle of the street. Feeling like an idiot, he chose a piece of gravel, rotated his shoulders to loosen them up and aimed at Cate's bedroom window.

# Three

Cate groaned and pulled the quilt up around her ears. That stupid squirrel was scratching around in the attic again.

After Isobel's birthday dinner on the mountain, Cate had tucked the old woman into bed as she had promised. Back at her own place, she wandered aimlessly in the bookstore for a long time. She plucked a book off the shelf, read a paragraph or two, replaced it and then repeated the restless behavior.

When she finally went upstairs, it took an hour or more of tossing and turning before she was able to fall asleep. Seeing Brody had unsettled her to a disturbing degree. And now this.

*Plink. Plink.* The distinctive pinging sound came two more times. And then once more. At last, the veils of slumber rolled away and she understood what was really happening. Brody Stewart. She would bet her signed, first-edition copy of *Gone with the Wind* that it was him.

Grumbling at having to abandon the warm cocoon of covers she had created, she stumbled to the window and looked out. The wavy panes of antique glass were unadorned. There was no one to peek at her from across the street. The owners of the general store used their upstairs square footage for inventory storage. Cate's modesty was safe from this angle, and she liked waking up with the sun.

The moment she appeared at the window, the barrage of gravel stopped. The man down below gesticulated.

Was he insane? Dawn was still hours away. Frowning—and wishing she was wearing something more alluring than flannel—she lifted the heavy wooden sash, leaned out and glared at him. "What do you want, Brody?" She shuddered as icy air poured into the room.

"Come down and unlock the front door. We need to talk."

Was that a socially acceptable way of saying he hoped to end up in her bed? Fat chance. "It's the middle of the night."

"I couldn't sleep. Please, Cate. It's important."

Nothing else he could have said at this hour would have induced her to let the wolf into the henhouse. The truth was, though, they *did* need to talk. Desperately, and soon. Her secret had been weighing heavily on her, and she was running out of time.

"Fine. I'll be down in a minute."

Despite the virtue-protecting properties of flannel, she wasn't about to meet Brody wearing her nightgown. Grabbing up a pair of jeans and a warm red cashmere sweater, she dressed rapidly and shoved her feet into a pair of fleece-lined slippers. Her hair was a tumbled mess, but she didn't really care. Making herself appear alluring to Brody Stewart was what had gotten her into this wretched state of affairs to begin with.

She didn't turn on any lights as she made her way downstairs. If any of her neighbors were awake, she'd just as soon not have them know she had a late-night guest. Gossip was the bread of life in Candlewick. Cate's personal situation had already edged into the danger zone.

Unlocking the dead bolt and yanking open the door, she shivered and jumped back when Brody burst into the shop. "Damn, it's cold out there," he complained.

"Where's your coat?" In the dark, he was bigger than she remembered from the autumn. More in-your-face masculine.

"I was in a hurry. I forgot it."

"Come on back to the office," she muttered, careful not to brush up against him. "I'll get the fire going."

He followed her down the narrow hallway without speaking and stood in silence as she lit the pile of kindling and wood chips beneath carefully stacked logs. Cate had a handyman who stopped by whenever she asked him—this time of year usually to clean out the grate and restock her woodpile. The fireplace and chimney had been cleaned and inspected regularly, so she had no qualms about using it. Another hearth upstairs in her tiny living room provided warmth and cheer for her apartment.

She wiped her hands on a cloth and indicated one of the tapestry wingback chairs in navy and gold. They were ancient and faded, but the twin antiques had come with the store. She loved them. "Have a seat, Brody. And tell me what's so important it couldn't wait until morning." She would let him speak his piece, and then she would find the courage to tell him the secret she had been hiding from everyone, *including* him.

Brody sat, but his posture indicated unease. She had purposely not turned on the lamps. Firelight was flattering. It also lent a sense of peace and calm to a situation that was anything but. In the flickering glow, Brody's profile was shadowed. Occasionally, when the flames danced particularly high, a flash of light caught the gold in his hair.

He leaned forward, elbows on his knees, and stared at

her, his expression impossible to read. "I owe you an apology," he said gruffly.

Her heart thudded. "For what?"

"For what I'm about to say."

Her stomach cringed. "I don't understand."

"Four months ago you and I had something pretty damned wonderful. I'd be lying if I said I didn't want to take you upstairs right now and make love to you for three days straight."

The utter, bald conviction in his words made her light-headed with yearning, but nothing he had said so far erased the certainty of impending doom. "I sense a *but* coming." She kept the words light. It took everything she had. Already her heart was freezing, preparing to shatter.

"But I can't fool around with *you* and still tend to Granny Isobel at the same time. I have a responsibility to discharge."

"How very noble," she mocked, her throat tight with painful tears she couldn't, wouldn't, shed.

His jaw tightened. "I never meant to return. My father was in contact with Granny from the moment I left until last week. Every time he spoke with her she told him things were fine. We assumed she had put the business and the house on the market immediately and would come back to Scotland as soon as the transactions were complete."

"Forgive me for stating the obvious, but I don't think any of you know her very well. It would take a stick of dynamite to blast her out of this town. If she wants to stay, she'll stay."

"Ach, Cate. I ken that very well…now. Do you think you could talk to her? As a favor to me?"

"I could, but I won't. It's not my place. She's my friend. My job is to support her."

"Surely you can see it's time for her to go."

"With you and Duncan..."

"Aye."

"Why couldn't one of you stay here?" Cate was fighting for her future. Isobel's happiness was important, but more was at stake.

Brody shook his head almost violently. "It doesn't make sense. Granny has lived a full and wonderful life. Seasons change, and now her time in Candlewick is done."

"Has anyone ever told you that you're an arrogant, blind, foolish ass of a Scotsman?"

"Don't hold back, Cate."

She leaped to her feet. "Don't worry. I won't." The words she needed to say trembled on her lips. *I'm pregnant, Brody. With your baby.* She had intended—any day now—to send a registered letter to Scotland. Terse. To the point. Morally correct. Absolving him of any responsibility.

It had seemed like a sound plan until Brody showed up in the flesh. Seeing him again was shocking. She hadn't expected to feel so giddy with delight. Nor so bleakly sure that this man was neither the answer to her problems nor the knight on the white horse.

She was still trying to come to terms with the news of her pregnancy. Her periods had never been regular, so she had been twelve weeks along before she went to the doctor and confirmed that her fatigue and queasiness were far more than a temporary condition.

The idea of having a baby had come completely out of the blue, but was not entirely unwelcome. She had always loved children. She was warming quickly to the notion of being a mother. She would do her best to be the kind of warm, nurturing parent she herself had never known. Her mother and father had gone through the motions, but their behavior had been motivated by duty, not gut-deep devotion.

Other worries intruded. What if Brody tried to take their child away from her...insisted the baby live in Scotland? Was that why she had struggled so over composing the letter? The Stewart-clan pride ran deep, centuries in the making. The mere thought of losing custody made her maternal instincts, hitherto unknown, scratch their way to the surface. She would fight Brody, if need be. She would fight all of them. This baby was hers.

Brody wouldn't be sticking around long this time, perhaps far less than the four weeks he devoted to his grandmother when he visited so soon after the funeral. Clearly, he didn't have any residual feelings for Cate. At least no more than the lust a man feels for a woman he's bedded. Otherwise, he wouldn't be making such a point of not resurrecting their affair.

If she could wait him out, avoid him, stay clear of the family drama, Brody would leave again and Cate would never have to tell him the truth.

She knew in her heart that idea was wrong. A man deserved to know he had fathered a child. Besides, wouldn't Miss Izzy let the cat out of the bag eventually? Cate's elderly friend was far from stupid or naive. She knew her grandson and her neighbor had spent a great deal of time together back in the autumn.

Even if Isobel hadn't guessed before now about Cate and Brody's sexual intimacy, once Cate's belly began to swell visibly, Isobel would do the math and realize that she was going to have another Stewart in the works.

Tension wrapped Cate's skull in a headache. She was an intelligent, educated woman. Surely there was a way forward.

*Tell him*, her gut insisted. *Tell him*. Postponing the truth would only make things more difficult. Still, she couldn't bring herself to say the words. What would he say? How would he respond? She felt fragile and helpless, and she hated both emotions.

The baby was only now becoming real to Cate herself. How much more unbelievable would conception seem to Brody? Because Cate's sex life had been nonexistent since moving to Candlewick, she hadn't been taking birth control pills when she met the handsome Scotsman. Brody had been happy to produce a seemingly never-ending supply of condoms.

But there had been that one time in the middle of the night, that poignant, dreamlike coupling, a series of moments as natural as breathing. They had found each other with hushed sighs and ragged groans in the mystical hours when the world slept. She had spread her legs for him, and he had claimed her as his. For all she knew, Brody might not even remember. He'd made love to her many times. Perhaps they all ran together for a man.

Cate remembered each one in vivid detail.

This was not the time to dwell on the past. Nor was it the moment to wallow in grief. She didn't know Brody Stewart well enough to let him break her heart. Love didn't happen so quickly.

She almost believed it.

While she paced, Brody leaned back in his chair, waiting. Judge and jury. He expected Cate to choose his side, to align herself with the grandsons and not Isobel.

If Cate had believed it was the right thing to do, she might have capitulated. Instead, her heart told her she had to fight for the old woman's happiness…and her own. At last, she stopped. She stood at his knees, her arms wrapped around her waist. "Go home, Brody, you and Duncan both. Give her a chance to settle back into the house. Now that she's been up there again, I think she'll quit living over the store."

"And then?"

She shrugged. "Then nothing. You live your life in Scotland. She lives hers here in Candlewick. I'll call you when the time comes."

"When she dies."

"If you want to be blunt about it, yes."

He straightened slowly, unfolding his tall, lanky frame and flexing his wrists until they popped. Despite his self-professed temporary vow of celibacy, he put his hands on her shoulders and massaged them.

Cate couldn't decide if he was attempting to comfort her, or if he was trying to avoid shaking her until her teeth rattled.

Maybe he subconsciously wanted to touch her. She didn't know.

Brody rested his forehead against hers. "You're trying to make me lose my temper, Catie lass, but it won't work. I came here to take care of my grandmother's affairs, and that's what I'm going to do."

"*Your* way."

"It's the *only* way, or at least the only way that makes sense."

His breath was warm on her face. The masculine scent of his skin filled her lungs when she inhaled sharply, imprinting on every cell of her body. Brody was not a man one could easily forget. She leaned into him, blaming her weakness on the late hour and her bone-deep distress. "I won't help you manipulate her, Brody. I won't."

His chest rose and fell in a sigh so deep it made her sad. "I suppose I can understand that. At least promise me you won't be deliberately obstructive. Duncan and I love Granny. We'll take care of her, Cate."

She nodded, her eyes damp. Was it hormones making her weepy or the knowledge that something miraculous had happened? She and Brody had created a baby. People did that every day in every way. But sheer numbers didn't make the awe she felt any less.

With her breasts brushing the hard planes of Brody's chest and her barely-there pregnant tummy nestled against him, she felt an incredible surge of hope mixed with despair. What she wanted from him was the stuff of fairy tales. The gallant suitor. The happy ending.

She made herself step away. "I need to go back to bed," she said. "Please leave."

Brody cupped her cheeks in his big, calloused hands. Years of handling rope and sails had toughened his body. Even without Isobel's estate, Brody's fleet of boats had made him a wealthy man. Isobel had bragged about it often enough. The eventual inheritance would secure his fortune.

His big frame actually shuddered, his arousal impossible to miss. "If it was going to be anybody, it would be you, Cate. But I've never been much for home and hearth."

"Thank you for being honest," she whispered.

Pressing his lips to hers, he kissed her long and deep. It was a goodbye kiss, bittersweet, painfully bereft of hope. The kind of kiss lovers exchanged on the dock when moviegoers knew the hero was never coming back.

Cate twined her arms around Brody's neck and clung. If this was all she would ever have of him, she needed a memory to sustain her. She could be a single mother. Lots of women did it every day. She wouldn't be any man's obligation.

There was a moment when the tide almost turned. Brody was hard and ready. His hands roved restlessly over her back and settled on her bottom, dragging her close. His hunger made him weak and Cate strong. But she had always been the kind of girl to play by the rules.

Only twice in her life had she broken them, and both times she had paid a high price.

Drawing on a dwindling store of resolve, she released him and eluded his questing hands. "Go," she said. "Go, Brody."

And he did.

# Four

Brody spent the following week working himself into a state of physical exhaustion so pervasive and so deep he fell into bed each night and was instantly unconscious. Six months of neglect had left Isobel's spectacular house with a host of issues and problems to be addressed.

He and Duncan made massive lists and checked them off with painstaking slowness. Damaged roofing shingles from a winter storm. Rotting wood beneath a soffit. Gutters clogged with leaves.

Some of the backlog of general repairs dated back to his grandfather's illness. The old man had suffered a stroke five months before he died. Virtually nothing had been done to the house, inside or outside, for almost a year.

Isobel was a wealthy woman. Brody and Duncan could easily have hired a crew to come in and do everything. But the two grandsons were silently paying penance for not coming sooner and staying longer.

The very depth of their guilt made Brody realize that returning to Scotland *without* their grandmother was going to be unacceptable.

No matter what Cate said, Candlewick was not Isobel's home anymore. Without her beloved American-born husband, she would be far better off to cross the ocean with her two devoted grandsons and settle in amongst the people of her youth.

On the eighth day, Brody and Duncan abandoned the house so a professional cleaning service could descend upon the mountaintop retreat and restore the estate to its previous glory.

While that refreshing and refurbishing was underway, the two men helped Isobel pack up her personal items downtown, everything she had taken with her when she moved into the apartment over her offices.

While Duncan carried a stack of boxes down to the car, Brody sat beside his grandmother and took her hands in his. "You know this is only temporary, Granny...a few nights for you to say goodbye to the house. I contacted a Realtor this morning about preparing the listing."

Isobel Stewart pursed her lips and straightened her spine. Her dark eyes snapped and sparked with displeasure. "I love you dearly, Brody, but you're a stubborn ass, exactly like your father and your grandfather before you. I am neither weak nor senile nor in any kind of physical decline. I'm old. I get it. But my age doesn't give you the right to usurp my decision-making."

Brody ground his teeth. "Duncan and I have lives we've put on hold. We did it gladly, because you're very important to us."

Her fierce expression softened. "I appreciate your concern. I truly do, my lad. But you're making a mistake, and you're being unfair. I'm moving back into my beautiful home—thanks to you boys—but I'm not returning to Scotland. My dear Geoffrey is buried in Candlewick. Everything we built together is here in the mountains. I can't leave him behind. I won't."

"It's dangerous for you to live alone," Brody said, incredulous to realize that he was losing the battle. Isobel would have been far safer to stay here in town where people could keep an eye on her. Now he and Duncan had convinced her to do the very thing they wanted to avoid.

"Life is a dangerous business," the old woman said, her expression placid. "I make my own choices. You can go home with no regrets."

Brody knelt at her side, putting his gaze level with hers. "Please, Granny. For me. Come to Scotland."

She shook her head slowly. "No. I've been away from Scotland too long. Candlewick is my home. Your grandfather and I, together, built something important here... a legacy. We spent so many happy days and months and years creating a host of memories that are all I have left of him. But I might consider a wee compromise if another party is agreeable."

He couldn't imagine any scenario that would make the situation palatable. "Oh?"

His grandmother stood and smoothed the skirt of her black shirtwaist dress that might have been designed anytime in the last six decades. Jet buttons marched all the way up to her chin. "I could ask Cate to move in with me. I'd offer her a modest stipend to be my companion. Keeping a bookstore afloat in the current economic climate is challenging. I'm sure the extra money would help. The girl works herself to death."

Brody bristled inwardly. "I would think Cate's family might help out if she's struggling financially or otherwise. Why does she need you?" Isobel was *his* grandmother, not Cate's.

"You're being churlish. Tell him, Duncan."

Brody's younger brother shut the door to the stairwell and leaned against it, grimacing. "I missed some of that. I love you, Granny. But I have to agree with Brody on this one. We don't want to leave you here in Candlewick all alone, and we can't stay much longer."

Isobel held out her hands. "My idea isn't entirely self-ish. Cate has no family of her own. I don't like to divulge her secrets, but you've left me little choice. Her parents are both deceased. They had Cate late in life…an accident."

Brody frowned. "What do you know about them?"

"They were academics. Valued education above all else. I get the impression they were not warm, nurturing people."

"How did she end up in Candlewick?" Brody asked.

"I suggest you ask Cate herself if you want to know. She's a private woman. But I trust her implicitly."

Duncan nodded. "You make a convincing argument. I like Cate. It's not altogether a terrible idea."

Brody glared at his brother. "I thought you were on *my* side, traitor."

Duncan wrapped his grandmother in his arms from be-hind and rested his chin on top of her gray-haired head. "It's not a war, Brody. I love you both, so don't make me choose. I don't know what the hell is the right thing to do anymore."

Isobel patted his hands and smirked at Brody. "Then I suppose one of you needs to call that very nice caterer and see if he can whip us up another of his wonderful meals this evening. We'll invite Cate to even out the numbers, and after we've plied her with wine and good food, I'll ask her to consider my proposition."

Cate drove up the mountain alone this time. Apparently, Miss Izzy's two grandsons had convinced her to leave her nest above the store.

While Cate applauded acknowledging grief and moving on, it was hard to imagine tiny Isobel sleeping all alone in a six-thousand-square-foot house. Even the thought of it squeezed Cate's heart.

She hadn't wanted to come tonight. The prospect of seeing Brody again turned her bones weak with dread. So many emotions. Guilt. Longing. Wishing for a miracle.

An hour ago she had almost canceled. Suddenly, overnight it seemed, none of her clothes fit. The waistbands of every pair of jeans she owned refused to button. Even her shirts and bras strained to confine her burgeoning breasts. Of course, she wasn't going to head up the mountain in anything but her Sunday best. So she found a loose, long-sleeved knit dress in a modern geometric print of blue and navy hiding in the back of her closet and put it on.

Only the most discerning glance would notice the swell of her pregnant belly. After sliding her feet into low heels and grabbing up a sweater in case the house was drafty, she turned her attention to her hair.

Her instinct was to leave it up in its usual knot on the back of her head. But something told her Brody would see the hairstyle as an in-your-face challenge. They had argued about it often enough. Cate liked her hair to be neat and under control. Brody said it was a sin to hide sunshine from the world.

Despite the current situation, when she remembered their flirtation—barely disguised as squabbles—she had to smile. Feeling Brody's hands in her hair had seduced her as surely as his kisses. He touched her gently but surely, clearly knowing that any token protest on her part was doomed to failure.

When the two of them had lain naked in bed together, Brody played with her hair endlessly. Even now, when she brushed the long, thick mass, she felt a frisson of sensation, of memory, snake down her spine. Most days her hair felt like a burden. When she was with Brody, he made her believe it was a sexy, feminine crowning glory.

*Hell's bells.* This was not the time to be thinking about

Brody. She put a hand to her stomach, flattened her fingers and tried to feel something, anything. Shouldn't she be able to detect the baby moving by now? Were all mothers-to-be this nervous and unsure?

She wanted desperately to have someone else to talk to about her pregnancy. By her deliberate choices, she had no friends in Candlewick close enough to be considered confidantes. Five years ago she had been too wounded and wary to cultivate deep relationships with other women her age. Once she was back on her feet emotionally, she had already gained a reputation as a loner.

Glancing in the mirror, she noted her flushed cheeks and wild-eyed expression. If she didn't get ahold of her pinballing, hormone-driven mental state, both Brody and Duncan, *and* Miss Izzy were going to know something was wrong.

Twenty minutes later she parked in front of Isobel's house, noting with interest, even in the fading light, the way the grounds had been spruced up already. Duncan met her at the door and welcomed her. Was that a deliberate snub on Brody's part? A signal that he'd been very serious about not picking up where they left off?

Perhaps she was being too sensitive. As it turned out, Brody and his grandmother were in the midst of a fiercely competitive game of chess. Duncan and Cate found them in the formal living room, seated on either side of a red-and black-lacquered gaming table.

Geoffrey and Isobel had traveled the world during the course of their marriage. Their home was filled with priceless artwork of all kinds.

Brody looked up when Cate entered the room. He lost his focus momentarily, and Isobel smirked. "Checkmate," she crowed.

"Nice job, Granny," he said absently. He stood and took

Cate's hand, lifting it to his lips. "You look stunning, Cate. In fact, if a Scotsman can be forgiven for hyperbole, you glow."

"Thank you," she said, her throat dry. She stepped away and broke his light hold. She couldn't bear to be so close to him with her emotions in turmoil.

The two Stewart brothers were clad in hand-tailored suits and crisp white dress shirts. Duncan's tie was blue. Brody's red. Either man could have graced the cover of *GQ*, but it was Brody whose intense stare made Cate's knees quiver. In more formal clothing, he carried an air of command that was the tiniest bit intimidating.

The other three seemed to be waiting on something. Cate lifted a shoulder. "So what's the occasion? Another birthday? Miss Izzy was very mysterious when she called earlier."

Duncan grinned. If Cate's heart hadn't been otherwise inclined, the younger Stewart brother might have won her over. "We have a proposition for you."

Cate shot Brody a startled glance. "Kinky," she muttered, low enough that Miss Izzy couldn't hear. The old woman's wits were razor-sharp, but her hearing was going.

Brody glared at her. "Behave, Cate. This is serious."

How dare he chastise *her*? "I'm terribly sorry, Mr. Stewart. Please. I'm all ears. What is this mysterious proposition?"

Isobel elbowed her way between her two strapping grandsons and linked her arm with Cate's. "We'll talk about it together over dinner, my dear. Our caterer is amazing, but he's somewhat temperamental. We don't want to keep him waiting."

Forty-five minutes later, with both the soup and salad courses behind them, Cate still hadn't heard anything of substance that warranted this fancy occasion. The food she had eaten rested heavy in her stomach, though it was undoubtedly haute cuisine.

Nerves made her jumpy and tense.

Unfortunately, the Stewart family decided it was a good time to talk about the ubiquitous Scottish dish haggis. Isobel shook her head. "I ate it as a lass, but I'd not be so eager to try it now."

Duncan's grin was mischievous. "What about you, Cate? Would you be game to try our native delicacy?"

*Please, God, let them be joking. Surely the American caterer wasn't going that route.* She gulped inwardly. "I've heard of it, of course. But to be honest, I'm not entirely sure what it is."

Brody stared at her. "I don't think Cate would be a fan."

"How would you know what I like?" she snapped.

He lifted one supercilious eyebrow. "A sheep's heart, lungs and liver? Chopped up and mixed with onion and oatmeal and all manner of other ingredients...then boiled in the sheep's stomach? Really, Cate? We may not know each other all that well, but you surprise me."

Bile rose in her throat. Her belly heaved in distress. "Oh. Well, no. I suppose not. Sounds revolting."

Duncan took pity on her and changed the subject. The shift gave her a few minutes to breathe and get herself under control. Brody, damn his sorry black-hearted hide, smirked as if he had bested her somehow. Not a chance. Not a damned chance in the world.

While they waited on the main course, Isobel finally grimaced. "Well, lass, here it is. The boys want me to sell out and go back to Scotland. I've let them know unequivocally that I'm not going to do that."

"Oh?" Cate felt as if she were treading a minefield. Neither Duncan nor Brody seemed in any way lighthearted or even at ease about this conversation. Was this some kind of trap for Cate? Did Miss Izzy need Cate to cast a deciding vote?

Isobel nodded, although Cate hadn't really said anything. "I offered a compromise. One the boys believe has merit."

"And that is?"

Izzy smiled gently. "I'd like you to consider moving in here with me as my paid companion. I wouldn't take you away from the bookstore, of course. Your wonderful shop is part of the charm of Candlewick. But my grandsons would feel better knowing that someone was officially looking after me."

"I already do that anyway." Cate frowned. "I care about you, Miss Izzy. And I'm happy to consider moving up here on the mountain with you, but I won't take any money. That's unacceptable."

Brody, the man whose flashing smile was the first thing she had noticed about him months ago, seemed to do nothing but frown at her now. His black scowl pinned her to her chair. "Try not to be difficult, Cate. Granny isn't a charity case. She can afford to pay for in-home help."

Cate was generally even-tempered, but Brody's condescending attitude nicked her on the raw. "Isobel is my *friend*," she said. "It seems to me this is an issue she and I can negotiate on our own. Or perhaps you and Duncan think I'll make the house too crowded."

"Oh, no," Izzy said. "The boys are leaving."

"Leaving?" Cate's tongue felt thick in her mouth. Her stomach clenched. "When?"

Duncan picked up the conversational ball, since his brother was sitting silent and stone-faced with his arms crossed over his chest. "Our tickets are open-ended, but probably in a couple of days. Granny has made up her mind. Since we won't be dealing with real estate issues,

we'll head on home and probably make another visit later…
in the summer, no doubt."

Cate's skin was clammy and cold, though she felt feverish and overheated from the inside out. Brody was leaving. Dear Lord. What was she going to do? She had to tell
him. Or did she?

Perspiration dotted her upper lip. Black spots danced in
front of her eyes. "Excuse me," she said. "I'll be back in a
moment." She stood up, deathly ill, desperate to make it to
the restroom before she broke down in tears.

Humiliation and rage and sheer distress tore her in a
dozen directions. Is this what hyperventilation felt like?
Nausea rolled through her belly. Not once in her shocking
pregnancy had she experienced more than mild discomfort. Now, at the worst possible moment, puking her guts
out was a very real possibility.

As she lurched to her feet, her chair wobbled and almost
overturned. She grabbed for something, anything. With one
hand she gripped the wooden edge of the seat back. With
the other, she reached blindly for the table.

"I'm sorry," she whispered. "I don't feel well."

She took a step toward the hallway. Her legs buckled.
She heard a trio of shouts. Then her world went black.

# Five

Brody leaped to his feet in horror, but he was too late to catch Cate. She crumpled like a graceful swan. Unfortunately, she was close enough to the sideboard to clip her head as she went down. A gash marred her high, pale forehead. "Bloody hell." He crouched beside her, his heart racing in panic. "Get some ice, Duncan."

Isobel sat awkwardly on the floor at Cate's hip. The old woman suffered from advanced arthritis in every joint, but she took one of Cate's hands and patted it over and over again. Her eyes glistened with tears. "Cate. Cate, dear. Open your eyes."

Cate was milk-pale and completely limp and unresponsive. Brody tasted real fear. "Damn it, Duncan! Where's the ice?"

Duncan appeared on the run, out of breath and agitated. "What's wrong with her?" The zip-top plastic bag of ice he carried was wrapped in a thin cotton dish towel.

"Hell if I know. I can't leave her on the floor, though. Hold the ice to her head while I move her." Carefully, Brody scooped Cate up in his arms. She was slender, but tall, so he grunted as he lifted her dead weight. Her gorgeous, sunlit hair cascaded over his arm. The scent of her shampoo and the feel of her feminine body in his arms excoriated him.

Ever since his visit to Cate's bookstore four nights ago, he had second-guessed himself a million times. His decision not to continue their physical relationship seemed like the mature, reasonable choice. It wasn't fair to Cate to pick up where they left off, and what he had told her was true. He needed time with his grandmother. More important, he wasn't a man who had any intention of settling down to family life.

Cate was not a one-night-stand kind of woman.

But God knew, he had vastly underestimated how hard it was going to be to stay away from her now that they were, at least for the moment, living in the same town. He strode down the hallway with only one destination in mind. Entering his bedroom, he motioned for Duncan to throw back the covers.

When that task was accomplished, Brody carefully deposited his precious cargo in his bed.

"Why isn't she waking up?" Isobel fretted.

"She doesn't look good," Duncan pointed out, voicing Brody's own thoughts.

Brody sat and chafed her cool, long-fingered hands. Duncan kept the ice bag against her temple. Isobel sagged into an armchair, suddenly looking every one of her ninety-two years.

Finally, after what seemed like a lifetime but was probably only another five or ten minutes, Cate's eyelashes fluttered and lifted. Her gaze was cloudy with confusion. "What happened?" she whispered.

Brody smoothed a lock of hair from her cheek. The golden strands clung to his finger. "You fainted."

Though she was ashen before, now she turned dead white, her expression both aghast and defeated. Her throat worked as she swallowed. "Sorry. Didn't mean to scare you."

Duncan moved to the end of the bed. "Could you be coming down with the flu, Cate? I heard in town yesterday that the clinic is seeing a big surge in new cases."

"If that's true," Brody said, "you shouldn't be around Granny. Flu can be deadly for people her age."

Duncan jumped in, clearly trying to temper his brother's unwittingly harsh comment. "Let's not race to conclusions." He smiled gently at Cate. "Do you feel feverish or nauseated?" he asked.

Cate clenched the sheets on either side of her, her fingers gripping the folds white-knuckled. "Yes."

"Damn." Brody gazed down at her, his chest tight. Young people also died from the flu. "I guess we should call the doctor."

Cate struggled to sit up despite their protests. She rested her back against the headboard and pushed the hair from her face. In Brody's big bed she seemed small and lost and defenseless.

Her mouth opened and closed. She licked her dry lips. "I don't have the flu," she said clearly. "I'm pregnant."

Duncan whistled long and slow.

Brody cursed and jerked backward, lurching to his feet. "That's not funny."

Isobel actually laughed and put her hands to her cheeks.

Cate lifted her chin, her eyes glassy with unshed tears. "Do I look like *I* think it's funny?" She turned toward Isobel, who should have been shocked, but instead, sat quietly with a look of Machiavellian concentration on her wrinkled face. "I can still take care of you, Miss Izzy. At least until the baby comes. Don't worry about a thing."

Brody felt his world caving in. "Whose is it?"

Isobel jumped to her feet and thumped his shoulder with

all her less-than-substantial weight. "Brody Stewart. You apologize right this instant."

Duncan frowned. "Granny's right."

Brody swallowed hard. Did men faint? He felt damn close himself. He grimaced at his brother and grandmother. "Why don't the two of you go eat before the caterer has apoplexy. Cate and I will stay here and talk."

Cate lurched out of bed. "Oh, no," she cried. "I'm not staying here with *you*." She gave Brody a look that could have melted steel, but the moment she tried to stand, she wobbled and fell over again. This time Duncan caught her, because he was close.

He helped her back onto the bed.

Brody fisted his hands, his chest heaving. "I'm sorry. You two go. Cate and I will be okay."

When Duncan and Isobel exited the bedroom and closed the door, the room fell silent. Brody knew he needed a conciliatory tone, but all he felt was fury and pain. "When were you going to tell me?" he shouted, totally unable to help himself.

Cate shrank back against the headboard, her arms wrapped so tightly around herself it was a wonder she didn't break. "I was working on it," she said, the words dull. "If you don't believe me, feel free to search my laptop. The letter is time-and-date-stamped. I started writing it two weeks ago. Right after I found out. You were an ocean away. It wasn't an easy thing to do."

"How far along?" He didn't mean for the question to sound accusatory; he really didn't.

But Cate took it as such. He saw it on her face. "Four months give or take."

"We used protection."

"Not that one time. In the middle of the night."

He blanched, suddenly remembering every detail. He'd

awakened hard and aching, already reaching for her in his sleep. She had been like a drug to him. The euphoria of taking her again and again shot him to the top and wrung him out. He'd been obsessed with her.

If he hadn't gone back to Scotland, they might have fucked themselves to death.

"Is there a chance anyone else could be the father?" He made himself ask the dreadful question.

Cate's green eyes sheened with tears. "Of course not, you stupid, thickheaded Scotsman." Her voice was tight. "If I weren't about to throw up on your priceless oriental rug right now, I'd get out of this bed and slug you in the stomach. Do you really think I found someone else so quickly after you left? Good Lord, Brody. You were the first man I'd slept with in five years. And that was a fluke. I wasn't looking for sex in the first place."

He knew she tried to stifle the sob at the end, but it slipped out. Why was he being such a prick? Perhaps because he had never been so scared and confused and guilty in his life. And ashamed. Conscience-stricken that he hadn't been with her during these traumatic weeks.

"Have you been sick from the beginning?" The only way to establish any sense of normalcy was to keep talking, but honest to God, his head spun, and he hadn't a clue what to do. It was like the time he took one of his boats out alone and got caught up in a wicked storm and nearly drowned.

Only tonight was much worse.

Cate shook her head slowly. "No. This is new."

He scraped both hands through his hair, trying and failing to come to terms with the fact that he was going to be a father. Nothing made sense.

"I'll provide for the child," he said, his jaw clenched so hard his temples screamed with pain.

Cate's emerald eyes went dark. "You needn't bother with

speeches, Brody. The only reason I was going to tell you about the baby at all was to soothe my conscience. I make a decent living. I have a nest egg from my parents. I don't want or expect anything from you. You're free to go back to Scotland. The sooner, the better, in fact. Isobel doesn't need you and neither do I."

Fury, hot and wild, pounded in his veins. But when he looked at her, sitting so defeated and miserable in his bed, he forced himself to swallow the words of angry confrontation that he wanted to throw at her. Cate carried his child. She was sick and confused and vulnerable.

"Clearly, there are decisions to be made," he said quietly. "Now is not the time. I know you don't feel well, but you need to eat. Let's go back to the dining room and give it a try."

"You go," she said stubbornly. "I'll stay here and rest."

He managed a smile and wondered if it seemed as strained and false as it felt to him. "I can tell you're feeling better," he said. "Your cheeks have color in them again. Don't fight me on this, Cate. You'll only make things worse."

Ignoring her sputtered protests, he kissed her on the forehead and picked her up again. "You'll wear yourself out fighting, Little Mama. Take a break tonight. Talk to Duncan and Granny. Tomorrow the sun will come up and you'll feel better, I swear. We both will."

Her head lolled against his shoulder, her breath warm on his neck. "I hate you, Brody."

A mighty sigh lifted his chest and rolled through him with a tsunami of regrets. "I know, Cate. I know."

An hour later Brody stood at the front door and watched as the taillights of Cate's car disappeared down the hill. He had lost the violent argument about whether or not she would drive herself back to town. Only when brave, beautiful Cate broke down in tears did he make himself back down. He didn't know much about pregnant women, but her mental state seemed precarious at the moment, so he acquiesced reluctantly. It felt like an eternity before he at last got her text saying she was safely at home.

The caterer was long gone and the countertops pristine. Brody prowled the darkened kitchen, scrounging in the refrigerator for a piece of the key lime pie he had been too upset to eat earlier.

Though it was late, Brody was miles away from feeling sleepy. Maybe he was finally getting over his jet lag, and maybe tonight's news would give him permanent insomnia. Adrenaline pumped in his veins. He jumped when Duncan showed up unannounced in the dimly lit space.

Duncan sprawled in a cane-bottomed chair at the small table in the breakfast nook. "What are you going to do?"

That was Duncan. Cut to the chase. Don't dance around the issue.

"I haven't a clue," Brody said sullenly. "What would you do in my shoes?"

"Cate is an intelligent, beautiful, fascinating woman."

It pissed Brody that Duncan had noticed. Caveman instincts he didn't know he possessed clubbed their way to the speech center of his brain. "Don't get any ideas, little brother."

Duncan made a rude hand gesture. "If you don't want her, why shouldn't she find another guy who will value and appreciate her?"

Brody's teeth-grinding headache was back. "I never said I didn't want her."

"Oh, come on, Brody. I know you pretty damn well. You never date any woman long enough for her to get ideas about marriage. You might as well have it tattooed on your forehead. *Brody Stewart doesn't commit.*"

It was true. In fact, Brody had given Cate a version of the same speech. "You make me sound like a jackass."

"If the kilt fits."

"Very funny."

"Do you think there's any possibility she got pregnant on purpose? To force your hand?" Duncan's look held enough real sympathy to make Brody's throat tighten.

Brody swallowed hard. "No. Zero possibility. It was all on me." He'd made a mistake. A passion-driven, unthinking, hot and crazy, erotic mistake. That one unbearably sensual night had been emblematic of the two-week affair he couldn't forget. Now there was going to be a far more tangible reminder of his impulsive, testosterone-driven behavior.

Panic rose again, tightening his chest. "I don't know what to do, Duncan. Swear to God, I don't."

Duncan rolled to his feet and got a beer from the fridge. He popped the cap. "What do you *want* to do?"

"I want to rewind my life and go back to last week."

"Not an option, bro."

"You're no help."

"Look at it this way. We were both planning to go home in a few days. Now you can stay and make sure Granny is doing okay."

"I don't want to stay," Brody yelled, tempering the volume at the last minute to keep from awakening his grandmother.

"Then come back to Scotland with me. I'm sure Cate can manage without you."

Hearing the stark choices laid out so succinctly made Brody's blood chill. He glared. "Sometimes I wish I could still knock the crap out of you like I did when we were teenagers," he muttered.

"Your memory is faulty. I won at least half of those skirmishes. Face it, Brody. You're not the first guy to find yourself in this situation, and you won't be the last. But Granny complicates the equation. She won't let you walk away from your responsibilities."

"I appreciate your high opinion of me."

Duncan shrugged. "You live on another continent. Cate will do fine on her own. I, of all people, would understand if you set up a trust fund and let that be it. Do you even like kids?"

"How would I know? I could learn, I guess."

"I think the bigger question is whether or not Cate Everett means more to you than an easy lay." Duncan yawned. "I've got to get some sleep," he said, standing and tossing the empty bottle in the recycle bin. "I'll do whatever I can to help, Brody. But the first move is yours."

# Six

Now that Cate had fallen prey to pregnancy sickness, it settled in with a vengeance. The morning after the disastrous dinner party, she was late opening the store because she spent an hour hunched over the sink in the tiny antiquated bathroom of her upstairs apartment. Fortunately, tourists were not beating down her door in late February. Most people in town were busy with their own endeavors.

By the time she made it downstairs midmorning, the worst of the nausea had passed. Until noon, she was able to huddle by the fire and sip a cup of tepid tea and think. Apparently, *pregnancy brain* must be a real thing, because random thoughts bounced inside her skull like a drunken pinball game.

She was an inveterate list-maker as a rule. Though a blank pad lay on the table at her elbow, and a nearby antique coffee tin held an assortment of pens, she never actually wrote down anything at all. The future stretched before her, a terrifyingly blank canvas.

Would she set up a nursery in Miss Izzy's house? That wasn't part of the deal. It was a lot to ask of a woman Isobel's age to welcome an infant with all of the accompanying inconveniences and demands.

And what about the store? Would Cate have to find a manager? Could she afford to take maternity leave? It would be five years before the kid went to kindergarten.

At the moment an eerie and surprising calm wrapped her in a soothing cocoon. One hand rested on her stomach. This pregnancy was real. But she didn't feel any different. If it wasn't for the nausea, she could easily ignore the entire fiasco.

Only when she allowed herself to think about Brody Stewart did pain intrude. If there had ever been a man less pleased to hear he was going to be a father, she couldn't imagine it.

Brody had reacted to her news with shock and dismay and even anger. She winced inwardly, remembering his face. She couldn't really blame him. This situation was unprecedented for both of them.

To be honest, it was probably best he lived an ocean away. There would be no awkward encounters on the street, no need to take his feelings into account when she began making decisions about what kind of baby bed to buy, how soon to introduce solid foods and when to decide the kid was old enough for day care.

She didn't want or need Brody to take up parenting as a duty. No child deserved that. Neither did Cate.

Cate was in this all alone…for the duration. At least she had five more months to get used to the idea. The baby would be born in July. That was good. No worries about blizzards or nasty winter viruses. She would be able to go for long walks with the baby in the stroller and get back in shape after pregnancy strained her body.

She wanted to be elated and excited and exuberant about her situation. And she would be…probably. As soon as she got beyond feeling so sick and tired and overwhelmed. She hoped so.

She had actually dozed off in her chair when the bell over the front door jingled. With a yawn, she stood up and stretched. "Coming," she said. For some reason, finding Brody standing near the cash register caught her completely off guard. "What are you doing here?"

He lifted an eyebrow. "We have decisions to make."

Her heartbeat sped up drunkenly. "No," she said carefully. "*We* don't have to decide anything. This is my baby. All I owed you was the courtesy of information. Now that we have that out of the way, you're off the hook. Fly home with your brother."

He scowled. "I think we should get married."

She swallowed, and her eyes bugged out. "Um, no. Let's not do the dance, Brody. You have nothing to worry about. I've got this. Your boats need you."

"You and I are good together in bed."

The blunt challenge angered her and at the same time made her legs quiver. Heavens, yes. They definitely were. But so what? That didn't make a marriage. "And your point?"

"Lots of couples start with far less."

She rubbed two fingers in the center of her forehead. "A hundred years ago I'm sure there were shotgun weddings all over North Carolina. But, thank God, that's in the past. No one will bat an eye if I have this baby on my own. Seriously, Brody. You owe me nothing, nothing at all."

"You're carrying my baby." His gaze was stormy.

"But you don't really want to be a father, do you? Be honest. You don't even want to be a husband. Why would we put ourselves through a sham that will only lead to heartbreak?"

His brooding stare made her nipples tighten against the slippery fabric of her bra. She had never met a man as unflinchingly masculine as Brody Stewart. It was easy to imagine him in another time, a fiery chieftain leading his clan.

"I can't win this particular argument," he said, "since I was so blatant about not wanting to settle down and be a family man. But circumstances have changed, Cate."

"Not for you. Not really. I won't be an obligation you check off some moral list, Brody."

"Would marrying me be such a terrible fate?"

In his deep blue eyes, she saw a hint of the same turmoil she had carried with her every day since the baby became a reality. The prospect of being Brody Stewart's bride was a fantasy she had entertained briefly back in the fall. The intensity of their combustible attraction had raised the possibility that Brody might be *the one*.

Even now it would be far too easy to fall prey to the fairy tale. But she had done that once before and been burned. She was older...wiser.

Fortunately, more bookstore enthusiasts arrived, erasing any possibility of further substantive conversation.

Brody's lips tightened with frustration, but he waited more or less patiently as she greeted her customers. Then he caught her by the arm and drew her close. "I'll take you to dinner tonight. In Claremont. We'll talk."

Claremont was the next town over. Bigger. More cosmopolitan. Lots of lovely restaurants. "It won't change anything," she said.

He curled an arm around her waist and dragged her closer for one hard kiss. "Wear something nice," he said. "I'll pick you up at six."

The weather had finally moderated. The day was sunny with a hint of spring warmth. The hours crawled by, but at last Cate was free to put the *closed* placard in the front window and lock the doors.

Upstairs, she dithered over what to wear. Brody had taken her to eat in Claremont several times back in the fall. If he chose their favorite spot again, she would need to dress for the ambiance.

The only nice outfit she owned—that still fit—was a red jersey tank dress that left her shoulders bare. Her newly burgeoning breasts swelled against the scooped neckline. Pairing the sexy number with a sober black wool shawl would keep her warm and at the same time lend respectability to the above-the-knee frock. She didn't want to give Brody any ideas.

The larger-than-life Scotsman was punctual. It was one of the many things she liked about him. That and the way he charmed everyone they met, from strangers on the street to clerks and servers and anyone else who crossed his path. His thick, whiskey-colored hair, broad-shouldered masculinity and bone-melting accent were a trifecta that won over even the most curmudgeonly of acquaintances.

As he helped her into the car with a solicitous touch, she told herself she wouldn't be dazzled by something as shallow as sex appeal. So the man had a great smile and smelled like a crisp alpine forest. That wasn't enough. She was going to be a mother. She had mature decisions to make. Sex would only cloud the process.

Brody, perhaps correctly reading her reluctance, was on his best behavior. During the twenty-mile drive, they discussed movies and books and Isobel's determination to remain in her home.

Cate smiled. "It's hard for me to believe that one tiny old lady can stand up to a duo of strapping Scotsmen."

"We can't exactly tote her over our shoulder and kidnap her onto a plane. Granny has made up her mind. It complicates things for the family down the road, but we love her. Our father was naive to believe Duncan and I could sway her. But then again, none of us realized how much she loves it here in North Carolina. With Grandda gone, I thought Candlewick would hold too many painful memories."

"It's the memories that keep her going, I think."

"Seems so."

When they arrived at the restaurant, serious conversation was tabled for the moment. The tuxedo-clad host actually remembered them. He bent over Cate's hand with a theatrical French flair. "We are honored to have such a beautiful woman grace our humble restaurant."

The *humble* restaurant had three Michelin stars and an extensive wine cellar, so Cate took his effusive greeting with a grain of salt. "It's good to be back," she said.

Brody's lips twitched, but she gave him points for not rolling his eyes. The host seated them at a prime table in the corner near a large window that looked out over a scenic pond. Gardens, still clad in drab winter colors, nevertheless beckoned with tiny white lights strung in the branches of budding trees.

The last time she and Brody had patronized this particular establishment, they took a walk after dinner. He had pulled her into the shadows and kissed her desperately. They'd been so hungry for each other that the trip back to Candlewick had seemed endless.

The memory brought no pleasure. Cate had been giddy with infatuation back then. But soon after, Brody disappeared from her life.

Her dinner companion picked up on her wistful mood. After they ordered he leaned back in his chair and stared at her. "What's wrong? I thought this place was a favorite of yours."

She shrugged. "It was. It is. If I'm not mistaken, though, this is where you and I spent the evening before we went back to my place and…well, you know. Made a baby."

His face changed. "Ah, hell, lass. I'm sorry."

"It doesn't matter." Clearly, Brody didn't remember every moment of their affair.

The entrées arrived, derailing the awkward pause. Cate's stomach cooperated long enough for her to eat grilled salmon and sautéed squash. Brody's smile had gotten lost somewhere along the way. He consumed most of a strip steak and a baked potato, but his jaw was firm and his gaze hooded.

At last, the meal was done. Cate put down her fork and pulled her shawl more tightly around her shoulders. The restaurant wasn't cold, but she needed something to hold on to. She inhaled sharply. "Here's the thing, Brody. When and if I ever get married, I want it to be to a man who loves me and wants to be with me always. You're not that guy."

He couldn't argue the point. Not when he had so very carefully told her he wasn't interested in picking up where they left off.

"Circumstances have changed." He spoke carefully as if he was looking for exactly the right words to convince her.

"It doesn't matter. *You* haven't changed. I deserve better than a reluctant husband and father."

He winced. "I said a lot of things recently. Maybe I was a fool." He reached across the table and took one of her hands in his. His thumb stroked the pulse at the back of her wrist. "We could make it work, lass. For the baby."

Cate shivered inwardly. She could fall in love with Brody Stewart so easily. When he went back home last October, her world had gone flat for a while. The autumn leaves had seemed duller, the blue skies not as vibrant. Even the crisp mornings and warm afternoons—normally her favorite season of the year—had failed to lift her spirits.

Brody had crashed into her humdrum existence with the force and heat of a meteorite. She could no more have resisted his brash Scottish charm than she could have stopped the sun from coming up. He had wanted her and she had wanted him. They had wallowed in their mutual, intense attraction.

When he left, the physical realities of a harsher-than-normal North Carolina mountain winter had echoed the aching loss in her soul.

Having Brody, even briefly, and then losing him had hurt. A lot. Why would she ever let herself be so vulnerable again?

She pulled her hand away. Touching him or vice versa was dangerous. "We created a baby in a moment of physical need. It happened. I don't blame you. You're a nice man. You're honest. You care about your grandmother. If I thought you had any long-term interest in this child, I would make sure you could see him or her now and again. But be honest, Brody. You don't want to take on that kind of emotional responsibility for the rest of your life…do you?"

"I haven't had much time to think about it."

It wasn't an answer. Not really.

Perhaps she owed him more of her life than she had shared up until now. Maybe it would help him understand. "I know what it's like to be a child who's not wanted."

His face reflected shock. "You?"

"Yes. I wasn't an orphan. So you don't have to feel sorry for me. That's not the point of this story. My parents were both college professors. Sociologists. They chose not to have children because they wanted to be free to travel the world and research indigenous populations in remote places. They knew it wouldn't be fair to leave a child behind for someone else to raise."

"So what happened?"

"When my mother was forty-nine years old and approaching menopause, she found out she was pregnant.

Needless to say, it was a shock. She and my father were good, decent people. They didn't give me up for adoption. Instead, they put an end to their travels and settled into teaching year-round."

"But they resented you…"

His attempt to understand was almost comical. "Nothing so dramatic. They did everything parents are supposed to do. There were nannies, of course, when I was an infant and toddler, but good ones. When I was old enough for kindergarten, my mother and father began attending parent/teacher conferences and school programs."

"I don't understand."

"They were going through the motions. One reason they never wanted children was because they weren't 'kid' people, and they knew that about themselves. Instead of warmth and hugs and genuine parent/child bonding, it was more like playacting. They tried their best to perform the assigned roles, I really believe that, but it was a hollow effort."

"How old were you when you realized?"

An insightful question. Brody was sharp and intuitive.

"Seven, I think. That would have been the spring of first grade. My class put on a play. We had a dress rehearsal one Saturday morning, because we were to perform for the whole school the following Monday. On the day of practice, there were parents everywhere…laughing, talking, taking photographs. My best friend's mother brought cupcakes for everyone. Another kid's father videotaped the practice."

"And your parents?"

"They sat on folding chairs in a back corner of the auditorium. Never spoke to anyone. Never involved themselves in the chaos. I know I was very small, and it's possible I've embellished the details, but what stands out in my memory is the look of discomfort on their faces. Maybe that was the first time they realized they had committed themselves to more than a decade of this kind of thing."

"I'm sorry, Cate." Brody's gaze was troubled.

"Don't be. Over the years I came to understand that I was luckier than some. I had every material advantage and a safe place to sleep at night."

"Children need love."

"Yes, they do. That's what I'm trying to tell you. If babies aren't your thing, it would be best for all of us if we come to terms with that now."

Brody ignored her pointed advice. He drummed his fingers on the linen tablecloth. "What about the rest of your life?"

"I did well in school. Didn't make waves. When I went off to college, I think it was a relief for all three of us. My parents were finally free to live life as they pleased, and I was ready to be an adult."

"Granny told me your parents died before you came to Candlewick…is that right?"

"Yes. My father was diagnosed with lung cancer six years ago. One afternoon when my mother was driving him home from a doctor's appointment, a drunk driver ran a red light. They were killed instantly."

"Damn, Cate. I'm so sorry."

Her throat tightened to a painful degree. "Thank you. But it was a very long time ago. I grieved and moved on."

Brody frowned. "You and I could provide emotional security for this baby. I have family to share and to spare. It makes perfect sense for you to marry me."

"Stop pushing me," she said. "You think you can make everything work out simply by willing it to be the way you want it, but life is not that easy. Emotions are messy and complicated. Babies even more so…"

# Seven

Brody lifted a hand to summon the waiter. He wanted to pay the check and get out of this place. Hearing Cate's story haunted him. His own family saga wasn't much better. But at least his parents had been physically affectionate. Even if they hadn't been able to stay married to each other, neither of their sons had ever doubted they were loved.

On the steps of the restaurant, he put a hand beneath Cate's elbow. "Do you feel like walking? It's a beautiful night."

Beneath his fingertips, he felt her stiffen. But a moment later she murmured an affirmative. As they descended the steps, Cate's elegant shawl caught on a nail and slipped out of her grasp. Before he could retrieve it, another guest picked it up and returned it.

"Thanks," Brody said. When he swiveled back to Cate, his eyes widened. She had kept a death grip on her simple wrap the entire evening. This was the first time he had seen her without the shawl. He remembered the red dress from before. What he didn't recall were the voluptuous curves plumped up on display above the neckline. "Holy hell."

She crossed her arms defensively. "Yes," she said wryly. "I've got boobs now. Put your eyes back in your head."

He swallowed and carefully tucked the soft wrap around her shoulders. "You had beautiful breasts before, lass. Now there's simply more of you to admire."

Cate laughed. He hadn't realized how much he missed that sound. Things were so serious between them now. "Come on," he said gruffly. "Exercise is good for pregnant women."

"How would you know?"

He wrapped an arm around her waist and steered her down the path of small, smooth stones. "I downloaded a pregnancy manual on my iPad. I've made it to chapter three so far."

Cate stopped dead in the middle of the walkway and stared up at him. "You can't be serious."

Her incredulity stung. "This is important to me, Catie girl. It might not be what I wanted, but it's what I've got… what *we've* got. It pays to be prepared. I have a responsibility to you." He brushed a gentle fingertip over the wound on her head. "You've already passed out once," he muttered. "We can't let that happen again." She had covered the abrasion with makeup, but he could still see the swelling.

"I'll admit the knot does ache, but pain reliever helped, so it's nothing to worry about. Last night was stressful. I'm fine now. Honestly."

"We'll see."

Apparently, that annoying phrase translated across the globe. "Don't try to *handle* me, Mr. Stewart. I'm not one of your boats."

He chuckled, linking his hand with hers and squeezing her fingers. They strolled along in harmony. "Do you even like the water, Cate?"

"I don't dislike it," she said.

"I'd enjoy taking you sailing, lass. I have a honey of a boat called the *Mary Guinn*. She's sleek and fast and responds to my hand on the wheel like a cloud dancing across the sky. There's nothing like being out on the loch with the breeze whipping the water into a frenzy and the sun on your face. It's poetry, lass. Pure poetry."

"So is this Mary person a former lover?"

"No. But she *was* my first teenage crush. Two years older than me and sweet as a spoonful of honey. I was madly in love with her for an entire spring."

"She must have been really something to inspire you to name a boat after her."

He stopped and pulled her to face him, holding her narrow shoulders between his two hands. "Are ye jealous, Cate?"

Her chin lifted. "Of course not. Don't be absurd."

He hadn't meant to kiss her. Not tonight. Not with so much at stake. But the way her wary green eyes gazed up at him lit a fire in his belly. "God, I've missed you."

He slid his hands beneath her hair and cupped her head, diving in deep for the first kiss, then lingering and savoring the second. He'd half expected her to slap his face and run away. Instead, she leaned into him and curled her arms around his neck.

"I missed you, too, Brody."

This time when the shawl fell, neither of them cared. His hands shook. How had he made himself believe he could stay away from this woman? Even with an ocean between them he had remembered the way her body fit his so perfectly. Was that a happy coincidence or a portent of something greater?

Tongue tangling with hers, he breathed raggedly. In his arms, she felt like home. "Do ye believe in fate, Catie girl? The Scots are a superstitious people. We come from a long line of seers and prophets. Sometimes life steers us in ways we're meant to go."

She pulled back for a moment, her lips swollen from his kisses, her cheeks flushed. The moonlight painted her in silver. "Don't make something out of nothing, Brody. Sex is sex. It doesn't mean we're the folk heroes of a Celtic legend. I like sleeping with you. You knocked me up. End of story."

He put a hand over her mouth. "Don't talk like that. You're not meant to be flippant."

She nipped his fingers with sharp teeth. "For a man who said 'no more sex' in no uncertain terms, you're creating a very compromising situation."

Cate was right. They had wandered about as far away from the restaurant as it was possible to go. No one could see them here in the copse of trees unless they stumbled upon them. And that was unlikely. Other diners were inside keeping warm.

He ran his hands up and down her arms. "I want ye badly, lass. I don't know what I was thinking."

"Did you sleep with other women when you went home?"

The question knocked the wind out of him.

Cate clapped a hand over her mouth, her expression aghast. "Forget I said that, Brody. It's none of my business."

He was stunned. Not by her question, but by his own calculations. He'd told himself the boat business had kept him too busy over the winter to get laid. What a pile of horseshit. Apparently, he'd not actually been tempted by any of the women who crossed his path. None of them had been Cate.

"The answer is no," he said bluntly.

She went still. "Really?"

He shrugged. "Really."

"Then why the big speech last week?"

"Maybe I'm a damned fool. Come here, little Cate. Let me kiss you again."

She put a hand in the center of his chest, holding him

momentarily at bay. "I'm five foot ten. Not little at all. And I won't let you coerce me with sex. This baby is none of your business."

"I'll be honest, woman. Right now I've no' got a thought for anything but touching you." He shimmied her skirt up to her hips. "Damn, your skin is soft." He was losing control. He recognized his fraying resolve. Tonight was supposed to be about solving the mess he had made. Now he was perilously close to compounding his transgressions.

"Brody..." She whispered his name with such yearning the hair on his nape stood up.

His next discovery fried his reasoning. "Lord, God, woman. Are you no' wearing any underwear?" She had gooseflesh all over, so he shrugged out of his suit jacket and tucked it around her.

"It's a thong," she muttered. "It keeps me from having lines in my dress."

He wrapped his fingers in the tiny sliver of satin and ripped it with a satisfying jerk. "No lines at all, my sweet. You're welcome."

Scooping her up, he urged her legs around his waist and backed her against the nearest tree, knowing his coat would protect her skin. "Tell me to stop, and I'll stop." It would kill him, but he would. He'd already changed Cate's life irrevocably with this pregnancy. He needed to know what she expected from him.

She cupped his face in her hands. "I want you to quit talking, Brody. Hurry. Before someone finds us out here."

Although Cate didn't get the words exactly right, she had her hand on his zipper, so he was definitely clear about where this was going.

What happened next was both clumsy and exhilarating. With both of them breathless and urgent and trying to help the other, at last he was inside her. "Ah, damn, my Cate."

"Brody, Brody…" She clung to him tightly.

Except for her bunched-up dress and his still-buttoned shirt, they were as close as two humans could be. He caressed her smooth, firm bottom. "Is it weird that I'm really turned on 'cause you're pregnant?"

Her laugh was a choked gasp. "I don't think so. Besides, I don't *feel* pregnant. All I can think about is how long it's been since we did this."

"Too long," he groaned. Already he was close to coming, and that was unacceptable.

Cate bit his earlobe and whispered something naughty in his ear. His temperature shot up a hundred and fifty degrees. "Stop that," he pleaded. "I'm trying to make this last."

Cate shivered hard. It was far too cold to be fooling around outside, but she didn't care. Brody was making love to her. So many lonely nights she had dreamed of this. When she told herself time and again that the sex couldn't have been as earth-shattering as she remembered, she tried to believe that was so. Only now Brody was back and the truth stared her in the face.

Whatever this was between them was magic.

His big, ruggedly masculine body radiated heat despite the air temperature. Each time he moved in her, the hard length of him probed sensitive spots that made her close her eyes and arch her back, aching for something just out of reach.

Even in the midst of physical euphoria, her brain offered irritating explanations. Probably Brody was using this interlude to coax her into doing things his way. He thought if they were lovers, she would say yes to him across the board.

She shoved away the unwelcome thoughts. His strength

made her feel intensely feminine. Despite her years of education and her dedication to women's empowerment, the fact that he was able to hold her so easily spoke to some deep unevolved corner of her psyche.

Brody was a protective male. He would keep her safe if she allowed it.

He muttered her name and rested his forehead against hers. His big body quaked. "I've lost my bloody mind."

His coffee-scented breath was warm on her cheek. She wanted to gobble him up. "Are you complaining, Brody?" She squeezed him intimately with inner muscles.

"No," he croaked. "Never." He adjusted the jacket he had wrapped around her. "Am I hurting you?"

The tree bark had scraped her hip bone when the coat fell, but she barely noticed. "I'm good."

He pulled back and reached between their joined bodies to give her the extra bit of stimulation she needed to hit the peak. "Come for me, lass."

She was primed and ready. The sweet tide rolled through her and left her limp in his arms. Brody thrust his way to completion moments later and heaved a great sigh, his body shuddering in the aftermath.

In the echoing silence that followed, Cate yawned unexpectedly. The intense fatigue of early pregnancy sapped her energy. Under the circumstances, Brody had taken whatever bit of strength she had left.

He chuckled and carefully disengaged their bodies, setting her on her feet and holding her arm until she was steady. She had lost a shoe, so they had to scramble in the dark to find it. She leaned against him, replete, weary, oddly unconcerned about the future. Just being near him gave her a deep sense of peace.

She didn't examine those feelings too intently. It was difficult enough to come to terms with impending motherhood. She didn't have the mental fortitude to deal with how Brody fit into the picture.

He insisted on carrying her back to the car, which was embarrassing and sweet, and yet in some odd way, frightening. He'd been back in Candlewick such a short time, and already she was letting him take charge.

That couldn't happen.

Like a famous Southern heroine, Cate would think about it tomorrow.

Back at the bookstore, they argued. Brody wanted to come upstairs and spend the night. Cate needed space and time to think.

She faced him on the sidewalk, wrapped once again in her cozy black shawl. "You said it first, Brody," she pointed out. "We shouldn't and *can't* pick up where we left off last October. You have concerns about helping your grandmother, but now I have responsibilities, too."

He cursed beneath his breath, his grumpy displeasure evident. "So what happened back there at the restaurant? Or in the woods, to be more exact."

Cate shrugged, feeling tears prick her eyes. This hormonal roller coaster made it difficult to be wise. "We lost our heads. It was nice to be together again. Maybe you were trying to sway me to your way of thinking."

He put a finger under her chin and tipped her face up to his. In the glow of the streetlight, his eyes flashed with temper. "I didn't make love to you to win points, Cate. I hadn't planned for that to happen at all. But I'm not sorry."

"I'm not asking for an apology."

"Then what do you want from me?"

"My life is changing whether I want it to or not. I'll move up to the house and stay with Miss Izzy. You and Duncan can feel free to go home."

"And what about the baby?"

"I'll figure it out."

Brody knew he had made a major misstep. Earlier—before picking Cate up for dinner—he had realized sex would cloud the issue, but he hadn't been able to help himself. It had been so long, so damn long, since he left Candlewick. He'd been away for sixteen, seventeen weeks, give or take, and in all that time, Cate Everett had been an incandescent memory haunting his dreams.

The drive back up the mountain was relatively short. Certainly not enough time to unravel the many challenging aspects of his current situation.

He hadn't even kissed her good-night, damn it. Cate had unlocked the bookshop door and slipped inside, leaving him to stand on the street like some lovesick adolescent and wait for her bedroom light to come on so he would know she was okay.

When he finally pulled up in front of his granny's house and got out of the car, the last person on earth he wanted to see was his brother. Apparently, Duncan had been waiting up for him. They stood outside on the driveway, speaking in low voices.

Duncan didn't mince words. "I'm packed for my flight out tomorrow morning. Have you decided if you're coming with me?"

Brody thought about his fleet of beautiful and sturdy boats, and his comfortable house in the glen, and the way his buddies gathered at the local pub at the end of the week to share a pint and celebrate everything or nothing at all. He slammed a fist on the hood of the car. "I can't leave. Not yet. Nothing is settled."

"You don't think Cate can deal with this on her own?

She has Granny, and Cate strikes me as an eminently capable woman."

"It's *my* baby," Brody said. Why did no one understand that?

Duncan shrugged. "One lucky sperm doesn't make you father of the year. Don't break Cate's heart, Brody. Right now you're caught up in wanting to make a grand gesture. Ye've got to think carefully, man."

"Would you leave if you were me?" The words came out sharp and angry, taking Brody by surprise. He hadn't known his mood was so volatile.

The silence stretched from seconds to minutes. Duncan leaned against the side of the car, his gaze focused somewhere out in the dark night. At last, he sighed and faced Brody. "I can't say for sure. But I think it would depend more on the baby's mother than the kid itself. I saw how you looked at Cate. Are you in love with her?"

Brody felt his face heat and was glad Duncan couldn't see. "Of course not. I barely know her."

"Looks like you know her plenty well to me." The comeback was wry and pointed.

"People have sex without being in love."

"Aye. So I'll rephrase the question. Do you think Cate is in love with you?"

# Eight

*Do think Cate is in love with you?* Duncan's question haunted Brody for hours. When the sun came up, he had barely slept. He drove Duncan to the airport.

Once his brother had checked in and was ready to go through security, Brody hugged him tightly. "Thanks."

Duncan lifted an eyebrow and smiled, not appearing to notice the female TSA official who was giving him the eye. "What did I do?"

"Ye're family. The best part, in fact. Are you sure you're willing to take over the business for a few weeks?" He'd told Duncan at breakfast that he was going to stay in Candlewick until important decisions were made.

"I already handle all the boring business part," Duncan said, grinning. "I think I can survive the rest."

"I love you, man." Surely that wasn't panic slugging through his veins. Duncan was making a clean getaway. Brody was trapped.

Duncan picked up his carry-on and cuffed his brother on the shoulder. "You'll figure this out, Brody. I have complete faith in you."

When Brody's last and most final connection to Scotland walked away and disappeared into a queue of travelers, Brody returned to his car and made the drive back to Candlewick. When it had been the two of them arriving ten days ago, Brody had been confident and buoyed by the knowledge that a duo of Stewart men could deal with just about anything.

Now here he was, all alone. Duncan was happily bound for Scotland. Granny wasn't going *anywhere*. And Cate Everett was pregnant with Brody's baby. God help him.

When he made it back to his grandmother's house, he found her in the study going through a drawer of her husband's private correspondence. "Well," he said, forcing cheer, "Duncan's on his way home."

Isobel stood up from the desk and stretched. "Ye look half sick, my boy. Things will all work out."

So much for pretending. "What are you up to, Granny?" he asked, ignoring the subject he didn't want to discuss.

She grimaced. "Trying to decide what to pack away and what to pitch. Your grandda was a dab hand with pen and words. I see his beautiful, spidery writing, and I want to keep every scrap of paper." She ran a hand across the smooth cherry of the desk. "It's daft, I know."

He hugged her and then sprawled on the love seat. "Not daft. Not at all. There's no rush, is there?"

"Not really, but with our Cate moving in, I thought it would be a nice gesture to give her this office. So she could deal with bookstore matters and not go to town every single day."

Brody frowned. "You think she'll close the shop occasionally?"

"It's already closed on Sundays and Mondays. That's when she normally does her accounting and ordering. Maybe she'll close on Tuesdays, as well, now that she's pregnant. And I'm guessing she'll be hiring some help when the time comes. After the baby gets here, who knows?"

Brody couldn't understand why his indomitable and out-spoken grandmother wasn't putting the screws on him to make an honest woman out of Cate.

"I told her we need to get married," he said, wincing inwardly at the defensive note in his voice.

Isobel rolled her eyes. "Ye can't club the lass over the head with a broadsword and expect her to do yer bidding. Cate has a mind of her own, boy. Things were different in my day. But this is the modern era. She doesn't need you to *save* her."

Nausea swirled in his belly. Deep inside, he'd been counting on his grandmother to swing the vote his way. "I see," he said slowly. "Then tell me why I'm not on the plane with Duncan right now."

His grandmother limped over and kissed the top of his head. "Ye're the only one who can answer that question, my lad. And ye'd better get it right, because if you hurt my lovely Cate, I'll have your head on a platter, grandson or no grandson."

Cate stood in the middle of her small bedroom and surveyed the piles of clothing strewn across the bed. Packing to move up to Miss Izzy's house had seemed like a simple chore until she realized that very few of her clothes would be suitable for pregnancy.

One or two unstructured dresses. A few loose tops. A skirt with an elastic waistband. None of her pants. It seemed her first chore would be to go online and order the basics of a new wardrobe.

She was finding it harder and harder to concentrate. Fortunately, today was Sunday. She had the whole day ahead of her to organize her life and gather what she needed to relocate. Even now she had deep reservations. Not about helping Miss Izzy. That was a given. But putting herself more deeply into the bosom of the Stewart family could make things awkward when the baby came.

The child would carry Isobel's blood. Knowing how the old woman felt about her Scottish heritage meant this baby would be a symbol, a link to Geoffrey, a tangible reminder of all that Isobel had given up to become a bride in America.

Cate paused in front of the mirror over the dresser and pulled her soft ivory knit top flat across her belly. Her stomach definitely pooched out. Sometimes that new physical manifestation scared her. This morning, with the sun shining and the nausea temporarily at bay, her little baby bump made her smile.

Unlike her own childhood, this baby was going to be smothered in love. Boy or girl, it didn't matter. Having a little daughter to dress in soft fabrics and colors would be joyful and sweet. On the other hand, a tiny boy crafted in Brody's image would steal her heart just as quickly.

It was easier to imagine herself as the single parent of a daughter. After all, Cate knew what it felt like to have crushes and periods and acne and friends who did stupid things. But boys? That was another worry entirely.

Even so, raising a male infant and toddler and young boy would be doable, surely. It was the future that gave her nightmares. When Cate's teenage son or daughter grew old enough to make his or her own decisions. Like defiantly hopping on a plane for Scotland and choosing to live with the father they had never known.

How would she explain that Brody had not wanted children? That this conception, like Cate's own, was an accident.

Her parents had done the right thing. They hadn't abandoned their daughter. Nor had they distanced themselves physically. It was the intangibles she had missed out on.

Things like affection and humor and genuine familial bonds. Those gaps had left emotional scars. As a child, she filled the void with books and reading and an active imagination. Later in life, when she was finally out on her own, she continued to look for something she had never known, but in that instance, the consequences were tragic and painful.

In the midst of her soul-searching, the bell at the top of the stairs tinkled. It was linked to the front door of the bookshop, which meant she had a visitor. When she peeked out the front window, her breath whooshed out of her lungs and fogged the glass. Although the angle was such that she couldn't see the person who stood at her door, the vehicle parked at the curb was Brody's rental car.

With her heart pounding wretchedly fast, she glanced in the mirror again and groaned. She hadn't been expecting anyone to drop by. She'd barely even brushed her hair, and a little lip gloss would have been nice.

Now she didn't have time for such simple luxuries. The bell rang again. She could almost *hear* Brody's impatience in the rapid dinging.

All the way down the steps, she gave herself a lecture. No kissing. No arguing. And definitely, no physical contact of any kind.

When she turned the bolt and pulled open the door, Brody swept in like a conquering hero. He scooped her up and kissed her on the forehead before setting her on her feet. "Granny sent me to help you pack," he said. "Show me where the boxes are, and we'll get started."

Cate counted to ten slowly, telling herself that one platonic kiss couldn't derail her determination. "I could definitely use help moving boxes later today, but for now, I have things under control."

They were both being so polite it was almost comical.

Was Brody thinking the same thing she was? That the shop was closed and she had a very comfy and cozy bed just up the stairs?

He frowned. "I'm here. I know how to pack clothes."

She folded her arms across her chest. "Why aren't you on a plane with your brother?" She refused to let him know she was desperately glad to see him.

"Do we have to stand here for this conversation?"

"Fine," she said. The stairwell was narrow. Was he looking at her butt as they climbed the steps? Flustered and embarrassed at the mess she had created, she waved him to a chair at her tiny kitchen table. "Sit, Brody."

He cooperated, but the look in his eyes told her he was only biding his time.

She opened the fridge. "You want a beer?"

"No. I'm here to help you move."

"I don't need help *packing*. I've already told you that. Come back after dinner."

"Nope. Granny says you're in a fragile state. She doesn't want you exerting yourself."

"And what do *you* think, Brody?" Ah, hell. She was flirting again. Anytime she was around the handsome Scotsman, it seemed as natural as breathing. She handed him a Coke and opened one for herself, joining him at the table.

"Aren't you supposed to give up caffeine?" he said.

"Stop it. Right now. I refuse to take pregnancy advice from a man who has probably never even changed a baby's diaper."

He lifted an eyebrow. "Have you?"

"No. but that's beside the point. Seriously, Brody. You'll be in the way right now. I think I can load a few boxes without fainting."

He popped the tab on his soft drink and took a swallow.

When he set the can on the table, his lips quirked. "Sorry, Cate. I can't go back up the mountain without you."

She pointed a finger. "You're scared of your grand-mother."

"Damned straight. Besides, I thought you and I could make plans for the wedding while I help you pack."

His bland smile infuriated her. "There's no wedding... nothing to plan. This baby is mine. This pregnancy is mine. You're off the hook. If Miss Izzy is pressuring you, I'll talk to her."

Brody got a funny look on his face.

"What?" she demanded.

"Actually, Granny told me not to press the marriage thing."

Cate swallowed, refusing to admit her feelings were hurt. Did the tiny Scotswoman think Cate wasn't good enough for her grandson? "I see." She took a quick breath. "It's just as well. I told you it was a bad idea."

Brody leaned forward, elbows on the table, his gaze direct and intent. "You can trust me, Cate. I would never cheat on you, I swear. And our kid will have every ad-vantage."

"I'm not interested in your money, Brody."

"Money isn't evil."

"Maybe not. But it's not a substitute for love. You said it yourself. You don't want to settle down. It's okay. Re-ally it is."

"Damn it, Cate." He jumped to his feet and paced, all evidence of the relaxed Brody wiped away in an instant. "You have to understand. My parents divorced when Dun-can and I were children."

"I know. Isobel told me. And I'm sorry. But that's all the more reason not to jump into marriage."

"That's what I thought, too. Up until now. I felt like such

a stupid clueless kid when they split up. I thought they were pretty cool parents, actually. I never heard them arguing or fighting. At least not until they decided they were done. After that things got bad fast. That's when Duncan and I came to the States and spent a few months with Grandda and Granny."

"You were lucky to have them."

"More than you know. What I'm trying to say is that I spouted off some stupid stuff to you. But I want to retract that self-righteous speech. I need a do-over. Please, Cate."

Her chest burned. "You and I wouldn't stand a chance."

"You don't know that." He paused behind her chair and stroked the back of her neck. "We have something powerful between us, Cate," he said quietly. "We could make it work."

She stood up to face him. The fact that she wanted so badly to say yes told her she had to fight. "I can't do this right now. You're pressuring me, and it's not fair."

"So you'll think about it?" His lopsided smile was disarming.

"If I say yes, will you leave me alone?"

He brushed the back of his hand over her cheek. "If you're expecting me to be honest, you won't like my answer."

"Forget it," she muttered.

He caught a flyaway strand of her hair and rubbed it between his fingers. "May I ask you a personal question?"

"I suppose…" But she tensed inwardly.

His shoulders hunched the tiniest bit as if he was uncomfortable. "Would it be weird if I touched your stomach? I'd like to feel it. The baby, I mean."

"Oh." She swallowed. "I don't think it's weird. You do remember I was half-naked with you last night?"

His chuckle sounded raspy. "I might have been a tad

single-minded. Plus, you distracted me with your Amazonian breasts."

"Oh, please. They're not *that* big." She couldn't help giggling, and then was mortified.

"Made you laugh."

His satisfied masculine smile caught something deep in her heart and squeezed it hard. Being with Brody was like the first day of summer vacation. Everything seemed exciting and new, bursting with possibilities.

She bit her lip and told herself this tiny moment was no big deal. Lifting her shirt with one hand, she lowered the zipper on her old faded jeans. The pants hadn't been buttoned anyway. When she glanced up, Brody's cheeks were flushed and his eyes had a weird unfocused look to them.

"Go ahead," she said. "It's fine."

Slowly, he reached out and laid his large, warm palm flat on her swollen belly. Her navel and the surrounding real estate had never been particularly erogenous zones. But when Brody Stewart caressed the barely-there mound from the baby they had created together, her knees weakened, and she felt everything inside her melt.

She thought he might jerk his hand away. Seeing and touching the reality of conception was much different from a theoretical discussion about babies and marriage. Still, far from seeming squeamish about the pregnancy, Brody's gaze held wonder. "What does it feel like, Cate?"

"Odd. Wonderful. As if I have a secret, and I want to savor it." Did he even realize he was stroking her? Back and forth. Softly. Gently.

"Do you know if you want a boy or a girl?"

"I've thought about it, of course. I understand girls better than I do boys. The latter idea scares me, to be honest."

Having Brody touch her like this eroded all her high-minded notions of keeping distance between them. She should step away…break the connection. But how could she move when he was so obviously spellbound by the changes in her body?

# Nine

Brody was flooded with all sorts of disconcerting emotions. He wanted to coddle Cate and at the same time, he was consumed with a throbbing, urgent desire that went way beyond simple physical lust. Her gently convex tummy fascinated him. She was carrying a brand-new life. How incredible...

Only when goose bumps covered her skin did he realize how long he had been touching her. It was a struggle, but he made himself break the connection. "Thank you," he said gruffly.

She flushed adorably, tugging down her shirt and fussing with the zipper on her jeans. "Of course."

"Does it make me an insensitive male if I say I'll enjoy watching you get bigger?"

Cate wrinkled her nose. "I think *fat* is the word you're looking for..."

Brody chuckled. "I won't win this argument. C'mon, lass. Let's get started on your packing. The sooner I get you up to Granny's house, the happier she'll be."

In the end, it took them barely an hour to fill three suitcases and seven boxes, but they still weren't done. When Cate insisted on unloading the entire small bookshelf beside her bed, he winced and scratched his head. "Ye own a bookstore, woman. And I happen to know you have an e-reader. Why in the devil are we taking all these?"

His grandmother's houseguest-to-be thrust out her jaw, her expression mulish and determined. "My books make me happy and comfortable. I didn't know there was a limit on how much I was allowed to bring with me."

He held up both hands in surrender. "No limit. My apologies. But don't blame me if this won't fit into the two cars."

Cate sat down on the bed and burst into tears.

"What did I say? Is this a hormone thing?" Dear Lord, he was out of his depth already.

His question only made things worse. With a sigh of resignation, he joined her on the mattress and put an arm around her, tugging her head onto his shoulder. "It's going to be okay, my sweet Catie girl. Don't cry."

Seeing the capable, unflappable woman dissolve into an emotional mess shook him to the core. How was he supposed to support her and help her if she wouldn't let him get close?

Intuitively, he kept his mouth shut and simply held her. It pleased him that her hair was down. He stroked it absently, feeling the silken strands beneath his fingers. When Cate's sobs finally dwindled to sniffles, he reached for a box of tissues on her nightstand and handed it to her.

While she blew her nose, he studied her face…saw the smudges beneath her eyes. "You didn't sleep well last night, did you?" he asked.

Cate grabbed another tissue, her gaze wary and embarrassed. "How do you know that?"

"You get weepy when you're tired. I remember."

She bit her lower lip. "How can I sleep when my whole world is about to change?"

"I have a solution for that." He pulled back the comforter. "You need a nap, lass. It's Sunday. We've most of the packing done. When you wake up, I'll take you out for lunch or we'll order pizza."

"I'm not a child," she huffed. But she scooted underneath the covers and yawned.

Brody smoothed the sheets and pulled everything up to her chin. "Do you mind if I stay here with you? I've had a few sleepless nights lately myself."

Her eyes narrowed in suspicion. "We're *not* having sex."

"No, ma'am. I understand. But turns out, there are other things a man and a woman can do in bed together. I'll even stay on top of the covers if that will make you happy."

"It would make me happy if you had gone back to Scotland," she grumbled. But her protest was halfhearted at best.

Brody kicked off his shoes and stretched out with a sigh. The brief hint of spring had come and gone quickly. It was cold again. And damp. Cate must have turned the heat down when she was working. Now the air in the apartment seemed frigid.

When he shivered involuntarily, Cate snorted. "Oh, for Pete's sake. Get under the blankets, you big ornery Scotsman. But if you lay a hand on me, I'll scream."

He hurried to take her up on the offer before she changed her mind. As he settled in beside her, his muscles and bones relaxed instinctively. *Ah, bliss.* Four months ago he had spent a lot of time in this very room, though little of it sleeping. Cate's bed was a wrought iron antique, painted white. The crisp cotton sheets carried a hint of lavender.

They were both lying on their backs. When he turned on his side to face her, her eyes were open, her head turned toward him. Green irises with flecks of gold were shadowed with thick lashes a shade darker than her hair. She had one arm extended over her head, her fingers grasping a curlicue in the headboard.

On one memorable occasion he had tied her wrists to that sturdy metal. He shuddered in remembrance.

Cate closed her eyes. "I'm so tired I can't see straight, Brody. Would you, could you, just hold me? Please…"

He dared to tease her. "What about that screaming thing?"

"Oh, shut up and spoon me."

"I thought you'd never ask."

She turned her back to him, and he scooted in close. For a split second it was as if the world spun backward, and it was October, and he and Cate had just met.

He put his left arm around her and tucked it beneath her breasts, careful not to do anything that would get him kicked out. "Better?"

"Hmm…"

She was already half asleep. He listened to her steady breathing and kissed the nape of her neck softly. Holding her like this would cost him, but it was worth it. When Cate let down her guard, it was as if the past four months had never happened.

For a long time, he simply breathed in the scent of her. Where her bottom nestled in the cradle of his pelvis, his sex responded painfully. Everything about Cate was perfect for him. The warm, responsive, feminine body. Her sharp wit. A deep compassion for his crotchety granny.

He didn't know which was the right thing to do anymore. Didn't this baby deserve a father? Granny seemed to think that pressuring Cate into marriage was wrong. It wasn't what Brody thought he wanted. Even Cate seemed reluctant. Yet if he went home, he was almost positive the window of opportunity to secure her trust would be gone forever.

He closed his eyes and exhaled, feeling the air from

deep in his chest escape. If he were at home on the Isle of Skye, he'd be out on the water by now. Boats were the place where he could think. Candlewick was a quaint, charming town, much like a small Scottish village in many ways. But it was landlocked, and Brody felt bereft.

He must have dozed. His body was comfortable, even while his brain wrestled with weighty matters. Dreams wrapped him in spiderwebs of sensation. Struggling, confused, he pursued something always out of reach.

When he finally surfaced, Cate was sprawled half on top of him, one of her legs trapping his. She was still asleep.

He blinked and strained to see his watch. It was almost one thirty, which explained why his stomach was growling. "Catie," he whispered. If she slept too long, she'd be awake again tonight. "Catie girl. Wake up."

"Mmph." She buried her face in his neck. "Don't wanna," she muttered.

He grinned, palming her bottom and squeezing. "Fair warning, lass. If you stay on top of me much longer, something is going to happen, promise or no promise."

One eye opened. Apparently, she hadn't grasped the compromising nature of her current position. "Did you try to start something with me asleep?"

"Hey," he said, genuinely indignant. "You're the one who moved, not me. Now either go back to your own pillow, or—"

She put a hand over his mouth, her grin mischievous. "Or what?"

His little Cate was feeling amorous after her nap, but he couldn't afford another misstep on his part. He removed her hand. "You said *no sex*," he pointed out calmly, although he had an erection that could hammer steel.

"We've both said things we regret," she said, her tone

airy and teasing. "Situations change." She nipped his bottom lip with sharp teeth and then kissed him lazily.

He swallowed hard. "You're not playing fair, lass."

"Make me forget, Brody," she whispered. "Turn back the clock. I liked being crazy and impetuous with you."

Something about that last bit bothered him. Was he Cate's walk on the wild side? "We need to talk," he said, trying to ignore the way her breasts thrust against the soft cotton knit of her top.

She unfastened the top three buttons of his shirt and licked his collarbone. "Later, Brody. Later."

A man could only withstand so much provocation. "Ah, hell." He gave in, because to resist her would be insane on multiple levels. Jerking her top over her head and tossing it aside, he sighed with pleasure at the sight of her voluptuous breasts spilling out of her standard-issue white bra. "Being pregnant suits you, lass. Ye're a feast for the eyes."

They attacked each other, ripping at buttons and zippers and laughing as they rolled over and over in the bed. "Don't let me fall," she said, the words husky and low.

"Never, Catie girl. Never."

He moved over her and into her and sucked in a startled breath at the tight fit. Despite last night's insanity at the restaurant gardens, he felt as if he hadn't had her in days. Greedy and hungry, he thrust to the hilt, pressing the mouth of her womb. Cate's low groan urged him on.

Cate whimpered when Brody pistoned his hips wildly. What had started as lazy afternoon sex quickly escalated. Sharing this bed with him was at once familiar and new. She carried his child. He wanted her to marry him.

Wrapping her legs around his waist, she canted her hips, begging him wordlessly for more and then more. Her body was like a stranger to her. Nerve endings and sensations sprang to life, carrying her along on a tide of wanting so intense, she felt as if she literally might die if he stopped.

Though the room had been cold before, they were both damp with sweat. Brody was still half dressed, one leg of his jeans down around his ankle. Her bra was trapped somewhere, the strap digging into her arm. Nothing mattered. "Brody," she gasped. "Brody…"

His chest heaved with the force of his ragged breaths. Her orgasm bore down on her like a wild, runaway horse straining for freedom. She wanted to feel it all, every incandescent second, but she shattered in his arms, crying out his name again and shuddering endlessly as her body found blissful release.

Brody cursed and went rigid, filling her with his life force. Then he collapsed on top of her and moaned into her tangled hair.

Long seconds passed as they struggled for oxygen.

He stirred at last. "Holy God." It was more prayer than profanity.

"I always heard that some pregnant women were insatiable when pregnant. Never thought it would be me."

She expected him to laugh. Brody always found a way to make her smile. But for once he was oddly silent. When he eventually levered himself off her and started pulling on his clothes, her stomach growled loudly.

Brody stood and tucked his shirt into his pants. "How 'bout I grab us a pizza?"

She nodded, abashed at his odd mood. "That sounds good."

"Back in a few." He scooped up the key to the street entrance and tucked it in his pocket.

When the door at the top of the stairs closed behind him, she grimaced. Brody was right. They needed to talk. But first, she had to finish the job they had started. Fortunately, the upstairs apartment was small. It didn't take long to eye-ball closets and drawers and make sure she hadn't forgotten anything. Who knew if it would be six months or six weeks before she returned to this familiar nest? She and Miss Izzy might not get along on a daily basis.

Because her parents had structured almost every aspect of her life growing up, uncertainty was a hard thing to accept. Not only was she pregnant, but she had also agreed to look after a woman who might live forever or might keel over tomorrow. Cate was no nurse, but she was happy to keep an eye on Brody and Duncan's grandmother if it would give the family a feeling of security.

Brody returned in just under forty-five minutes bearing a box that smelled like heaven. Since she had cleaned up the kitchen already in preparation for leaving, she opted for paper plates and plastic cups.

They ate in an awkward silence that only increased in intensity as the minutes ticked by. Brody finished off his fourth piece to her two and drummed his hands on the table. "Tell me something, Cate."

The bite of pizza stuck in her throat. "Okay."

His mood was hard to pin down, somewhere between challenge and grumpiness, which was mighty strange for a man who had just had what Cate thought was the best sex of their relationship to date.

Since she couldn't read him, she allowed the silence to build. Let him take the conversational lead.

Finally, he leaned his chair back on two legs in a familiar pose. "A while back I asked Granny to tell me why you came to Candlewick five years ago. She said if I wanted to know, I'd have to ask you myself."

"I see." Her heart sank.

"So I'm asking." His beautiful cerulean eyes were stormy. His hands clenched in fists on the table.

The story didn't paint her in a flattering light. Maybe if she admitted the truth he would finally understand that marriage was out of the question. Where to start? After a pause to gather her thoughts, she shrugged. "You remember I told you that my parents were killed in a car accident?"

"Yes."

"It happened just as I started my first year of med school in southern California."

His brows flew to his hairline. "You're a doctor?"

"Not even close. I didn't make it until Christmas, unfortunately."

"What happened?"

"I fell in love."

He went pale beneath his tan. "Oh? With another student?"

"No. One of my professors. He was young, charismatic. I'd been traumatized by my parents' deaths. I was so damned lonely and vulnerable. It makes me sick to think about it. I was hungry for someone to care about me, Brody. How pathetic is that?"

He recovered some of his composure. "Makes sense, I suppose. You've told me your childhood left emotional wounds. With the tragedy on top of that, and you heading into a new environment… I guess I'm not surprised it was a hard time."

"He was married, Brody. A wife and two kids on the other side of town. Nobody knew. Certainly not me."

"Hell, Cate." He looked genuinely ill.

"The affair had been going on from the end of September until almost Thanksgiving break. Then one day it all came crashing down. The wife showed up on campus. Pitched a huge screaming fit. The board demanded his immediate resignation. And I was just the poor stupid woman who had fallen for his lies. Gullible. Pitiful. I packed up my tiny apartment, loaded my car and never looked back."

"Why Candlewick?"

"I did a real estate search for places as far away from the Pacific Ocean as I could imagine. Found the bookstore for sale. I had the life insurance money from my parents. This was the place I ran to…and meeting Miss Izzy was a bonus."

"I don't know what to say." Some of his pallor lingered.

She shrugged, feeling twinges even now of shame and self-loathing. "You don't have to say anything. The fact is, I'm a lousy judge of relationships. I won't marry you, Brody. I thought I had found the love of my life, and it turned out to be a gigantic lie. I can't go through that again. I like being on my own. It's safer that way."

# Ten

Brody had never been more confused. Cate was having his baby. That gave him a moral imperative to try to create a family. Didn't it? But he could hardly expect her to follow him to Scotland, not when she had baldly confessed that trust was hard for her.

As for Candlewick? There was nothing for him here, not one damned body of water bigger than a fish pond. Back in the Highlands he owned a whole fleet of boats, everything from sleek sailing vessels to tourist charters to workaday fishing trawlers. Water was his life. His ancestors had carved an existence from the icy waters of lochs and oceans.

The only alternative he could see was to work alongside his grandmother and try to help her as best he could. The prospect of never returning home to Scotland made him break out in a cold sweat. How had he let his life get so fucked up?

Unfortunately, the day deteriorated after Cate's confession. They loaded up both cars and locked the store, making it up the mountain to Isobel's home just before five. Unloading took another hour. Soon, Cate was ensconced in a luxurious bedroom just across the hall from Brody's.

His grandmother's suite of rooms was at the far end of the corridor.

Was Isobel playing matchmaker? Surely not. She hadn't been enthusiastic when Brody admitted he had more or less proposed to Cate.

For the time being, Brody's grandmother had hired a young woman from the town to come in and prepare dinner each evening. The presence of another person in the house made it virtually impossible to carry on any kind of personal conversation during the meal.

After dessert, Cate pleaded fatigue and disappeared.

Brody shoved back from the table and ran both hands through his hair. "I don't know if I can stay here, Granny. Maybe I should rent a place of my own for a few weeks."

"What are you afraid of, Brody?"

He jerked back, mouth agape. "I'm not *afraid* of anything, damn it. You were the one who said I needed to give Cate some space."

"Don't curse at me, young man."

"Sorry, Granny." He felt his neck heat. "I can't figure her out. Women are impossible."

"I may be ancient, but I still remember what it was like when your grandda and I were keeping company. I thought he was an arrogant American ass."

"Really?" Brody chuckled. "I didn't know that."

"Oh, aye. The upstart thought he could sweep me off my feet and shower me with presents. I sent him packing more than once."

"How did he finally win you over?"

"He loved me," she said, the words simple and direct. "When I understood that, everything was easy."

Brody changed the subject awkwardly and spent the remainder of the evening pretending everything was normal when it was anything but. This house was not an unfamiliar place. He'd visited many times over the years. Still, it wasn't *home*. Like a new shirt that didn't fit exactly right, somehow he knew that Candlewick and even his grandmother's beautiful and luxurious home were not where he was supposed to be.

Which brought him back to his original problem. What was he going to do about Cate?

He was still prowling the darkened hallways at midnight, unable to sleep, when he stumbled upon Cate raiding the refrigerator. She turned guiltily, her expression illuminated by the small appliance bulb, and tried to hide a piece of pie behind her back. "I thought everyone was asleep," she said.

"I'm not the food police." He kept his tone light. "Isn't this the one time in a woman's life when she's supposed to be able to eat anything she wants, guilt-free?" He rummaged in a drawer for a couple of forks. "Come sit. I'll join you if there's more." He hadn't been interested in dessert earlier…too much on his mind.

"There's plenty," Cate said. "I love this new cook. Butterscotch meringue pie. Haven't had anything like it since I was a child."

They sat at the small table elbow to elbow. Neither of them opted for the overhead light. Instead, a small decorative Tiffany lamp cast just enough glow for them to see their plates. At first, they ate in silence. The pie filling was smooth and creamy, and the topping was exactly right.

Brody came up with a dozen sentences in his head and cast them aside. There was too damn much at risk for him to alienate Cate. At last, he set his fork on his empty plate and reached out to take one of her hands in his. She jerked, startled, when he touched her, but she didn't pull away.

"Cate…"

"Yes, Brody?"

She was wearing thin flannel pajama pants and a peach

thermal top that made her skin glow. With her hair down around her shoulders, she looked far too young to be anyone's mother.

He traced her knuckles. Her long, slender fingers were bare. "I know I said I wouldn't push, but I'm torn, lass. Having us both live under this roof, given the circumstances, seems artificial at best. I want you, and I think you want me, but I can't see us sneaking around like two teenagers. It's disrespectful to Granny. I love her too much."

"I completely agree."

"So how do we get past the fact that I ache for you, Cate? Am I the only one?"

She shook her head slowly. "No. I feel the same way."

"If you married me, we could share a bed and a life."

Her expression was pained, her eyes dark with misery. "If you count the days we've actually spent together, Brody, we've known each other less than a month."

"True." He rubbed the heel of his hand against his brow where a headache pounded. "I understand what you're saying. On the surface, the idea is ridiculous. But over the centuries, people have married for far less practical reasons. We *like* each other, Cate. And we have sexual chemistry in spades. We've created a baby who carries our DNA. Why can't we give it a chance?"

"My doctors are here, Brody. And my health insurance. What would you do every day?"

He shrugged. "I don't know. Help Granny with the business. Look after you."

"Why is this so important to you?"

If he could answer that, his gut wouldn't be in a knot. "Honestly?" he said. "I'm not entirely sure. But I can't imagine walking away from you and our child, nor going back to Scotland and pretending my life is the same as it's always been. It's *not* the same, Cate. It can't be."

"What would you do about your boat business?"

Was he winning? Did he sense a softening in her? Elation filled his veins, but he tamped down his compulsion to press for the outcome he wanted. "Duncan is my partner. He's been handling the financial side for some time. The man is a whiz with numbers. If I ask him, he'll keep things running while I'm gone."

"And then what?"

"Damn it, Cate. Can't we make it up as we go along?"

She wrapped her arms around her waist. "If I'm going to agree to this, it would have to be for a set period of time. Let's say a year. We draw up legal documents that outline all the eventualities. After twelve months, if you go back to Scotland, the baby stays with me."

He clenched his jaw so hard, his headache tripled. "You expect me to leave my bairn?"

"That's why this won't work, Brody. You think getting married will solve something."

"It's a start," he said sullenly.

Suddenly, she grinned at him. "Wouldn't it be easier to live in sin?"

"Is that some kinky American custom I don't know about?"

"Oh, shoot. I forget you're not from around here."

"Are you casting aspersions on my intelligence?"

"Not your intelligence, Brody. Just your knowledge of American idioms. Living in sin is the same as shacking up."

"Shacking up?"

"Is there an echo in here?"

"Say what you mean, Catie girl."

She leaned a hip against the kitchen table, looking tired but incredibly sexy. "I don't think abstinence is going to work for us. Miss Izzy is less of a traditionalist than you think. I'll talk to her about it if you want me to."

"No," he said forcefully. The thought of having his lover discuss their sex life with his ninety-two-year-old granny freaked him out. "So let me get this straight. You won't marry me, but you're willing to fool around with a chaperone just down the hall?"

"Not a chaperone, Brody. Besides, she doesn't hear a thing at night when she takes out her hearing aids."

He put his hands over his face. "I'm in hell."

"Don't be so dramatic. I'm the one whose body is going to morph into a giant whale."

"Quit fishing for compliments. You're gorgeous and sexy. I can't look at you without wanting you. That's not going to change just because you have a cute little pregnant belly."

"It won't be *little* for long," she muttered.

He lifted her hand and kissed her fingers, lingering over the caress until Cate squirmed. "Do ye think you can sleep now?"

Heavy-lidded eyes looked up at him. "Will you be there?"

He stood, drew her to her feet and curled an arm around her waist, urging her toward the hall. "Aye. But I don't ken how much sleepin' there'll be."

Three weeks passed in the blink of an eye. Cate felt as if she were living two separate lives. She followed her usual schedule at the bookstore Tuesdays through Saturdays. The work kept her mind occupied, and when shipments came in, the job was physically challenging, as well.

All the hustle and bustle was good because otherwise, she would have spent her time incessantly wondering if she was falling in love with Brody Stewart. She experienced all the signs. Increased heart rate. Butterflies in her stomach when he walked into the room.

The same urgent desire that had catapulted her into a physical relationship with a near stranger now bound her to him infinitely more. She *liked* him, and that was dangerous.

On Sundays and Mondays, Cate spent quality time with Miss Izzy. The moment had come, in the old woman's estimation, to clean out her husband's personal effects. The task was heart-wrenching and poignant. Cate helped sort clothing, but Isobel had to make the final calls.

A few things were set aside for the grandsons. A pocket watch. A well-used shaving set with sterling silver handles. Most of the items—the bulk of them—went to a local charity.

Cate didn't know what Brody did all day every day, and she didn't ask. She assumed he and his grandmother were dealing with things at the company headquarters. Isobel thrived having her grandson nearby, and she relished having Cate under her roof, as well.

The mundane routine of Cate's daily activities was underscored with a breathless happiness. Brody came to her bed every night, but he always returned to his own room before dawn. It was doubtful they were fooling anyone. Still, Isobel didn't challenge them. Even the housekeeper who cleaned twice a week couldn't know for sure.

Cate and Brody's lovemaking was at times tender and sweet. Other nights he took her forcefully, as if trying to prove without words that they were a couple. Cate told herself she was living on borrowed time. This *pretend* situation couldn't last. Perhaps it was the pregnancy that enabled her to ignore all the ramifications lurking just beyond the bend in the road.

The pleasant fiction of her self-indulgent days was rudely ripped apart one afternoon in March. She had closed the bookstore early—given the lack of customers—and rushed up the mountain, eager to spend the evening with the man who was becoming far more to her than just the father of her unborn child, or even the lover who warmed her bed at night.

Brody was insinuating his way into her heart. His generosity and caring made her feel more special than anyone ever had. The man was almost unfailingly positive. He coddled her and showered her with gifts and made her feel sexy and desirable, even as her body bloomed with the changes of pregnancy.

The day that became a turning point gave no sign of what was to come. The only thing she could later recall was the old maxim that eavesdroppers rarely heard good of themselves. When she hurried through the house to find Brody and show him the stack of books she had ordered for the baby, she stopped short, just outside the den, when she heard her name.

Miss Izzy's voice was unmistakable. "Tell me, Brody," she said. "Why is this marriage to Cate so important to you?"

Cate's heart clenched in her chest, terribly afraid to hear his answer.

Brody's reply was oddly weary. "I don't know, Granny. Part of it is pride, I suppose. I don't want people thinking I got Cate pregnant and didn't do right by her."

"So it's about *you* and not the baby."

"Not *just* that," he said, definitely irritated by his grandmother's prodding. "I want to be listed on the birth certificate as the father. I want the kid to have my last name."

"And you don't think Cate will accommodate your wishes regardless of your circumstances?"

"Maybe. I suppose."

"Stewart men have always had a knack for thinking with something other than their brains."

"Granny!"

Cate could almost feel Brody's face flushing.

Isobel chuckled. "It's understandable. You've helped create a new life. But I have to ask you, dear boy. Do you love Cate?"

Where Cate stood, the pause seemed to last forever.

At last, Brody replied. "I think I *could* love her. We only met a few months ago, and I was gone for most of that. But when we're together…"

He trailed off.

Isobel didn't mince words. "You *want* her, Brody. And you feel possessive. But it's not enough. Once lust and desire transmute into something less urgent, you have to have more. To sustain a marriage, there has to be a foundation of some kind, something more than physical."

"Or I'll end up like Mom and Dad."

Isobel snorted audibly. "Your parents are both wonderful people—individually. Unfortunately, their relationship turned toxic, and you and Duncan became collateral damage."

"I don't want to fail at marriage."

Cate forced herself to enter the room, even though her stomach heaved and she felt like throwing up. "That's why we're not getting married." She gave Isobel as much of a glare as she could muster for her petite, elderly friend. "I appreciate your concern, Miss Izzy, but this is between Brody and me."

Brody's pupils had dilated as if he was alarmed or embarrassed or both. "I didn't say anything to Granny that I haven't said to you," he muttered.

*Except to admit that you aren't in love with me.* The raw truth hurt like hell. Only then did Cate realize she had been weaving painfully naive fantasies. She knew better than most that men used honeyed words and sex to get what they were after. Brody was far more honorable than the professor who had humiliated her, but at the end of the day, he wanted certain things, and he was willing to try everything in his power to sway her to his way of thinking.

"I'm not angry, Brody." She kept her voice completely even. Calm. All the while, her heart shattered into a million painful fragments. She turned back to Miss Izzy. "If Brody and I were ever to get married—and that's a big if—it would be for practical reasons, and it would be temporary only. We would have a lot of details to work out before that time comes."

Isobel sniffed. "In my day we'd say you put the cart before the horse, sweet, stubborn Cate."

Brody put his arm around Cate. "This is *our* problem, Granny. You'll have to trust us to deal with it in our own way and in our own time."

Cate stiffened when Brody touched her. She couldn't bear his nearness. Not right now. And his words poured salt in the wound that was her bruised and aching heart. She jerked free and wrapped her arms around her waist. Her voice wobbled despite her best efforts. "I don't consider this child a *problem*, Brody Stewart. I'm sorry that you do. If you'll excuse me, I think I'll skip dinner and have an early night. I'll see you both in the morning."

# Eleven

A man knew when he had been summarily dismissed. *Hell*.

Isobel's worried expression underscored his own unease. She shook her head. "I'm sorry, lad. Do you think she heard the whole conversation? I shouldn't have butted in."

Given his grandmother's obvious distress, Brody didn't have it in him to chastise her. "Not to worry," he said lightly. "I'll smooth things out with Cate."

"Not tonight."

"No," he said ruefully. "It won't be tonight."

Only when he undressed at 1 a.m. and crawled naked into his lonely bed did he realize how much he had come to anticipate the sweet hours with Cate at the end of each day. Her changing body was a miracle to him.

The wounded look he had seen in her eyes earlier troubled him. Was he at fault in this situation? He'd proposed marriage, damn it. What more could she expect from him?

A restless sleep did nothing for his disposition. He spent the long hours alternating between unsettling dreams and awakening to find himself with a painful erection. By the time he arrived in the kitchen the following morning, he was in a foul mood. It didn't help that Cate barely acknowledged his presence. Isobel had not made an appearance. One of the signs she was slowing down at all was that she liked to sleep in until nine or ten.

Brody poured himself coffee. The American custom was one he had embraced eagerly. Today he would have mainlined the caffeine if he could. Instead, he downed the first cup and started in on a second.

Cate sat at the small table in the breakfast nook, her head buried in a pregnancy magazine.

He took the chair at the opposite side of the table and stared at her, hoping to force a confrontation. Apparently, her ability to ignore him was greater than his patience for being ignored. "Look at me, Cate," he said, forcing the words between clenched teeth.

She glanced up, wrinkled her nose dismissively and returned to her reading.

Brody counted to ten. "I don't understand why you're so pissed at me," he said, aggrieved and truculent.

Very slowly, she folded down the corner of the page she had been reading, closed the magazine deliberately and met his ill humor with a bland green-eyed gaze. "You called our baby a *problem*," she said. "I wasn't aware that my child and I were such a great hindrance to your welfare. I *would* tell you to get the hell on a plane and head back to your precious moors, but you're not a man known for taking direction well, now, are you?"

Her snotty tone sent him into the red zone. "You don't want to mess with me this morning, Cate," he said, each word distinct and as threatening as he could make them.

His attempt at cowing her bounced off as if she had sealed her emotions in a deep freeze. "Go away, Brody. Let me have my breakfast in peace."

This time he had to count to twenty. He was angry and horny and completely out of his depth. No woman he had ever known could yank him in so many directions at once. "Tell me what you want, damn it. I'm tired of guessing and coming up short."

Her chin shot up and fire flashed in her eyes. "I don't want *anything* from you. I thought I had made that abundantly clear. In fact, I don't care if I ever—" She stopped dead and hunched over the table, her expression equal parts stunned and startled.

"What is it?" he snapped. "What's wrong?"

She didn't reply. Her gaze focused somewhere on the far side of the room. Her body had frozen into complete stillness.

He jumped to his feet and put his hands on her shoulders, shaking her gently. "Talk to me, lass. Are you ill?"

Her head fell back against his chest and a tiny smile crept across her face. "I'm fine."

He stroked her cheek. "You're scaring me."

"It's the baby, Brody. I think I felt the baby."

He sat down hard in the nearest chair, loath to admit that his knees were wobbly. "Is that normal? Does it hurt?"

She bit her lip, still with that look of intense concentration. "Normal? Yes, I think. I'm almost five months. It's time. I'm not sure what it should feel like, but there was something…"

"May I?" He reached across the small space separating them, not waiting for permission. Reverently, he placed his hand on the rounded swell of her belly. "Where, Cate? Show me where."

"Here." She took his fingers and shifted them a few inches. "I don't know if you can feel it from the outside."

But he did. Distinctly, yet subtly. A delicate flutter that rippled beneath her skin and warmed his fingertips. "Good God." The baby had been ephemeral to him until this moment. A tiny, unspecified, barely-there idea.

His breath lodged in his chest and his eyes grew damp. The flutter stopped. He glanced up at her, alarmed. "Why can't I feel it now?"

Cate shrugged. "I don't know. Maybe she's sleepy."

"He," Brody said with certainty. "A Stewart male to carry on the line."

"Good grief." Cate rolled her eyes, but when she looked at him, her earlier antagonism had vanished, replaced by a sense of dawning wonder. He recognized it, because the very same feeling snaked through his veins, making him the slightest bit nauseated. Such wild, unfamiliar emotion was unsettling.

"I'm sorry about yesterday," he said, stroking her hair from her face. "I hurt your feelings, but that wasn't my intention at all."

Some of her open joy faded away. She eluded his touch and stood, placing a hand on the table to steady herself as if her feet weren't on solid ground. "I'm sorry, too," she said, her expression sober. "I understand, I think. Or I'm trying to. I've been reading a lot, and everybody says men are at a disadvantage in the beginning, because the baby doesn't seem real."

Brody nodded slowly. "At the risk of sounding like a jerk, I'd say that's true. I've been more focused on you and how you're feeling."

"For me," Cate said, her eyes pleading with him to understand, "it's like everything I've known about myself is changing at once. My body. My emotions. My future. As scared as I was in the beginning, and as distraught, I never once thought about giving this child up for adoption. But that's on *me*, not on you. I won't let one crazy middle-of-the-night sexual encounter where I was fully participatory dictate the rest of your life. It's not fair to you, and it's not really fair to me."

"Why is it not fair to you, lass?"

She bit her bottom lip, her eyes shiny with tears. "Because I deserve to have someone by my side who is crazy in love with me. Maybe that won't ever happen. I don't know. But I do know that a lukewarm marriage of convenience and practicality sounds like a wretched, lifelong prison sentence."

Brody absorbed the hit without flinching. After knowing what Cate's parents had been like and then finally hearing the story of the man who had betrayed her trust and love by lying to her and humiliating her, he couldn't fault her logic.

Slowly, he nodded his head, his mind spinning. "I see what you're saying. I really do. But—"

She held up her hand. "Stop. Just stop. To you, this pregnancy is a problem, one you're trying so very hard to solve. I appreciate the fact that you're interested and that you care and that my welfare and the baby's are important to you. But I won't be any man's *problem*, Brody. I've spent my whole life being a problem for *somebody*. Now I'm on my own, and this baby is a miracle. I refuse to look at it any other way."

He swallowed the urge to argue and held up his hands. "Understood. Perhaps we could call a truce?"

Cate yawned suddenly, telling him that her night might have been equally as unsettled as his own. "Yes," she said simply. "I don't have the energy to do battle with you, Brody. But promise me you'll think about going back to Scotland. I'm very serious about that."

"Fine. I'll think about it." Still, no matter how much he missed his old life, he couldn't see himself walking away.

Cate struggled against an overwhelming tsunami of fatigue. She hadn't slept well without Brody in her bed. Admitting that weakness, even to herself, was alarming.

On top of her sleepless night, this latest confrontation had left her wiped out. "I'll see you tonight," she said, hoping to slip past him without incident. She needed to get to work.

He caught her arm as she walked by. "Thank you," he said gruffly.

They were so close she could inhale the masculine scent of his sleep-warmed skin. "For what?"

"Sharing that *first* with me. The baby moving. I'm glad you wanted our child, Cate. Pregnancy suits you."

She closed her eyes and allowed herself one brief moment to lean her head against his shoulder and absorb his strength. "You're a silver-tongued devil, Brody Stewart, but I'll take the compliment."

Stroking her hair, he chuckled. "Could you use any help at the bookstore today? Granny has decided not to go into work. She told me last night. The two managers are doing very well, and she wants them to know she trusts them. Actually, I was afraid the business would be in chaos with Grandda dying and Granny grieving, but things are solid."

"I'm glad." Cate sighed. Actually, she wanted nothing more than to climb back into bed. But the bookstore was her responsibility and her livelihood. "I'd love some company," she said. "Let me get a few things together and we'll leave in fifteen minutes… Does that work for you?"

He kissed her forehead and released her. "I'll have the car waiting."

Cate brushed her teeth and grabbed the large canvas tote that held the things she would need for the day. It was still packed from the afternoon before. On top were the handful of books she had been so excited to share with Brody. *Goodnight Moon. Pat the Bunny.* Two different Sandra Boynton board books. Already she was looking forward to snuggling with the baby at bedtime and singing silly songs as she rocked her son or daughter.

Wistfully, she removed the books from the tote and left them on the dresser. She had let herself get too far ahead on a road that went nowhere. There was a very good chance that Brody would not even be around for the birth. She still had four months to go.

Already, she struggled with the notion of where to set up a nursery. Did Brody and Duncan really want her to stay with Miss Izzy in the long-term? Cate was happy to keep her friend company, but Isobel's beautiful home was filled with priceless antiques and objets d'art. As soon as the baby started crawling and walking, the environment would become imminently unsuitable.

Cate was trying, really she was, to live in the moment and not to worry so much. With each day that passed, however, new questions arose.

Brody was as good as his word. When she stepped out the front door, he was waiting with the vehicle. But the car parked on the flagstone apron was not the nondescript rental sedan in which he and Duncan had first arrived. This beauty was a shiny, black, luxury SUV with tinted windows.

"What's this?" she asked, running an appreciative hand over the spotless hood.

Brody jingled the keys in his hand. "I bought it yesterday. Didn't make sense to keep the rental any longer since I'm going to be sticking around for a while."

"I see."

He opened the passenger-side door and helped her in. As he did, new-car smell wafted out to mix with the crisp morning air. Cate breathed in the appealing scent and fastened her seat belt with a sigh of appreciation. The seats were high-end leather, buttery soft and oh-so-comfortable.

Brody chuckled and reached out to turn on the radio. "I'm glad you like it. I listed your name alongside mine on the contract. If and when I go back to Scotland, you and the baby will have a safe, reliable means of transportation. The crash-test ratings for this model are impeccable."

"Brody?"

"Hmm?" He glanced in the rearview mirror and pulled out onto the winding road that led to town.

"You're doing it again."

"Doing what?"

"Trying to take charge of my life. I'm a grown woman. I already have a car, a perfectly reliable means of transportation."

His frown was quick and unmistakable. "You do have a car," he said, "but it's a dozen years old, and besides, it's way too close to the ground. When you're eight or nine months pregnant you won't be able to get in and out. Not only that, this car is perfect for a car seat. You can put the baby in and out without having to bend over and break your back."

"And I suppose you've already bought the car seat, as well?"

"No," he said. "I assumed you'd want to choose that for yourself."

Blatant sarcasm wasn't satisfactory at all when the object of her retort was too impossibly arrogant to realize she was making a dig at his expense. *She* kept drawing a line in the sand, and Brody continued to step right over it. If she wasn't careful, he'd end up in the delivery room helping some poor doctor deliver the baby.

Luckily for Brody, Cate was far too tired to put up a fuss about the car. She closed her eyes and catnapped during the quick trip into town. It was nice having someone looking after her. If she allowed it, Brody would wrap her in cotton wool and protect her from every difficult situation and challenging decision.

Unfortunately, she was going to have to develop a backbone very soon. Otherwise, the alpha-male Scotsman was going to take over her life entirely.

When they parked in front of the bookstore, all the businesses up and down Main Street were beginning to open for the day. The bank. The dry cleaners. The corner diner. An assortment of retail shops offering everything from clothing to candy. A handful of professional offices that accommodated lawyers and title companies and an acupuncture therapist.

Cate loved Candlewick's small-town ambience and relished the knowledge that her business was an integral part of the community. If she hadn't gotten pregnant, her life would have ticked along year after year with very little variation along the way.

This town and its residents had welcomed her when she arrived broken and alone. Izzy, in particular, had taken her under her wing. The old woman had seen Cate's lost soul and had coaxed Cate into wholeness and healing with homemade bread and cups of coffee and long, wonderful conversations about books and authors and whether or not the digital age was going to ruin intellectual curiosity.

While Cate was lollygagging and lost in thought, Brody had exited the driver's side and come around to open her door. "C'mon, woman. It's getting late."

His intervention startled her. She recovered quickly and hopped out of the car. Once she had unlocked the bookstore door and turned off the alarm, she turned to Brody. "Make yourself at home. Browse the shelves. I have a couple of things to do straightaway, and then I'll see if I can find a project for you."

He grinned, his eyes this morning the blue of a springtime sky. "Don't *invent* jobs for me, lass. I'm quite content to hang out and watch you work."

She left him in the New Fiction section, still laughing.

Her small office was tucked away in a corner at the back of the building. The antique rolltop desk that was her pride and joy always seemed to be stacked with catalogs and bills and advance reading copies. She had thought more than once about hiring help, but it had taken several years before she finally began showing a profit. Not only that, Cate was a very private person. It couldn't be just anyone she brought into her special spot.

This bookstore had saved her life. It was her home.

When the bell over the front door chimed a warning, Cate poked her head out of the office to see who it was. Brody was in the midst of greeting Sharma Reddick and her four-year-old twins.

Cate hurried out to meet them. "Hey, Sharma. I haven't seen you in weeks." The young mother shopped often at Cate's bookstore.

Sharma grimaced. "The boys had the flu. We're only now rejoining the land of the living. They were driving me crazy, so I promised if they cleaned up every one of their toys, I would bring them down here." She turned to Brody. "Cate is a genius. She fixed up that little corner over there several years ago. Now it's the best spot in town for parents who want a few minutes of peace and sanity while they shop."

Brody grinned and eyed the two mischievous boys. They were happily playing on a six-by-six, brightly colored rug. Cate had added a small train table, a container of plastic building blocks, a tub of Matchbox cars and an old-fashioned school desk that opened up and held crayons and paper for budding artists.

"Impressive," he said.

Sharma beamed at him. "Do you have children, Mr. Stewart? I'm a single mom, so I'm always on the lookout for child-rearing tips."

*Or fresh meat.* Cate maintained her smile…barely. Sharma was a dear, but that didn't mean Cate wanted her panting after Brody. "Brody is Miss Izzy's grandson, Sharma. He's here visiting and helping with the cabin business."

"I see." Now Sharma's eyes held a new appreciation. Gorgeous *and* rich? What woman could resist that?

Cate took Sharma's arm and steered her away from Brody. "Let me show you the new kindergarten level prereaders. I think the boys would love them, and it wouldn't hurt to get them interested before school starts in the fall."

Fortunately, the ploy worked. Brody was able to go back to perusing the Biography section, and he was close enough to the kiddie corner to make sure the boys weren't doing anything dangerous.

Sharma picked out two books each for the brothers and headed for the cash register, plucking her credit card out of her pocket. "It's a good thing my parents love reading, too. Now that they know about Dog-Eared Pages, they send the kids checks every few weeks to buy more books."

"Works for me," Cate said cheerfully. When she finished ringing up the sale, she glanced across the counter and grimaced inwardly. It would take her half an hour to clean up the mess. But Sharma was a great customer, so the inconvenience was worth it.

Brody was keeping his distance. Once, when Sharma wasn't looking, he shot Cate a comical look over the tops of the nearest shelves. Cate grinned at him. Sharma's pool of eligible men in Candlewick was limited. It made sense that she would see Brody in a positive light.

The woman, who was only a few years older than Cate,

gathered up her progenies and headed for the front door. "I'll be back soon," she promised. "Tell Miss Cate good-bye, boys."

Cate followed them, smiling, and then gasped as she stepped on something and her foot slid out from under her. She went down hard, landing on her right hip and banging her elbow on the floor.

# Twelve

Brody's head snapped up when he heard Cate cry out. Sharma and her twins were not even out the door yet. Cate was sprawled on the floor.

"Oh, Cate," Sharma cried. "I am so sorry."

Apparently, a small toy had unwittingly brought about the accident. Brody's heart stopped. Cate had fainted several weeks ago, but this was far worse. Had she bruised her abdomen?

Heart in his throat, he crouched beside her. Cate struggled to sit up. "Wait a minute," he said gruffly. "I need to make sure nothing is broken. It was an awkward fall." He ran his hands along her arms and then her legs.

Sharma hovered, squawking and apologizing and generally getting on Brody's nerves. "I'm all the time stepping on little toys at home. *See*, boys. See what you've done to poor Miss Cate."

The twins appeared suitably chastened.

Brody managed a smile. "I think it's best if we close the store so I can take Cate to the doctor. Do you mind turning the sign on your way out?"

"Of course."

Sharma took her dismissal well. She shooed her kids

out to the sidewalk, flipped the *open* sign to the opposite side, and closed the door behind her.

Brody sighed. "Good Lord." He picked up a tiny car. "Is this the culprit?"

Cate nodded. "It was my own fault. I didn't see it. I hit the floor so hard my teeth rattled."

She was trying to be funny, but Brody could see that she was hurting. "We need to get you checked out," he said firmly.

"My obstetrician's office is forty-five minutes away at the regional medical center. Honestly, Brody, I don't want to deal with that today. I'm fine, really. I'm sure I'll have some wicked bruises, but there's nothing the doctor can do for that."

"True. But you can't tell me you aren't worried about the baby."

She couldn't deny it. Those beautiful summer-grass eyes were dark with anxiety. "Of course I am," she muttered.

"Is there no doctor here in town who would see you?"

"Only a walk-in clinic. I've never met the people, but you don't need an appointment to get in."

"We'll start there, then." He bent and scooped her into his arms.

"I can walk, Brody," she protested.

"Humor me, lass."

He carried her out to the car and deposited her in the passenger seat. Then he made a quick jog back inside to retrieve her purse and lock up the store. He was gone, all in all, maybe four minutes.

When he returned, Cate had both hands on her belly.

"Are you hurting?"

She nodded. "Yes. But it's muscles and bones. I don't think the baby is in trouble. I can feel her moving around."

"Thank God." Relief made him light-headed.

The clinic was located on the outskirts of town in an area that was far less scenic than Main Street. The strip mall was home to a loan company, the clinic and a nail salon. Apparently, this was a busy time of day, because every parking spot was taken.

Before he could stop her, Cate had her hand on the door and was climbing out. "I can get in on my own, honestly."

"Damn it." He watched her walk gingerly inside. The stubborn woman was obviously in pain.

It took him three times around the block before he was able to find a legal parking space. He threw the car in Park, jumped out and hustled to the clinic. Though the storefront was uninspiring, the woman at the reception desk was friendly enough.

"Hello," she said. "May I help you?"

Brody scanned the mostly empty waiting room. "I need to go back with Cate Everett."

The woman eyed him with some suspicion. "Are you her husband?"

For a split second he thought about lying, but karma was a bitch, and he couldn't take any chances. "No."

"Family member?"

"No."

Her smile was kind, but her response firm. "I'm sorry. You'll have to wait out here."

Brody came close to losing it. He couldn't very well storm the castle, though. Cate had walked in under her own steam. Surely she wasn't in any real danger. Then again, what did these people know about babies?

His wait stretched from thirty minutes to an hour. Then half an hour more. He couldn't even text Cate because she had left her phone on the seat of the car. When he stood up to pace, the receptionist frowned, but didn't stop him.

In the interim, a few patients came out and left. A handful more checked in. What in the hell was taking so long?

When Cate finally appeared, Brody had worked himself into a frenzy. Only by studying her face was he able to put his fears to rest. She looked tired, but normal.

Once she had taken care of the bill, Brody took her arm and walked her slowly outside and down the sidewalk to where he had parked the car. "I told Granny I was taking you out for dinner," he said.

"It's only three o'clock," Cate protested.

"But you missed lunch, and that's not good for a pregnant lady. If you feel like riding in the car, I thought we'd go over to Asheville. I haven't been there since I was a teenager. Grandda took Duncan and me to a concert once."

Cate nodded. "I'd like that."

"We need to talk, Cate, and as much as I love my grandmother, we don't need an audience."

They were in the car and on the way by now, so he couldn't look at Cate directly, but she nodded slowly. "Okay. But no talking now, please. All I want to do is take a nap." She leaned her seat back and kicked off her shoes.

"Of course." He tuned the radio to a soothing station and adjusted the air. "Do you need a snack on the way?"

"They gave me crackers and two bottles of water. I still have one in my purse."

His hands clenched the wheel. "What did they say? Are you sure we don't need to get you to a hospital?"

She bent her knees and curled up in an awkward position. "Very sure. The nurse called and made me an appointment with my ob-gyn tomorrow. As a precaution. But I'm fine. They poked and prodded and checked all my vitals a dozen times. I think it freaked them out that I was already bruising. That's normal for me, though. The curse of fair skin."

He reached out and took her hand in his. "You scared the hell out of me, lass. I heard the thud when you hit the floor."

"It wasn't a picnic for me, either, Brody. And poor Sharma…"

"Serves her right if she was upset. She should have taken the time to clean up after those wild boys."

"They're not bad kids," Cate protested. "Just very active."

"If you say so."

Cate didn't try to pull her hand away. He was glad. He and Duncan had grown up every bit as rambunctious as the two little monsters who had visited the bookstore earlier. The Stewart brothers had suffered through broken bones and stitches and countless thrashings from their father. Even in the worst of those situations, he never remembered fearing for his *own* safety.

But when it came to Cate… Damn. He couldn't bear the thought of anything happening to her.

She was asleep almost instantly. He'd checked the route with his GPS during the long wait at the clinic. Now all he had to do was follow the road and think.

Summer would be here before he could blink, and with it, the need to return to Skye. The bulk of his tourist business took place during June, July and August. It wasn't fair to expect Duncan to cover for him that long.

Could Brody go back to Scotland for a couple of months and then return for the birth? Would his absence during that time create a rift between him and Cate that could not be repaired? Already, he felt guilty for leaving her when they first met. It made no sense, not really.

Never at any moment had Cate expected him to stay. He'd been in Candlewick back in October for the express purpose of checking on his grandmother and reporting back to the family. He'd been entirely up front with Cate about that.

The two of them falling into bed had been a complication he never saw coming.

Now they were having a baby.

No matter how many times he parsed the information, he couldn't come up with any clear answers.

He hit the outskirts of Asheville at rush hour. Though the mountains encircled the town, it was still a city, after all. Everybody was in a hurry to get home after work.

Cate didn't wake up until he had to slam on the brakes to avoid rear-ending a delivery truck that stopped without warning. "Sorry," he muttered.

She rubbed her eyes. "Please tell me we're close. I'm starving, Brody."

He chuckled. "Almost there." He'd Googled restaurants and found one in the heart of town that promised romantic fine dining. Neither he nor Cate were dressed formally, but it was only five o'clock, so he was counting on the early hour to make their attire unexceptional.

The small dining room was actually part of a boutique hotel. The maître d' welcomed them cordially and led them to an alcove partially hidden behind flowering trees. The corner booth was constructed of high-backed, dark, carved wood and cushions covered in crimson damask.

"This is beautiful," Cate said, smiling as she took in the white linen tablecloth and the crystal, silver and china.

"I was hoping you would like it." He seated her and slid into the adjoining bench. The ninety-degree angle of the booth meant he was close enough to touch her, but he could look at her, as well. That tiny detail was helpful, because this was an important moment, and he needed to be able to gauge her mood.

Their waitress was attentive but not obtrusive.

Cate gave the woman a bashful grin. "Don't judge me for this order. I'm eating for two and I skipped lunch."

"Not a problem, honey. I had three kids of my own. You'd better let yourself be pampered now. It's all downhill from there."

Brody passed Cate the basket of hot yeast rolls as the server walked away. "I hope she was kidding."

"How would I know?"

"Are you scared, Cate?" It was a question that had been on his mind a lot in the past few days.

She spread butter on the fragrant bread and took a bite, her expression reflective. "Scared? No. Not really. More like anxious and overwhelmed and totally unprepared. I know I still have months to get ready, but I'm not entirely sure what *ready* means."

It worried Brody that she had no mother or older sister to help her. Miss Izzy wouldn't be much of an asset, either. His grandmother's single childbirth experience happened about a million years ago. Everything about having babies had changed since then.

Over a meal of chicken Madeira and spinach salad and angel hair pasta, Brody touched on impersonal topics. Politics. The summer schedule at the bookstore. Miss Izzy's upcoming health checkup. With the server constantly coming back and forth, there were too many interruptions to say what had to be said.

At last, the dinner was done. The only thing left was to consume the rich slices of salted caramel cheesecake. For this course, they were left in peace. It helped that the restaurant had become progressively more crowded.

Brody put down his fork and took a deep breath. "I have to go back to Scotland soon, Cate. But I want you to marry me before I leave. Not so I can control you," he said hastily, "but because I want to have legal rights to protect you and the child."

Her expression was impossible to read. With her gaze focused on her dessert, he couldn't even see her eyes. "Why, Brody?"

The question was blunt. Unadorned.

"You know the reason. I've explained half a dozen times."

"I don't know why you're so worried about *protecting* me. You didn't even bother to come back and sit with me at the clinic. I was worried and bored and where were you? Checking email? It's not my problem that you need a piece of paper to ease your conscience, Brody Stewart."

Emerald eyes blazed at him. Cate was furious…probably had been the entire time since they left Candlewick.

His own temper kicked in. "Really? This is my fault now? Good God, Cate. I was pacing the floor. But I'm nothing to you, at least not as far as the doctor's office was concerned. I *wanted* to be with you. Of course I did. They wouldn't let me go back to the exam room."

"Oh." She deflated visibly. "I didn't think of that."

"Why didn't you tell somebody to come out and get me?"

She gnawed her lip. "I didn't want to seem needy. I just assumed you were happy where you were."

He grimaced and sat back in his chair. Cate, wearing a soft cotton sweater that matched her eyes, looked as if she was about to cry.

"We're not handling this very well, are we?" he said.

"No." She shook her head and used the cloth napkin to wipe her eyes.

The waitress approached with their ticket, but Brody waved her off. "Marry me, Cate," he said quietly. "Please. We can take a quickie honeymoon and then be back here to set up the nursery before I go."

"Before you go to Scotland, you mean..." It wasn't a question. Cate recognized his responsibilities almost as well as he did.

"Yes. I'll be gone eight weeks, ten at the most. That will put me back in Candlewick in plenty of time for the birth."

"And after the baby comes?"

This was the part that tightened his throat and wrenched his stomach. "I don't know yet. You'll have to trust me to figure that out." It was asking a lot of a woman whose vulnerabilities had been built betrayal by betrayal.

Her face was pale, her expression set. "I don't want to be married in a church. Not when we both know this won't last."

The stubborn tilt of her chin threatened to ignite his temper again, but he forced himself to see beyond her truculence to the many ways she had been let down by the people in her life.

"If that's what you want. We can have a civil ceremony." Already, regret trickled through his veins. This wasn't how it was supposed to be. Cate deserved so much more.

"Swear to me you'll never try to take my baby away from me."

He said a word beneath his breath that he rarely used. Her lack of faith cut deep. "You have my word, Catie girl. You can trust me, I swear."

# Thirteen

A week later Cate stood in front of the cheval mirror in her bedroom at Isobel's house and examined her reflection with dismay. Buying a wedding dress for a simple ceremony when a woman was almost six months pregnant was not an easy task. Particularly in a place like Candlewick.

Because Cate hadn't felt up to a shopping trip in the nearby county seat, she had resorted to a trio of purchases online and had the packages overnighted. Unfortunately, none of the gowns worked.

Cate had in mind something simple but elegant. The first one was frillier than it had appeared in the photograph. She hated it so much she didn't even try it on. The next dress draped tightly and showed her tummy far too much. This last one was the wrong shade of cream, making her look washed out.

She undressed and tried not to panic.

By the time she and Isobel had repacked the order and passed the box off to Brody with instructions on how to handle the shipping, Cate was exhausted and near tears again. She hated the weepy feeling.

Isobel urged her to sit. "All right, my sweet lass. Let's

take another tack. Would ye perhaps be interested in seeing my wedding dress? It's old-fashioned, of course, but it's been in a cedar chest since the week I wore it, and 'tis in good condition. It might suit."

Cate sniffed. "I'd love to see it." Miss Izzy was tiny. This would never work. But she didn't want to hurt the old woman's feelings. "Of course I would."

She followed the Stewart matriarch down the hall to the large master suite. Isobel hadn't changed a thing since returning home as far as Cate could tell. Geoffrey's pipe still lay on the dresser.

The cedar chest sat at the end of the massive four-poster. Isobel raised the lid, bent and carefully lifted out a tissue-wrapped bundle. She carried it around to the side of the bed and laid it reverently on the mattress. Suddenly, she stopped and put her hands to her face. "Ah, heavens, lass. I'm sorry. I didn't think this would make me weep. I miss my Geoffrey."

Cate put an arm around her and sighed. "We're a pair, aren't we? You grieving and me hormonal. It's a wonder Brody hasn't run for the hills. Are you sure you're okay with him marrying me? I wouldn't do anything in the world to cause you more heartache."

Isobel leaned her head on Cate's shoulder and wiped her eyes with a dainty lace-edged handkerchief. "I think it's the right thing to do, Cate. Giving the bairn a legitimate birth. And as for you and Brody, well, time will tell."

The quavering words were hardly a ringing endorsement. But Isobel, like many of her countrymen, was practical and down-to-earth. She'd lived a long time and seen it all.

Cate stepped away and touched the tissue-wrapped bundle. "I don't think we should disturb the dress, Miss Izzy. I'm a lot taller than you are. And not as thin."

"Nonsense." Isobel straightened her spine. "The differences in our heights will make it tea length, which is perfectly acceptable for a courthouse wedding. And I wasn't always so scrawny. I started shrinkin' when I got old."

Cate couldn't help laughing. "If you're sure."

"Take it there in the bathroom and have a go at it. I have a notion ye'll be surprised."

Isobel's wedding gown was a dream, a romantic, exquisite vision of times gone by. Cate undressed, slipped it on and looked in the mirror.

From bodice to hem, the fit was perfect, thanks in most part to the timeless design. Heavy cream satin. Cut on the bias. Not a single pearl or bead or speck of lace. It was astonishingly perfect.

The wide, low-cut neckline showcased Cate's assets. The fabric was designed to cinch beneath the breasts and fall freely to the floor. The fact that the hem landed a couple of inches below her knees proved Miss Izzy's point. On Cate, the wedding gown was tea length.

The rich, lustrous material was soft to the touch. It slid over her rapidly increasing belly gently—by no means hiding her pregnancy—but instead, subtly emphasizing her condition. With one last glance in the mirror, Cate opened the bathroom door and stepped out.

Isobel's eyes brightened, and she exclaimed, "Ah, lass. Ye're a vision, 'tis true. Please tell me you like it. Lie if you have to. I've got my heart set on it now, you wearing my dress, that is."

Cate shook her head in bemusement. "Of *course* I like it," she said. "I feel like a princess."

"Don't move," Isobel said. She scurried across the room to the dresser. Lifting the lid on a large, carved wooden box, she examined the contents, then scooped something out.

She turned back to face Cate. Her hands were cupped

together, hiding the prize. "Don't look, Cate. I've another surprise for ye. In fact, close your eyes. Don't peek until I give ye the word."

"Yes, ma'am." Cate stood in one spot obediently, not sure what Isobel had up her sleeve next. Moments later she felt the old woman's small, gnarled fingers brush the back of her neck.

"Geoffrey gave me these on the day we were wed," Isobel said. "The puir man nearly bankrupted himself, but he was determined his bride would have a suitable wedding gift." She steered Cate toward the mirror. "Ye can look now, lass."

Cate opened her eyes and gasped softly. "Oh, wow. They're gorgeous, Miss Izzy." The strand of pearls was perhaps twenty inches long. It fell just at the tops of Cate's breasts. The color of the aging pearls matched the dress perfectly. Cate touched the creamy beads reverently. "I don't think I can wear them, though. I'd be terrified they might break. I do appreciate the thought."

Isobel got up in her face and shook a finger. "Don't talk back to yer elders, my girl. Brody's grandfather picked these out, and now Brody's bride will wear them."

"This isn't a real wedding, Miss Izzy. You know that. It seems disrespectful at the very least."

Isobel harrumphed. "Ye'll still be legally wed, no matter what nonsense you and my grandson have cooked up between you. History means something to we Scots, Cate." She touched Cate's baby softly. "This bairn inside you carries the blood of Highland clansmen. Strong. Honorable. Wed to the land they loved. And by the by, I can't believe you and Brody are being so stubborn. It's the twenty-first century. We should know by now if this wee one is a boy or a girl."

Cate grinned, still stroking the pearls warmed by her

skin. "It's going to be a surprise. To all of us. Brody and I want it that way."

"Makes no sense to turn yer back on technology," Isobel muttered. Her criticism was not new. She was like a little child anticipating Christmas when it came to this baby.

Cate took one last look in the mirror and exhaled. "I suppose we're done here. The dress. The pearls. I already own a pair of ivory sandals that will work. Thank you for doing this, Miss Izzy. You saved me."

Brody stood in the foyer of his grandmother's elegant home and wrestled with the knot in his tie. Under other circumstances, he would be wearing his full dress kilt on his wedding day. Instead, he'd been forced to settle for a dark, hand-tailored suit. The uniform of the wealthy American male was perfectly acceptable, but Brody was Scots to his bones.

He should be wearing his kilt.

The two women in his life were supposed to have met him fifteen minutes ago. The delay stretched his nerves. His hands were clammy. His stomach churned.

When Cate appeared without fanfare from the hallway, his breath caught in his chest. "C-cate," he stuttered.

Her smile was tentative. "Hey, Brody. We're almost ready. Your grandmother forgot her hearing aids and went back to get them."

"Ah." He cleared his throat. "You look incredible, lass." Her hair fell like liquid gold in softly curving waves.

Cate smoothed her skirt self-consciously. "This is your grandmother's wedding dress. I couldn't find anything that would work, so she offered me her gown. It's not too much, is it?" Big green eyes stared at him.

He shook his head. "Not at all. You look like a Madonna." He wanted to say more, but she seemed as nervous as he felt, and he didn't want to venture into intimate territory when they weren't going to be alone.

Since Isobel arrived moments later, he was glad he had held his tongue.

Soon, they were on their way down the mountain. The county seat was thirty-five miles away. Isobel and Cate sat in the back of the car, leaving Brody alone with his thoughts. The old adage about it being bad luck for the groom to see the bride before the wedding wasn't really practical in this situation. There was no one to drive the females to the courthouse but Brody.

He had asked Cate in a roundabout way if there was someone she would like to have with her during the ceremony. She had said no. That worried him. Shouldn't Cate have at least one or two girlfriends to confide in? Isobel was a wonderful woman, but several decades separated her and Cate.

He glanced in the rearview and unexpectedly caught Cate staring at him. Her cheeks were flushed, her expression hard to read. Was she thinking about backing out of this wedding? The possibility made him antsy.

At the courthouse, their little trio elicited few stares. Despite the pregnant bride and her elderly attendant, Brody, Cate and Isobel were far from being the most unusual people waiting to be wed.

At last, it was their turn. Brody was so rattled it took him three tries to find the pocket where he had tucked Cate's wedding ring. Suddenly, the whole thing felt wrong.

Cate picked up on his unease. "Brody?" She scanned his face. "Are you sure this is what you want?"

"I didn't mean for it to be so clinical," he muttered. "We should at least have had a minister."

Cate lifted one beautiful shoulder and let it fall. "You needed legalities," she said quietly. "This will suffice."

Soon, the judge was speaking. Brody couldn't have repeated a single word or phrase of the ceremony afterward, even if he'd been faced with a firing squad. His whole brain went blank. All he could do was stare at his bride and mutter his responses at the appropriate places.

The only one that really registered was *with this ring, I thee wed*. He repeated the words and slipped the circle of platinum onto Cate's slender finger. Too late, he wished he had bought her an engagement ring, as well.

She curled her fingers into a fist and exhaled audibly. To his surprise, she had a ring for him, too. It was heavy and wide, the gold etched with a Gaelic pattern. When she took his hand in hers and pushed the ring against his knuckle, her touch made him shudder.

Suddenly, he wanted her. Intensely. Inappropriately, given the witnesses around them. Hoping that his jacket hid the state of his arousal, he helped her with the ring and kept her hand in his for the final words.

At last, it was over. Granny Isobel cried and hugged them both. Cate smiled, but she was pale, too pale.

Brody took Cate's shoulders in a gentle grasp and bent his head. "Happy wedding day, Mrs. Stewart." He kissed her long and deep, his heart slamming in his chest. Cate's lips clung to his. Her scent filled his lungs.

Slender arms came up around his neck, and she clung to him. "Aye, Mr. Stewart," she whispered. "I suppose it is."

He held her carefully, very aware of her baby bump. Isobel interrupted his concentration. "Tell her about the surprise, Brody," she said, her eyes twinkling with excitement. "Tell her."

Cate pulled away and smoothed her hair. "Surprise?"

Brody gave his grandmother the stink eye and waved her off. Escorting Cate to a corner of the room, he bent his head and kissed her temple, because he couldn't help himself. Touching her was an addiction. "Mrs. Tompkins is going to stay with Isobel for a few days. Granny packed your bags. They're in the back of the car. I've booked us a four-night honeymoon in Key West."

Far from being excited, his new bride frowned. "That's not necessary. You know this wedding isn't the real thing. A honeymoon would be inappropriate and over-the-top."

He held his temper with difficulty. "Make no mistake, Cate. We're married. *For real.* You are my wife, and I'm your husband." Saying the words aloud gave him an odd feeling.

"For now," she said, her expression both mulish and panicked.

His momentary anger faded as rapidly as it had come. Poor Cate looked overwhelmed. "Don't make a big deal about it," he said gently. "Everyone knows that life with a newborn is difficult and chaotic. If it makes you feel better, think of this as a pre-baby, relaxing getaway. You deserve to be pampered."

"I'm not sure I feel like flying in my condition."

"I've chartered a small, private jet. We'll be the only passengers. You'll have plenty of privacy and room to be comfortable."

"I suppose you've thought of everything." She bit her lower lip.

He took a gamble. "I won't make you go, Cate. I can cancel if that's what you want."

She reached for his lapel, adjusting the single white rosebud pinned there. Brody had bought her an enormous, expensive bouquet of matching roses with freesias and eucalypti. "I've never been to Key West."

"Neither have I. We can explore together."

"And share a bed?" Those cat eyes stared at him blandly.

"It *is* a honeymoon," he pointed out. "And it's our wedding day."

Sexual tension shimmered between them. For a moment he flashed on an image of him lifting her satiny skirt and taking her up against the wall. Sweat beaded his forehead. "Yes or no, Catie girl. What's it going to be?"

He saw the muscles in her throat work as she swallowed. This close to her, he could see the deep valley between her breasts.

"Take me to Key West, Brody. I want to be alone with you before you go back to Scotland."

# Fourteen

Cate felt like a fairy-tale princess if one overlooked the fact that she was six months pregnant. Isobel had hugged her and cried as they left the courthouse. Both Brody *and* his grandmother had insisted that Cate continue to wear her wedding dress and carry her bouquet. There was no hiding the fact that she was a very unusual bride.

During the brief drive to the Asheville airport, Brody behaved himself. When he held her and kissed her after the ceremony, she had felt the evidence of his arousal. Knowing he still wanted her went a long way toward soothing her doubts. Perhaps Brody was right when he said that many couples began a life together with much less in common.

She had dreaded the usual airport ordeals, but her fears were groundless. Apparently, Brody's money made a host of hurdles disappear. In no time at all, they boarded the sleek private jet and strapped themselves into large, comfy seats. Although there was no flight attendant, the small, luxurious plane was stocked with every conceivable amenity.

While the pilot and copilot ran through the pre-flight checklist, Brody offered Cate a flute of sparkling cider.

"To my blushing bride," he said, touching his glass lightly to hers.

He was incredibly handsome in his tailored suit that fit his masculine, athletic frame perfectly.

Cate drank thirstily. It had been hot in the courthouse. She felt limp and rumpled. Because she had been too nervous to eat before the ceremony, now she was starving. "Are those sandwiches?" she asked, trying not to let Brody see how totally freaked out she was.

His grin was indulgent. "Aye." He opened the container and offered it to her. "We'll have a special dinner tonight, but this should hold us until then."

Cate was glad of the meal for more reasons than one. Eating gave her a way to ignore Brody to some extent. Only a narrow aisle separated their seats. The whole cabin was small, and Brody was a large man. His presence made her shaky. Or maybe she was getting airsick.

At this point in their relationship, her feelings for him were a weird mélange of excitement and dread.

Fortunately, by the time she finished eating, there was plenty to occupy her attention outside her small window. The pilot had flown south and east, and now their route hugged the coastline. She spotted miles of ocean sparkling far below.

Brody startled her when he touched her shoulder. "How are you feeling, Cate?"

She turned her head reluctantly. This man was her husband. *Her husband.* "Um, fine, I suppose."

His grin was lopsided. "Hardly a glowing affirmation on your wedding day." He caressed her elbow, his warm fingers sending gooseflesh down her spine and everywhere else.

Out of nowhere, stupid tears threatened again. "Stop it,

Brody. Don't pretend. Playacting isn't necessary. I already feel like a fraud. You'll only make it worse."

His lighthearted smile was instantly replaced by a scowl. Blue eyes turned icy, and his jaw tightened. "Make no mistake, Catie girl. This marriage is real. Ye may not have had ten bridesmaids and a string quartet, but you *are* my wife. For better or worse." The utter determination in his gravelly voice sent a frisson of unease through her belly.

"And what if it's for worse? What then?" Despite her best efforts, tears spilled over and rolled down her cheeks.

Brody's expression hardened. He released her. "You know the options. We stay married for the bairn, or we get divorced."

"I don't know why you made us do this," she cried.

He stared at her, his expression glacial. "I never forced you, Cate. That's not fair."

She swallowed hard. He was entitled to his anger. Gripping the armrests, she sniffed and then wiped her face with the back of her hand. "I apologize. You're right, of course. It's been a difficult few weeks. At the risk of sounding like a cliché, these stupid pregnancy hormones are making me a little crazy."

He nodded, his gaze hooded. "Why don't you rest? I'll wake you up when we land."

The closer they came to Key West, the more Brody fumed and brooded. He had only himself to blame for this colossal mess. He'd pushed her too hard. And the hell of it was, he was not at all sure he had done the right thing. Not when it made Cate so skittish.

She had been more comfortable with him back in October when they barely knew each other.

Now those wary cat eyes constantly watched him. What was she thinking? How was he supposed to guess?

She kept her emotions so damned guarded all the time. Why couldn't she relax and trust him? Was that so much to ask?

He studied her while she slept. Her hair was caught up today in a fancy concoction that was nothing more than a challenge to a hungry male. Already he imagined removing each pin until the entire mass of soft, silky waves tumbled into his hands.

When she rode him, that curtain of hair would fall across her full breasts. The image in his brain sent a signal to his groin, increasing his discomfort. In his gut, he believed that sex was the place they connected. Maybe if he kept Cate in bed for the next four days they would find enough common ground to survive this marriage.

She slept deeply, her head tilted to one side. It was no wonder he had fallen instantly in lust with her last October. She was exquisite. Creamy skin. Classic features. Only now did he acknowledge the stubborn tilt to her chin. It should have been a tip-off.

Still, he would have pursued her regardless. Nothing short of a wedding ring or an outright no on her part could have dissuaded him from exploring the intense sexual attraction that had tormented him from the first moment he saw her.

A quiet ding interrupted his troubled thoughts. The copilot appeared in the doorway. "We'll be landing shortly, Mr. Stewart."

"Thank you."

When the man disappeared, Brody shook Cate's arm gently. "Wake up, Cate. We're almost there."

She surfaced slowly, her expression groggy. "That was fast."

"You were out for a long time."

"Sorry," she muttered, smoothing her skirt.

"I'm glad you rested," he said simply. "Stress is exhausting."

"And what about you?"

"I dozed a time or two."

"That's not what I meant. I want to know if all this has been stressful for you?"

"Of course it has," he said. "Look, Cate." He stopped, weighed his words and sighed. "I propose a truce. We could both use a holiday, right?"

She nodded. "Definitely."

"Then let's do that," he said. "We'll agree not to talk about the wedding or the marriage or the baby at all. Just two people running away from home to have a little fun in the sun."

Cate held up her left hand, the one wearing his ring. "And I'm supposed to forget about this?"

He grimaced. "Take it off if you want to. I wouldn't expect you to be uncomfortable."

She leaned across the aisle and took his hand in hers. "I don't want to take it off, Brody," she said earnestly. "But I like your idea. No more squabbling until we're back in North Carolina. It's a deal."

The feel of her warm, slender fingers twined with his larger, rougher, masculine ones settled something in his gut. "You think we can go four whole days without fighting?" he teased.

At last, her smile was genuine, her eyes unclouded. "We'll give it our best shot."

After that, the afternoon improved. Their landing and deplaning in Key West was low-key and uneventful. Brody and Cate both were taken aback at how tiny the airport was. Even so, the car Brody had ordered was right outside, ready to whisk them away to their waterfront hotel.

There were no natural beaches in Key West. The island

was built on the remnants of an ancient coral reef, rocky and remote. Still, who needed sand when brilliant blue waters and tropical breezes made the island a haven for artists and musicians and writers and tourists like Cate and Brody.

Despite Brody and Cate's détente in regard to the wedding, the hotel was prepared to give them the full bridal experience. It was too late for Brody to wave off the fanfare, so he stood by in silence, groaning inwardly as the manager greeted them effusively and insisted on procuring a crystal vase for Cate's bouquet.

Finally, the flurry of hotel employees departed, leaving the newlyweds alone in what was by any description an incredible suite. Cate threw open the double French doors and exclaimed. "Oh, Brody, this is amazing."

The air was warm and soft and fragrant with the scent of bougainvillea. Their rooms were on the top floor of a three-story building. As she leaned over the railing to look below, he had to remind himself not to hover. Cate was a grown woman. She was in no danger of falling.

"I'm glad you like it," he said. "I thought about booking a B and B, but I decided we might enjoy a little more privacy."

She looked over her shoulder at him. Her face was solemn, but her eyes danced. "Just to be clear, we're talking about sex, right?"

He felt his face heat. "*You're* the noisy one," he pointed out.

Her eyebrows went up. "Brody Stewart. That's not a polite comment."

"But factual."

When Cate laughed, something inside him relaxed. This was the place where he and Cate worked best. The intersection between carnal and casual. If they could keep their relationship easy and uncomplicated, this trip would be well worth the emotional and financial cost.

He shrugged out of his suit jacket, loosened his tie and unbuttoned the top buttons of his shirt. "I made dinner reservations for seven. Does that suit you? I thought we'd stay here in the hotel since it's our first night."

"Sounds perfect. I'll shower and change."

"You could still wear the dress," he said, hating to see it go.

Cate wrinkled her nose. "I'm rumpled and damp. I brought several new things. I won't embarrass you, Mr. Stewart." She handed him the strand of pearls. "Stash these in the safe, will you?"

He took the pearls and dropped them on a nearby table. "Come here, woman. I haven't kissed you in hours."

Dragging her close, he found her lips with his and dove in. The taste of her destroyed his good intentions. He'd intended to remind her that she was his now. What he discovered instead was that the ground beneath his feet was alarmingly unsteady.

Kissing Cate Everett, his lover, was one thing. Kissing Cate Stewart, his wife, was entirely another. Feelings he hadn't expected buffeted him from all sides. Tenderness. Protectiveness. Raw, urgent need.

He tamped down his lust with great effort. Cate leaned into him trustingly, her arms linked around his neck. "I'm too fair-skinned for many hours in the sun," she whispered. "I think we'll need to spend a lot of time in our suite."

"In bed," he muttered. It wasn't a question.

She wriggled closer. The slick fabric of her dress rubbed against his suit, creating some kind of erotic friction that threatened to incinerate him from the inside out. "Yes," she said, the word drawn out on a sigh.

In desperation, he thrust her away, holding her at arm's

length until her eyes opened, and she stared at him. "I think we should pace ourselves," he said desperately. He wouldn't be accused of using sex to get his way.

Cate pouted dramatically. "I thought honeymooners usually slammed the door and went at it like rabbits."

"What would you know about it?" he asked, deliberately snarky to give himself time to ratchet down. "Have you ever been on a honeymoon before today?"

"No. Have you?"

"Hell, no. But I'm damned sure the groom is supposed to provide romance leading up to the main event."

"Romance isn't all it's cracked up to be," she said, her eyes reflecting memories he wanted to obliterate, memories of the idiot who had hurt her so badly.

He ran the back of his hand across her cheek. "Maybe you've been with the wrong person before," he said softly. "Could be that you and I are exactly the right combination, Mrs. Stewart."

"We aren't supposed to mention weddings and honeymoons and my new marital status," she reminded him.

"You started it," he said. "Go take your shower, Catie girl. I'll wait for you." He would wait forever if need be.

# Fifteen

Cate stepped out of her unique wedding dress with more than a little wistfulness. Today, standing beside Brody Stewart and saying her wedding vows in front of a judge, she felt beautiful and desired. The fact that it was more sex with Brody than soul-mates-until-the-end-of-time was a distinction that didn't bother her at the moment.

She was in Key West with a sexy, ruggedly handsome man who wanted to make love to her nonstop for four days. That kind of thing was good for a woman's self-esteem. Particularly when she was growing out of all her clothes and already finding small silvery stretch marks.

The bath enclosure was decadent in the extreme—four separate showerheads and walls of beautiful taupe marble veined in gold. She wrapped a towel around her head to protect her hair and stepped in with a sigh of pleasure. As she washed with the expensive shower gel she found in the caddy, she got hot and shaky as she thought about the hours to come.

Was it normal to feel so wanton, so out of control? The thought of his hands caressing her breasts made her knees wobbly.

When she was clean and dry, she tweaked her hair and

then rifled through her collection of brand-new maternity clothes. At her recent doctor's appointment, the scales had reflected an increase, but nothing too terrible. Tonight was her wedding night. She wanted to look extra special.

Fortunately, one dress fit the bill. Since joining a couple of social media groups for expectant moms, she had discovered all sorts of helpful advice. One designer in particular was known for creating special-occasion dresses that would expand along with a pregnant woman's waistline.

Cate had researched and ordered a slender tank dress made of ribbed cotton gauze that fell to her ankles. Spaghetti straps braided from the same fabric were intertwined with tiny gold metallic strands. The colors were an impressionist canvas of celadon, ivory, tangerine and gray.

The soft translucent fabric was lined with a similar thin gauze in ecru. Though the dress clung from shoulders to knees, the style and the fabric were flattering in the extreme.

After touching up her mascara and adding a bit of eye shadow for evening drama, Cate stepped back and examined her reflection in the mirror. Her eyes danced with excitement. Maybe Brody was right. Once the baby came, it would be a very long time before Cate had the same freedom she enjoyed now. It made sense to enjoy this trip and her companion.

She tiptoed back into the living room, hoping to surprise him. Instead, she was the one to suck in a startled breath. Brody lay sprawled on the sofa deeply asleep. He had unbuttoned his shirt all the way, giving her a tantalizing glimpse of hard male abdomen.

The man was ridiculously ripped. All that boating, presumably.

She knelt beside him on the rug. The evidence of late-day stubble shadowed his jaw. His eyelashes were long and thick, his nose straight and masculine. If her baby was a boy, she wanted him to look like Brody.

Without warning, the truth washed over her, drowning her in a sea of dismay and giddy certainty. She was in love with Brody Stewart. Despite her Ivy League academic education and her twenty-first–century feminist sensibilities that might pooh-pooh the idea of love at first sight, she had met him last October and fallen head over heels almost the first instant.

Why else would she have broken her sexual dry spell in a way that was so unlike her usual behavior?

She sat there for minutes, maybe even an hour. Who knew? All she wanted to do was watch the steady rise and fall of his broad, sculpted chest. Even as she clung to the sweetness of the moment, she knew she would never have all of him. Knew it and accepted it. Just as she knew and accepted the fact that he would leave her and break her heart.

Brody was a man not easily tamed or housebroken. He wanted to do his duty by this baby, though that would not be a full-time job. Like her parents, he would provide for Cate's needs, but he would move on.

In those quiet moments, she made peace with her future. It hurt. The pain was a great jagged wound, ripping her in two. Even so, she said her prayers and accepted her fate. She had Brody for a time. That would have to be enough.

At last, he stirred, those movie-star lashes lifting slowly. "Sorry," he muttered. "I must have been more tired than I thought."

She managed a smile. "It's okay. I like watching you sleep."

His grin held only a fraction of its usual wattage. "Isn't that the man's line?"

Leaning forward, she kissed him softly. "I think we're inventing our own rules," she said.

He curled a hand behind her neck and held her close when she would have pulled away. "I like the dress," he muttered. "Can't wait to take it off you."

"Dinner first," she reminded him, trying not to let him see how completely undone she was. She would have to get a handle on her careening emotions, or he would know something was up.

She was strong. She could handle many difficult challenges and situations. But having Brody know she was in love with him was not one of them.

It was bad enough that he felt obligated by this tiny unborn baby. Cate refused to be the poor, pitiful woman who pleaded for his love.

She stood up as gracefully as she could, given the circumstances, and held out a hand to help him to his feet. "The shower's all yours," she said lightly.

He nodded, though his gaze was keen as he looked her over. "You okay, Catie girl? Your cheeks are pink."

"I'm great. But if you wait much longer, I'm going down to dinner without you."

He held up his hands. "I'm going. I'm going."

Much later, Cate leaned her chin on her hand and yawned. "I ate way too much," she said.

On the other side of the linen-clad table, Brody took a sip of his wine and smiled. "It was a verra good meal," he drawled. He had changed into a fresh suit and tie, this one with a blue shirt that emphasized his eyes.

They had talked about innocuous subjects over dinner. Now she wanted more from him. "Tell me about the ocean," she said. "How did you end up loving boats?"

Brody's hand stilled midsip. He finished his drink and set the glass aside. Shrugging, he shot her a strange look. "Don't really know. My parents didn't own boats, but many of their friends did. I think I probably spent time out on the water with people we knew when I was very young. Loving the water goes as far back as I can remember…when I was only a wee lad."

"Wasn't that odd? For a child to be out on the water? Isn't it dangerous?"

"Not if you teach a bairn how to follow the rules. I knew how to sail a small craft on my own by the time I was thirteen."

"I see."

"I don't know that you do, lass. Skye is a small place. Everybody knows everybody else. For teenagers, the isolation and lack of amenities can be suffocating. For me, getting out on the water was a means of escape. The world was bigger out there."

"And somehow your passion turned into a business?"

"Aye. Eventually. I went away to university in Edinburgh. Studied business. Came home to Skye and bought my first commercial fishing vessel. It was small and dirty and stank like rotten fish, but I turned a profit the second year. By then I was hooked, pardon the pun. I'd never been able to see myself as the kind of bloke who holed up in an office and wrangled numbers. Making a living from the sea is very satisfying, whether it be fishing or entertaining tourists."

"But you don't technically have to do the work yourself anymore, right? You've become successful."

He frowned slightly. "I could sit at home and count my money, if that's what you mean. Aye. They don't need me on a day-to-day basis. The various endeavors run fairly well without me. But a ship without a captain at the helm can wander off course. I have to make the major decisions."

"Makes sense…" Did he think she was lobbying for him

to stay in the US? She would never do that, even if there was a chance he would agree. It was beyond clear that Brody Stewart was a Scotsman to the core, and one who needed home to flourish.

To be honest, she would have entertained the idea of moving to Scotland permanently for a man who loved her, heart and soul. But that man was not Brody, and he had never once even hinted at the idea of Cate relocating as a possibility.

With an inward sigh, she finished her last bite of key lime tart and tried not to think about how many calories it had. This was her honeymoon, damn it.

Brody summoned the waiter with their check. "We don't want to miss sunset," he said.

While Brody was in the shower earlier, Cate had read a pamphlet about the history and quirks of Key West. According to the travel guide, the locals hosted a sunset celebration every night of the year, weather permitting, at Mallory Square. From their suite, she and Brody could overlook the festivities, but he had suggested a walk after dinner. Cate had jumped at the chance.

Outside, the night was humid but not terribly hot like it would be later in the summer. Crowds had gathered all along the waterfront. Street performers of every kind plied their trades and posed for tips. Acrobats. Mimes. Musicians and artists. The atmosphere was something like Times Square on New Year's Eve but on a much smaller and more laid-back scale.

Brody tucked an arm around her waist. "Tell me when you want to go back," he said. He steered a lazy path through the crowds, careful to keep Cate from being crushed. Anytime she stopped to look at something, he smiled indulgently and stayed at her side. She couldn't resist buying a small, red, hand-painted Christmas ornament.

The ball was dated for the current year. Was it a good thing or a bad thing that Cate would have a reminder of this trip?

They paused momentarily when the excitement in the square picked up. The sun—a huge, red-gold orb—dropped low in the sky, kissed the horizon and sank into the ocean with a dramatic splash of color.

Hundreds of people clapped and cheered.

"I see why everyone celebrates," she said, leaning into Brody and soaking up the moment.

Brody nodded. "I'm partial to home, but even I have to admit the sunset here is spectacular." He kissed her temple. "A nice way to mark the day."

On the far side of the square they found themselves at the edge of the charming shopping district. The famous Duvall Street stretched for over a mile, filled with quirky shops and unique restaurants. Though the Keys had been hard hit by a recent hurricane, the area was rebounding slowly but surely. The locals were determined to reclaim paradise.

Brody tugged her to a halt. "I want to go in here," he said.

Cate glanced at the storefront. The elegant window display was filled with expensive jewelry. "Why?"

He rolled his eyes. "You're not that naive. I want to buy you a wedding gift. Something, in fact, that I should have given you before now."

"Oh, but I—"

Brody ignored her protest and steered her inside. The proprietor took one look at the tall, well-dressed Scotsman and beamed a greeting.

"How may I help you, sir? Ma'am?"

Brody lifted Cate's left hand. "We need an engagement ring. It was a fast wedding, and this bride deserves a stone as special as she is."

"No, Brody," Cate stuttered beneath her breath. A fake wedding didn't require jewelry.

He ignored her. "I'd like to see loose stones. Emeralds to match her eyes."

"Of course." The man reached beneath the counter and opened a safe. Muttering to himself, he sorted through several small packets until he found the one he wanted. "Here we go," he said triumphantly. He held out his hand, palm flat. The jewel he had selected was a deep, brilliant green. It caught the light and sparkled beautifully.

Brody picked up the emerald and examined it under the nearby microscope. "Very nice," he said.

Freaking understatement of the year. "Brody," she whispered. "I don't need something that expensive. I'm fine with the wedding ring you gave me."

He frowned at her. "Well, I'm not." He pinned the merchant with a sharp gaze. "Origin? Size?"

"Colombian. Three carats. As fine a stone as I've seen in the past twenty years."

"We'll want a setting to match the wedding ring. Something plain. I don't want to detract from the stone." He turned to Cate. "Do you like it, Catie girl? I can buy a diamond if you'd rather have that."

She gulped. "Um, no. No diamonds. The emerald is incredible. But seriously, Brody, I—"

He had already turned away and was examining the tray of platinum settings. A moment later he selected a traditional six-prong style that would cradle the emerald. The salesman scribbled something on a small slip of paper. He showed it to Brody. Brody nodded.

And it was done. Brody handed over his credit card.

The man practically danced with joy. "Give me an hour," he said. "And I'll have it ready for you."

Outside, Cate fretted. "I know that ring costs a fortune,

Brody. You want to provide for the baby, and I appreciate your help. But I don't need an engagement ring, really I don't."

"Too late," he said blandly. "The deed is done."

"I'll give it back when the marriage is over."

For a brief moment she quailed at the fire in his eyes. Fury blazed. But he brought himself under control rapidly. "Ye're being rude, lass. It's a gift between lovers. We agreed not to discuss other topics, remember?"

He had his hands on her bare shoulders. Because of the press of people on the street, they were standing close, her rounded belly touching him. She stared into his eyes, trying to decide if she noted anything there other than male hunger. "I'm sorry," she said. "I'm not accustomed to having men give me extravagant presents."

His lips quirked in a wry smile. "This is verra new to me, as well, lass. Do ye want to go to the hotel while we wait for the ring?"

She took a chance and went up on her tiptoes to kiss him square on the mouth. The shock on his face was worth any momentary discomfort at being the first one to make a move. The man needn't think he was in charge all the time. "My doctor said walking is good for me. It's a perfect evening. I'm up for a leisurely stroll."

Brody blinked. "Well, okay, then. Let's walk."

For Cate, it was a night filled with magic. She might be a shotgun bride with a baby on the way, but romance was definitely in the air.

All along Duvall Street, humanity ebbed and flowed, bracketed with tropical flowers and steel drum melodies. Music spilled from bars and restaurants. Laughter and chatter filled the air.

Brody held her hand, his grip firm as if he was afraid she might disappear into the crowd. Cate shut her mind to the past and the future and concentrated on the present. No matter what happened down the road, she would have the memories of this night to sustain her.

At last, they turned around and made their way back to the jewelry store. The salesman—whom they discovered was actually the owner—was ready for them. He held up a small black-and-gold bag. "All set, Mr. Stewart. I've put it in one of our very best boxes. Though I'm guessing the lady would like to wear it."

His arch smile was too much for Cate. She hung back.

Brody took the bag. "I don't know about the lady, but *I* want to see the emerald on her finger."

He opened the box, removed the ring and then tucked the packaging into his inside coat pocket. Going down on one knee, he took both of Cate's hands in his. "I've mucked this up, Catie girl. But will you agree again to be my bride?" Without waiting for permission, he gently pushed the ring onto the appropriate finger of her left hand until it nestled against the wedding band.

"Oh, Brody."

The ring was exquisite, perhaps the most beautiful piece of jewelry she had ever seen, much less owned. His big thumb caressed her knuckles. "I can't get off this damned hard floor until you give me an answer."

Cate laughed softly. "Aye, Mr. Stewart. I'll be your bride."

At last, he stood and kissed her, apparently unconcerned they were being observed.

Cate's stomach fell to her knees and whooshed upward again like the elevator at the Empire State Building. Too much excitement for one evening. She was dizzy with happiness.

"Brody," she whispered. "Let's go back to our room."

His eyes darkened to navy. "I'm no' an experienced groom, but I know a good offer when I hear one."

As they made their way to the hotel, all of Cate's doubts returned a hundredfold. How could she make love to him and still protect herself? How terrible was it when one loved and the other did not?

Once Brody unlocked the door to their suite and they stood in the elegant sitting room, everything became awkward. They had already eaten and showered. There was nothing left to do except for that thing newlyweds enjoy on their wedding night.

Her heart was beating so fast and so hard she was afraid she might get sick again or faint.

Brody was no fool. He cupped her face in warm hands. "You're trembling, Catie girl. What's wrong? Talk to me."

"Nothing's wrong," she lied. "Not exactly. But I got married today, and things are different." *And I know now that I'm in love with you.*

He shook his head, folding her close against his chest and stroking her hair. "Not different at all, lass. We're the same two people. We want each other, and we're going to spend a long, wonderful night together. Nothing has changed, I swear. No need for nerves."

Brody was trying to comfort her, but every word he uttered underscored the bitter truth. For him, this was a marriage of convenience. For Cate, the mockery of what this relationship *ought to be* rubbed salt into a wound. Brody could brush aside the implications of the marriage license and the vows because they meant little to him. He wasn't in love with her.

But it was painfully different for Cate.

# Sixteen

Brody knew something was wrong, but he hadn't a clue how to fix it. Cate was almost rigid in his embrace. Her distress was palpable. He played with her hair and murmured to her in Gaelic until at last her body relaxed. Only then did he scoop her up in his arms and carry her into the bedroom.

Though his instinct was to bend her over the lace-covered bed and take her wildly, he kept a tight leash on his hunger. Women put great stock in things like romantic wedding nights. He wouldn't ruin the moment for Cate.

He set her on her feet and played with the narrow straps at her shoulders. "Are ye wearing anything underneath this dress, Catie girl?"

Finally, a small smile tilted her lips. "Not much. Feel free to explore."

He sucked in a deep breath and exhaled slowly. The soft, gauzy fabric of Cate's outfit had neither buttons nor zippers. After a few moments of study, he deduced that all he had to do was peel it carefully over her body in order to remove it.

To keep himself in check, he started slowly. He tugged the straps down her arms to her elbows. The bodice bunched up just above the tips of her breasts. His hands were clammy.

Very deliberately, he tugged again and sighed as she was bared to him from what once was her waist all the way up.

"I still can't get used to these curves," he said. He brushed her nipples with his thumbs and cupped the warm weight of her in his two hands.

Cate stood unmoving, her gaze downcast.

"Look at me, lass."

When she finally raised her head and her eyes met his, he realized with no little shock that his Cate was as aroused as he was. Her cat eyes sparkled, and her cheeks were flushed.

Experimentally, he rolled the tips of her breasts between his fingers and tugged. Cate's low groan went straight to his groin and hardened his erection to a painful degree.

"Don't move," he said raggedly.

He ripped his shirt from his pants and dragged at the buttons, popping loose at least two in the process. With his tie strangling him, he shrugged out of the shirt and finally managed to ditch the tie, as well.

Cate's eyes fastened on his chest. She laid a palm flat over the spot where his heart hammered wildly. "You're a beautiful man, Brody Stewart," she whispered, stroking him until he could barely breathe.

"You keep stealing my lines," he croaked. How far was it to the bed? He was losing control.

Cate touched his belt buckle. "May I?"

He couldn't have answered either way if his life depended on it. His throat closed up entirely.

Her small, deft hands dealt with button and zipper and fly. Soon, she grasped him and sighed.

Brody steeled himself. Letting Cate play when he wanted to rush headlong to the main event was virtually impossible. Her fingers squeezed and measured and stroked with careful reverence that destroyed him.

"Cate…" The single syllable was guttural.

She looked up at him. "Too much?" Her eyes were huge. "Not enough."

He took the reins again and gently finished removing her dress. Now her only adornment was silver hoop earrings, strappy, high-heeled sandals and the rings he had placed on her finger.

Her ripe, lush body was incredibly beautiful and alluring—like a Gauguin he had once seen in the Louvre during a school trip. As a teenage boy, he had understood the lust of male for female, but not the deep, wrenching need to please a woman.

Feeling remarkably light-headed, he kicked off his shoes, removed his socks and stepped out of his trousers. His erection stood flat against his belly. Cate's eyes rounded slightly as if she had never seen him like this before.

Suddenly, he lost his nerve. This was Cate's wedding night. He'd told her it didn't matter, but he was wrong. It mattered a hell of a lot. He had given her his name and his ring, if not his heart. Tonight she deserved to be wooed and taken with every ounce of finesse he could muster.

He took one of her hands in his. "Come with me."

The bed was tall and covered in pillows. He tossed them all aside but two and folded back the fancy duvet. The sheets were crisp and cool to the touch. Again, he lifted her, intending to lay her on the mattress. But this time she was naked. The feel of her in his arms fried his brain.

He felt like a caveman faced with a glorious princess. "You're the most beautiful thing I've ever seen," he muttered. "When I first set eyes on you last October, I knew you were going to be trouble." He said it teasingly, but the truth of that statement resonated in his gut.

Something about Cate Everett made him a little insane. Her hands were linked behind his neck. When she kicked her feet, both shoes went flying. "Are we going to talk all night?"

Her little pout forced a choked laugh from his parched throat. "God, I hope not."

He dropped her on the bed and chuckled when she bounced and protested. Then he was down beside her, his hands roving her body like a blind man learning the curves and valleys of a perilous journey.

Cate was larger now, and infinitely more lovely. He pressed his fingertips on either side of her navel and bowed his head when Baby Stewart kicked in protest. "Is the sex okay?" he asked. "Do we have to be careful?"

"No more careful than usual," she said.

Suddenly, he wanted her on top more than any other position he could think of. "How about this for starters?" He sprawled on his back and helped her move astride him.

She bit her lip, her expression anxious. "Are you sure, Brody? I must look like a cow from this angle."

He scowled. "Don't be absurd. I want you so badly I'm shaking, Cate. Do I seem like I'm repulsed by you?"

"Oh," she said, chastened. "Okay. I thought maybe you were just being nice."

He took her fingers and wrapped them around his rigid sex. "There's nothing nice about this, lass. I'm going to have ye now."

He grasped her hips and guided her down onto his erection. Her body took his eagerly, stretching to accommodate him, gloving him in warm, wet heat. *Holy hell.*

He closed his eyes and tried to breathe as he tried not to come inside her. Not yet. Damn, not yet.

Cate leaned forward, her hands on his chest. "Brody? Are you okay? Your face looks weird."

He started laughing and couldn't stop. Each time he laughed, her body slid another millimeter down onto him.

"Ye're killin' me, Catie girl. I'm like a green lad with his first woman. I'm about to embarrass myself and you haven't even crossed the first gate yet."

His pregnant lover wriggled her hips and groaned. "I'm not as far behind as you think, stupid man. Do something. Move. *Please*."

For the first time it dawned on him that his beautiful Cate was as wildly reckless with lust as he was. "Aye." That was all he could manage. One short word. He thrust his hips and found the mouth of her womb with the head of his sex.

"Yes…" Cate was flushed all over, her face rosy-red. "More," she demanded. "More, Brody."

He lost it. All thoughts of rings and babies and wedding-night romance flew out the window. Passion consumed him, that and the need to make Cate irrevocably his. He worked her up and down on his erection wildly, knowing her pale hips would bear the mark of his hands.

"Cate. Ah, God, Cate." His climax slammed into him, rendering him rigid in release for what seemed like eons, and then lax with pleasure. With his last vestige of sanity, he found her pleasure spot and rubbed it.

She came apart and cried out his name.

He rolled to his side and cuddled her.

Cate floated in a haze of contentment, blinking blear-ily as she realized that the pinks and golds of dawn had sneaked into the room. She and Brody had only slept in snatches all night long. The man was voracious. Not that she was complaining.

With a smug smile, she turned her head and examined his now-familiar face. Her *husband* slept deeply, obviously worn out from his many hours of vigorous activity. Surely Brody felt *something* for her. He was so tender, so sweet. Even in the middle of the night when they were half-asleep, he played with her hair. She had lost most of the pins along the way.

Though it pained her to leave him, nature called. After a quick trip to the bathroom, she washed up, donned one of the fancy hotel robes and tried to do something about the disaster that was her hair. She found the few remaining pins, removed them and brushed out what was left of her bridal hairstyle.

Though it would be nice to spend all day in bed, it did seem a shame to miss seeing more of Key West. Maybe they could order room service and then head out...

When she returned to the bedroom, Brody was awake and staring at his phone. Something about the rigid set of his jaw told her he wasn't in quite as good a mood as she was. He was still nude, but he had wrapped a coverlet from the foot of the bed around his waist.

"Brody? What is it? What's wrong?"

He shot her a glance. "There's been an accident. In Scotland. One of our boats rammed another one in the Skye harbor. Multiple injuries. There may be fatalities."

She went to him and slid her arms around his from behind. "I am so sorry. Is there anything I can do?"

He shrugged free of her light embrace, crossed the room to get his suitcase and began dressing with jerky motions. "I have to get back."

Her jaw dropped. "To Scotland? But we're on our honeymoon. Can't Duncan handle things?"

Brody turned around and shot her an incredulous look. "We may be sued."

"Don't you have insurance?"

"Cate," he said forcefully. "You aren't listening. You don't understand. If victims start suing my company, I could lose everything. *Everything*."

Perhaps she hadn't understood the first time, but she

did now. When Brody said the word *everything*, he clearly wasn't including Cate and the baby. The *everything* he was so passionate about was all back in Scotland. His wife and his child were no more than inconvenient incidentals.

From the beginning she had known that loving Brody and losing him was going to hurt. She just hadn't expected it to end so soon.

The next hours passed in a haze of frustration and incredulity. Brody was on the phone constantly, wheeling and dealing and cajoling to change tickets and book new ones. By noon they had boarded a plane to Fort Lauderdale. When they landed, Brody quick-marched her to another terminal and another gate. He handed her a ticket. "I've booked you a first class seat to Asheville. And I arranged for a car to pick you up on the other end and take you to Candlewick." He paused. "I'm sorry about Key West, Cate. We'll go another time."

She hid every ounce of her hurt and despair. "Of course. When does *your* flight leave?"

He glanced at his watch. "Four hours. But it's from Miami. I'm renting a car. I'd better get over there."

"Yes. You should."

He took her by the shoulders and kissed her forehead. "Take care of yourself, Little Mama. I'll be in touch soon."

"Goodbye, Brody." She made herself walk away from him calmly, spine straight, eyes dry. This might well turn out to be the shortest marriage in the history of record books. When she entered the waiting area and found a seat, she waited a full ten seconds and then turned her head to look for him.

Brody was gone.

# Seventeen

Brody had been running on autopilot ever since he received Duncan's text. Only by clamping down on his feelings and compartmentalizing every detail of the incredible night before was he able to function.

He had returned the rental car, checked in for his overseas flight and boarded the huge jumbo jet. Twelve hours later Brody tipped the driver and got out of the taxi. He'd spent a fortune today, and had nothing to show for it.

After landing in London, he'd taken a commuter jet to Glasgow. Now here he was, on Duncan's doorstep. Brody hadn't wanted to go to his own place, because the air would be hot and stale, and he had no food at home. His stomach curled with nausea. He wouldn't think about Cate. He couldn't.

Duncan opened the door almost immediately, his face reflecting shock. "What in the hell are you doing here? You're supposed to be on your honeymoon."

Brody shoved him aside, went into the house and collapsed onto the sofa. "Give me an update about the accident."

Duncan continued to stare at him in bemusement. "Definitely our fault. It was the new guy you hired four months ago. He and the wife had a falling out. She tossed him in the street. He had a few too many pints at the pub before going on board for his shift, and the rest is history."

"The victims?"

"Stable. Eleven in all. Three are children."

"Hell."

"Exactly." Duncan grimaced. "I can't believe you didn't trust me to handle this."

Brody blinked. "Of course I trust you. Implicitly."

"Then why are you here?" Duncan's dark eyes judged Brody and found him wanting.

"I've put everything I have into the business. My boats are an extension of me. They're who I am. Cate or no Cate, I had to be here. Not because I don't trust you, but because I…" Brody stopped, scrubbed his hands over his face. *Because being with Cate scared me shitless, and I seized on this disaster as a chance to put some distance between us.* He sucked in a ragged breath. "The point is, I'm here to help."

Duncan scowled as the landline began to ring. "There's nothing you can do at the moment."

He picked up the phone and after a few moments of listening, his face sobered. He looked like someone had punched him in the belly. "Sure, Granny," he said. "Do you want to talk to Brody?" Her response was loud enough for Brody to hear the volume if not the actual words. Duncan held the phone away from his ear, wincing. After a few moments he seized a break in his grandmother's rant. "I'll tell him. Don't worry."

When Duncan hung up, Brody stood, swaying with exhaustion. "What is it?"

Duncan's expression held both sympathy and pity, enough to curl Brody's stomach. "Cate is in the hospital. She's had some heavy bleeding. The doctor says she may lose the baby."

* * *

Cate picked at a loose thread on the thin hospital blanket and tried not to think about Brody. He was gone. She was in this alone. Even if he came back for the birth, it meant nothing. And besides, there might be nothing to come back for. Tears she couldn't stem leaked down her face.

She'd sent Isobel home hours ago. This was day two of Cate's hospitalization. The old woman was too frail for a vigil. Now it was dark outside, and there was nothing to do but wait.

The stack of mail Brody's grandmother had brought was little more than a distraction, but Cate reached for the yellow envelope and extracted the single piece of cardstock to read it a second time. Her friends in Candlewick were throwing her a baby shower. They were indignant and perplexed that she didn't know the sex of the child, hence the yellow card. Sharma was spearheading the party-planning.

In the midst of her fear and panic, Cate was touched and grateful that she actually *had* friends who cared. She had locked herself away emotionally for the past five years. It was a wonder she hadn't scared them all away.

A slight noise from the doorway brought her head up.

"Cate," Brody said. That was all. Just her name.

She shook her head, not entirely sure she wasn't dreaming. "You look like hell," she said flatly. She was dead inside. Nothing could penetrate the ice in her heart. She wasn't upset that Brody had abandoned their honeymoon for a business emergency. That would be petty and immature. No, what cut to the bone was the way he had made it so very clear that his damned boats were everything to him.

"So do you." He hadn't shaved since she last saw him. His face was gaunt with exhaustion. His hair stood on end.

"I thought you went back to Scotland." She knew he had. She had tracked his flight online.

"I did. I was there for all of forty-five minutes before Granny called Duncan and I headed back for the airport."

She shrugged. "You shouldn't have bothered. That was foolish."

"How are you feeling?"

She shrugged again. "How do you think I feel? You broke my heart, Brody. I thought you and I were getting closer, but you cut and ran at the first sign of trouble. I thought I was part of your everything. Now I know I'm not. And on top of that, I may lose my baby. I love you, Brody. But it doesn't matter, because you made your choice. At least I didn't have to guess where you stand."

Her cold, cutting tone made him go pale beneath his tan. "They said you're bleeding."

"Off and on. Apparently, it's common. There's some danger, and they've given me meds. Now I wait and see."

"I love you, Cate."

Brody blurted it out, uncensored. He'd figured out the truth sometime during the middle of his second transatlantic voyage. Cate blinked but didn't seem particularly overjoyed. "Go back to Scotland, Brody."

"I can't leave you."

"Correction. You can and you did. *Everything* you cared about was in jeopardy, remember?"

It was worse than he thought. Hearing Cate quote his callous words back to him was agonizing. "My mother often called my father a thickheaded, stubborn male when I was growing up. Apparently, I'm more like him than I realized. I'm sorry, Cate. I didn't know."

"Didn't know what?" Her air of calm showed cracks. "Never mind," she said. "Get out." Each word was an icy command. "I don't want you here."

"Can you feel the baby?"

"I'm not discussing this with you. If I miscarry, we'll have the marriage annulled. That's all you need to know."

"It's my baby, too. For God's sake, Cate. Don't be absurd."

A nurse came hurrying in and scowled at him as Cate's monitor began to beep loudly. "You'll have to leave, sir. Visiting hours were over long ago. You're upsetting my patient." She checked Cate's blood pressure efficiently and frowned. "Don't make me say it again. You need to go."

"I'm her husband," Brody said desperately.

The woman raised an eyebrow. "You're Mr. Everett?"

"No," Brody stuttered. "I'm Brody *Stewart*."

"Well, this woman is registered as Cate Everett, so I'd suggest you leave before I call security."

Brody turned to the silent woman in the bed. "Tell her, Cate. Tell her who I am."

Cate stared at him impassively. Those vibrant green eyes were dull and lifeless. "You're nothing to me. Go away."

Brody staggered into the hall and slumped against the wall, eventually ending up on his butt with his head on his knees. God, he was tired. Never in his life had he felt such overwhelming fear. The black hole inside his chest was sucking away every shred of hope he'd managed to cling to for the past unbearable hours. The only day that came close to being this dreadful was the one when he had finally understood his parents were divorcing.

Even that hadn't been as bad, because he'd had Duncan and Grandda and Granny. Tonight he had no one.

Why had he been so slow to realize the truth? Cate was his everything, not some stupid boat. At a deep, barely conscious level, he had been dealing with that realization for months. The truth had been terrifying, so he had stayed away from North Carolina. How could he have been so stupid? His deliberate, obtuse refusal to recognize the wonder that was right beneath his nose had ruined everything. He had let fear consume him. Fear of pain and loss.

And now the damage was done. All he could do was pray for answers. He had to figure out a way to fix this. He had to... Failure was not an option.

Fortunately, the night shift was sparsely populated. Nurses and aides walked around him gingerly, but no one actually tried to boot him out. At last, his body shut down. With his throat thick with tears, he slept.

Why did doctors have to do their rounds so damned early? Cate had finally managed a good stretch of rest somewhere after 5 a.m., and now, barely two hours later, her ob-gyn awakened her.

"Let's take a look," the perky, too-cute-for-school doctor said. The woman's hands were gentle as she folded back the sheet and lifted Cate's hospital-issue gown. She pursed her lips and probed delicately. At last, she lifted her head. "Breathe, honey, before you black out."

Cate hadn't even realized she was holding her breath. "Oh, sorry. Well, how am I?"

The doctor smiled. "As far as I can tell, the bleeding has stopped completely." She held her stethoscope to Cate's belly and listened. "That little one is dancing around in there. I think you're in the clear. But we'll keep you until tomorrow morning just to be on the safe side."

"Thank you, Doctor."

The woman left, and Cate burst into tears, noisy, ugly sobs that made her chest hurt. The relief was overwhelming.

Suddenly, someone sat on the side of her bed and took her hands. "I'm so sorry, Catie girl. So damned sorry. Please don't cry. It's killing me."

She sucked in a deep breath and wiped her face with the

sheet. Brody's presence befuddled her. "I told you to go. How did you get back so early?"

"I slept on the floor outside your door. I saw the doctor leave. I heard you crying. I'm sorry, Cate." He pulled her close, his big, strong arms wrapping around her and holding her tight.

"You smell like stale French fries," she said, sniffing and still crying a little bit.

"I've been wearing the same clothes for three days. It's no wonder." He sat back and smoothed the hair from her face. "Are they sure?" His throat worked. "About the baby, I mean?"

Cate felt as if she were having an out of body experience. "The baby is fine. He's fine. I was crying because I was so relieved and happy."

Brody went still. "He?" His eyes widened.

"I wanted to pray for our baby, and I needed to know if it was a him or a her, so I made the doctor tell me."

"A boy…"

Brody looked poleaxed.

Cate felt far too fragile to handle any more emotional drama. "I'm fine, too, Brody. Please go. I don't know why you stayed last night. They're keeping me one more day, but it's just a precaution."

"I love you."

She took a deep breath and exhaled. "We had a scare. It's over. Back to business as usual."

"No," he shouted, slamming his hand on the bed rail.

She shrank back in the bed. "I don't understand."

He took her face in his hands and stared into her eyes. "I'm in love with you, Cate."

"No. You're not. You made your choice obvious when you left. You've had several shocks in a row. And you probably haven't had a good Scottish breakfast in days. You're off your game. But things will get better. Go or stay. I don't care."

He stood up and glowered at her. "I'm neither a Victorian maiden nor an elderly aunt. I'm completely clearheaded. And I love you."

"Go pickle a herring," she said, her heart racing. "I don't want to hear your fanciful tales."

"Where's the ring?" he snapped, his gaze zeroing in on her bare left hand.

"They don't let you have jewelry in the hospital. It's a hazard. But not to worry. I left it with Isobel. I'm sure you can sell it on eBay. Or do they even have eBay in Scotland?" She was babbling.

Brody put his hand over her mouth. "Shut up, Cate. And listen to me." His words were perfectly polite, but she sensed the steel behind them. "I love you. This isn't a game."

Cate was tired and overwrought and wearing nothing but an ugly hospital gown. And that wasn't even counting the fact that she was still supposed to be on her honeymoon. She shoved his hand away. "If you care for me even the tiniest bit, Brody Stewart, you will walk out of this room and leave me alone until I can go back to Candlewick. By then I might be willing to have a civil conversation with you. But I make no promises."

Brody's face darkened. She held all the cards. No man in his right mind was going to argue with a pregnant woman who almost lost her baby, particularly if that very same man was responsible for ruining her and his honeymoon.

"Okay," he said quietly. "If that's what you want."

She stuck out her chin. "It is," she said.

When Brody walked out the door, she burst into tears again, only this time she cried into her pillow so no one would hear. She didn't know if he was out in the hall again, and she didn't want to know.

Somehow she had to pull herself together and make plans, plans that didn't include Brody. The baby would be the focus of her time and attention and love. No matter how badly she wanted to believe in Brody's impassioned about face, she dared not risk being wrong about him again.

For the remainder of the day she divided her time between watching stupid programs on the TV and talking on the phone with Isobel. Brody's granny didn't mention her grandson, and neither did Cate.

At eight the following morning, Cate's doctor signed her dismissal papers. "No strenuous activity for a week," she said. "And no sex." The last instruction was said with a grin. "I've seen that brawny Scotsman out in the hall, but you tell him I said to keep it in his pants for a few more days."

"Doctor Snyder!" Cate muttered, utterly mortified.

The other woman just chuckled and opened the door. "You can come in now."

Brody entered the room looking only a shade better than he did the last time she had seen him. When she cocked her head and gave him the evil eye, he held up his hands. "Granny said I had to come take you home." He held up a bag. "I brought clean clothes." He sat on her bed. Again.

Cate snatched the leather tote out of his hands. "Go back in the hall while I get dressed."

"I've seen you naked," he reminded her.

The gentle teasing weakened her defenses. He was being so darned sweet and gentle. How was she supposed to resist him? Tears welled in her eyes. Brody, his expression strained, held her as she cried. "Sorry, lass."

This time the storm didn't last as long. Cate gathered

herself together and sniffed. "Stupid hormones. Give me fifteen minutes to get ready, and we'll go."

He bent his head, looking searchingly into her eyes. "Are you really okay? And the baby, too?"

She nodded, unable to meet his gaze. "We're both fine."

Brody stood. "That's good." He shifted from one foot to the other. "Should I call a nurse? Do ye need help with your clothes?"

"I don't need anything. Go, please."

The near-tragedy had left her shaky and emotional, and on top of that, she had to figure out what to do about Brody. Could she risk a marriage that wasn't emotionally equal? She adored the man. Now, seeing his reactions to this latest scare, she did believe he cared about her and the baby. But love? His declaration was suspect at best. He was feeling guilty on several counts. She didn't want a convenient marriage. Eventually, if Brody didn't love her the way she loved him, the entire thing would unravel. The best thing she could do was absolve him and send him back to Scotland.

# Eighteen

Brody was worried about Cate. She was pale and quiet, too quiet. No conversational gambit he tried succeeded in coaxing her out of her silence. At last, he gave up. Pushing her would only upset her. He had done enough of that already.

Without asking, he had decided to choose the longer route home. Taking a section of the Blue Ridge Parkway would add only twenty minutes to their forty-five-minute trip. But it would also provide several opportunities to pull off and look at the view, thus getting Cate out of the car.

He was hoping like hell that something, anything, would help him break through her brittle shell. He loved her. Sooner or later he had to convince her that was true. And though it scared him, he had to offer her a way out. One that wasn't what he wanted, but a choice to prove that he wasn't trying to control her life.

While she had made one last trip to the loo in preparation for leaving the hospital, he had read through the paperwork the doctor left with Cate. She was supposed to drink plenty of water, have regular mild exercise and not ride in a car or airplane for extended periods.

Now, after waiting for Cate to be wheeled out to the

exit per hospital procedure, they were in the SUV he had bought for her, and the air was thick with tension. Seeing a turnout up ahead, he eased the car off the road. "Let's get out and stretch," he said.

Cate shot him a look but didn't say anything. They had barely been driving half an hour.

Unlike Key West, here in the mountains, the air was crisp and cool. He handed her a water bottle and watched as she drained half of it. "I brought some food," he said. "Granny thought you might be hungry before we got home."

His companion brightened visibly. "Anything to sit on?"

"A blanket. You want a picnic table or the hood of the car?"

"That picnic table is in the shade." She pointed. "But let's sit on top."

"Of course." Concrete benches weren't designed for pregnant women.

While Cate stood and stretched, he retrieved the basket of food and the blanket. He spread the blanket over the table and set out the containers. When he offered Cate his hand to step up onto the bench, she pretended she didn't see and hopped up on her own.

Granny and the cook between them had provided fresh roasted chicken, a fruit salad and homemade croissants. There was even an insulated carafe of iced tea. Brody would have preferred a beer, but the tea would do.

They ate in silence. Cate sat as far away from him as possible given the confines of the tabletop. She stared out into the distance where ridge after ridge of mountains stretched for miles.

Brody wiped his fingers and leaned back on his hands. "Are you in love with me, Cate?"

Her body jerked, but her answer was flat. "No."

He absorbed the hit, though it left him breathless. "Do you want to annul our marriage?"

The silence lasted for hours, it seemed. At last, she half turned to face him. "I'm not sure. I thought you wanted the baby to have your name. Legalities and all that."

"I did. I do. But I've hurt you too much. Like most everyone else in your life. So from now on, I only want what you want."

Her smile was wry. "So docile. So tame. You can't fool me, Brody Stewart. You would never let a woman call the shots."

"I'm sorry for everything, Cate. I know you don't believe me, but I love you."

For one brief instant he caught a glimpse of the pain in her beautiful green eyes. Knowing he was responsible for that distress turned the knife in his gut. His lovely Cate was hurting. Badly. And he was to blame.

She wrinkled her nose and swatted at a fly that had shown up uninvited to their picnic. "Here's the thing, Brody. I think you're right. You do belong in Scotland. So it makes my life very difficult. I don't want to keep a father from his son."

"Then come back with me," he said, not even realizing the words were about to tumble from his lips. "Live there with me. Or in a separate house. The Scots love bookstores. We could make a good life."

Her lips trembled. "We've made such a mess of things, Brody. I don't know what to think anymore."

"We have to make decisions," he said. "You know I'm right."

Jamming her hands in the pockets of her lightweight jacket, she stared at him. "I see the guilt on your face. But none of this is your fault, at least no more than mine. You're wearing a hair shirt and trying to do penance, for what? I don't blame you for leaving Key West. I truly don't. Maybe at first, but not now."

"I never should have abandoned our honeymoon," he said.

"It wasn't real, was it? We both knew that."

"Cate, I—"

She held up a hand. "I need time." The words were dull. "Time to think this through. Maybe an annulment is the answer. Please take me home so I can see Isobel and let her know I'm okay. I don't want to keep her waiting anymore."

Brody tasted panic, but he was going to fight. "I'll give you what you ask," he said quietly, "but I won't stop loving you."

For an entire week Brody bided his time. Isobel, for once, had chosen to stay out of the middle of the mess Brody and Cate had created. She hovered over her young friend, clearly worried, but not offering advice. As for Cate, she read books, chatted with Brody's grandmother, spent time online creating a baby registry at Sharma's request and generally avoided speaking to Brody.

The three of them had meals together, but that was as far as it went. Brody slept in his original bedroom, Cate in hers.

Their marriage had lasted all of twenty-four hours.

At the end of the seventh day, Brody decided they couldn't wait any longer for a showdown. He had promised Cate time, but despite his best intentions, he was desperate. He had to win her over now, for both their sakes. Cate had to understand how he felt. It was critical for their happiness and for their future.

Decisions had to be made. Duncan was keeping him updated daily about the situation in Scotland, but Brody was far more worried about his bride, who seemed to be losing weight when she should be gaining.

Her face was thinner, her eyes underscored with shadows. Cate had been excited about her pregnancy. Now she drifted through the house like a listless ghost.

Tomorrow morning he would take her for a walk or a drive so they could have privacy, and he would lay his cards on the table.

He prowled the darkened hallways restlessly. Maybe he should have insisted on sleeping in the same bed. Now the gulf between them was so deep and so wide, he might never find a way across.

He had played the gentleman, trying to give Cate space and time to heal emotionally and physically. But was that the right thing to do? He knew the incident had terrified her, because it had scared the hell out of him, too.

He had waited this long. Surely twelve more hours wouldn't kill him. Even so, he found himself standing outside her room like a lovesick swain.

Resting his forehead against her door, he tried not to think about the nights she had welcomed him eagerly into her bed. He ached to hold her, to bury his face in her hair and inhale the scent that was uniquely Cate's. She was strong and funny and smart and sexy.

How could he not have known he was in love with her? All those months in Scotland over the winter, he had been restless and grouchy. He'd written it off to the terrible weather and work stress.

The answer was so much simpler.

With a deep sigh, he straightened and prepared to walk away. And then he heard it. A small, muffled sound, but unmistakable. Cate was crying.

His gut twisted. His heart fell to his knees. Somehow, he had to fix this. Without waiting for an invitation, he opened the door. The room was familiar to him. Even in the dark, he found her. She was huddled beneath the covers.

"Cate," he said, sitting down on the edge of the mattress. He tugged back the covers. She'd had them pulled over her head. "It's me. Talk to me, Catie girl. I can't stand to hear you cry." She was wearing a soft T-shirt, tiny bikini panties and nothing else.

"What are you doing here, Brody? It's late."

Her voice was husky and raw. There was no welcome in her words. But she didn't throw him out immediately. He took heart from that.

"May I turn on the little lamp?" He needed to see her eyes, to gauge her reactions when he talked to her.

After a long silence, she sighed. "I suppose so."

The light from the low-wattage bulb was sufficient for him to tell that she had probably been crying for some time. Her hair was tousled, and her face was damp. He rubbed her cheek with his thumb. "I never meant to ruin your life. From the day I met you last October, your smile has haunted my dreams. I went home to Scotland for the winter, but somewhere deep inside, I regretted that decision every day. All I can tell you is that I didn't know what love was. How precious. How rare. You are everything I want, Catie girl."

"What about the boating business?"

There was no accusation in her question, but he flinched. "I can sell it if that's what we decide is best. Move here. Help with Granny."

"I saw how you reacted in Key West, Brody. You were beside yourself."

"Turns out, it wasn't the boating accident that freaked me out."

She frowned. "Of course it was. I saw you."

He shook his head slowly. "I was crazed and irrational,

yes. But it was our wedding night that did it. I thought I had my whole life planned out so neatly, but after that night with you I was ready to chuck everything I had worked for. It terrified me. I've never felt for anyone the way I feel about you, Catie love. I'm sorry I handled things so badly."

"You couldn't get away from me fast enough."

He swallowed hard. "Aye. That's true. But when I arrived in Scotland, I came to my senses. It wasn't my finest moment. I ran away, lass, plain and simple. It shames me to my core. The only thing I can say in my defense is that our wedding night shook the foundations beneath my feet. It was incredible. I couldn't breathe for wanting you."

"And you thought that was a bad thing…" Her bottom lip trembled.

"Ah, hell, don't look at me like that. I've always prided myself on being in control of the world. When it comes to you, Cate Everett, I don't even know who I am. But I want to figure it out, and I want to do that with you at my side. You told me you don't love me. If that's true, I guess I deserve it. But if you were lying, I'd give everything I own for another chance to make you happy."

"My name is Cate *Stewart*," she said. She didn't smile when she said it, but she leaned into him and rested her forehead against his chest. "I've been so scared and tired and unsure of myself, Brody. I didn't know what love was, either. I'm worried I'll be a parent like *my* parents. I worry that I didn't know my professor was a cheating, lying scumbag. Then there's you. How do I know what I feel for you is real?"

His heart stopped. Nothing in the room moved. Not a whisper. Not a breath. He kissed her temple. "What *do* you feel for me, Catie girl?"

She pulled back and looked up at him with a wavering,

lopsided smile. "I love you, Brody. Madly. Passionately. Like in the movies, only better. You protect me, but you don't smother me. You believe in me. You let me know without making a big deal about it that you think I'll be a good mother." She paused. "And at the risk of sounding shallow, you're a beautiful, sexy man, and I love the way you whisper to me in Gaelic when we make love."

His mouth dried and his throat closed up. He had to try twice before he could speak. "Thank God." His hands trembled as he smoothed her hair. "*Mo chridhe*. My heart. I swear I'll never leave you again. I can't. I couldn't."

"Then I've made up my mind."

Alarm skittered through his veins. "About what?"

"It doesn't make sense to move now. I'm too pregnant, and I want to stay with my doctor. But as soon as the baby is old enough to travel, I'm going back to Scotland with you. I want to see the water you love so well and the wild Highlands and the heritage that runs in my son's veins. We'll figure out some way to take care of Isobel. I want to go home with you, Brody. Your home will *be* my home."

He shuddered at the prospect of what he had almost lost. "Ach, my dear, wonderful Cate. Ye're so much more than I deserve."

She linked her arms around his neck and kissed him softly. "Neither of us planned on love, Brody. Somewhere, somehow, we found each other. Maybe the timing was off, and maybe we shouldn't be having a baby so soon. It doesn't matter. As long as I have you, I can handle anything."

"I love you, Catie girl."

"And I adore you, you big, opinionated, gorgeous Scotsman."

He smirked. "It was the accent, wasn't it? Gets 'em every time."

\* \* \*

Cate was floating. Though her body was large with child, she felt as if she were light as a cloud or a feather. Happiness effervesced in her veins. "Make love to me, Brody," she whispered. "I've missed you."

He stiffened in her embrace. "We can't, my love. It's dangerous."

"It's been a week. I counted. I'm fine, Brody. Healthy as a horse. And we'll be gentle and easy. Please."

The man was torn. She could see that. But she wanted her husband, and she wasn't prepared to wait a minute longer. Fortunately, he was barely dressed. She ran her hands over his hard, bare chest, feeling the ripple of muscle and the delineation of bone and tendon.

Brody exhaled on a ragged sigh. His large frame was rigid as if he was exercising mighty control. "You'll tell me the moment anything hurts you?"

"Of course." Sliding her hands around his waist, she eased inside his elastic-waist sleep pants and raked his taut buttocks with her fingernails. "It was a great wedding night. Now I want to see what you can do with ho-hum sex."

He reared back and stared at her, his blue-eyed gaze sharp and mildly offended. "Ho-hum? I'm no' familiar with that one, but I think I've been insulted."

She nipped his earlobe with sharp teeth. "Sex can't always be like it was in Key West. I'm sure we'll lose our edge eventually."

"Woman," he growled, his tone terse with determination, "ye'd better shut yer mouth before I have to put you over my knee. I'll never get tired of making you mine. So ye'd best get used to it."

Before she could do more than gasp in shock, he ripped off her nightclothes and his own and thrust her down on her back spread-eagled on the bed. He gripped her wrists in two big hands, pinning them to the sheets. Then he stroked her pregnant belly with his erection.

She panted as her nipples pebbled and her skin tightened with gooseflesh. "I want you, Brody." She was desperate. It had been a long, miserable week. "Don't make me wait."

His jaw was clenched, his smile tight with arousal. "Waiting is good for the soul, Little Mama." He bent and suckled one breast. Her body arched and tightened in longing.

He smelled like warm, aroused male. The look in his eyes, even more than words, told her that he loved her. The brilliant blue was alight with happiness and something far deeper.

"I love you, Brody." Her throat was thick with tears. She had almost lost everything. Her baby. Her lover.

He bent and kissed her softly, careful not to crush her. "No more tears, sweet bride. We're together now. You, me and our son."

With gentle hands, he rolled her to her side and entered her from behind, spooning her in an erotic position that left his hands free to play with her sensitive breasts. She moaned when he cupped them and squeezed them together.

"Oh, yes," she whispered, already near the peak after long days of wanting him.

He nuzzled the back of her neck, his breath warm on her skin. "When I'm inside you," he muttered, "I don't want it to end."

He was large and filled her irrevocably from this angle. Her role was more passive. She sensed that even now, he was trying to protect her. She moved restlessly, so close to shattering that her body strained for the peak. Grabbing his hand, she gripped it tightly. "Don't stop," she panted.

"Never," he swore as he thrust harder, faster. And then, he touched her where their bodies joined and made her fly...

Brody felt definitely strange, but it was the best damned feeling of his life. The woman he adored was in his arms, and they were both trying to breathe. "I think it's after three," he groaned. "Maybe we should sleep." At least one of them should show some sense. He was going to be a father. He needed to practice making mature decisions.

Cate wrapped her fingers around his penis. "I'll bet we could try for another."

"Cate," he warned, halfheartedly slapping her hand away. "You need your rest."

"What I *need*," she said, flopping onto her back, "is calories. I'm starving."

"Now that you mention it, so am I. I hope Granny has eggs in the fridge."

"And toast with butter and jam?"

He rolled to his feet and helped her out of bed. "Anything the little mama wants."

"Wow," Cate said, laughing. "I guess there are perks to this pregnancy gig, after all."

He slapped her on the butt and rescued her underwear and shirt. But then on second thought, he tossed them on the bed and caressed her rounded belly. "I have an idea."

"I hope it involves feeding me."

He perched on the edge of the bed and drew her closer. "Soon," he swore. His sex surged and flexed. "I have an urge to sit you on my lap."

"Sounds kinky." She giggled.

"You can bet on it, Cate."

As he joined their bodies, his lover sighed and rested her head on his shoulder. "This is the real thing, isn't it?"

He gripped her bottom and pulled her in, taking her deeper. "Aye, Cate, it is. I love you, my dearest wife."

"And I love you, Brody."

"Until death do us part?"

"Longer than that."

"That's all I needed to hear." And then he took them home.

# Epilogue

Duncan Stewart strode into the hospital with his blood pumping and his stomach in a knot. The long-awaited moment was finally happening. Somewhere inside the walls of this vast medical facility, a tiny baby was being born, first in the next generation of Stewarts.

It was a great day, a glorious day. Brody and Cate, still newlyweds, were over the moon and wildly in love. Soon, they would be leaving North Carolina and going back to Scotland.

But not Granny. Stubborn, wonderful Granny Stewart was determined to stay in the home she had shared with her husband and to continue running the business they had built with their bare hands. No going back to Scotland for her.

Which meant that "someone" had to be sacrificed on the altar of familial responsibility.

Duncan felt the invisible noose tighten around his neck. He was single. He had nothing and no one to tie him down. It made perfect sense for him to be the one to stay with Granny Stewart and help her keep Stewart Properties afloat.

So what if Duncan was giving up his job and his home and his friends?

He was happy to do it. Isn't that what he had said to everyone who asked? His brother? His parents? His dear, ancient grandmother?

Everyone of them had praised his selflessness and his kind heart.

Duncan punched the elevator button, grim-faced, and stewed in his own deceit. He was a damned hypocrite. He was going to stay, of course he was. But only because there was no way out…

\* \* \* \* \*

# COMING SOON!

We really hope you enjoyed reading this book. If you're looking for more romance, be sure to head to the shops when new books are available on

# Thursday
# 14th June

To see which titles are coming soon, please visit
**millsandboon.co.uk**

MILLS & BOON

# LET'S TALK
## Romance

For exclusive extracts, competitions
and special offers, find us online:

**f** facebook.com/millsandboon

**○** @millsandboonuk

**y** @millsandboon

Or get in touch on 0844 844 1351*

For all the latest titles coming soon, visit
millsandboon.co.uk/nextmonth